Witold Gombrowicz

· · · · · · · · · · · · ·

Ferdydurke

Translated from the Polish by Danuta Borchardt

Foreword by Susan Sontag

Yale Nota Bene

Yale University Press / New Haven & London

First published as a Yale Nota Bene book in 2000.

Published with assistance from the Alfred Jurzykowski Foundation,
Inc., and from the Kosciuszko Foundation, Inc.,
An American Center for Polish Culture, New York, New York.

For information about this and other Yale University Press
publications, please contact:
U.S. office   sales.press@yale.edu
Europe office   sales.yaleup.co.uk
Designed by Nancy Ovedovitz and set in Minion type by Keystone
Typesetting, Inc. Printed in the United States of America.

Library of Congress Cataloging-in-Publication Data
Gombrowicz, Witold.
[Ferdydurke. English]
Ferdydurke / Witold Gombrowicz ; translated from the Polish by
Danuta Borchardt ; foreword by Susan Sontag.
p. cm.
ISBN 0-300-08239-8 (cloth : alk. paper) — ISBN 0-300-08240-1 (pbk.)
1. Borchardt, Danuta, 1930–   II. Title.
PG7158.G669 F4713 2000   99-058269

A catalogue record for this book is available from the British Library.

10   9   8   7   6   5   4

Contents

Foreword

Susan Sontag

S tart with the title. Which means . . . nothing. There is no character in the novel called Ferdydurke. And this is only a foretaste of insolence to come.

Published in late 1937, when its author was thirty-three, *Ferdydurke* is the great Polish writer's second book. The title of his first, *Memoirs of a Time of Immaturity* (1933), would have served beautifully for the novel. Perhaps this is why Gombrowicz opted for jabberwocky.

That first book, whose title was pounced on by the Warsaw reviewers as if Gombrowicz had made a shaming confession inadvertently, was a collection of stories (he'd been publishing them in magazines since 1926); over the next two years more stories appeared, including a pair ("The Child Runs Deep in Filidor" and "The Child Runs Deep in Filibert") that he would use, with chapter-long mock prefaces, as interludes in *Ferdydurke,* as well as a first play, *Princess Ivona*; then, in early 1935, he embarked on a novel. Had the title of his volume of fanciful stories seemed—his word—"ill-chosen"? Now he would *really* provoke. He would write an epic in defense of immaturity. As he declared toward the end of his life:

"Immaturity—what a compromising, disagreeable word!—became my war cry."

Immaturity (not youth) is the word Gombrowicz insists on, insists on because it represents something unattractive, something, to use another of his key words, *inferior*. The longing his novel describes, and endorses, is not, Faust-like, to relive the glory days of youth. What happens to the thirty-year-old who, waking up one morning roiled in the conviction of the futility of his life and all his projects, is abducted by a teacher and returned to the world of callow schoolboys, is a humiliation, a fall.

From the start, Gombrowicz was to write, he had chosen to adopt a "fantastic, eccentric, and bizarre tone" bordering on "mania, folly, absurdity." To irritate, Gombrowicz might have said, is to conquer. I think, therefore I contradict. A young aspirant to glory in 1930s literary Warsaw, Gombrowicz had already become legendary in the writers' cafés for his madcap grimaces and poses. On the page, he sought an equally vehement relation to the reader. Grandiose and goofy, this is a work of unrelenting *address*.

Still, it seems likely that Gombrowicz did not know where he was going when he began the novel. "I can well remember," Gombrowicz declared in 1968, a year before he died (*did* he remember? or was he massaging his legend?),

that, when I started Ferdydurke, *I wanted to write no more than a biting satire that would put me in a superior position over my enemies. But my words were soon whirled away in a violent dance, they took the bit between their teeth and galloped towards a grotesque lunacy with such speed that I had to rewrite the first part of the book in order to give it the same grotesque intensity.*

But the problem was less (I suspect) that the first chapters needed a further infusion of lunatic energies than that Gombrowicz did not anticipate the freight of argument—about the nature of eros, about culture (particularly Polish culture), about ideals—his tale would carry.

Ferdydurke starts with a dreamlike abduction to an absurd world, in which the big become small and the small monstrously big: those great buttocks in the sky. In contrast to the landscape Lewis Carroll conjured up for a prepubescent girl, Gombrowicz's wonderland of shape-shiftings and re-sizings seethes with lust.

Everything was expanding in blackness. Inflating and widening, yet at the same time shrinking and straining, evading something, and some kind of winnowing, general and particular, a coagulating tension and a tensing coagulation, a dangling by a fine thread, as well as transformation into something, transmutation, and furthermore—a falling into some cumulative, towering system, and as if on a narrow little plank raised six stories up, together with the excitement of all organs. And tickling.

In Alice's story, a child falls into an asexual underworld governed by a new, fantastic but implacable logic. In *Ferdydurke*, the grownup who is turned into a schoolboy discovers new, puerile freedoms for giving offense and owning up to disreputable desire.

Starts with an abduction; ends with an abduction. The first (by Professor Pimko) returns the protagonist to the scene of true, that is, unmanageable, feeling and desire. The second abduction shows the protagonist making a provisional flight back into so-called maturity.

If someone were to spot me in the hallway, in the darkness, how would I explain this escapade? How do we find ourselves on these tortuous and abnormal roads? Normality is a tightrope-walker above the abyss of abnormality. How much potential madness is contained in the everyday order of things—you never know when and how the course of events will lead you to kidnap a farmhand and take to the fields. It's Zosia that I should be kidnapping. If anyone, it should be Zosia, kidnapping Zosia from a country manor would be the normal and correct thing to do, if anyone it was Zosia, and not this stupid, idiotic farmhand . . .

Ferdydurke is one of the most bracing, direct books ever written about sexual desire—this without a single scene of sexual union. To be sure, the cards are stacked from the start in favor of eros. Who would not concur in the silencing of *this* social babble by the clamor of rumps, thighs, calves? The head commands, or wishes to. The buttocks reign.

Later, Gombrowicz referred to his novel as a pamphlet. He also called it a parody of a philosophical tale in the manner of Voltaire. Gombrowicz is one of the super-arguers of the twentieth century— "*To contradict,* even on little matters," he declared, "is the supreme necessity of art today"—and *Ferdydurke* is a dazzling novel of ideas. These ideas give the novel both weight and wings.

Gombrowicz capers and thunders, hectors and mocks, but he is also entirely serious about his project of transvaluation, his critique of high "ideals." *Ferdydurke* is one of the few novels I know that could be called Nietzschean; certainly it is the only comic novel that could be so described. (The affecting fantasia of Hesse's *Steppenwolf* seems, in comparison, riddled with sentimentality.) Nietzsche deplored the ascendancy of slave values sponsored by Christianity, and called for the overthrowing of corrupt ideals and for new forms of masterfulness. Gombrowicz, affirming the "human" need for imperfection, incompleteness, inferiority . . . youth, proclaims himself a specialist in inferiority. Swinish adolescence may seem a drastic antidote to smug maturity, but this is exactly what Gombrowicz has in mind. "Degradation became my ideal forever. I worshipped the slave." It is still a Nietzschean project of unmasking, of *exposing*, with a merry satyr-dance of dualisms: mature versus immature, wholes versus parts, clothed versus naked, heterosexuality versus homosexuality, complete versus incomplete.

Gombrowicz gaily deploys many of the devices of high literary modernism lately re-labeled "post-modern," which tweak the traditional decorums of novel writing: notably, that of a garrulous, intrusive narrator awash in his own contradictory emotional states. Burlesque slides into pathos. When not preening, he is abject; when not clowning, he is vulnerable and self-pitying.

An immature narrator is some sort of candid narrator; even one who flaunts what is usually hidden. What he is not is a "sincere" narrator, sincerity being one of those ideals that make no sense in the world of candor and provocation. "In literature sincerity leads nowhere . . . the more artificial we are, the closer we come to frankness. Artificiality allows the artist to approach shameful truths." As for his celebrated *Diary*, Gombrowicz says:

> Have you ever read a "sincere" diary? The "sincere" diary is the most mendacious diary . . . And, in the long run, what a bore sincerity is! It is ineffectual.
>
> Then what? My diary had to be sincere, but it could not be sincere. How could I solve the problem? The word, the loose, spoken word, has this consoling particularity: it is close to sincerity, not in what it confesses but in what it claims to be and in what it pursues.
>
> So I had to avoid turning my diary into a confession. I had to show myself "in action," in my intention of imposing myself on the reader in a certain way, in my desire to create myself with everyone looking on. "This is how I would like to be for you," and not "This is how I am."

Still, however fanciful the plot of *Ferdydurke*, no reader will regard the protagonist and his longings as anything other than a transposition of the author's own personality and pathology. By making Joey Kowalski (as the Polish name of the protagonist-narrator is here rendered in English) a writer—and the author of an unsuccessful, much derided book of stories entitled, yes, *Memoirs of a Time of Immaturity*—Gombrowicz dares the reader *not* to think about the man who wrote the novel.

A writer who revels in the fantasy of renouncing his identity and its privileges. A writer who imagines a flight into youth, represented as a kidnapping; a discarding of the destiny expected of an adult, represented as a subtraction from the world in which one is known.

And then the fantasy came true. (Few writers' lives have so clearly taken the shape of a destiny.) At the age of thirty-five, a few days short of the fateful date of September 1, 1939, Gombrowicz was dropped into unexpected exile, far from Europe, in the "immature" New World. It was as brutal a change in his real life as the imagined turning of a thirty-year-old man into a schoolboy. Stranded, without any means of support, where nothing was expected of him, because nothing was known about him, he was offered the divine opportunity to lose himself. In Poland, he was well-born Witold Gombrowicz, a prominent "vanguard" writer, who had written a book many (including his friend, the other great Polish writer of the same period, Bruno Schulz) considered a masterpiece. In Argentina, he writes, "I was nothing, so I could do anything."

It is impossible now to imagine Gombrowicz without his twenty-four years in Argentina (much of which was spent in penury), an Argentina he made to suit his own fantasies, his daring, his pride. He left Poland a relatively young man; he returned to Europe (but never to Poland) when he was nearing sixty, and died six years later in the south of France. Separation from Europe was not the making of Gombrowicz as a writer: the man who published *Ferdydurke* two years earlier was already fully formed as a literary artist. It was, rather, the most providential confirmation of everything his novel knows, and gave direction and bite to the marvelous writings still to come.

The ordeal of emigration—and for Gombrowicz it was an ordeal—sharpened his cultural combativeness, as we know from the *Diary*. The *Diary*—in three volumes in English, and anything but a "personal" diary—can be read as a kind of free-form fiction, postmodern *avant la lettre*; that is, animated by a program of violating decorum similar to that of *Ferdydurke*. Claims for the staggering genius and intellectual acuity of the author vie with a running account of his insecurities, imperfections, and embarrassments, and a defiant avowal of barbaric, yokel prejudices. Considering himself slighted by, and therefore eager to reject, the lively literary milieu of late 1930s Buenos Aires, and aware that it harbored one indisputably great writer, Gombrowicz declared himself "at opposite poles" from Borges. "He is deeply rooted in literature, I in life. To tell the truth I am anti-literature."

As if in agreement, shallow agreement, with Gombrowicz's entirely self-serving quarrel with the idea of literature, many now regard the *Diary* instead of *Ferdydurke* as his greatest work.

No one can forget the notorious opening of the *Diary:*

> *Monday*
> *Me.*
> *Tuesday*
> *Me.*
> *Wednesday*
> *Me.*
> *Thursday*
> *Me.*

Having got *that* straight, Gombrowicz devoted Friday's entry to a subtle reflection on some material he had been reading in the Polish press.

Gombrowicz expected to offend with his egocentricity: a writer must continually defend his borders. But a writer is also someone who must abandon borders, and egotism, so Gombrowicz argued, is the precondition of spiritual and intellectual freedom. In the "me . . . me . . . me . . . me" one hears the solitary émigré thumbing his nose at "we . . . we . . . we . . . we." Gombrowicz never stopped arguing with Polish culture, with its intractable collectivism of spirit (usually called "romanticism") and the obsession of its writers with the national martyrdom, the national identity. The relentless intelligence and energy of his observations on cultural and artistic matters, the pertinence of his challenge to Polish pieties, his bravura contentiousness, ended by making him the most influential prose writer of the past half century in his native country.

The Polish sense of being marginal to European culture, and to Western European concern while enduring generations of foreign occupation, had prepared the hapless émigré writer better than he might have wished to endure being sentenced to many years of near total isolation as a writer. Courageously, he embarked on the enterprise of making deep, liberating sense out of the unprotectedness of his situation in Argentina. Exile tested his vocation and expanded it. Strengthening his disaffection from nationalist pieties and self-congratulation, it made him a consummate citizen of world literature.

More than sixty years after *Ferdydurke* was written, little remains of the specifically Polish targets of Gombrowicz's scorn. These have vanished along with the Poland in which he was reared and came of age—destroyed by the multiple blows of war, Nazi occupation, Soviet dominance (which prevented him from ever returning), and the post-1989 ethos of consumerism. Almost as dated is his assumption that adults always claim to be mature.

In our relations with other people we want to be cultivated, superior, mature, so we use the language of maturity and we talk about, for instance, Beauty, Goodness, Truth . . . . But, within our own confidential, intimate reality, we feel nothing but inadequacy, immaturity . . .

The declaration seems from another world. How unlikely it would be for whatever embarrassing inadequacies people feel now to be covered over with hifalutin absolutes such as Beauty, Goodness, Truth. The European-style ideals of maturity, cultivation, wisdom have given way steadily to American-style celebrations of the Forever Young. The discrediting of literature and other expressions of "high" culture as elitist or anti-life is a staple of the new culture ruled by entertainment values. Indiscretion about one's unconventional sexual feelings is now a routine, if not mandatory, contribution to public entertainment. Anyone now who would claim to love "the inferior" would argue that it is not inferior at all; that actually it's superior. Hardly any of the cherished opinions against which Gombrowicz contended are still cherished.

Then can *Ferdydurke* still offend? Still seem outrageous? Exception made for the novel's acidic misogyny, probably not. Does it still seem extravagant, brilliant, disturbing, brave, funny . . . wonderful? Yes.

A zealous administrator of his own legend, Gombrowicz was both telling and not telling the truth when he claimed to have successfully avoided all forms of greatness. But whatever he thought, or wanted us to think he thought, that cannot happen if one had produced a masterpiece, and it eventually comes to be acknowledged as such. In the late 1950s *Ferdydurke* was finally translated (under auspicious sponsorship) into French, and Gombrowicz was, at last, "discovered." He had wanted nothing more than this success; this triumph over his adversaries and detractors, real and imagined. But the writer who counseled his readers to try to avoid all expressions of themselves; to guard against all their beliefs, and to mistrust their feelings; above all, to stop identifying themselves with what defines them, could hardly fail to insist that he, Gombrowicz, was not *that book*. Indeed, he has to be inferior to it. "The work, transformed into culture, hovered in the sky, while I remained below." Like the great backside that hovers high above the protagonist's half-hearted flight into normality at the end of the novel, *Ferdydurke* has floated upward to the literary empyrean. Long live its sublime mockery of all attempts to normalize desire . . . and the reach of great literature.

Translator's Note

For several years the question has been whether *Ferdydurke* could be translated into comprehensible English, and if so, would it still be *Ferdydurke?*

Ferdydurke was published in Poland in 1937 and translated into Spanish in 1947 in Buenos Aires, the result of a collaboration between Gombrowicz and his Hispanic literary friends. In the early 1960s it was translated into French and German. An English version was derived from the French, German, and possibly the Spanish translations, but some of the most beautiful and important passages were omitted. This is the first unabridged English translation, and it is taken directly from Gombrowicz's original text. I hope that it will establish that it is possible to translate *Ferdydurke,* at least for the most part.

I arrived at the task of translating *Ferdydurke* by a circuitous route. I was born in Poland, and my mother tongue is the language in which Gombrowicz was creating his works and on which he was already exerting an influence. I began to learn English at the age of thirteen when, as a refugee during World War II, I found myself living in England and Ireland. I settled in the United States in 1959 and began, some years later, to write short stories in English—rather idiosyncratic in content and style—and discovered an affinity with Gombrowicz's writing. After reading Gombrowicz's last novel, *Cosmos*, in Polish, I thought that it would sound beautiful in English. I translated the first chapter of *Cosmos*, as well as some of Gombrowicz's short stories, and began to explore the possibilities of having them published. This brought me into contact with publishers and scholars, and with Gombrowicz's widow, Rita Gombrowicz. They all encouraged me to translate *Ferdydurke*, Gombrowicz's first major work.

I decided at the outset to use American rather than British English because it is less formal and therefore better suited to Gombrowicz's style. My own English is influenced by my having learned it in London and Dublin. For this reason, and also because the translation was going to be from a native language to an acquired one, it became apparent that I would need the assistance of a born speaker of American English. My husband's reviews of the many drafts proved to be most useful in this respect. In some instances, however, when he would interject, "But we don't say it this way," my reply would be, "In Polish we don't either; it's pure Gombrowicz"—and this would be the final court of appeal. Clearly I was dealing with yet another language: Gombrowicz's Polish.

Gombrowicz had availed himself of four idioms: colloquial Polish; literary Polish; the language of the intelligentsia and the landed gentry; and the language of the peasantry. But he also introduced his own idiosyncrasies by playing *with* and *on* words, by changing nouns into verbs and adjectives, by using unusual phraseology, and by inventing new forms, some of which have entered colloquial Polish. Had I not worked as a psychiatrist with English-speaking schizophrenics who invent their own languages, I may not have felt comfortable "neologizing" English in such crucial words and phrases as "proffed" and "he had dealt me the *pupa*." The Polish word *pupa* (pronounced "poopa") presented a special problem. It means the buttocks, behind, bum, tush, rump, but not one of these (nor any others that I considered) adequately conveys the sense in which Gombrowicz uses "pupa" in the text. While the "mug" is Gombrowicz's metaphor for the destructive elements in human relationships, the pupa is his metaphor for the gentle, insidious, but definite infantilizing and humiliation that we inflict on one another. We made the decision to stay with the Polish word.

Ferdydurke is a tragi-farce, in which events are often tragic and comic at the same time, and in which the mug and the pupa are the metaphors for violence and belittlement. Names of body parts are given meaning beyond the usual, often through wordplay. This wordplay is, whenever possible, translated literally. Some plays on words are impossible to translate—for example, Gombrowicz uses the fact that the Polish term for fingers and toes is same word to create wordplay between "fingers" and "tiptoeing."

I had to bear in mind that in English the sequence of words is crucial to meaning, whereas in Polish there is a more complicated grammar that clarifies the meaning of a sentence. Mishaps such as "he threw his mother from the train a kiss" do not occur in Polish.

Gombrowicz delighted, it seems, in compressing the abstract into the concrete: it is not the thought of the farmhand but the farmhand himself that "paints the morning in bright and pleasant colors," or, "she was generally a bit disgusted with mother," instead of "mothering."

Gombrowicz's long sentences and paragraphs, frequent use of dashes, and his grouping of entire conversations into single paragraphs were part of his style, and I preserved these. The same applies to his repeating a word rather than providing its synonym; by doing so he evokes a sense of emphasis and rhythm.

I was equally faithful to Gombrowicz's changes of tense between past and present in the same paragraph and even in the same sentence. The metamorphosis of a thirty-year-old man into a teenager is often indicated by past tense becoming present. Also, the change of tense imbues the story with a surreal sense of time.

In translating idioms I sometimes had to use an English one that had the same meaning as the Polish but was entirely different. For *z palca*—"from the finger"—I substituted "out of thin air." However, the English idiom "the end justifies the means" was changed to "the end sanctifies the means," preserving a nuance of the Polish.

In Polish, the use of diminutives imparts, in many instances, an aura of affectation and artificiality, and they often sound ridiculous. Gombrowicz spared no effort in pointing this out by his frequent and exaggerated use of diminutives. I have tried to capture this with diminutive adjectives, as in "cute little head," or by using the ending "-ie."

In Poland, French was not the language of the aristocracy, as it had been in Russia until the early 1800s, but the occasional use of French and other languages was, nonetheless, a common affectation and a fruitful field for Gombrowicz's satire. I have followed Gombrowicz in not offering a translation of familiar foreign words and phrases.

Two important names—Kneadus (from the verb "to knead") and Youngblood—were translated into English because they have definite connotations in Polish that contribute to the meaning of the tale. The title itself, *Ferdydurke*, has no meaning in Polish, although there is some conjecture that the word was a contraction and alteration of the name Freddy Durkee, the chief character in Sinclair Lewis's *Babbitt*, which was widely read in Poland in the early 1930s. Gombrowicz himself never explained the title.

Gombrowicz has presented us with a remarkable novel in a bold and innovative style—with élan, humor, beauty. No translation is final, but it was incumbent on me to make a valiant effort to transfer the original text to the English-speaking reader with fidelity and with the verve inherent in the original; my guiding principle was to approach Gombrowicz with humility and the reader with audacity.

The following texts were used in this translation.

Witold Gombrowicz, *Ferdydurke* (Paris: Institut Littéraire, 1969). Includes changes by Gombrowicz.

Gombrowicz, *Ferdydurke,* translated into English by Eric Mosbacher (London, 1961).

Gombrowicz, *Ferdydurke,* translated into French by George Sédir (Paris, 1973).

Gombrowicz, *Ferdydurke,* translated into Spanish, based on 1947 translation (Buenos Aires, 1964).

Gombrowicz, *Polish Reminiscences and Travels Through Argentina* (in Polish).

Gombrowicz, *Diary* (in Polish).

Michał Głowiński, *Witold Gombrowicz's "Ferdydurke"* (in Polish).

Acknowledgments

It is my pleasure to acknowledge the unfailing support of Professor Stanisław Barańczak in this difficult and challenging endeavor. Coming from such an esteemed translator, it meant a great deal to me. When I cried to high heaven for succor, he always gave me encouragement and valuable suggestions.

My gratitude also goes out to my husband, Thom Lane, whose familiarity with American colloquial English and slang, as well as his wide reading of European literature, were of great assistance to me. He also helped me clarify complex passages through his mindful reading of my translation drafts.

I also want to thank Dr. Richard Fenigsen for his careful verification of my translation from the Polish, and for his helpful remarks.

No less appreciation is due my family, friends, and colleagues for their support during the long process of the translation, and for their comments.

And, last but not least, I want to thank Jonathan Brent of Yale University Press for his willingness to let this work reach the light of day.

D. B.

1 Abduction

Transition time
Twilight

Tuesday morning I awoke at that pale and lifeless hour when night is almost gone but dawn has not yet come into its own. Awakened suddenly, I wanted to take a taxi and dash to the railroad station, thinking I was due to leave, when, in the next minute, I realized to my chagrin that no train was waiting for me at the station, that no hour had struck. I lay in the murky light while my body, unbearably frightened, crushed my spirit with fear, and my spirit crushed my body, whose tiniest fibers cringed in apprehension that nothing would ever happen, nothing ever change, that nothing would ever come to pass, and whatever I undertook, nothing, but nothing, would ever come of it. It was the dread of nonexistence, the terror of extinction, it was the angst of nonlife, the fear of unreality, a biological scream of all my cells in the face of an inner disintegration when all would be blown to pieces and scattered to the winds. It was the fear of unseemly pettiness and mediocrity, the fright of distraction, panic at fragmentation, the dread of rape from within and of rape that was threatening me from without—but most important, there was something on my heels at all times, something that I would call a sense of inner, intermolecular mockery and derision, an inbred superlaugh of my bodily parts and the analogous parts of my spirit, all running wild.

The fear had been generated by a dream that plagued me through the night, and finally woke me. The dream took me back to my youth, a reversal in time that should be forbidden to nature, and I saw myself as I was at fifteen or sixteen, standing on a rock near a mill by a river, my face to the wind, and I heard myself saying something, I heard my long-buried, roosterlike squeaky little voice, I saw my features that were not yet fully formed, my nose that was too small, my hands that were too large—I felt the unpleasant texture of that intermediate, passing phase of development. I woke up laughing and terrified both, because I thought that the thirty-year-old man I am today was aping and ridiculing the callow juvenile I once was, while he in turn was aping me and, by the same token, each of us was aping himself. Oh, wretched memory that compels us to remember the paths we took to arrive at the present state of affairs! Further: as I lay awake but still half dreaming, I felt that my body was not homogeneous, that some parts were still those of a boy, and that my head was laughing at my leg and ridiculing it, that my leg was laughing at my head, that my finger was poking fun at my heart, my heart at my brain, that my nose was thumbing itself at my eye, my eye chuckling and bellowing at my nose—and all my parts were wildly raping each other in an all-encompassing and piercing state of pan-mockery. Nor did my fear lessen one iota when I reached full consciousness and began reflecting on my life. On the contrary, it intensified even as it was interrupted (or accentuated) by a giggle my mouth could not hold back. I was halfway down the path of my life when I found myself in a dark forest. But this forest, worse luck, was g r e e n.

For in my waking life I was just as unsettled and torn apart—as in the dream. I had recently crossed the unavoidable Rubicon of thirty, I had passed that milestone and, according to my birth certificate and to all appearances, I was a mature human being, and yet I wasn't—what was I then? A thirty-year-old bridge player? Someone who happened to be working, attending to life's trivia, meeting deadlines? What was my status? I frequented bars and cafés where I exchanged a few words, occasionally even ideas, with people I ran into, but my status was not at all clear, and I myself did not know whether I was a mature man or a green youth; at this turning point of my life I was neither this nor that—I was nothing—and my contemporaries, already married and established, if not in their views on life, at least at various government agencies, treated me with understandable mistrust. My aunts, those numerous quarter-mothers, tacked-on, patched-on, though they loved me dearly, had long been urging me to settle down and be somebody, a lawyer, or a civil servant—they seemed exceedingly irked by my vagueness, and, not knowing what to make of me, they didn't know how to talk to me, so they just babbled.

"Joey," they would say between one babble and another, "it's high time, dear child. What will people say? If you don't want to be a doctor, at least be a womanizer, or a fancier of horses, be something . . . be something definite . . ."

And I heard them whispering to one another that I was socially awkward, inexperienced, and, as they wearied of the blank that I was creating in their heads, they would resume their babbling. True, this state of affairs could not continue indefinitely. The hands on nature's clock move relentlessly, inexorably. When I cut my last teeth, my wisdom teeth, my development was supposed to be complete, and it was time for the inevitable kill, for the man to kill the inconsolable little boy, to emerge like a butterfly and leave behind the remains of the chrysalis that had spent itself. I was supposed to lift myself out of mists and chaos, out of murky swamps, out of swirls and roars, out of reeds and rushes, out of the croaking of frogs, and emerge among clear and crystallized forms: run a comb through my hair, tidy up my affairs, enter the social life of adults and deliberate with them.

Oh, sure! But I had already given it a try, I had already made that effort, yet I could only shake with laughter at the results. And therefore, to make myself presentable, my hair neatly combed, and to explain myself as best I could, I set out to write a book—strange that I should think my entrance into the world needed an explanation, even though no one has yet seen an explanation that was anything but obfuscation. I wished, first of all, to buy my way into people's good graces with my book so that, in subsequent personal contact, I would find the ground already prepared, and, I reasoned, if I succeeded in implanting in their souls a favorable image of me, this image would in turn shape me; and so, willy-nilly, I would become mature. So why did my pen betray me? Why did holy shame forbid me to write a notoriously trivial novel? Instead of spinning lofty themes from the heart, from the soul, I spun my themes from more lowly quarters and filled my narrative with legs, frogs, with material that was immature and fermenting, and, having set it all apart on the page by style, by voice, by a tone that was cold and self-possessed, I indicated that I wished, herewith, to part ways with those ferments. Why did I, as if thwarting my own purpose, entitle my book *Memoirs from the Time of Immaturity?* * In vain my friends advised me against using such a title, saying that I should avoid even the slightest allusion to immaturity. "Don't do it," they said, "the concept of immaturity is too drastic, if you think of yourself as immature, who will think of you as mature? Don't you understand that first and foremost you must think of yourself as mature, otherwise—nothing doing?" Yet it just didn't seem appropriate to dismiss, easily and glibly, the sniveling brat within me, I thought that the truly Adult were sufficiently sharp and clear-sighted to see through this, and that anyone incessantly pursued by the brat within had no business appearing in public without the brat. But perhaps I took the serious-minded too seriously and overestimated the maturity of the mature.

Memories, memories! My head tucked under my pillow, my legs

---

*This was Witold Gombrowicz's first book, later completed by the author and published as *Bakakaj*.

under the covers, tossing about between fear and laughter, I took stock of my entrance into the adult world. There is too much silence about the personal, inner hurts and injuries inflicted by that entrance, the grave consequences of which remain with us forever. Men of letters, those men who have a God-given talent to write on the subject of such remote and indifferent matters as, for example, the grief in the soul of Emperor Charles II caused by Brunhilde's marriage, shudder at the thought of mentioning the most important issue—their metamorphosis into a public and social being. They prefer, it seems, to have everyone think of them as writers inspired by the grace of God, not man, and to imagine that they have dropped from the sky, talent and all; they are too embarrassed to shed any light on the concessions they had to make as individuals, on the personal defeats they had to endure in order to acquire the right to expound on Brunhilde or, for that matter, on the lives of beekeepers. No, not a word about their own lives—only about the lives of beekeepers. Indeed, having produced twenty books on the lives of beekeepers, one can be immortalized—but what is the connection, where is the bond between the king of beekeepers and the inner man, between the man and the youth, between the youth and the boy, the boy and the child that, after all, he once was, what comfort is the king to the little brat in you? A life unmindful of these bonds, a life that does not evolve in unbroken continuity from one phase to another is like a house that is being built from the top down, and must inevitably end in a schizophrenic split of the inner self.

Memories! Mankind is accursed because our existence on this earth does not tolerate any well-defined and stable hierarchy, everything continually flows, spills over, moves on, everyone must be aware of and be judged by everyone else, and the opinions that the ignorant, dull, and slow-witted hold about us are no less important than the opinions of the bright, the enlightened, the refined. This is because man is profoundly dependent on the reflection of himself in another man's soul, be it even the soul of an idiot. I absolutely disagree with my fellow writers who treat the opinions of the dull-witted with an aristocratic haughtiness and declare: *odi profanum vulgus*. What a cheap and simplistic way of avoiding reality, what a shoddy escape into specious loftiness! I maintain, on the contrary, that the more dull and narrow-minded they are, the more urgent and compelling are their opinions, just as an ill-fitting shoe hurts us more than a well-fitting one. Oh, those judgments, the bottomless pit of people's judgments and opinions about your wisdom, feelings, and character, about all the details of your personality—it's a pit that opens up before the daredevil who drapes his thoughts in print and lets them loose on paper, oh, printed paper, paper, paper! And I'm not even talking about the heartfelt opinions so fondly held by our aunts, no, I mean the opinions of those other aunts—the cultural aunts, those female semi-writers and tacked-on semi-critics who make pronouncements in literary magazines. Indeed, world culture has been beset by a flock of superfluous hens patched-on, pinned-on, to literature, who have become finely tuned to spiritual values and well versed in aesthetics, frequently entertaining views and opinions of their own, who have even caught on to the notions that Oscar Wilde is passé and that Bernard Shaw is a master of paradox. Oh, they are on to the fact that they must be independent, profound, unobtrusively assertive, and filled with auntie kindliness. Auntie, auntie, auntie! Unless you have ever found yourself in the laboratory of a cultural aunt and been dissected, mute and without a groan, by her trivializing mentality that turns all life lifeless, unless you have ever seen an auntie's critique of yourself in a newspaper, you have no concept of triviality, and auntie-triviality in particular.

Further, let us consider the opinions of men and women of the landed gentry, the opinions of schoolgirls, the narrow-minded opinions of minor office clerks, the bureaucratic opinions of high officials, the opinions of lawyers in the provinces, the hyperbolic opinions of students, the arrogant opinions of little old men, and the opinions of journalists, the opinions of social activists as well as the opinions of doctors' wives, and, finally, the opinions of children listening to their parents' opinions, the opinions of underling chambermaids and of cooks, the opinions of our female cousins, the opinions of schoolgirls—a whole ocean of opinions, each one defining you within someone else, and creating you in another man's soul. It's as if you were being born inside a thousand souls that are too tight-fitting for comfort! But my situation was even more thorny and complex, just as my book was more thorny and complex than the conventionally mature reading matter. It brought me, to be sure, an array of fine friends, and, if only those cultural aunts and other members of the populace could hear how splendidly I was feted in a small circle that was closed to them and not accessible even to their aspirations, a circle of the Esteemed and the Splendiferous, and how, at those lofty heights, I carried on intellectual conversations, they would fall prostrate before me and lick my boots. Yet there must have been something immature in my book, something that encouraged undue intimacy and attracted those transitory individuals who were neither fish nor fowl, that most awful stratum of semi-intelligentsia—as if the time of immaturity had lured the demimonde of culture. It is conceivable that my book, too subtle for dullards, was at the same time not sufficiently lofty or puffed up for the rabble who respond solely to the outer trappings of what is important. And, as so often happened, I would leave one of those hallowed and esteemed places where I had just been pleasantly and reverently celebrated, to be faced, in the street, by some engineer's wife or a schoolgirl who would unceremoniously treat me like one of her own, like an immature kinsman or fellow traveler, slap me on the back and exclaim: "Hello, Joey, you silly, you're, you're—immature!" And so I seemed wise to some, silly to others, notable to some, hardly noticed by others, commonplace to some, aristocratic to others. Spread-eagled between loftiness and lowliness and chummy with both, respected and disparaged, admired and disdained, as chance or circumstances would have it! My life was torn apart as it had never been in the quiet days I spent in the shelter of my home. And I no longer knew whether I belonged to those who valued me, or to those who did not.

But, worse still—hating the semi-educated rabble, hating it with a vengeance, perhaps as no one has ever hated it before—I played into their hands; I shunned the elite and the aristocracy, and flew from their friendly and open arms into the boorish paws of those who considered me a juvenile. H o w one organizes oneself and t o w a r d w h a t one directs oneself is actually of primary importance and crucial to one's development—in actions, for example, in speech and twaddle, in one's writing—whether one directs oneself solely toward those who are mature and fully evolved, toward a world of crystal-clear ideas, or whether one lets oneself be constantly plagued by the specter of the rabble, of immaturity, of schoolboys and schoolgirls, of gentry and peasantry, of cultural aunts, of journalists and columnists, by the specter of the shady, murky demimonde that lies in wait to slowly entwine you in the green of its creepers, lianas, and other African plants. Not for one moment could I forget the little not-quite world of the not-quite-human, and yet, terrified and disgusted as I was and shuddering at the very thought of that swampy green, I could not tear myself away from it, mesmerized by it like a little birdie by a snake. As if some demon were tempting me with immaturity! As if I were favoring, against my very nature, the lower class and loving it—because it held me captive as a juvenile. Even if I strained all my faculties I would not have been able to speak with intelligence, not even for a moment, because I knew that somewhere in the provinces a doctor would think that I was silly anyway, and would expect nothing of me but silliness; and I could not be on my best behavior, nor comport myself decently in social situations, because I knew that schoolgirls, someplace, expected nothing of me but indecencies. Truly, in the world of the spirit, rape is the order of the day, we are forced to be as others see us, and to manifest ourselves through them, we are not autonomous, and what's more—my personal calamity came from an unhealthy

delight in actually making myself dependent on green youths, juve-
niles, teenage girls, and cultural aunts. To have that cultural aunt
forever on your back—to be naive because someone who is naive
thinks you are naive—to be silly because some silly person thinks you
are silly—to be green because someone who is immature dunks and
bathes you in greenness of his own—indeed, that could drive you
crazy, were it not for the little word "indeed," which somehow lets
you go on living! To brush against a higher and more mature realm
and yet be unable to penetrate it, to be but a step from refinement,
elegance, wisdom, dignity, from mature judgments and mutual respect, from hierarchy and acknowledged values, and yet to merely
lick those sweetmeats through the shop window, and have no access
to these matters, to be superfluous? To associate with adults and still
imagine, as at sixteen, that you are merely pretending to be an adult?
To pretend you're a writer, a man of letters, to parody literary style
and mature, fanciful phrases? To join publicly, as an artist, the merciless fray for the survival of your true "self," while at the same time
covertly siding with your enemies?

Ah yes, at the outset of my public life I did receive a less-than-
glorious consecration, and I was duly anointed by the lower class. Yet
what complicated matters even more was the fact that my social
demeanor left much to be desired, I was fumbling along, inadequate
and helpless in relation to those semi-brilliant men of the world. My
awkwardness, stemming from contrariness, or perhaps from anxiety,
would not let me identify myself with any aspect of maturity, and,
out of sheer panic, I would quite often pinch the very person whose
spirit reached out to my spirit with approval. I envied those literary
men, exalted and predestined to higher things from the cradle,
whose Soul—its backside prodded with an awl—strove continually
upward; those writers who in their Soul took themselves seriously,
and who, with inborn ease and in great creative torment, dealt with
matters so high and mighty and forever hallowed that God himself
would have seemed to them commonplace and less than noble. Why

isn't everyone called to write yet another novel about love or to tear apart, in pain and suffering, some social ill or other, and become the Champion of the oppressed? Or to write poems, and become the Poet who believes in the "glorious future of poetry"? To be talented, and with one's spirit to lift and nourish the wide masses of untalented spirits? Yet what pleasure is there in agonizing and tormenting oneself, in burning on the altar of self-sacrifice, be it in the realm of the high and the sublime and—the mature? To live vicariously through thousand-year-old cultural institutions as securely as if one were setting aside a little sum in a savings account—this could be one's own, as well as other people's, fulfillment. But I was, alas, a juvenile, and juvenility was my only cultural institution. Caught and held back twice—first by my childish past, which I could not forget, and the second time by the childishness of other people's notions of me, a caricature that had sunk into their souls—I was the melancholy prisoner of all that is green, why, an insect in a deep, dense thicket.

A rather unpleasant and, what's more, a dangerous situation. For there is nothing that the Mature hate more, there is nothing that disgusts them more, than immaturity. They will tolerate the most rabid destructiveness as long as it happens within the confines of maturity, they are not threatened by the revolutionary who fights one mature ideal with another mature ideal and abolishes Monarchy in favor of the Republic, nor by one who nibbles at the Republic and then devours it with Monarchy. Indeed, it gives them pleasure to watch the thriving business of maturity and of all that is sublime. However, let them as much as sniff immaturity, let them sniff a juvenile or a sniveling brat in someone and they will pounce on him and, like swans that peck a duck to death, they will kill him with sarcasm, derision, and mockery, they will not allow a foundling from the world that they have renounced long ago to befoul their nest. And how will it all end? Where will this road take me? How did I become imprisoned in my own underdevelopment, I wondered, where did my infatuation with all the greenness have its origins—is it because I come from a country rife with uncouth, mediocre, transitory individuals who feel awkward in a starched collar, where it is not Melancholy and Destiny but rather Duffer and Fumbler who moon about the fields in lamentation? Or is it because I've lived in an era that, every five minutes, emits new fads and slogans, and, at the slightest opportunity, grimaces convulsively—a transitory era? . . . A pale dawn was seeping in below the half-open window shade and, as I was thus taking stock of my life, I blushed and shook with an obscene little laugh between my bed sheets—and I began to explode with an impotent, bestial, mechanical, knee-jerk kind of laughter, as if someone were tickling my foot, as if it were not my face but my leg that was giggling. It was high time to put an end to it, cut the ties with my childhood, make a decision and start anew—do something! Forget at last, forget the schoolgirls! Dismiss the fondness of cultural aunts and peasant girls, forget the minor and pretentious office clerks, forget about the leg and my heinous past, snub the sniveling brat and the juvenile—settle myself squarely on mature turf, and yes, finally assume that extremely aristocratic stance and despise, despise! No longer stimulate, titillate, and attract the immaturity of others with immaturity, as I have done thus far, but, on the contrary, elicit my own maturity and with it evoke their maturity, speak from my soul to their soul! The soul? And forget the leg? The soul? How about the leg? How can one forget the legs of cultural aunts? And what if, no matter how hard I try, I do not succeed in conquering the green that is budding, pulsating, growing all around (and I'm almost sure not to succeed), what if I treat people maturely and they persist in treating me immaturely, what if I address them with wisdom and they respond with stupidity? No, no, I'd rather be the first to act immaturely, I don't want to expose my wisdom to their stupidity, I'd rather direct my stupidity against them! And yet no, no, that's not what I want, I'd rather be at one with them because I love them, I love the little buds and sprouts, the little sprigs of green, oh!—and all at once I felt them grabbing me again, catching me in their love embrace, and again I roared with that mechanical, knee-jerk laughter and sang a frivolous little ditty:

> In the town of Little Zanich
> In the bedroom of Miss Bozek
> Hid two bandits in a closet

. . . when suddenly the taste in my mouth turned bitter, my throat went dry—I realized that I was not alone. There was someone else in the room, in the corner by the stove where it was still dark—another person was there.

But the door was locked. Not a person then, but an apparition. An apparition? The devil? A ghost? A dead person? I suddenly sensed that it was not someone dead but someone alive, and all at once my hair stood on end—I sensed another human, like a dog smells another dog. My mouth dry, my heart pounding, I was hardly able to catch my breath—when I realized that it was I standing by the stove. And this time it was not a dream—it really was my double standing by the stove. I noticed however, that he was more scared than I was; he stood with his head lowered, his eyes downcast, his hands hanging by his side—and his fear gave me courage. I peeked from under my covers at a face that was mine and yet it wasn't mine. It loomed from a deep and dark greenness, itself a brighter green—it was my own countenance as it had always been. Here were my lips . . . my ears . . . my nose, they were my home. Hail familiar nooks and crannies! And how familiar! How well I knew the twist of those lips hiding tension and fear. The corners of my mouth, my chin, my ear partially torn off by Ziggy long ago—all the signs and symptoms of a twofold impact, a face that two forces, an outer and an inner, had ground between them. It was all mine—or maybe I was it—or maybe it was all someone else's—and yet it was I.

I suddenly thought that it was not I. I felt like someone who unexpectedly looks into a mirror and for a split second does not recognize himself, so did the startling concreteness of the form surprise me and cut me to the quick. The quaint short hairstyle, the eyelids, pants just like mine, organs of sight, hearing, and breathing—were these my organs, was it really me? The minute details, the clarity and precision of the outline . . . all too clear. He must have noticed that I saw those details, and, embarrassed, he smiled uneasily and waved his hand with a hesitant motion that seemed to recede into the darkness.

And yet, as the light from the window grew brighter, his form became more and more vivid—his fingers and fingernails now came into view—and I saw . . . but the ghost, realizing that I saw him, crouched slightly and, not looking at me, began to signal me with his hand not to look. Yet I could not refrain from looking. Because that's the way I am. Strange indeed, like Mme Pompadour. And unpredictable. But why? An ephemeron. His faults and blemishes creeping into the light of day, he crouched like one of those nocturnal animals made easy prey by the light—like a rat caught by surprise in the middle of the room. The details emerged more and more clearly, more and more horribly, body parts creeping out of him everywhere, one by one, clearly defined and real . . . to the limits of their disgraceful clarity . . . to the limits of disgrace . . . I saw his finger, his fingernails, his nose, his eye, his thigh, and his foot, everything was now out in the open, and, as if hypnotized by all the details, I stood up and took a step toward him. He shuddered and waved his hand as if in apology, and he seemed to say "that's not it, never mind—let me be, forgive me, leave me alone" . . . but my movement, initiated as just a warning, ended despicably—I continued to move toward him, and, unable to stop the sweep of my outstretched hand, I struck him in the face. Off with you! Off! No, this is not me at all! This is something randomly thrust upon me, something alien, an intrusion, a compromise between the inner and outer world, it's not m y body at all! He groaned and—with a leap—he vanished. I was left alone but actually not alone—how could I be alone when I wasn't even there, I had no sense of being there, and not a single thought, gesture, action, or word, in fact nothing seemed to be mine, but rather it was as if it had all been settled somewhere outside myself, decided for me—because in reality I was quite different! And this upset me terribly. Oh, to create my own form! To turn outward! To express myself! Let me conceive my own shape, let no one do it for me! My agitation pushes me toward writing paper. I pull out a few sheets from the drawer, it is morning now, sunlight pours into my room, the maid brings my morning coffee and bread rolls while I begin, amid shimmering and finely chiseled forms, to write the first pages of my very own *oeuvre*, which will be just like me, identical with me, the sum total of me, an *oeuvre* in which I will be free to expound my own views against everything and everyone, when suddenly the bell rings, the maid opens the door, and T. Pimko appears—a doctor of philosophy and a professor, in reality just a schoolteacher, a cultured philologue from Kraków, short and slight, skinny, bald, wearing spectacles, pin-striped trousers, a jacket, yellow buckskin shoes, his fingernails large and yellow.

> Do you know the Professor?
> Have you met the Professor?
> Professor?

Stop, stop, stop, stop, stop! At the sight of this horribly banal and utterly commonplace Form I threw myself on my texts, covering them with my whole body, but he sat down, so I too had to sit down, and having sat down he proceeded to offer me his condolences on the death of my aunt, who died long ago and whom I had totally forgotten.

"The memory of the dead," said Pimko, "is the ark of the covenant between the new times and the old, just like the songs of the people (Mickiewicz). We live the life of the dead (A. Comte). Your aunt is dead, and this is a good reason, even a compelling reason, to extol her contribution to cultural thought. The deceased had her faults

Abduction

(he enumerated them), but she also had her good points (he enumerated them) which benefited everyone, all in all not a bad book, that is, I meant to say a 'C plus'—well then, to make a long story short, the deceased was a positive force, my overall assessment of her is rather favorable, which I consider it my pleasurable duty to tell you, since I, Pimko, stand guard of the cultural values your aunt undoubtedly still personifies, especially since she's dead. And besides," he added indulgently, "*de mortuis nihil nisi bene,* and although one could criticize this or that, why discourage a young author—I beg your pardon, a nephew . . . But what is this?" he exclaimed when he saw my notes lying on the table. "Not only a nephew, but also an author! I see we're trying our wings, are we? Chirp, chirp, chirp, author! Let me look it over, and encourage you . . ."

And, still seated, he reached across the table for my papers, put on his spectacles, all the while remaining seated.

"It's nothing . . . it's just . . ." I mumbled, still in my seat. My whole world suddenly collapsed, his talk of the aunt and the author upset me no end.

"Well, well, well," he said, "chirp, chirp, little chickie." He wiped one eye as he said this, he then took out a cigarette and, holding it between two fingers of his left hand, proceeded to squeeze it with two fingers of his right hand; at the same time he sneezed because the tobacco irritated his nose, and, still seated, he began to read. And sitting squarely on his wisdom, he went on reading. I felt sick at the sight of him reading. My world collapsed and promptly reset itself according to the rules of a conventional prof. I could not pounce on him because I was seated, and I was seated because he was seated. For no apparent reason, sitting itself assumed prime importance and became an obstacle to everything else. Not knowing what to do or how to behave I fidgeted in my seat, moved my leg, looked around at the walls and bit my nails, while he went on sitting, logically and consistently, his seat fairly and squarely filled with that of a prof, reading. This went on for a terribly long time. Minutes weighed on me like hours, seconds stretched and stretched making me feel like someone trying to drink the ocean through a straw. I groaned:

"For God's sake, not your prof stuff! You're killing me with it!"

The rigid, angular prof was indeed killing me. But he continued to read in the manner of a true prof, and, like a typical prof, he went on absorbing my rambunctious texts, holding the paper close to his eyes, while outside the window a brownstone building stood, twelve windows wide and twelve windows deep. A dream?! An apparition? Why had he come here? Why was he sitting? Why was I sitting? How on earth was everything that preceded this—dreams, memories, aunts, torments, ghosts, my *oeuvre* only just begun—epitomized now by this commonplace prof sitting here? My whole world shrank into this trite prof. How unbearable! It made sense for him to keep sitting (because he was reading), but it made no sense for me to be sitting. I strained to get up, but just at that moment he looked at me indulgently from under his spectacles, and suddenly—I became small, my leg became a little leg, my hand a little hand, my persona a little persona, my being a little being, my *oeuvre* a little *oeuvre*, my body a little body, while he grew larger and larger, sitting and glancing at me, and reading my manuscript forever and ever amen—he sat.

Do you know what it feels like to be diminished within someone else? Oh, to be diminished within an aunt is unseemly enough, but to be diminished within a huge, commonplace prof is the peak of unseemly diminishment. And I noticed that the prof was like a cow grazing on my greenness. It's a strange feeling—to see a prof nibbling at the green of your meadow, which is actually your apartment, to see him sitting in your chair and reading—yet actually nibbling and grazing. Something terrible was happening to me, and, at the same time, I was surrounded by something stupid and brazenly unreal. "A spirit!" I exclaimed, "That's me, a spirit! Not a little author! A spirit!

A living spirit! That's me!" But he just went on sitting, sitting, and sitting, stuck to his seat—an act of sheer stupidity—yet incredibly powerful. He took his spectacles off his nose, wiped them with his handkerchief, and placed them back on his nose, the nose that had now become indomitable. It was a truly nasal nose, trite and inane, consisting of two parallel, finite tubes. And he said:

"What do you mean, a spirit?"

"My spirit!" I exclaimed.

He then asked:

"You mean the spirit of your home, your country?"

"No, not of my country, my own spirit!"

"Your own?" he asked amiably, "we're talking about your spirit then? But are we at least familiar with the spirit of King Ladislas?"

What, King Ladislas? I felt like a train suddenly shunted to the siding of King Ladislas. Stopped in my tracks, my mouth open, I realized that I was not familiar with the spirit of King Ladislas.

"And are we familiar with the spirit of the times? How about the spirit of Hellenic civilization? And the Gallic, and the spirit of moderation and good taste? And the spirit of the sixteenth century bucolic writer, known only to myself, who was the first to use the word 'umbilicus'? And the spirit of language? Should one say 'use' or 'utilize'?"

His questions caught me by surprise. Ten thousand spirits suddenly smothered my spirit, I mumbled that I didn't know, he then pressed on: what did I know about the spirit of the poet Kasprowicz and his attitude toward the peasantry, he then asked about the historian Lelewel's first love. I cleared my throat and quickly glanced at my nails—they were blank, no crib notes there. I turned my head as if expecting someone to prompt me. But of course there was no one there. What a nightmare, for God's sake! What was happening? O God! I quickly turned my head back to its usual position and looked at him, but with a gaze that was no longer mine, it was the gaze of a schoolboy scowling childishly and filled with hatred. I was suddenly seized with an inappropriate and rather old-fashioned itch—to hit the prof with a spitball right on the nose. Realizing that I was losing it, I made a supreme effort to ask Pimko in a genial tone about recent events in town, but then, instead of my normal voice a broken, squeaky sound came out, as if my voice were changing back, so I fell silent; and Pimko asked about adverbs, told me to decline *mensa, mensae, mensae,* to conjugate *amo, amas, amat,* he then winced and said: "Well, yes, we'll have to work on it." He took out his notebook and gave me a bad grade, all the while sitting, and his sitting was absolute and final.

What? What's this? I wanted to scream "I'm not a schoolboy, it's all a mistake!" I tried to run for it, but something caught me in its claws from behind and riveted me to the spot—it was my puerile, infantile pupa.* I was unable to move because of my pupa while the prof, still seated, and while sitting, projected such perfect prof-authority that instead of screaming I raised my hand to speak, like boys do in school.

"Sit down, Kowalski. Not to the bathroom again?"

And so I sat through this surreal nonsense, gagged and steam-rolled by the prof, I sat on my childish little pupa while he, seated as if on the Acropolis, wrote something in his notebook. Finally he said:

"Well, let's go to school, Joey."

"To what school?"

"To Principal Piórkowski's school. A first-rate educational institution. There are still vacancies in the sixth grade. Your education has been sorely neglected, and first of all we must make up what is lacking."

"But to what school?!"

"To Mr. Piórkowski's school. Don't be scared, we teachers love you little chickies, chirp, chirp, chirp, you know: 'suffer the little ones to come unto me.'"

*See Translator's Note.

"But to what school?!!!"

"To Mr. Piórkowski's school. He asked me the other day to fill all the vacancies. The school must stay open. There would be no school without pupils, and no teachers without schools. To school! To school! They'll make a student out of you yet."

"But to what school?!!!"

"Oh, stop fussing! To school! To school!"

He called the maid and told her to bring my coat, but the girl could not understand why this strange gentleman was about to take me away, and she broke into wails, so Pimko pinched her—there was no way for a pinched servant girl to continue her wailing, so she bared her teeth and burst out laughing like a pinched servant would—he then took me by the hand and led me out of the house, and in the street houses stood as usual and people walked about!

Help! Police! This was ridiculous! Too ridiculous to be real! Incredible because it was so ridiculous! Too ridiculous even to fight back . . . I couldn't anyway—against this inane prof, this trivial prof. Just as you can't when someone asks you an inane and trivial question—so I couldn't either. My idiotic, infantile pupa had paralyzed me, taking away all my ability to resist; trotting by the side of this colossus who was bounding ahead with huge steps, I could hardly keep up because of my pupa. Farewell, O Spirit, farewell my *oeuvre* only just begun, farewell genuine form, my very own, and hail, hail, oh terrible and infantile form, so callow and green! Tritely proffed by him, I ran in mincing steps by the side of the giant prof who muttered on: "Chirp, chirp, little chickie . . . The sniffling little nose . . . I love, ee, ee . . . Little fellow, little, little man, ee, ee, ee, chirp, chirp, chickadee, Joey, Joey, little Joey, tiny Joey, tinier and tinier, chirp, chirp, tiny, tiny little, little pupa . . ." Ahead of us a refined lady was walking her little pinscher on a leash, the dog growled, pounced on Pimko, ripped his trouser leg, Pimko yelled, expressed a unfavorable opinion of the dog and its owner, pinned his trouser leg with a safety pin, and we walked on.

2 Imprisonment and
Further Belittlement

And now before us—no, I don't believe my eyes—is a low building, a school, and Pimko drags me there by my little hand despite my tears and protestations, then pushes me in through a wicket gate. We arrived during lunch hour, and we saw in the school yard human beings of that transitional age between ten and twenty walking in circles and eating lunch, which consisted of bread and butter or bread and cheese. There were cracks in the fence surrounding the school yard through which mothers and aunts, never tiring of their little darlings, were peeking. Pimko, relishing the school aroma, breathed it in through his thoroughbred nasal tubes.

"Chirp, chirp, chirp, little fellow," he called out, "little, little fellow..."

At the same time an intelligent-looking man with a limp, a teacher on lunch-hour duty, no doubt, approached and greeted us, with all due servility to Pimko.

"My dear colleague," said Pimko, "here's little Joey whom I would like to enroll into the ranks of your sixth-grade students, Joey, say 'hello' to the professor. In a moment I'll have a chat with Piórkowski, but in the meantime I'll leave him with you, break him in to school life." I wanted to protest, but instead I scraped the ground with my foot, a light breeze came up, branches of trees moved slightly and with them a tuft of Pimko's hair. "I hope he'll be on his best behavior," said the old pedagogue, patting me on my little head. "How are the youngsters doing?" Pimko asked, lowering his voice. "I see they're walking in circles—that's very good. They're walking about, chatting, while their mothers are snooping—very good. There's nothing better for a school-age boy than having his mother close by, behind the fence. No one can bring out that fresh baby pupa better than a mother, well placed behind a fence."

"Even so, they are still not naive enough," the teacher complained sourly, "they just refuse to take on that new-potato look. We set their mothers on them, but even that's not enough. We're just not able to bring out that youthful freshness and naiveté. You won't believe, my dear colleague, how stubborn they are and reluctant to comply in this respect. They simply don't want to."

"That's because you're amiss in your pedagogical skills," Pimko sternly chastised him. "What? They don't want to? But they have to! I'll show you how to bring about naiveté. I bet that in half-an-hour their naiveté will be doubled. My plan is as follows: I'll start by watching the students, and I'll show them in the most naive manner possible that I think they are naive and innocent. This will infuriate them of course, they'll want to show me that they are not naive, and you'll see how this will plunge them into genuine naiveté and innocence, so sweet to us pedagogues!"

"Don't you think, though," asked the teacher, "that instilling naiveté in the students is a somewhat outdated, antiquated pedagogical trick?"

"Precisely!" replied Pimko, "give me more of those antiquated tricks! The more antiquated the better! There is nothing better than a truly antiquated pedagogical trick! The little cuties, educated by us in this perfectly unreal atmosphere, yearn for life and real experience, and therefore nothing bothers them more than their innocence. Ha, ha, ha, let me suggest to them right now that they're innocent, box them up in this amiable concept, and you'll see how innocent they become!"

With that he slipped behind the trunk of a huge oak tree growing to one side of the school yard, while the teacher took me by my little hand and, before I could explain or protest, led me to the other students. Having done so, he let go of my hand and left me in their midst.

The students walked about. Some snapped their fingers or poked each other in the ribs, others, having blocked their ears with their fingers and stuck their heads in their books, crammed their lessons without a break, some played copycat or tripped one another, their vacant and dumb stares slid off me, not recognizing the thirty-year-old that I was. I stepped up to one of the students closest to me—I had no doubt that this cynical farce must soon come to an end.

"Hello," I began, "you must surely realize I'm not . . ."

But he yelled:

"Look, fellahs! N o v u s c o l e g u s!"

They surrounded me, one of them screamed:

"A n d w h a t p e r f i d i o u s w h i m s a n d a i r s h a v e p e r c h a n c e c a u s e d t h e p e r s o n o f m y d e a r S i r t o p r e s e n t h i m s e l f s o t a r d i l y a t t h i s d u m p o f a s c h o o l?"

Another one squeaked and laughed like an idiot:

"C o u l d i t b e t h a t a m o u r s f o r a d a m s e l h a v e d e l a y e d o u r c o l e g u s v e n e r a b i l i s? I s t h i s p e r-c h a n c e w h y o u r p r e s u m p t u o u s c o l e g u s s o l a n-g u i d u s e s t?"

I fell silent at this grotesque talk as if someone had tied my tongue into knots, but they went on, unable to stop it seemed—the more atrocious their words, the greater their delight—and with a maniacal stubbornness they befouled themselves and everything around them. And they went on—t h e f a i r s e x, d a m s e l, w e n c h, P h o e-b u s, l o v e-l u s t, g n o m e, p r o f e s s o r u s, l e s s o n u s polonicus, perfectus, sexus. Their movements were clumsy—their faces looked stuffed and bloated, their topics—sex organs in the younger group, sexual exploits in the older group, all of which, in conjunction with archaisms and Latin endings, created a singularly disgusting cocktail. They seemed stuck in something, ill-placed, off-track in space and time, furtively peeking at the teacher or at their mothers behind the fence, clutching their pupas, all the while aware of being watched, which made it rather difficult for them to eat lunch.

I stood there flabbergasted by it all, unable to see the rhyme or reason, and I realized that the farce was not about to end. When those formalists noticed a strange man observing them closely and keenly from behind the oak tree, they became exceedingly nervous, and whispers spread that a school inspector had arrived and was snooping from behind the tree. "A school inspector!" some said, reaching for their books and ostentatiously approaching the oak. "A school inspector!" said others, walking away from the oak, but none of them could take their eyes off Pimko who, standing discretely behind the tree, was making notes with his pencil on a scrap of paper torn out of his writing pad. "He's taking notes," they whispered right and left, "he's writing down his observations." Suddenly Pimko tossed the scrap of paper into the air with a deft movement of his hand, as if the wind had blown it. The note said:

On the basis of my observations conducted during lunch hour at school X, I came to the conclusion that our male youth is innocent! This is my deepest conviction. And my evidence: their mien, their innocent conversation, as well as their cute and innocent pupas.

T. Pimko

September 29, 193 . . . Warsaw

When the note reached the students the school swarmed like an anthill. "What? We're innocent? We, today's youth, innocent? We, who already screw women?" Laughter and tittering grew, impassioned yet secretive, and the air teemed with sarcasm. "Oh, what a naive fuddy-duddy! What naiveté! Hey, what naiveté!" I soon realized however, that the laughter had lasted far too long . . . instead of abating it became louder, and, while asserting itself, it seemed unduly contrived in its fury. What was happening? Why was the laughter not subsiding? Not until later did I realize the kind of poison that the satanic and Machiavellian Pimko had injected into them. Because, in truth, those puppy dogs, confined to school and distanced from life—were indeed innocent. Yes, they were innocent, and yet they were not innocent! They were innocent in their desire not to be innocent. Innocent when they held a woman in their arms! Innocent when they struggled and fought. Innocent when they recited poetry, and innocent when they played billiards. Innocent when they ate and slept. Innocent when they behaved innocently. Ever threatened by a sacrosanct naiveté, even as they spilled blood, tortured, raped, or cursed—they did everything to avoid falling into innocence!

Therefore their laughter, rather than calming down, grew and grew, some students held back at first from reacting while others could not—and slowly at first, then faster and faster, they lapsed into filthy talk that would have made a drunken cabby proud. And feverishly, rapidly, they muttered among themselves the most brutal profanities and opprobrious invectives, while others chalked graffiti on the walls; and the limpid autumn air swarmed with words a hundredfold worse than those to which they had treated me in the beginning. I thought I was dreaming—because it is in a dream that we fall into a situation more stupid than anything we could imagine. I tried to stop them.

"Why do you say 'f . . .'?" I feverishly asked one of them, "why do you say that?"

"Oh, shut up, you puppy dog!" the rogue replied, jabbing me in the ribs. "It's a terrific word! You say it too, c'mon, say it," he hissed and stepped painfully on my foot. "Say it, now! It's our only defense against the pupa! Can't you see that the inspector behind the tree is treating us to the pupa? You wimp, you French poodle, if you don't talk dirty this minute I'll twist your ear. Hey, Mizdral, come here and keep an eye on this new fellow so he behaves himself. And you, Hopek, tell us a filthy joke. Go for it, gentlemen, or he too will treat us to the pupa!"

Having given these orders the vulgar scamp, whom they called Kneadus, sneaked up to the oak tree and carved upon it four letters that neither Pimko nor the mothers behind the fence could see. A subdued titter brimming with hidden delight came from all around, and when the mothers behind the fence and Pimko behind the tree heard their youngsters laughing they too joined in with their benevolent laughter—a twofold laughter resulting. Because, having duped their elders, the laughter of the young was full of mischief, while the laughter of the older people, in reaction to their youngsters' carefree gaiety, was good-natured and benevolent—and so in the calm autumn air the two forces struggled with each other amid the leaves falling from the tree, amid the hustle and bustle of school life, the elderly janitor sweeping litter into a dustpan, the grass turning yellow, the pale sky . . .

Yet suddenly it all seemed so naive—Pimko behind the tree, the scamps crowing with delight, the toadies with noses in their books—the whole situation became so disgustingly naive that I felt I was drowning, along with all my unspoken protestations. And I did not know whether I should rescue myself, my schoolmates, or Pimko. I moved slightly closer to the tree and whispered:

"Professor, sir."

"What?" Pimko asked, also in a whisper.

"Please come out of there, sir. They've written a dirty word on the other side of the tree. That's why they're laughing. Please, sir, come out."

And as I whispered these fatuous words into thin air, it occurred to me that I had become some kind of mystical conjurer of stupidity, and my own position frightened me—my hands cupped over my mouth, by an oak tree, in a school yard, whispering something to Pimko standing behind a tree . . .

"What?" asked the professor, crouching behind the tree, "what have they written?"

A car honked in the distance.

"A dirty word! They've written a dirty word! Please come out, sir!"

"Where did they write it?"

"On this oak tree. On the other side. Please, sir, come out and put an end to this! Don't let them make fun of you! You wanted to make them think they're naive and innocent, but instead they've written a dirty word for you . . . Stop this teasing. That's enough. I can't go on like this, talking into thin air. I'll go crazy. Please, sir, come out! Enough's enough!"

Gossamer threads of Indian summer drifted about while I thus carried on in whispers, leaves were falling . . .

"What? What's this?" Pimko exclaimed, "am I to doubt the purity of our youth? Never! You can't tell this to an old dog like me, and a pedagogue at that!"

He stepped out from behind the tree, and at the sight of this figure of a potentate the students burst into a wild roar.

"My dear young men!" he said after they calmed down somewhat. "Don't imagine that I don't know that you use foul and obscene language among yourselves. I'm well aware of it. But don't you worry, neither this nor any of your other transgressions will shake my deepest conviction that at bottom you are modest and innocent. Your old friend here will always think of you as pure, modest, and innocent, he will always believe in your modesty, purity, and inno-cence. As to dirty words, well, I know you're just repeating them after some servant girl, not really understanding them, just to show off. Well, well, well, there's nothing wrong with that, on the contrary— it's more innocent than you think."

Imprisonment and Further Belittlement

He sneezed, wiped his nose with great satisfaction, and proceeded to the administration building to discuss my case with Principal Piórkowski. Mothers and aunts behind the fence were ecstatic, they fell into one another's arms and reiterated: "What a seasoned pedagogue! Oh, what cute little pupas, pupas, pupas our little darlings have!" But among the students his speech evoked nothing but dismay. Dumbfounded, they watched Pimko walk away, but as soon as he was out of sight a hail of invectives followed. "Did you hear that?" roared Kneadus, "we're innocent, shit, screw that! He thinks we're innocent—he takes us for innocents! He insists we're innocent! Innocent!" And in no way could he extricate himself from the word that had entrapped and shackled him, and was now killing him, yet it somehow grounded him ever more in naiveté and innocence. Just at that moment a tall, well-built youth whom his classmates called Syphon—it was now his turn to be swept into the naiveté that was raging in the air—said to himself, yet so that everyone could hear, in the clear and limpid air which made a voice sound like cowbells in the mountains:

"Innocence? And why not? Innocence is a virtue . . . One should be innocent . . . And why not?"

No sooner did he say it than Kneadus pounced on his words.

"What? You believe in innocence?"

And he took a step back, because it sounded so silly. This annoyed Syphon, who in turn pounced on Kneadus' words.

"I believe in it! And why shouldn't I? I'm not childish in this respect."

This in turn annoyed Kneadus, who started hurling mockeries into the echoing air.

"Did you all hear that? Syphon is innocent! Ha, ha, ha, Syphon the innocent!"

Cries of "Syphonus innocentus! Has the arrogant Syphon perchance not been with a woman?" came from everywhere. A shower of lewd epigrams in the style of poets Rey and Kochanowski rained down, and for a brief moment the world became soiled again. But the epigrams annoyed Syphon even more, and he dug in his heels.

"Yes, I am innocent—and what's more, I don't know anything about such things, and I don't see why I should be ashamed. Friends, surely not one of you can seriously maintain that filth is better than purity."

And he took a step back, because it sounded so awkward. Everyone fell silent. Finally there was whispering:

"Syphon, you're not joking? You don't know about the facts of life, really? Syphon, it can't be true!"

And they all took a step back. Kneadus spat on the ground.

"It's true, gentlemen! Just look at him! It shows! Ugh! Yuck!"

Then Mizdral exclaimed:

"Syphon, that's impossible, you're bringing shame on us, go ahead, get initiated into the facts of life!"

Syphon

"What? Me? I'm supposed to get initiated?"

Hopek

"For heaven's sake, Syphon, think, this isn't only your concern, you're bringing shame on us, on all of us—I won't dare to look at a gal again."

Syphon

"There are no gals, there are only lasses."

Kneadus

"La . . . did you hear that? Maybe only lads then, eh? How about lads?"

Syphon

"That's right, you took it right out of my mouth—'lads'! Friends, why should we be ashamed of this word? Is it worse than any other? And why should we, in this reborn country of ours, be ashamed of our 'lasses'? On the contrary, we should cultivate them in our hearts! Why, may I ask, should we be ashamed, merely for the sake of some contrived cynicism, of such pure words as 'lad,' 'eaglet,' 'knight,' 'falcon,' 'lass'—they're surely closer to our hearts than the vulgar lingo with which our friend Kneadalski is polluting his imagination."

"Hear, hear!" seconded a few.

"You toady!" shouted others.

"Colleagues!" Syphon exclaimed, now really carried away, relentless, and intoxicated with his own innocence. "Lift up your hearts! I suggest we take an oath this moment never to renounce the lad nor the eaglet! *We'll never forfeit the land of our birth!** Because our birth springs forth from the 'lad' and the 'lass'! 'Lad' and 'lass'—that's our land! Whoever is young and noble, follow me! Our slogan—youthful zeal! Our password—youthful faith!"

In response to this call a few of Syphon's followers, carried away by youthful zeal, raised their hands and, with faces suddenly solemn and radiant, took the oath, and, in the air so limpid and clear Kneadus pounced on Syphon, who became furious—but fortunately they were separated before a fight broke out.

"Gentlemen!" reviled Kneadus, "why don't you kick this eaglet, this lad, in the butt? Don't you have any guts? Where's your pride? Kick him, why don't you kick him? Only a kick can save you! Show him your manhood! Show him that we're guys who go with gals, not some lads who go with lasses!"

He ranted and raved. I looked at him, drops of sweat on my brow, my cheeks shrouded in pallor. Yet a glimmer of hope sustained me, I thought that after Pimko's departure I would somehow regain my bearings and manage to explain things—but how was I supposed to regain my bearings when a couple of steps away, in the cool and bracing air, naiveté and innocence were on the rise. The pupa had rolled over the lads and the guys. The world seemed to have collapsed and reset itself in the mode of the lad and the guy. I took a step back.

Now the irate Syphon called out into the pale blue expanse, as he

---

*From a patriotic song.

stood on the hard ground of the school yard, which was covered with veins of shadow and blotches of light:

"Excuse me, Kneadalski is talking nonsense, he's setting us up! I suggest we ignore him and act as if he doesn't even exist, off with him, my friends, he's a traitor, a traitor to his own youth, he has no ideals!"

"What ideals, you ass? What ideals? Your ideals, no matter how beautiful, can't be any better than you are," fumed Kneadus, his words gathering steam, "don't you all realize, can't you see that his ideals are fat and pink with large noses? You dogs! It will be a disgrace to show ourselves in the street! Don't you see how real guys, the sons of janitors and peasants, apprentices of all sorts, handymen and farmhands our age, are poking fun at us! They think we're nothing! Defend the guy against the lad!" he pleaded in all directions. "Stand up for the guy in us!"

Indignation grew. The students, their cheeks flushed, went at each other, Syphon stood immobile, his hands folded on his breast, while Kneadus clenched his fists. Behind the fence mothers and aunts, without quite grasping what was going on, were also highly excited. Yet the majority of students were undecided, and, stuffing themselves with bread and butter, simply reiterated:

"Is the presumptuous Kneadus perchance a ribald? Is Syphonus an idealistus? Noses to our books, let's cram, cram, cram or we'll flunk!"

Others, preferring not to be mixed up in all this, led tactful conversations about sports and pretended to be greatly interested in a football match. But now and then one or another, evidently unable to resist the scorching and burning issues of the dispute, would listen, ponder awhile, and, cheeks flushed, join either Syphon's or Kneadus' camp. The teacher dozed off on a bench in the sun and, from afar, smacked his lips at the youthful naiveté. "Hey, the pupa, the pupa," he purred. Only one student had not been swept away by the general ideological excitement. He stood to one side, dressed in a knit shirt, soft flannel pants, a delicate gold chain round his left wrist, calmly warming himself in the sun. "Hey, Kopyrda!" each side called to him, "Kopyrda, join us!" He seemed to be the subject of general envy, both hostile camps wanted to win him over, but he did not heed either side. He moved one foot forward and wiggled it to and fro.

"We don't give a hoot for the opinions of janitors' sons, apprentices, and all the street riffraff!" exclaimed Pyzo, a friend of Syphon's, "they're all dumb."

"And what about schoolgirls?" Mizdral anxiously asked, "don't you care about the opinions of schoolgirls? Just imagine, what will schoolgirls think?"

Shouts came from all around:

"Schoolgirls love those who are pure!"

"No, no, they prefer the filthy ones!"

"Schoolgirls?!" Syphon mouthed disdainfully, "we care only about the opinions of noble-minded lasses, and they are on our side!"

Kneadus walked up to him and said, his voice breaking:

"Syphon! You wouldn't do this to us, would you?! Take back what you've just said, and I will too! Let's both drop it, shall we? I'm ready to . . . to apologize to you, I'm ready to do anything . . . as long as you retract your words about those 'lads' and . . . let yourself be initiated. Retract 'lads.' And I'll retract 'guys.' This isn't just your own personal matter, you know."

But before answering, Syphon Pylaszczkiewicz gave him a bright and gentle look, yet a look that was full of inner strength. With such a look must come a strong reply. Taking a step back, he therefore said:

"I'm ready to give my life for my ideals!"

But Kneadus had already moved in on him, his fists clenched.

"Onward! Charge! Get him, guys! Beat the lad! Kill him, kill him, beat him up, kill the lad!"

"Here, lads, here!" exclaimed Syphon Pylaszczkiewicz, "stick up for me, I haven't lost my innocence yet, I'm your lad, stick up for me!" he went on with a piercing voice. And hearing his call many of them were moved within by the "lad" against the "guy." They formed a tight circle around Syphon, and they stood their ground against the followers of Kneadus. Blows fell, Syphon jumped up on a rock, rousing his own to resist, but now Kneadus' followers had the upper hand and Syphon's retinue was retreating and breaking up. Suddenly, in the face of defeat, and with what remained of his strength, Syphon intoned the *Falcons' March:**

> Hey, lads and Falcons, give him vigor and brawn,
> Wake him up from the dead, make him rise and live on!

The song, which they took up instantly, grew and swelled, crested and rolled like a wave. They stood motionless, singing, and, with Syphon's lead, fixed their gaze on a distant star and also at the very noses of their assailants. Whereupon the assailants' clenched fists dropped helplessly to their sides. They no longer had any idea how to get at their opponents, how to provoke or taunt them—while the others sang with ever greater power, ardor, and fervor, aiming their star-inspired song straight at the noses of their assailants. One after another of Kneadus' followers whispered something under his breath, fidgeted in his place, shifted aimlessly this way and that, then stepped aside, until finally there was nothing left for Kneadus to do but clear his throat uneasily and walk away.

. . . Sometimes a morbid dream will take us to a land where everything chokes us, corrupts and inhibits us because it pertains to the t i m e of o u r y o u t h and is therefore young, yet it has now become outworn, old, and archaic, and there is no torment equal to the torment of such a dream, such a land. There is nothing more horrible than to delve into issues one has long outgrown, the old

---

*Sokoły in the original text. It means "falcons" and is probably based on *Sokols,* gymnastic societies in Czechoslovakia promoting festivals in which as many as ten thousand gymnasts participated simultaneously (Encyclopeadia Britannica, vol. 10, 1970).

issues of youth and immaturity that have long since been pushed into a corner and settled . . . for example the question of innocence. Oh, threefold wise are they who live solely by today's concerns, the concerns of maturity and of the prime of life, leaving outdated problems to elderly aunts. Because making the choice as to the subject matter and the issues one will address is immensely important to the individual, just as it is to entire nations, and we so often see that a person who is mature and sagacious in his dealings with mature matters becomes, in the twinkling of an eye, painfully immature when confronted with matters that are too puerile or too far in the past—and incompatible with the spirit of the times and the rhythm of history. Truly, there is no easier way of inflicting naiveté and infantilizing humanity than by presenting it with problems of this kind, and I must admit that Pimko, with a masterly skill worthy of the most eminent and consummate of all profs, embroiled me and my schoolmates in a dialectic and in a set of problems that were more infantilizing than one could ever imagine. I thus found myself in the epicenter of a tirelessly belittling and devaluing dream.

A flock of pigeons flew by in the autumn sun and air, then swept in over the roof, touched down on the oak, and flew off again. Kneadus, unable to stomach Syphon's triumphant song, dragged himself, along with Mizdral and Hopek, to the far corner of the school yard. After a while he recovered and regained his speech. He stared vacantly at the ground, then finally exploded:

"Well—and what now?!"

"What now?" replied Mizdral, "nothing, except that we must redouble our energies, and go on using the choicest obscenities we know! Four-letter words, four-letter words—that's our only weapon. That's a guy's weapon!"

"What, again?" Kneadus asked. "Again? Till they're sick of it? Round and round in circles? Keep repeating our tune just because Syphon is humming his tune?"

He broke down. He opened his hands, retreated a couple of steps, and looked around. The heavens above drooped, light, pale, cool, and sneering, while the tree—that stalwart oak in the school yard—turned its back and the old janitor by the gate laughed up his sleeve and walked away.

"A farmhand," whispered Kneadus, "a farmhand . . . think of it—what if some farmhand overheard our intellectual drivel . . ." And, suddenly terrified, he tried to escape, he wanted to make a run for it in the limpid air. "Enough, enough, I've had it with the lad and the guy, I've had enough . . ."

His friends caught up with him.

"Hey Kneadie, what's the matter with you?" they said, bathed in the limpid air, "you're our leader! We can't manage without you!"

Seized and held by his wrists, Kneadus bowed his head and said bitterly:

"Tough luck . . ."

Mizdral and Hopek were shocked and speechless. In his distraction Mizdral picked up a piece of wire and absentmindedly poked it through a hole in the fence, injuring the eye of one of the mothers. But he threw the wire away immediately. The mother groaned behind the fence. Finally Hopek asked timidly:

"Well, Kneadie, what next?"

Kneadus shook off his momentary dejection.

"There's no other way—we must fight!" he said, "fight till we drop!"

"Hooray!" they exclaimed. "That's what we want to hear! You're our man, our old Kneadus!"

But the leader again waved his hand with an air of hopelessness.

"Oh, save your breath! Your cries are no better than Syphon's song! However, what must be must be. You want to fight, do you? But fighting isn't the answer. Let's say we knock his teeth out, so what? That's playing right into his hands—we'll make him a martyr, and then you'll see what unshaken yet oppressed innocence he'll lord over us. Besides, even if we were to launch an attack, you saw what happened—they'll put on such a pretense of bravery that even the toughest in our group will turn tail and run. No, that won't do! And all the rest of it—curses, misdemeanors of all sorts, filth—it's all useless, useless! It's only grist for his mill, I tell you, it's just baby's milk for his 'lad.' I'm sure he's counting on it! No, no, but fortunately," and here Kneadus' voice became strangely rabid, "as luck would have it, there is another way . . . that's more effective . . . we'll take away, once and for all, his inclination to sing."

"How?" they asked with a glimmer of hope.

"Gentlemen," he said, dryly and to the point, "since Syphon isn't willing, we'll have to initiate him by force. We'll capture him and tie him up. As luck would have it, there is a way to get inside him— through the ears. We'll tie him up, and we'll initiate him so that even his own mother won't recognize him! We'll destroy the little treasure once and for all! But be quiet! Get some ropes ready!"

I listened to this plot with bated breath, my heart pounding in my chest, but at that moment Pimko appeared in the door of the school building and beckoned me to come with him to Principal Piórkowski. The pigeons were back again. Flapping their wings, they settled on the fence behind which the mothers were peeking. I walked down the long corridor, frantically seeking a way to explain myself, to protest, but I couldn't do it because Pimko was spitting into every spittoon we passed along the way and told me to do the same . . . I just couldn't speak out . . . and so, spitting and walking, we reached Principal Piórkowski's office. Piórkowski, a giant among giants, sitting there with absolute power and authority, received us graciously, then promptly gave me a fatherly pinch on the cheek and, with an air of cordiality, stroked my chin, so I bowed instead of protesting while he, speaking above my head, addressed Pimko in a bass-baritone.

"Oh, the pupa, pupa, pupa! Thank you for remembering us here, dear Professor! And God bless you, dear colleague, for the new pupil! If everyone were as good at belittling as you are, our school would be twice as big! The pupa, pupa, pupa. Would you believe that when we artificially belittle and infantilize adults we get better results than we do with children in their natural state? Oh, the pupa, the pupa, there would be no school without pupils, and no life without school! I commend myself to you, my institution doubtless continues to deserve support, our methods of turning out the pupa have no equal, and the teaching body is meticulously selected with that in mind. Would you like to see the body?"

"But of course, my pleasure," Pimko replied, "as you well know—nothing influences the spirit as much as the body does." The principal half-opened the door to the staff room, both men peeked in, and I with them. I was appalled! In the large room teachers sat at a table drinking tea and munching on bread rolls. Never before had I seen a gathering of so many, so hopeless little old men. Most of them were sniveling, one was chomping on his food, a second one was smacking his lips, a third was sucking his tea, a fourth was slurping, a fifth was bald and sad, while the French teacher's eyes watered, and she kept wiping them with the corner of her handkerchief.

"Yes, Professor," the principal said proudly, "the body has been carefully chosen for their exceptionally disagreeable and annoying qualities, there is not one pleasant body here, all strictly pedagogical, as you can see for yourself, and, if once in a while circumstances force me to hire a younger teacher, I make sure that he has at least one repulsive trait. Take the history teacher, for instance—he is, regretfully, in the prime of his life and at first glance appears to be all right, but please note that he is cross-eyed."

"Yes, but the French teacher seems pleasant enough," Pimko said in an informal tone.

"She stutters, and her eyes are always watering."

"Ah yes! You're right, I didn't notice it at first. But isn't she rather interesting?"

"Not at all, I can't converse with her for more than a minute without yawning at least twice."

"Ah, well, I see your point! But do they have enough experience and tact to teach, are they sufficiently aware of the magnitude of their mission?"

"These are the soundest brains in the capital," replied the principal, "but not one of them has a single thought of his own in his head; if one of them should spawn a thought, I'd be sure to chase away either the thought or the thinker. They're actually a bunch of harmless duffers, they teach only what's in their worksheets, and, no, they don't entertain a single thought of their own."

"That's the pupa, the pupa," said Pimko, "I can see I'm placing my Joey in good hands. Because there is nothing worse than teachers who are personable, especially if they happen to have opinions of their own. Only a truly irksome pedagogue can inculcate the pupils with that adorable immaturity, that engaging helplessness and clumsiness, that lack of *savoir vivre* that should be the hallmark of our youth so they'll provide a target for us, the earnest and inspired pedagogues that we are. And we need the help of such well-chosen staff to infantilize the whole world."

"Tst, tst, tst," said Principal Piórkowski, pulling Pimko by the sleeve, "sure, that's the pupa, but be quiet, don't talk about it too loudly."

At that moment one body turned to another and asked:

"Ho, ho, hmm, well, what's up? What's up, my dear colleague?"

"What's up?" replied the other body, "I thought prices had gone down."

"Gone down?" said the first body, "I thought prices had gone up."

"Gone up?" asked the second body, "I thought they had gone down slightly."

"The price of bread rolls just isn't going down," muttered the first body, and tucked away the rest of his unfinished roll into his pocket.

"I keep them on a diet," whispered Principal Piórkowski, "this assures their anemic condition. Only with food conducive to anemia can the *age ingrat* warts, warts of graceless old age, flourish in full.

Suddenly the penmanship teacher noticed the principal standing with a strange and impressive-looking gentleman at the door, she choked on her tea and shrilled:

"School inspector!"

At this cry the bodies trembled, stood up, and flocked together like a covey of partridges, but the principal, not wanting to scare them further, gently closed the door, then Pimko kissed me on the forehead and said solemnly:

"Well, Joey, go to your classroom, the lessons are about to begin, in the meantime I'll look around for some lodgings for you, and I'll fetch you after school and take you home." I wanted to protest, but this despot of a prof had proffed me with his absolutist prof so suddenly that I could not, so I just bowed, and, full of unspoken protests and roars that drowned all protests, I went to class. And the class was roaring too. In the general ruckus the students were taking their places at their desks and shouting as if in a moment they would cease to speak forever.

And, seemingly from nowhere, a teacher appeared at the podium. It was the same sad and pallid body that had so gravely opined in the staff room that prices were going down. He sat and opened the attendance book, brushed a speck of dust off his waistcoat, rolled up his sleeves so they would not wear out at the elbows, tightened his lips, stifled something within himself, and crossed his legs. He then sighed and tried to speak. The rumpus redoubled in strength. Everyone yelled except for Syphon, who, with an air of self-assurance, pulled out his notes and books. The teacher looked at the class, straightened one of his cuffs, pursed his lips, then opened and closed them again. The students screamed. The teacher knit his brow and winced, checked his cuffs, drummed with his fingers, pondered something far away—pulled out his watch and placed it on his desk, sighed, again stifled something, or gulped, or maybe yawned and, having finally worked up enough energy, banged the attendance book on the desk and exploded:

"That's enough! Calm down, will you! The lesson is about to begin."

Whereupon the whole class, as one man (except for Syphon and his cohorts), voiced an urgent need to go to the bathroom.

The teacher, popularly known as Ashface for his sickly and ashen complexion, smiled sourly.

"That's enough!" he exclaimed mechanically. "So you want to be excused, do you? The soul hankers after paradise, eh? And why is it that nobody excuses me? Why do I have to stay put? Sit down, all of you, no one is excused, and I'm writing Kneadalski and Bobkowski into the class log, and if I hear so much as a peep from anyone, I'll call him to the blackboard!" Whereupon no fewer than seven students presented notes which said that, due to such and such an illness, they had not been able to do their homework. Four others claimed migraine headaches, one broke out in a rash, another threw himself into jerks and convulsions. "I see," said Ashface, "and why is it that no one writes a note for me saying that, for reasons beyond my control, I could not prepare the lesson? Why is it that I can't have convulsions? Why, I ask you, instead of having convulsions, do I have to sit here, day in and day out, Sundays excluded? Off with you, your notes are fake, your illnesses are fake, sit down, I know what you're up to!" But three of the most brazen and eloquent students approached the teacher's desk and proceeded to tell a funny story about the Jews and the birds. Ashface blocked his ears. "No, no," he moaned, "I can't stand this, have pity on me, stop tempting me, this is supposed to be a class, what would happen if the principal walked in on us."

He trembled at the thought and, pale with fear, looked uneasily at the door.

"And what if the school inspector should catch us? Gentlemen, I warn you, the inspector is visiting the school! That's right! . . . I warn you, gentlemen . . . This is no time for foolishness!" he groaned with fear. "In the face of this higher authority, let's pull ourselves together.

Well . . . hmm . . . which one of you has mastered the subject for today? Cut out this nonsense, this is no time for joking around! Come on, speak up. What?! Nobody knows anything? You'll be the ruin of me! Come on, maybe at least one of you, come on, my friends, come forward, don't hesitate . . . Ahh, boys—Syphon Pylaszczkiewicz, you say? God bless you, Pylaszczkiewicz, I've always thought you an admirable fellow. Well, Pylaszczkiewicz, and what have you mastered? *Konrad Wallenrod?* Or *Forefathers' Eve?* Or maybe the general characteristics of romanticism? Tell me, Pylaszczkiewicz."

But Syphon, the "lad" now well entrenched in him, stood up and answered:

"I'm sorry, Professor, but I cannot. If you call on me when the school inspector is here, I'll answer to the best of my knowledge—but in the meantime I can't reveal what I have mastered, because by revealing it I would not be true to myself."

"Syphon, you'll be our ruin," said the others, terror-stricken, "c'mon, speak up!"

"Well, well, Pylaszczkiewicz," Ashface said in a conciliatory tone, "why don't you come out in the open, Pylaszczkiewicz? We're among friends, aren't we? Tell me the truth, Syphon Pylaszczkiewicz. Surely you don't mean to ruin the two of us, do you? If you don't want to speak openly, let me know somehow . . ."

"Sorry, sir," replied Syphon, "but I can't do it because I'm above wheeling and dealing, and I am not about to betray my principles, nor to betray myself."

And he sat down.

"Tut, tut," mumbled the teacher, "these are honorable sentiments, Pylaszczkiewicz, and much to your credit. And don't take all this to heart, I was just making a private joke of it. Yes, of course, one should always remain incorruptible, so, what do we have for today?" he said sternly and checked his worksheet. "Ah, yes! Elucidate and explain to the students why Słowacki inspires our love and admiration? Well then, gentlemen, I'll recite for you my lesson, and then in your turn you'll recite yours. Quiet!" he yelled, and they all sprawled themselves on their desk tops, resting their heads on their arms, while Ashface inconspicuously opened the appropriate textbook, tightened his lips, sighed, stifled something within himself, and began his recitation:

"Hmm . . . hmm . . . Well then, why does Słowacki inspire our love and admiration? Why do we weep with the poet when we hear the Aeolian strings of his poem *In Switzerland?* Or, why are we swept away when we hear the heroic and stalwart verses of the *Spirit King?* And why can't we tear ourselves from the wonders and magic of *Balladyna,* why do the wails of *Lilla Weneda* tear our hearts to pieces? And why are we so willing to rush and speed to the rescue of the hapless king? Hmm . . . why? Because, gentlemen, Słowacki—oh, what a great poet he was! Wałkiewicz! Why? Repeat why, Wałkiewicz. Why the admiration and love, why do we cry, why the rapture, why the heartbreak, why do we rush and speed? Why, Wałkiewicz, why?"

It seemed to me I heard Pimko all over again, but a Pimko on a more modest salary and lacking the wider horizons.

"Because Słowacki—oh, what a great poet he was!" Walkiewicz repeated, while other students carved their desk tops with pocket knives or made tiny paper balls, the tiniest they could make, and pitched them into their inkwells. They pretended these were fish in make-believe ponds, and, using their hair as fishing lines, they tried to catch the fish but, alas, the paper would not bite. So instead they tickled their noses with the hair, and they signed their names in their notebooks over and over again, with or without curlicues, while one of them practiced his penmanship all over the page: "Why, w-h-y, w-h-y, Sło-wac-ki, Sło-wac-ki, Sło-wac-ki, wac-ki, wac-ki, Wa-cek, Wa-cek-Sło-wac-ki and a f-l-y and a f-l-e-a." They all looked miserable. What happened to the fervor, to the disputes and discussions of just a few moments ago? Only a few fortunate ones seemed to have forgotten the world around them as they immersed themselves in E. Wallace's writings. Even Syphon had to exert all the strength of his character to keep his principles of self-discipline and self-amelioration intact, but he could do it only because, for him, distress was a source of bliss and a measure of the strength of his character. Whereas the others cupped their hands into hollows and hillocks and blew air through them, Russian-style: hey, hey, hillocks and hollows, hillocks and hollows . . . The teacher sighed, stifled something within himself, looked at his watch, and continued:

"A great poet! Remember that, it's important! And why do we love him? Because he was a great poet. A great poet he was indeed! You laggards, you ignoramuses, I'm trying to be calm and collected as I tell you this, get it into your thick heads—so, I repeat once more, gentlemen: a great poet, Juliusz Słowacki, a great poet, we love Juliusz Słowacki and admire his poetry because he was a great poet. Please make note of the following homework assignment: 'What is the immortal beauty which abides in the poetry of Juliusz Słowacki and evokes our admiration?' "

At this point one of the students fidgeted and groaned:

"But I don't admire it at all! Not at all! It doesn't interest me in the least! I read two verses—and I'm already bored. God help me, how am I supposed to admire it when I don't admire it?" His eyes popped, and he sat down, thus sinking into a bottomless pit. The teacher choked on this naive confession.

"For God's sake be quiet!" he hissed. "I'll flunk you. Gałkiewicz, you want to ruin me! You probably don't realize what you've just said?"

Gałkiewicz

"But I don't understand it! I don't understand how I can admire it when I don't admire it."

Teacher

"How can you not admire it, Gałkiewicz, when I told you a thousand times that you do admire it."

Gałkiewicz

"Well, I don't admire it."

"That's your private business. Obviously, Gałkiewicz, you lack the intelligence. Others admire it."

Gałkiewicz

"Nobody admires it, I swear. How can anybody admire it when nobody reads it besides us, schoolboys, and only because we're forced to . . ."

Teacher

"Quiet, for God's sake! That's because there aren't many people who are truly cultured and up to the task . . ."

Gałkiewicz

"But the cultured ones don't read it either. Nobody does, nobody. Absolutely nobody."

Teacher

"Listen, Gałkiewicz, I have a wife and a child! Have pity on the child at least! There's no doubt, Gałkiewicz, that we should admire great poetry, and Słowacki was, after all, a great poet . . . Maybe Słowacki doesn't move you, Gałkiewicz, but you can't tell me that Mickiewicz, Byron, Pushkin, Shelley, Goethe don't pierce your soul through and through . . ."

Gałkiewicz

"They pierce nobody. Nobody cares, they're bored by it all. Nobody can read more than two or three verses. O God! I can't . . ."

Teacher

"This is preposterous! Great poetry must be admired, because it is great and because it is poetry, and so we admire it."

Gałkiewicz

"Well, I can't. And nobody can! O God!"

Sweat covered the teacher's brow like dew, he took a snapshot of his wife and child out of his wallet and tried to move Gałkiewicz, but the latter repeated his "I can't, I can't" over and over again. And the piercing "I can't" proliferated and grew infectious, mutterings of "we can't either" came from all corners, and a generalized inability threatened everyone. The teacher found himself at a terrible impasse. Any moment there could be an outbreak of—of what?—of inability, at any moment a wild roar of not wanting to could erupt and reach the headmaster and the inspector, at any moment the whole building could collapse and bury his child under the rubble, and here was this Gałkiewicz with his "I can't, I can't."

The hapless Ashface felt that he too was threatened by inability.

"Pylaszczkiewicz!" he yelled, "you, Pylaszczkiewicz, why don't you show me, and show Gałkiewicz and everybody else, the beauty of some splendid passage! But hurry up, or else *periculum in mora!* Pay attention, everybody! If I hear as much as a squeak I'll give you all a class assignment! We must shake this inability, we must, or woe to my child!"

Syphon Pylaszczkiewicz stood up and began to recite a poem.

And he recited. Not for an instant did he succumb to the general and suddenly prevailing inability, on the contrary—he was totally able, because he derived his ability from the inability of others. He recited then, and he recited with the proper intonation, he recited with emotion and from the depths of his soul. What's more, he recited beautifully, and the beauty of his recitation, enhanced by the beauty of the poem, by the greatness of the poet, and by the majesty of art, imperceptibly transformed itself into a monument to all possible beauty and greatness. What's more, he recited mysteriously and with reverence; he recited in all earnestness and with inspiration; and he sang the song of the bard as a bard's song should be sung. Oh, what beauty! What greatness, what genius, and what poetry! Wall, fly, ink, fingernails, ceiling, blackboard, windows, oh, the danger of inability was averted, the child saved and the wife likewise, everyone said yes, yes, because they now could, and they implored him to stop, because it was all too much. I also noticed that my neighbor was smearing my hand with ink—he had already smeared his own and was now starting on mine (because he couldn't very well take off his shoes to smear his feet), yet someone else's hands were awful too because they were actually just like one's own, but so what? Nothing, that's what. How about legs? Swing them? What for? After a quarter-of-an-hour even Gałkiewicz groaned that he'd had enough, that he gets it, that he retracts all he said and agrees with everything, that he apologizes, that now he can.

"See, Gałkiewicz? There's nothing like school to inculcate the adoration of great genius!"

But strange things were happening to the listeners. All differences had vanished, and everyone, be it under the colors of Syphon or of Kneadus, writhed equally under the weight of the bard and the poet, of Ashface and his child, and—of stupor. The bare walls, the black school desks with their inkwells, ceased to provide diversion, and through a window one could see a brick sticking out of a wall with an inscription gouged in it: "He's been kicked out." The only choice remaining was between the pedagogic body and one's own body. Therefore those who were not busy counting the hairs on Ashface's scalp or studying the complex lacing of his shoes tried to count their own hairs and to dislocate their necks. Mizdral fidgeted, Hopek tapped mechanically, while Kneadus kneaded himself, so to speak, in painful exhaustion, some were lost in reverie, others gave in to the awful habit of whispering to themselves, some tore off their buttons, destroying their clothes, and jungles and deserts of eerie gestures and bizarre actions blossomed everywhere. The only one among them who thrived was the perverse Syphon—the greater the general misery the better he felt—because he had that special inner mechanism for turning poverty into riches. And the teacher, still preoccupied with his wife and child, went on and on: "Towiański, Towiański, Towiański, his messianism and his 'forty and four,' Poland—the Christ of Nations, flame eternal, sacrifice, inspiration, suffering, redemption, heroes, and symbols." The words entered my ears and tortured my mind while faces, contorting more and more horribly, mangled, weary, crumpled, and stripped of any notion of a face, seemed ready to assume any face—one could make those faces into anything one wished—oh, what an exercise for the imagination! And reality was also spent, also wrung out, crumpled and ruined—*all that had been real slowly, imperceptibly turned into a world of ideals, oh, let me dream now, let me!**

Ashface went on: "He was a bard! He sang! Gentlemen, I beg you, let's repeat once more—we admire him because he was a great poet, and we revere him because he was a bard! That's the key word. Ciemkiewicz, please repeat!" Ciemkiewicz repeated: "He was a bard!"

I realized that I had to run away. Pimko, Ashface, the school, my schoolmates, all my experiences since this morning suddenly whirled in my head and, as in a lottery, the ticket dropped out at—run away. But where? Where? I didn't know, but I knew I had to run, otherwise I would fall prey to all the freakishness that was crowding in on me from all sides. Yet instead of running away I wiggled my toe inside my shoe, and the wiggling paralyzed me and foiled my intentions to run, because how was I to run while I was still wiggling my toe, here on the first floor of the school? Run—run! Run from Ashface, run from unreality and boredom—but in my head was the bard, squeezed in there by Ashface, while down below I wiggled my toe, how could I run then—my inability to run was more serious than the inability that had earlier affected Gałkiewicz. In theory nothing seemed easier—just walk out of the school and don't come back—Pimko would not call the police to look for me, the tentacles of his pupa pedagogy surely did not extend that far. All I needed was—the will to run. But I lacked the will. Because to run one needs the will, but where is the will to come from when one is wiggling one's toe and one's face is nothing but a face of boredom. And I now understood why no one could run from the school—it was their faces, their whole being in fact, that killed their ability to run, everyone was a prisoner of his own ghastly face, and even though they should have run they couldn't, because they no longer were what

*Based on a poem by Zygmunt Krasiński.

Imprisonment and Further Belittlement

they should have been. To run meant not only running from school but, first and foremost, running from oneself, oh, to run from oneself, from the sniveling brat into which Pimko had turned me, abandon the brat, be the man I once was! But how is one supposed to run from something one i s, where is the reference point, the foot-hold from which to oppose it? Our form permeates us, imprisons us from within as well as from without. I felt sure that, had reality asserted itself for one moment, the incredibly grotesque situation in which I found myself would have become so glaringly obvious that everyone would have exclaimed: "What is this grown man doing here?" But against the background of the general freakishness the case of my particular freakishness was lost. Oh, give me one uncon-torted face next to which I can feel the contortion of my own face, but instead—all around me were faces that were twisted, mangled, and turned inside out, faces that reflected my own like a distorting mirror—and this mirror image of reality truly held me down! Was it a dream? An apparition? At that moment Kopyrda—the one in flan-nel pants, suntanned, the one who, that time in the school yard, had smiled superciliously at the word "schoolgirl"—drifted into my field of vision. Equally indifferent to Ashface as to Kneadus and Syphon, he bent over nonchalantly, looking just fine, normal, in fact—his hands in his pockets, well groomed, spry, easygoing, just so, and pleasant—he sat rather disdainfully, crossed his legs, and watched one of his legs. As if sidestepping school with his legs. A dream? An apparition? "Could this be an ordinary boy at last?" I wondered. "Not a lad, not a guy, but just an ordinary boy? Maybe thanks to him we would regain the ability we had lost . . ."

3 Caught with His Pants Down
and Further Kneading

The teacher looked at his watch more and more often, the students took out their watches and also looked. Finally the saving bell rang, Ashface broke off in mid-sentence and disappeared, the students came to and exploded—only Syphon remained quiet, focused and self-absorbed. But no sooner did Ashface leave than the issue of innocence, stifled earlier by the boredom brought on by the bard, flared up again. Leaving officially sanctioned musings behind, the students again bashed their faces into the lad and the guy, and all that had been real slowly turned into a world of ideals, oh, let me dream now, let me! Syphon did not take part in the dispute but just sat, coddling himself—while Pyzo was rallying Syphon's followers and Hopek was promoting Kneadus' cause. And, in the thick and stifling air, cheeks flushed again and controversy grew—various theories and the names of doctrinaires were catapulted and sped into battle—here world views grappled with each other high above hot-heads, there a troop of liberated and liberating damsels charged at the obscurantism of the conservative press with the vehemence of sexual neophytes. "Our nationalism! Bolshevism! Fascism! Catholic Youth! Falcons! Boy Scouts! Be prepared! Knights of the Sword! Ancient tribes of Poland!"—and ever more fanciful words were falling. It was obvious that each political party had stuffed the students' heads with its brand of the ideal boy, and on top of that, individual thinkers had loaded them with their own tastes and ideals, while films, romantic novels, and newspapers had also done their job. And so all types of lad, guy, communist youth, athlete, juvenile, youngblood, scoundrel, aesthete, philosopher, and skeptic rose into the air above the battlefield and, red with anger, spat at one another, while from below one could hear only moans and groans of "You're naive!" "No, it's you who are naive!" Because all their ideals, without exception, were narrow, awkward, constrained, and inept; they spat them out in the heat of the dispute, then recoiled like catapults, scared of what they had done and unable to retract their callow words. Having totally lost touch with life and with reality, mangled by all kinds of factions, trends, and currents, constantly subjected to pedagogy, surrounded by falsehood, they gave vent to their own falsehood! They talked through their hats! Their pathos was artificial, their lyricism was odious, they were dreadful in their sentimentalism, inept in their irony, jest, and wit, pretentious in their flights of fancy, repulsive in their failures. And so their world turned. Turned and proliferated. Treated with artifice, how else could they be but artificial? And being artificial how else could they talk but in ways that were dishonorable? Consequently a terrible impotence hung in the stifling air, and what had been real slowly turned into a world of ideals, while Kopyrda was the only one to resist being sucked in by it all, nonchalantly tossing his nail file and looking at his legs . . .

In the meantime, Kneadus stood to one side with Mizdral, getting the ropes ready, and Mizdral, trying to oblige, took off his suspenders. Shivers went down my spine. If Kneadus were to carry out his plan of initiating Syphon through the ears, then indeed—reality . . . reality would turn into a nightmare, freakishness would take over, and escape would become impossible. One had to take action against all this, at any cost. But how could I act alone, against all of them, and with my toe still stuck in my shoe? No, I could not. Oh, give me a single face that's still uncontorted! I approached Kopyrda. He stood by the window, in his flannel pants, looking at the school yard and whistling through his teeth, and I thought at least he would not be harboring any ideals. But how was I to begin?

"They want to violate Syphon," I said simply. "It would be better to dissuade them from it. If Kneadus violates Syphon, the school atmosphere will become completely unbearable."

And I anxiously waited for the sound, the ring of Kopyrda's voice . . . But he did not say a word, and with his legs straight, just as he stood, he jumped out the window and into the yard. Once in the yard he went on whistling through his teeth.

I was left there, totally bewildered. What happened? He ducked my question. Why did he jump instead of answering me? This was not normal. And why legs—why had his legs come to the fore, to the forefront? His legs were on his forehead. I rubbed my forehead with my hand. Was I dreaming? Or was this real? But there was no time to think. Kneadus jumped toward me. Only now did I realize that, standing nearby, he had overheard what I said to Kopyrda.

"Why are you butting in?" he yelled. "Who gave you permission to talk to Kopyrda about our business? He doesn't care! Don't you dare talk to him about me!"

I took a step back. He exploded with the most awful invectives.

I whispered pleadingly:

"Kneadus, don't do it to Syphon."

No sooner did I say that when he exploded again:

"He is a pain in the ass and so are you, with all due respect!"

"Don't do it," I begged him. "Don't get mixed up in this! Can you see yourself doing it? Listen, just imagine it! Look! Here is Syphon, on the ground, all tied up, and you're initiating him—by force, through the ears! Can you see yourself doing it?"

He twisted his face even more hideously and said:

"I see that you're quite a lad yourself! Syphon has pulled you into his camp too! Your 'lad' is also a pain in the ass, with all due respect!"

And he kicked me in the shin.

I searched for words, which, as usual, failed me.

"Kneadus," I whispered, "drop it . . . You're making an ass of yourself too. Does Syphon's innocence entitle you to depravity? Drop it."

He looked at me.

"What is it you want from me?" he asked.

"Don't make a fool of yourself!"

"A fool?" he mumbled, his eyes became misty. "Stop making a fool of myself," he went on wistfully. "Indeed, there are guys who don't make fools of themselves. There are guys—journeymen, farmhands, sons of caretakers—these guys cart water, sweep the streets . . . They must really laugh at Syphon and me, at all our poppycock!" He fell into one of his pained musings, for a moment he abandoned trifling talk and uncouth mannerisms, his face relaxed. But suddenly he jumped as if burned with a red-hot poker. "Oh, what a pupa! A pupa!" he exclaimed. "No, I won't have it, I won't have the students taken for innocents. I have to rape Syphon through the ears! F . . . f . . . f . . . !" And his face twisted again into a disgusting grimace, he splattered a ton of filth—I had to take a step back.

"Kneadus," I mechanically whispered, horrified, "let's run away, let's run from here!"

"Run?"

His ears were up. He stopped spluttering and looked at me inquisitively. He looked more normal now—I seized on this like a drowning man would clutch at a straw.

"Let's run, Kneadus, run away," I went on whispering, "drop it, let's run!"

He hesitated, his face sagging with indecision. I realized that the thought of escape was having a positive effect, and, trembling with fear lest he resume his freakishness, I desperately searched for a way to egg him on.

"Run! To freedom! To those farmhands, Kneadus!"

Aware of his yearning for the journeyman's real world I thought I could bait him with the farmhand. Oh, I couldn't care less what I said, I just wanted to keep him away from the grotesqueness, from suddenly contorting his face again. And indeed, his eyes began to sparkle, and he gave me a brotherly poke in the ribs.

"Would you like to, really?" he asked softly, intimately, and he laughed with a laughter that was soft and pure. I too laughed softly.

"To run away," he murmured, "to run . . . To the farmhands . . . To those real guys who tend their horses by the river, who bathe . . ."

But then I saw something terrible—something new had come over his face—a longing, a kind of beauty unique to a schoolboy running away to farmhands. He switched from brutality to musicality. Taking me for one of his own he stopped acting, and instead he gave vent to his yearnings and lyricism.

"Hey, hey," he sang softly, "hey, to eat black bread with farmhands, to ride horses bareback over a meadow . . ."

His lips parted with a strange and bitter smile, his body turned supple and slender, and a kind of self-betrayal settled on his back and shoulders. He turned into a schoolboy longing for the freedom of farmhands—and now, quite openly, and throwing all caution to the wind, he flashed his teeth at me. I took a step back. I found myself in an awful predicament. Should I flash my teeth in return? If I didn't flash, he was likely to start spitting and swearing again, but what if I did flash . . . wouldn't the flashing make things worse, wouldn't the clandestine beauty that he proffered here be even more grotesque than his ugliness? Damn it, damn, why did I induce him to dream about the farmhand? I decided against flashing my teeth, I pursed my lips instead and whistled softly, and so we stood facing each other, flashing, whistling, or laughing softly, while the whole world seemed to have broken down and reorganized itself in the mode of a flashing, fleeing boy, when suddenly, a derisive roar came from a few steps away and all around us! I took a step back. It was Syphon and Pyzo, together with half a dozen other Syphonists—they were clutching their innocent bellies, chortling and roaring, an indulgent yet sneering expression on their faces.

"What?!" exclaimed Kneadus, caught with his pants down. It was too late.

Pyzo bellowed:

"Ha, ha, ha!"

While Syphon shouted:

"Congratulations, Kneadalski! Now we know what's going on! We've caught you, my friend, with your pants down! So you're hankering after a farmhand, are you?! You'd like to go trotting with a farmhand over a meadow, would you?! You pretend to be a realist, a brute, you fight the idealism of others, while deep down you're a sentimentalist yourself. A farmhand sentimentalist!"

Mizdral spewed vulgarities as best he knew how: "Shut up! Son of a bitch! Shit! Damn!"—but it was too late. Not even the worst invectives could save Kneadus, caught *in flagranti* with his secret longings. He blushed blood-red while Syphon sneered triumphantly: "He fights the idealism of others, yet pulls beguiling faces at farmhands. Now we know why purity gets in his way!"

Kneadus was about to pounce on Syphon—but he didn't pounce. He was about to crush him with hyper-vulgar invectives, but he didn't crush him. Caught as he was *in flagranti* he couldn't—he stiffened and became cold and venomously polite.

"I see, Syphon," he rejoined quasi-nonchalantly, but mainly to gain time, "so you think I'm pulling faces, do you? And don't you pull faces?"

"I?" replied Syphon, caught off-guard, "not at farmhands, I don't."

"Only at ideals, eh? So I'm not supposed to pull faces at farm-hands, but it's all right for you to do it, because you pull fancy faces at ideals, is that it? Be so kind as to look at me. I'd love to see your face, if it's not too much bother."

"What for?" Syphon asked anxiously, and he took out his hand-kerchief, but Kneadus grabbed it from him and flung it to the floor: "What for? Because I can't stand the sight of your face! Stop putting on those pure and noble airs! I see, so it's all right for you to do it, is it? . . . Stop it, I tell you, or I'll screw up my face so horribly that you'll be sick of it all—sick of it . . . wait till I show you . . . I'll show you . . ."

"Show me what?" Syphon asked. But Kneadus went on ranting and raving feverishly: "I'll show you! I'll show you! You show me, and I'll show you! Enough talk, on with it, show us that lad of yours instead of talking about him, and I'll show you something too, and then we'll see who will run! Show me! Show me! Enough empty phrases, enough half-baked, timid airs, those little airs, to hell with those delicate, maidenly airs that we hide even from ourselves—damn it, damn it—I challenge you to pull real faces, great faces, no-holds-barred faces, and you'll see, I'll show you faces that will make your lad run with his tail between his legs! Enough talk! You show me, show me, and I'll show you too!"

What a crazy idea! Kneadus had challenged Syphon to a face-pulling duel. They all fell silent and looked at him as if he had lost his wits, while Syphon was thinking up all kinds of sarcasms. But the viciousness that spread over Kneadalski's face was so demonic that everyone easily grasped the deadly sincerity of his proposal. Pulling faces! Faces—a weapon and a torture, all in one! A fight with no holds barred! Some of the students shuddered, seeing that Kneadalski was pulling into the open this dreadful tool that, up to now, everyone had used with the greatest circumspection, freely and openly maybe only behind closed doors and in front of a mirror. And so I took a step back because I realized that Kneadus was at the end of his wits, gone mad, and that he wanted to pull those horrible faces to befoul not only Syphon and the lad, but also the farmhand, the guy, himself, me, and everything else besides!

"Got cold feet?" he asked Syphon.

"Why should I be ashamed of my ideals?" the latter replied, unable to hide his embarrassment. "Why should I be afraid?" but his voice trembled slightly.

"Well then, Syphon! The time—today, after school! The place—here in this classroom! Name your seconds, I name Mizdral and Hopek as my seconds, and for umpire (here Kneadus's voice became even more diabolical), for umpire I propose . . . this new fellow who just arrived in school today. He'll be impartial." What? Me? He proposed me for an umpire? Was I dreaming? Or was this real? But I couldn't be an umpire! Of course I couldn't! I didn't even want to watch this! I didn't want to see it! I tried to protest, but the general anxiety gave way to such an excitement that they all started screaming: "Great! It's settled! On with it!" while at the same time the bell rang, a little man with a short beard walked into the classroom and sat at the teacher's podium.

It was the same body that, in the staff room, had expressed the opinion that prices had gone up, an exceptionally friendly little old man, a little gray dove with a wart on his nose. He took out the grade book, and a deathly silence fell in the classroom—he beamed as he looked to the top of the list, and everyone whose name started with "A" trembled—he looked to the bottom of the list, and everyone whose name started with "Z" froze in fear. Because no one knew anything and, caught up in their discussions, they had forgotten to copy the Latin translation—with the exception of Syphon, who had already prepared his lesson at home and could deliver anything, whenever called upon, while others could not. But the little old man, totally unaware of the fear he was arousing, cheerfully gazed up and down the list of names, hesitated, reflected, bantered inwardly, then finally said with confidence:

"Slopowski."

But it soon became apparent that Slopowski couldn't translate Caesar, which was the assignment for today, and, worse still, he did not know that *animis oblatis* was in the *ablativus absolutus*.

"Oh, Master Slopowski," the gentle old man said with genuine reproach, "you don't know what *animis oblatis* means, nor do you know its grammatical construction? Why don't you know it?" And, truly upset, he gave him an F, but then he beamed again, and with a renewed surge of trust he called on "K"—Koperdillski, in the belief that by singling him out he was bestowing happiness, and, with looks and gestures full of the deepest trust, he egged him on to noble rivalry. But neither Koperdillski nor Kotecki nor Kabbaginski nor Kodowel had any idea what *animis oblatis* meant, they would go up to the blackboard and stand there, sulking, glum and silent, whereupon the little old man would express his fleeting disappointment with a brisk gesture, then, as if he had only yesterday arrived from the moon, from some other world, and, with a renewed upsurge of trust, he would again call upon someone else, each time expecting that the student, thus blessed and favored, would duly respond to his call. But no one did. He had already marked close to ten F's on the record sheet, and he still had not realized that everyone was trying to stave off his trust with a cold and deathly fear, that no one wanted all that trust—oh, he was such an extremely trusting little old man! And there was no remedy for all that trust! They tried in vain all means of persuasion, they presented sick-notes, excuses, ailments—to no avail, the teacher went on talking with compassion and understanding.

"What do you mean, Master Bobkowski! For reasons beyond your control you couldn't prepare your lesson? Well, don't worry, I'll ask you something from a previous text. What? You have a little bit of a headache? Great, I have just the thing for you, the interesting maxim *de malis capitis*. Now what—you have an urgent need to go to the bathroom? Oh, Master Bobkowski! What's your point? The ancients have done it already! Let me show you the famous *passus* from book five, where Caesar's whole army, having eaten spoiled carrots, succumbed to the same fate as you. The whole army, Bobkowski! Why bother with such a feeble attempt when you already have at hand a brilliant and classic description! These books, gentlemen, are life, life itself!"

Syphon and Kneadus were forgotten, the quarreling had stopped— everyone tried to cease to exist, to be no more, the students shrank, faded, and sank into the background, they pulled in their stomachs, hands, and legs, but not one student was bored, boredom was out of the question, because now each and every one of them was scared, and, in pained fear, grimly awaited his turn to be caught by the call of the childlike trust that had grazed on texts. And their faces—as faces are wont to do under stress and panic—turned into shadows, into illusions, until it was impossible to tell what was more insane, unreal, chimeric—their faces, the unfathomable *accusativs cum infinitivo,* or the hellish trust of a deluded old man and what had been real slowly turned into a world of ideals, oh, let me dream now, let me!

The teacher, however, having given Bobkowski an F and having finally exhausted *animis oblatis,* dreamt up a new problem, namely, what will *passivum futurum conditionalis* be in the third person plural of the reflexive verb *colleo, colleavi, colleatum,* and now this new idea caught his fancy.

"An amazing thing!" he exclaimed rubbing his hands, "amazing and instructive too! Well, gentlemen! This is an issue replete with subtlety! Here is a fertile field for showing off your intellectual prowess! Because if *ollandus sim* derives from *olleare* then . . . yes, then, then . . . gentlemen . . ." but the gentlemen had seemingly disappeared, terrified out of existence. "Right! Well? Well? *Collan . . . collan . . .*"

No one said a word. The little old man, still brimming with hope, went on repeating his: "yes, yes" and "*collan, collan,*" he beamed, he wooed them with his riddles, he encouraged and incited them, and— as best he knew how—he called for answers, for knowledge, for happiness and fulfillment. But suddenly he realized that no one wanted any of it, that he had been dancing while facing a blank wall. His lights dimmed, and in a hollow voice he said:

"*Collandus sim! Collandus sim!*" he repeated sadly, and, humiliated by the silence, he added: "How is it, gentlemen? Don't you appreciate any of it?! Can't you see that *collandus sim* develops intelligence, improves the mind, builds character, perfects us in every way and bonds us with ancient thought? Because, mark you, if *ollandus* is from *olleare,* then clearly *collandus* is from *colleare,* because *passivum futurum* of the third conjugation ends in *dus, dus, us,* with the exception of the exceptions. *Us, us, us*—gentlemen! There is nothing more logical than a language in which everything that's illogical is an exception! *Us, us, us,* gentlemen," he ended despondently, "what a great factor in evolution!"

At that moment Gałkiewicz jumped to his feet and groaned:

"Evolution, shmolution! How can it develop anything when it develops nothing? How can it perfect anything when it perfects nothing? How can it build something when it doesn't build anything? O God, O God—O God, O God!"

Teacher

"What's this, Master Gałkiewicz? The suffix *us* does not perfect you? You're telling me that this suffix does not perfect you? That the suffix *passivi futuri* of the third conjugation does not enrich you? Come, come, Gałkiewicz!"

Gałkiewicz

"That little tail ending does not enrich me! That little tail does not perfect me! Not in the least! O God! O God!"

Teacher

"What do you mean—doesn't enrich you? Master Gałkiewicz, when I say it enriches you, it most certainly does! And I'm telling you it does enrich you! Trust me, Gałkiewicz! Of course an ordinary mind cannot grasp these great benefits! In order to grasp them one has to, after years of extensive studies, first become an extraordinary mind oneself! For Christ's sake, in the course of the past year we've covered

Caught with His Pants Down and Further Kneading

seventy-three poems from Caesar, and in these poems Caesar describes how he positioned his cohorts on a hillock. Those seventy-three poems, just the words themselves, haven't they mysteriously revealed to you, Gałkiewicz, all the riches of antiquity? Haven't they taught you its style, its clarity of thought, its precision of expression, and its art of war?"

Gałkiewicz

"Nothing! Nothing! No art. I'm just scared of an F. That's all I'm scared of! Oh, I can't, I can't!"

Generalized inability was now threatening everyone. The teacher realized that it was threatening him too, and, worse still, if he did not redouble his trust to counter his own sudden lack of trust and will, he too would perish. Abandoned by all—"Pylaszczkiewicz!"—exclaimed the hermit in despair, "You, Syphon Pylaszczkiewicz, recapitulate at once the gains we've made in the last three months by revealing to us the full depth of thought and the delights of style, and—yes, I do trust, I do, Jesus, Mary, I do trust!"

Syphon, always ready—as mentioned before—and able on demand, stood up, and with great ease and fluency began:

The following day, having gathered his troops, Caesar chastised them for their hot-headedness and greed, and, surmising that they had used their own judgment, their own preconception as to where they should go and what they should do, and that they had decided, after the orders to retreat were given, that they would not be held back by any military tribunes or envoys, he explained to them the significance of an unfavorable site, such as Avaricum, where an otherwise assured victory eluded him even though he had seized the enemy without their leader and without their cavalry, and that they had, nonetheless, sustained major losses because the site was unfavorable. The spirit of those who will not be deterred by the fortifications of a camp, the height of mountains, or the walls of a city is to be much admired, but by the same token one has to condemn the undue willfulness and audacity of those who think they know more about victory and the outcome of things than their leader does, and in a soldier one wishes for modesty and restraint no less than for bravery and nobility of mind. Then, as he kept advancing, he made the decision and ordered the bugles to sound retreat so that ten legions would at once desist from battle, and this was carried out, but the soldiers in the remaining legions did not hear the sound of the bugles because they were separated from the rest by a wide valley. Therefore military tribunes and envoys tried to call them back, as had been ordered by Caesar, but the soldiers were so excited by the prospect of victory, of overpowering their enemy in his flight in the course of a propitious battle, all of which they could achieve through bravery and without resorting to flight, that they did not stop till they were at the walls and the gates of the city, then shouts were heard in all parts of the city, whereupon those terrified by the sudden uproar thought that the enemy was within the gates, and started running out of the city.

"*Collandus sim*, gentlemen! *Collandus sim!* What clarity, what language! What depth, what thought! *Collandus sim*, what a repository of wisdom! Oh, I can breathe again, I can breathe! *Collandus sim* forever and ever, to the very end *collandus sim, collandus sim, collandus sim, collandus sim, collandus sim*—suddenly the bell rang, and the students screamed wildly, the little old man gave a look of surprise and walked out.

At the same moment, abandoning these officially sanctioned musings, they all bashed full-face into their own private musings about the lad, the guy, discussions flared up again, and, what had been real slowly turned into a world of ideals, oh, let me dream now, let me! Kneadus had deliberately summoned me to be the umpire! He did it deliberately! So that I would have to watch, so that I would have to see it. His mind was set—by befouling himself he wanted to befoul me too, he could not bear the fact that I had been instrumental in revealing his momentary weakness for the farmhand. But how could I risk exposing my own face? I knew that if I became part of this aping, my own face would never return to normal, my chance of escape would be lost forever, no, no, let them carry on however they want, but without me, without me! Nervously wiggling my toe in my shoe I caught his sleeve, I looked at him imploringly and whispered:

"Kneadus . . ."

He pushed me away.

"Oh no, kiddo! That won't do! You are the umpire, and that's that!"

He called me "kiddo"! What a disgusting word! It was sheer cruelty on his part, I realized that everything was lost, and that we were heading full-steam toward that which I dreaded most, toward utter freakishness and grotesqueness. Meanwhile, even those who had until now been listlessly repeating "Could Syphonus perchance . . ." were seized with a wild and sick curiosity. Nostrils flaring, cheeks burning red, it was clear that the face-pulling duel would indeed be a duel with no holds barred, unto death, and not merely a duel of empty words! They surrounded the two contestants and shouted into the heavily laden air:

"Go ahead! Stick it to him! Get on with it! Go for it!"

Only Kopyrda calmly stretched himself, picked up his notes, and walked away on those legs of his . . .

And Syphon sat on that lad of his—all gloom and doom, as puffed up as a hen sitting on eggs—one could see that he was actually a little scared and would have preferred to back out! Pyzo, however, swiftly recognized what terrific chances Syphon's lofty beliefs and principles gave him. "We've got him!" he whispered into Syphon's ear to spur him on. "Don't be yellow! Think of your principles! You have your principles, and for the sake of these principles as such, you'll easily be able to pull faces, any number of them, while he has no principles, and he'll have to pull faces for his own sake, and not for the sake of principles, as such." As a result of these whisperings Syphon's face began to relax and soon to glow peacefully, because his principles were indeed empowering him to pull any number of faces, at any time. Mizdral and Hopek saw what was happening and, taking Kneadus aside, begged him not to risk certain defeat.

"Don't bring ruin on yourself and on all of us, better surrender right now—he's much better at pulling faces than you are—pretend, Kneadie, that you're sick, pass out, it'll blow over, we'll find excuses for you!"

But Kneadus merely answered:

"I can't, the die is cast! Off with you! Off! Do you want me to chicken out? Get those gawkers out of here! They're getting on my nerves! No one is to watch me from the side except the seconds and the umpire." But his face fell, and his initial doggedness gave way to obvious stage fright, which contrasted with Syphon's calm self-confidence so starkly that Mizdral whispered: "He's done for," and the others shuddered and slipped out of the classroom in silence, closing the door carefully behind them. Suddenly we found ourselves in the deserted classroom, behind closed doors, the seven of us, Syphon Pylaszczkewicz and Kneadus, Mizdral, Hopek, Pyzo, someone called Guzek (Syphon's other second), and of course myself in the middle as the superarbiter, as the dumbfounded superarbiter of all arbiters. And now Pyzo's voice resounded, sarcastic and awe-inspiring, and, looking slightly pale, he read the conditions of the engagement from a piece of paper:

The contestants shall stand facing each other and shall fire a salvo of faces, and to each and every one of Pylaszczkiewicz's inspiring and beatific faces, Kneadalski shall respond with an ugly and demolishing counterface. The faces—as personal as possible, totally individual, and intrinsically his own, as wounding and shattering as possible—shall be administered without a silencer, to the very end.

He fell silent—while Syphon and Kneadus took up their assigned positions, Syphon rubbed his cheeks, Kneadus slid his jaw from side to side—then Mizdral said through his chattering teeth:

"You may begin!"

And just as he said "you may begin," just at that moment when he said "begin," reality finally overstepped its bounds, all that was non-essential climaxed into a nightmare, and the outlandish event turned into a total dream—while I was stuck there in the middle like a fly caught in a web, unable to move. It seemed as if by way of long and hard exercise, the point at which one loses one's face had finally been reached. The empty phrase became a grimace, and the grimace—vacuous, sterile, idle, and futile—grabbed one and would not let go. It wouldn't have been at all strange to see Kneadus and Syphon take their faces in their hands and throw them at each other—no, nothing would have been strange any more. I mumbled: "Have pity on your faces, at least have pity on mine, a face is not an object, a face is a subject, a subject, a subject!" But Syphon had already presented and sallied his first face so violently that even my face curled on itself like a piece of gutta-percha.* Namely—he blinked like someone coming out of darkness into broad daylight, he then looked right and left in pious astonishment, rolled his eyeballs, shot them upward, ogled, opened his mouth, let out a soft cry as if he had spotted something on the ceiling, assumed an expression of rapture and so remained, entranced and inspired; he then placed his hand on his heart and sighed.

Kneadalski shrank, crouched, and hit him from below with a shattering, copycat counterface as follows: he too rolled his eyeballs, lifted them and ogled, he too opened his mouth in calflike rapture, and, his face thus prepared, he moved it in circles till a fly fell into his gaping mouth; he then ate it.

Syphon paid no attention to him, as if Kneadus' pantomime was not even taking place (because he had the advantage of acting for the sake of his principles, as such, and not for his own sake), but instead he burst into fervent, ardent sobs, and he sobbed and sobbed until he

---

*Gutta-percha is a tough plastic substance obtained from the latex of various Malaysian trees.

reached the peak of contrition, self-revelation, and emotion. Kneadus also began sobbing, and he sobbed long and hard till a drop of snot appeared at the tip of his nose—which he shook off into a spittoon, thereby reaching another peak of grossness. But the impudent blasphemy against all sacred feelings unnerved Syphon—he couldn't stand it any longer and he unwittingly glanced at Kneadus, then, exasperated by what he saw and still sobbing, he looked daggers at the daredevil! How unwise! Because Kneadus was ready for him! As soon as he realized that he had managed to turn Syphon's gaze toward himself and away from lofty heights, he immediately bared his teeth and pulled a face so filthy that Syphon, cut to the quick, hissed. It seemed that now Kndeadus had the upper hand! Mizdral and Hopek breathed a quiet sigh! But too soon! They breathed too soon!

Because Syphon—realizing in the nick of time that he had needlessly been carried away by Kneadus' face, and that in his exasperation he was about to lose command of his own face—quickly retreated, regrouped his features, and once again shot his eyeballs upward, moreover, he moved one of his legs forward, slightly tousled his hair, letting a cowlick slip onto his forehead, and so he remained, complete unto himself, with his principles and with his ideals; he then lifted his hand and quite unexpectedly pointed his finger upward! The blow was staggering!

Kneadus immediately stuck out the same finger and spat on it, he picked his nose with it, he scratched himself with it, he debased Syphon as much as he could, as he knew how, he defended himself by attacking, he attacked by defending himself, but Syphon's finger remained pointing to heaven on high, undaunted. To no avail did Kneadus bite his finger, dig his teeth into it, scratch the sole of his foot with it, and everything else humanly possible to befoul it—alas, alas—Syphon's unrelenting, undaunted finger remained pointing upward, and would not cede. Kneadalski found himself in desperate straits because he had exhausted all possible grossness while Syphon's finger continued pointing upward, on and on. The seconds' and the umpire's blood curdled! With a final, spasmodic effort Kneadus bathed his finger in the spittoon and, red in the face, covered in sweat, repulsive, he shook it at Syphon in despair, but Syphon paid no heed, nor did he move his finger, and what's more, his face turned as luminous as a rainbow after a storm, and the wondrous Eaglet-*Sokół*, the pure, innocent, uninitiated Lad, beamed in all of the seven colors of the rainbow!

"Victory!" shouted Pyzo.

Kneadus looked terrible. He retreated all the way to the wall and wheezed, let out a throaty rattle, foamed at the mouth, grabbed his finger and pulled on it, he wanted to tear it out, to tear it out by its root and throw it away, to destroy thereby any bond with Syphon and regain his independence! But he couldn't, no matter how hard he pulled, regardless of the pain! Inability reared its head again! While Syphon always could, always at the ready and as calm as the blue Skies, his finger uplifted not for Kneadus, as such, nor for himself, as such, but for his principles, as such! Oh, what horror! Here in one direction was Kneadus—contorted, baring his teeth, and there was Syphon doing it in the opposite direction! And there was I between them, the umpire, imprisoned perhaps forever, a prisoner of someone else's grimace, someone else's countenance. And my own face, like a mirror image of their faces, also turned freakish, while fear, disgust, and terror carved on it an indelible mark. A clown between two clowns, how could I attempt anything that would not be a grimace? My toe tragically seconding their fingers, I was grimacing, grimacing, and I knew that I was losing myself in that grimace. I thought I would never escape Pimko. Never be myself again. Oh, what horror! And what horrible silence! Because at times the silence was absolute, no weapons clanging, only face-pulling, and movements without a sound.

Suddenly Kneadus shrieked:

"Hold him! Grab him! Kill him! Hit him!"

What's this? Something new again? What now? Hasn't there been enough already? Kneadus lowered his finger, pounced on Syphon, and hit him in the mug—Mizdral and Hopek pounced on Pyzo and Guzek, and hit them in the mugs too! A tumult ensued. The mass of bodies lay entangled on the floor while I stood over them immobile, like some superumpire. In less than a minute Pyzo and Guzek were on the floor like two logs, tied up in suspenders, while Kneadus sat akimbo Syphon's chest, gloating horribly.

"What now, you little worm, you innocent Lad, you thought you had the better of me? Up goes your little finger, and you're pleased as Punch, eh? So you thought, you mama's boy (and he followed this with the most opprobrious expressions), that Kneadus wouldn't be able to handle this? That he'd let you twist him round your little finger? I have news for you: if nothing else works, that little finger will be pulled down by force!"

"Let go . . ." Syphon rattled with a throaty voice.

"Let go!? I'll let go in a minute! But I'm not sure I'll let you go just as you are. Let's talk first! Let's have your little ear! Fortunately, one can still get inside you . . . by force . . . through the ears . . . I'll get inside you all right! Give me your little ear, I tell you! Just wait, you little innocent, I'll tell you something . . ."

He bent over him and whispered—Syphon turned green, squealed like a stuck pig, and plopped like a fish out of water. Kneadus pressed down on him! And, in hot pursuit of Syphon's ears, Kneadus chased them with his mouth, first one ear then the other, while Syphon rolled his head from side to side to protect his ears, but, realizing that escape was impossible he started to roar, and he roared to deafen the murderous words that were tearing at his innocence, he roared horribly, grimly, he then stiffened, utterly beside himself in that desperate, primeval roar, and I could not believe my ears that ideals could roar like a wild ox in the wilderness. Then his torturer roared too:

"A gag! A gag! Gag him! You there, you goat-head! What are you gawking at? A gag! Use your handkerchief!"

He was screaming at me. I was the one to gag him with my handkerchief! Because Mizdral and Hopek, sitting akimbo their respective seconds, couldn't move. But I didn't want to! I couldn't! I stood motionless, and to move, to speak, to think of e x p r e s s i n g anything whatsoever filled me with disgust. Oh, what an umpire! Oh where was my thirty-year-old, my thirty-year-old, where was my thirty-year-old? Nowhere! And all of a sudden Pimko appears at the door of the classroom, and he stands there—in his yellow buckskin shoes, in his brown coat, cane in hand—he is there, standing . . . standing. And he stands there as absolutely as if he were seated.

4 Preface to "The Child Runs Deep in Filidor"

Before I continue these true reminiscences I wish to include, as the next chapter and by way of digression, a story entitled "The Child Runs Deep in Filidor." You saw how maliciously the doctrinaire Pimko had dealt me the pupa, you saw the idealistic nooks and crannies of our intelligentsia youth, their inability to embrace life, the hopelessness of their disparate aims, their dismal affectation, the boredom that plunged them into gloom, their ridiculous fantasy life, their anguish over their anachronisms, the folly of their pupas, faces, and other body parts. You have heard words, words, vulgar words waging war on high-flown words, and you have heard other equally vacuous words uttered in class by their teachers—you were the silent witnesses to the way that a mishmash of inane words came to a bad end in the form of a freakish grimace. It is in the prime of youth that man sinks into empty phrases and grimaces. It's in this smithy that our maturity is forged. In a moment you'll see yet another reality, another duel—a fight unto death between Professors G. L. Filidor from Leyden and Momsen from Colombo (with the genteel title of "anti-Filidor"). And words, as well as various body parts, will play their part in that reality, but one should not look for an exact connection between the two parts of the said whole; and whoever thinks that by including this story, "The Child Runs Deep in Filidor," my sole aim was not merely filling space on paper and reducing slightly the enormous number of white pages before me, is sorely mistaken.

But if notable scholars and connoisseurs, all those Pimkos adept at fabricating the pupa out of texts by pointing to the faulty construction of a work of art, reproach me that—in their opinion—a desire to fill space is a purely private matter and insufficient reason for writing, and that one shouldn't stick everything one has ever written into a work of art, I will reply that in my humble opinion individual body parts form an adequately aesthetic-artistic linkage with words. And I will prove that my construction is in no way inferior, as far as precision and logic are concerned, to even the most precise and logical constructions. Look—that basic body part, the tame and kindly pupa is the basis, therefore, it is from the pupa that all action begins. It is from the pupa, as from the trunk of a tree, that the branching of individual parts, namely the toe, hands, eyes, teeth, ears, begins, and, at the same time, all those parts imperceptibly pass from one part to another in delicate and skillful transformations. And the human face, otherwise known as the mug, is the crown, the foliage of a tree whose individual parts grow out of the trunk of the pupa; the mug closes the cycle that began with the pupa. And having arrived at the mug, what is there left for me to do but to retrace my steps, through the individual parts, back to the pupa?—and this is the purpose of the short story "Filidor." "Filidor" is a construction in reverse, a passage or, strictly speaking, a coda, it's a trill, or rather a twist, a twisting of the gut, without which I would never have reached the calf of my left leg. Isn't this an ironclad skeleton for a construction? Isn't this enough to satisfy the most exacting requirements? And what if you penetrate deeper, into the linkages between the individual parts, into the pathways from the finger to the teeth, into the mystical meaning of some of your favorite parts, and further, into the significance of individual joints, of the sum of the parts, as well as into all the parts of parts? I assure you, such a construction is invaluable as far as filling space is concerned, one could fill three hundred volumes with critical research on the subject, thus filling even more space, reaching thereby an even higher place, and seating oneself even more squarely and comfortably in that place. Do you like blowing soap bubbles by the lakeside at sunset when carp splash about and a fisherman s i t s in silence, looking at himself in the mirrorlike sheet of water?

And I recommend repetition as the method for enhancing the vigor of your work, because by systematically repeating certain words, phrases, situations, and parts I intensify them, thereby heightening the impression of uniformity of style to the point of near-mania. It's by means of repetition, repetition that mythology is most readily created! Take note, however, that this construction from particles is not a mere construction, it is actually an entire philosophy which I'll present here in the frivolous and frothy form of a carefree magazine article. But what do you think, tell me—in your opinion, doesn't the reader assimilate parts only, and only partly at that? He reads a part, or a piece of it, then stops, only to resume reading another piece later, and, as so often happens, he starts from the middle or from the end, then backtracks to the beginning. Quite often he'll read a couple of segments then toss the book aside, not because he has lost interest in it, but because something else came to his mind. And even if he were to read the whole—do you think that he can visualize it in its entirety and appreciate the relationship and harmony of its individual parts unless he hears it from an expert? Is it for this that an author toils for years, cuts his material and bends it into shape, tears it apart and patches it up again, sweats and agonizes over it—so that an expert may tell the reader that its construction is good? But let's go on, on, and into the realm of the reader's everyday personal experience! Might not just a phone call, or a fly, interrupt his reading precisely at the point where all the individual parts unite in a dramatic resolution? Or what if, at that very moment, his brother

Preface to "The Child Runs Deep in Filidor"

(for instance) comes into the room and says something. The author's noble-minded pains go for naught *vis à vis* the brother, the fly, or the phone call—fie! nasty little flies, why do you bite human beings who have lost their tails long ago and have nothing to swat with? What's more, let us consider whether your work, this unique, outstanding, and elaborate work is merely a particle of some thirty thousand other works, equally unique, which make their appearance year in, year out and on the principle of "each year be sure to add, whether bad or good, a new *oeuvre* to your brood"? Oh, horrid parts! Is this why we construct a whole, so that a particle of a part of the reader will absorb a particle of a part of the work, and only partly at that?

It's hard not to play little games and make fun of the subject. Making fun is the name of the game. Because we've learned long ago to make fun of that which too scathingly makes fun of us. Will there ever be a sufficiently serious-minded genius who will look life's trivia in the eye without bursting into a dumb giggle? Someone whose greatness will ever be a match for triviality? Hey-ho, I'm setting here a tone, a tone for my carefree feuilleton! But let's note further (to drain the chalice of particles to the last drop) that the cannons and principles of construction to which we so slavishly adhere are also the product of a mere part, and a rather minuscule part at that. It's only an insignificant part of the world, a scant circle of experts and aesthetes, a small world no bigger than one's little finger, a world that could fit in its entirety into one café, that constantly shapes itself, squeezing out ever more refined postulates. But what's worse, their tastes are not actually tastes—no, their fancy for the construction of your work is only a small part, the larger part being their fancy for their own expertise on the subject of construction. Is this why an author tries to show his skill in the way he constructs his work, so that an expert may show off his expertise on the subject? Quiet, shush, something mysterious is happening, here before us is a fifty-year-old author, on his knees at the altar of art, creating, thinking about his masterpiece, about its harmony, precision, and beauty, about its spirit and how to overcome its difficulties, and there is the expert thoroughly studying the author's material, whereupon the masterpiece goes out into the world and to the reader, and what was conceived in utter and absolute agony is now received piecemeal, between a telephone call and a hamburger. Here is the writer who with all his heart and soul, with his art, in anguish and travail offers nourishment—there is the reader who'll have none of it, and if he wants it, it's only in passing, offhandedly, until the phone rings. Life's trivia are your undoing. You are like a man who has challenged a dragon to a fight but will be yapped into a corner by a little dog.

But to go on, I want to ask you (to take one more swig from the chalice of particles)—in your opinion—does a work that obeys all the cannons express a whole or only a part? Indeed! Doesn't all form rely on the process of exclusion, isn't all construction a process of whittling down, can a word express anything but a part of reality? The rest is silence. And finally, do we create form or does form create us? We think we are the ones who construct it, but that's an illusion, because we are, in equal measure, constructed by the construction. Whatever you put down on paper dictates what comes next, because the work is not born of you—you want to write one thing, yet something entirely different comes out. Parts tend to wholeness, every part surreptitiously makes its way toward the whole, strives for roundness, and seeks fulfillment, it implores the rest to be created in its own image and likeness. Out of the turbulent sea of images our mind catches a certain part, let's say an ear or a leg; then, right at the beginning of a work, the ear or the leg drifts under our pen, and henceforward we can no longer extricate ourselves from this part, so we continue with it, it imposes on us all the remaining body parts. We wrap ourselves around that part like ivy round an oak tree, the beginning sets up the end, and the end—the beginning, while the middle evolves between the beginning and the end. A total inability to encompass wholeness marks the human soul. What are we then to do with a part that has turned up and is not in our likeness, as if a thousand lustful, fiery stallions had visited the bed of our child's mother—and hey! if only to save some semblance of paternity we must, with all the moral power at our disposal, try to resemble our work, but it doesn't want to resemble us. Indeed, I remember a writer I knew years ago who, at the outset of his career, happened to write a heroic book. With his first words, and quite accidentally, he struck a heroic chord—he could equally well have struck a skeptical or lyrical note—but the first few sentences happened to sound heroic, therefore, out of consideration for the harmony of construction, he couldn't help but to go on enhancing the heroism, step by step, to the very end. And he continued rounding off the edges of his material, polishing and perfecting it, revising it, matching the beginning with the end, and the end with the beginning, until the work emerged like a living thing, full of deep convictions. But what could he do with those deep convictions? Could he then turn around and deny them? Can an author who is responsible for his every word admit that he just stumbled upon a heroic theme, that those deep convictions are not his deep convictions at all, that they had somehow crept in from outside and had crawled over, ambled, and clambered into his text? Absolutely not! Because such trite methods as stumbling upon, crawling over, or creeping in have no place in a sophisticated piece of work, they are a makeshift approach suitable only for a frothy and playfully unimportant magazine article. In vain did our hapless heroic writer hide in embarrassment and try to weasel out of the part that caught hold of him, while the part, once having grabbed him, would not let go, and he had to adapt to it. And he continued to become more and more like the part until, at the end of his writing career, he became just like it, and just as heroic— though a rather weakly victim of his heroism. And he avoided his colleagues and companions from the time of immaturity like the plague, because they marveled at the whole that had so closely been matched with the part. And they called to him: "Hey, Bolek! Do you remember that fingernail . . . the fingernail . . . Bolek, Bolek, little

Bolek, do you remember the fingernail on the green meadow? The fingernail? That fingernail, Bolek-boy, where is it now?"

These are then the basic fundamental and philosophical reasons that have induced me to build a work on a foundation of individual parts—treating the work itself as a particle of the work, man as a union of parts, and mankind as a composite of parts and pieces. But if anyone were to complain: this part-concept is not—if truth be known—a concept at all but sheer nonsense, a mockery and leg-pulling, and that I'm trying, instead of complying with strict rules and cannons of art, to evade them by mocking them—I would reply: yes, yes indeed, these and none other are my intentions. And—so help me God—I don't hesitate to admit it—I don't want to have anything to do with your Art, gentlemen, which I can't stand, just as much as I don't want to have anything to do with you . . . because I can't stand you, with your ideas, your artistic posturing, and all that artistic little world of yours.

Gentlemen, there are on this earth societies that are more or less ridiculous, more or less degrading, shameful and humiliating—and the amount of stupidity is also variable. So, for example, a guild of hairdressers may seem, at first sight, more prone to stupidity than a guild of cobblers. But what goes on in the world of art beats all for stupidity and degradation—and to such a degree that someone who has some sense of decency and balance can't help but lower his brow in burning shame when confronted with this childish and pretentious orgy. Oh, those inspired songs to which no one listens! Oh, the connoisseurs' clever talk and their enthusiasm at concerts and poetry readings, oh, the initiations, valorizations, discussions, and oh, the faces of those who recite or listen to poetry and collectively celebrate the mystery of beauty! By what painful paradox does everything you say or do transform itself, under these circumstances, into the ridiculous? When, over time, a society lapses into fits of stupidity, one can definitely say that its ideas are not in keeping with reality, that it simply stuffs itself with bogus ideas. And, without a doubt, your artistic concepts have also reached the peak of conceptual naiveté; but if you want to know how and in what sense they should be revised, I'll tell you soon enough—but you have to lend me your ear.

What is it that someone really desires these days when he feels a calling to take up the pen, the brush? He yearns, first and foremost, to be an artist. He yearns to create Art. He dreams of satiating himself and his fellow men with Beauty, Goodness, Truth, he wants to be their high priest of art and their bard by offering up all the riches of his talent to thirsting mankind. And perhaps he also wants to offer his talent in the service of some great idea as well as of his Nation. What lofty goals! What magnanimous undertakings! Wasn't this the role of all the Shakespeares and the Chopins? But, mark you, here is the catch: you are not, as yet, Chopins nor Shakespeares, you are not, as yet, fully fledged artists nor high priests of art; you are at most, in the present phase of your development, merely half-Shakespeares and quarter-Chopins (oh, those accursed parts again!)—and therefore your posturing does nothing but expose your miserable deficiencies—it's as if you wanted, at any cost, to jump onto a pedestal, thereby endangering your precious and sensitive body parts.

Believe me: there is a great difference between an artist who has realized his potential and a horde of half-artists and quarter-bards who merely dream of doing so. And that which befits a fully fledged artist has, when it comes from you, an entirely different ring. Yet you, instead of conceiving ideas to your own measure, ideas that fit your own reality, you adorn yourselves with someone else's feathers—and this is why you become mere hopefuls, forever inept, whose grades will never be more than a puny C, you servants and imitators, vassals and admirers of Art, which keeps you in its antechambers. Truly, it's a terrible thing to watch you try and not succeed, to watch you push on with new works and try to foist them on others even as you're being told "that's not quite it," to watch you boost yourselves with awful, second-rate little successes, pay each other compliments, arrange artistic soirées, and persuade yourselves and others to create ever new disguises for your own ineptness. And you don't have the consolation that what you write and concoct is of any value whatsoever, even to yourselves. Because all of it, I repeat, all of it, is mere imitation, it's been picked up from the masters—it's nothing but a premature illusion that your quality is being recognized, that you have attained a measure of worth. Your situation is false and, being false, must bear bitter fruit, therefore animosity, disdain, maliciousness grow ripe among you, and everyone looks down on everyone else and on himself in particular, you are a brotherhood of disdain—until you'll finally scorn each other to death. What is the situation, actually, of a second-rate writer if not one of major rebuff? The first and merciless rebuff is inflicted upon him by the ordinary reader who simply refuses to relish the writer's works. The second shameful rebuff is meted out to him by his own reality, which he has been unable to express. And the third rebuff, the most shameful of all and a real kick in the pants, is dealt him by art itself, the art to which he has turned for shelter but which regards him with utter disdain, as inept and inadequate. And this fills the cup of disgrace. This is where true homelessness begins. This is how the second-rate writer becomes the butt of ridicule from all sides, caught as he is in the crossfire of rebuff. Truly, what can be expected of a man rebuffed three times, each time more shamefully than the time before? And when he's dressed down like this, shouldn't a man pack his bags and leave, shouldn't he hide somewhere so he can't be seen? Can inadequacy which parades in the light of day and which craves honors be wholesome, won't it provoke one's nature to hiccup?

But first tell me this—in your opinion, are Anjou pears better and juicier than Bosc pears, aren't you more partial to the former than to the latter? And do you like to eat them while sitting comfortably in wicker chairs on the porch? For shame, gentlemen, for shame, shame, and shame again! I'm not a philosopher and theoretician, no—but I'm talking about you, I'm thinking about your life, do understand me, I'm purely and simply troubled by your personal

Preface to "The Child Runs Deep in Filidor"

situation. You just can't break free. Oh, this inability of yours to cut the umbilical cord that ties you to mankind's rebuff! A soul rebuffed—a flower unsniffed—a candy that wants so much to be tasty but pleases no one—a woman spurned—all these have always caused me sheer physical pain, I just can't bear this lack of fulfillment, and when I meet one of those artists downtown and realize to what extent an ordinary rebuff lies at the basis of his existence, how his every move, every word, how his beliefs, his enthusiasms, his every comma, his hurt ego, his pride, his crying shame and suffering, how they all give off the smell of an ordinary and unpleasant rebuff, I too feel shame. And I feel shame not because I commiserate with him but because I live side by side with him, because his grotesque nature touches me and everyone else whose consciousness it has penetrated. Believe me, it's about time to decide and settle the status of the second-rate writer, otherwise everyone will be left nauseated. Isn't it strange that people who dedicate themselves *ex professo* to form and therefore, one would think, are sensitive to style, give in without a protest to such a false and pretentious state of affairs? Can't you understand that from the point of view of form and style nothing can be more disastrous in its consequences—because whoever finds himself in such a false situation, in such entirely shoddy circumstances, cannot utter a single word that won't be shoddy.

How should we then—you'll ask—express ourselves in a way that would be congruent with our reality, yet at the same time be autonomous? Gentlemen, it's not within your power to transform yourselves, well, let's say from Tuesday to Wednesday, into mature masters, but you could save your dignity to some degree by distancing yourselves from Art, which sticks it to you with that disconcerting pupa. To begin with, part company forever with the word: art, and that other word: artist. Stop wallowing in these words and repeating them with such endless monotony. Isn't everyone a bit of an artist? Isn't it true that mankind creates art not only on paper or on canvas, but also in every moment of everyday life—when a young girl pins a flower in her hair, when in the course of conversation a little joke escapes your lips, when we melt with emotion at the beauty of twilight's light and shadow, what is all this if not the practicing of art? Why then this odd and idiotic division into "artists" and the rest of mankind? Wouldn't it be more wholesome if you simply said: "perhaps I busy myself with art a little more than others do," rather than to proudly declare yourselves artists? Further, what use is it to you, this worship of the art contained within the so-called "works of art"—how did you dream it up, what's given you the daft idea that man has such a great admiration for works of art, that we swoon in heavenly bliss when we listen to a Bach fugue? Have you ever thought how impure, murky, and immature is the artistic aspect of culture— the aspect that you want to lock up within your simplistic phraseology? The mistake that you so commonly and flagrantly make is primarily this: you reduce man's communion with art to artistic emotion alone, and, at the same time, you define this communion in utterly egocentric terms, as if each one of us were experiencing art totally on our own—a single-handed, single-legged experience—and in hermetic isolation from your fellow men. Yet in real life we're dealing with a blend of many emotions, of many individuals who, acting on each other, create a collective experience.

And so, when a pianist bangs out Chopin in a concert hall, you say that the magic of Chopin's music, masterfully rendered by this master pianist, has thrilled the audience. Yet it's possible that actually no one in the audience has been thrilled. Let's not exclude the possibility that, had they not known Chopin to be a great genius, and the pianist likewise, they would have listened to the music with less ardor. It's also possible that when some listeners, pale with emotion, applaud, scream, carry on, writhe in enthusiasm one should attribute this to the fact that others in the audience are also writhing, carrying on, shouting; because every one of them thinks that the others are experiencing an incredible ecstasy, a transcendent emotion, and therefore his emotions as well begin to rise on someone else's yeast; and thus it can easily happen that while no one in the concert hall has been directly enraptured, everyone expresses rapture—because everyone wants to conform to his neighbor. And it's not until all of them in a bunch have sufficiently excited each other, it is only then, I tell you, that these expressions of emotion arouse their emotion—because we must comply with what we express. It's also true that by participating in the concert we fulfill something of a religious act (just as if we were assisting at the Holy Mass), kneeling devoutly before the Godhead of artistry; in this case our admiration is merely an act of homage and the fulfilling of a rite. Who can tell, however, how much real beauty there is in this Beauty, and how much of it is a sociohistorical process? Tut, tut, as everyone knows, mankind needs myths—it chooses this one or that one from among its numerous authors (but who can ever explore or shed light on the course that such a choice has taken?), whereupon it proceeds to elevate him above all others, to memorize his works, to discover in him its own mysteries, to subordinate its emotions to him—but if we were to elevate, with the same doggedness, some other artist, then he would become our Homer. Can't you see then, how many varied and often other than aesthetic elements (a list of which I could tediously extend *ad infinitum*) make up the greatness of the artist and his work? And you want to enclose this muddled, complicated, and difficult communion with art in the naive phrase: "the poet sings with inspiration, the listener lends his ear in admiration"?

Stop then pampering art, stop—for God's sake!—this whole system of puffing it up and magnifying it; and, instead of intoxicating yourselves with legends, let facts create you. And once you open your minds to Reality this alone may bring you great relief—at the same time stop worrying that it will impoverish and shrivel your spirit—because Reality is always richer than naive illusions and idle notions. And I will soon show you what riches await you on this new path.

Certainly art is the perfecting of form. But you seem to think—and here is another of your cardinal mistakes—that art consists of creating works perfect in their form; you reduce this all-encompassing, omni-human process of creating form to the turning out of poems and symphonies; and you've never been able to truly experience nor explain to others what an enormous role form plays in our lives. Even in the field of psychology you haven't been able to secure form its proper place. You still seem to think that emotions, instincts, ideas govern our behavior, while you're inclined to consider form to be a superficial appendage and a simple gewgaw. When a widow who walks behind her husband's casket cries and wails to the point of splitting her sides, you surmise she's wailing because she's overcome by her loss. Or when some engineer, doctor, or lawyer murders his wife, children, or friend, you think that he let himself be seized by bloodthirsty instincts. Or when a politician says something stupid, you think that he's stupid because he's talking nothing but nonsense. But in Reality matters stand as follows: a human being does not express himself forthrightly and in keeping with his nature but always in some well-defined form, and this form, this style, this manner of being is not of our making but is thrust upon us from outside—and this is why one and the same individual can present himself on the outside as wise or stupid, as bloodthirsty or angelic, as mature or immature—depending upon the style he happens to come up with, and in what way he is dependent on others. And just as beetles, insects chase after food all day, so do we tirelessly pursue form, we hassle other people with our style, our manners while riding in a streetcar, while eating or enjoying ourselves, while resting or attending to our business—we always, unceasingly, seek form, and we delight in it or suffer by it, and we conform to it or we violate and demolish it, or we let it create us, amen.

Oh, the power of Form! Nations die because of it. It is the cause of wars. It creates something in us that is not of us. If you make light of it you'll never understand stupidity nor evil nor crime. It governs our slightest impulses. It is at the base of our collective life. For you, however, Form and Style still belong strictly to the realm of the aesthetic—for you style is on paper only, in the style of your stories. Gentlemen, who will slap your pupa which you dare turn toward others as you kneel at the altar of art? For you form is not something that is human and alive, something—I'd say—practical and everyday, but just a feature for the holidays. And while you're leaning over a piece of paper you forget your own self—you don't care about perfecting your own individual and concrete style, you merely practice an abstract stylization in a vacuum. Instead of art serving you, you serve art—and with a sheeplike docility you let it impede your development, and you let it push you into the hell of indolence.

Now consider how different the stance would be of someone who, instead of feeding on the words of the concept makers, would sweep the world with a fresh look and with an understanding of the boundless importance of form in our lives. If he were to take up the pen it would not be for the sake of becoming an Artist but—let's say—to better express his individuality and explain it to others; or else to put his internal affairs in order, and also, perhaps, to deepen and sharpen his relationship with his fellow men because other souls exert an immense and creative influence on our soul; or, for example, to try to fight for a world as he would like it to be, for a world that is indispensable to his life. He would, of course, spare no effort to have his work attract people and win their hearts with its artistic charm— but in this case his chief goal would not be art but the expression of his own person. And I say "his own," not "someone else's," because it's high time you stopped thinking of yourselves as creatures of a higher order who are here to edify and enlighten someone else, to lead and raise someone else into the sublime, or to improve someone else's morals. Who has granted you this superiority? Where does it say that you now belong to a higher class? Who has promoted you to aristocracy? Who gave you a patent on Maturity? Oh no, this writer, the one I'm talking about, will not write because he considers himself mature but because he is aware of his immaturity, because he knows that he doesn't know everything about form, he knows he is still climbing and has not quite yet crawled to the top, that he is in the process of becoming but has not yet become. And if he happens to write something inept and silly he'll say: "Great! I've written something stupid, but I haven't signed a contract with anyone to produce solely wise and perfect works. I gave vent to my stupidity and I'm glad of it, because the animosity and harshness of others that I've aroused against me will now form and shape me, it will create me as if anew, and here I am—reborn." Which shows that the bard who has such a sound philosophy, one who is so well-grounded within himself that neither stupidity nor immaturity can threaten nor harm him, this bard can, his head raised high, express himself even as he is being indolent, while you, you can no longer express much of anything because fear deprives you of speech.

With all this in mind, the reform I recommend should bring you considerable relief. One must add, however, that only a masterly writer cognizant of these matters would be equal to grappling with this problem, which, thus far, has dealt you the worst possible pupa— and the problem which I raise here is, very likely, the most fundamental, the most awesome, and the most brilliant (I have no hesitation in using this word) of all the problems of style and culture. Here is a graphic way of formulating the problem: imagine that the adult and mature bard, leaning over a piece of paper, is in the process of creating . . . but on his back a youth has squarely settled himself, or some semi-enlightened fellow from the semi-intelligentsia, or a young maiden, or some nondescript slouch of a soul, or some kind of juvenile, lowbrow, ignorant creature, and then—this creature, this youth, this maiden, or lowbrow fellow, or for that matter any muddle-headed son of the unenlightened quarter-culture—suddenly pounces on his soul and drags it down, constricts it, kneads it with his paws, yet at the same time, by embracing this soul, by soaking it up, sucking it in, he rejuvenates it with his youth, seasons it with his immaturity, and prepares it to his own liking, then he brings it down to his own level—and oh, into his arms! But this author, instead of pitting himself against his assailant, pretends that he does not see him and—what idiocy!—he thinks he'll avoid being violated by putting on a face as if he were not being violated. Isn't this exactly what happens to you, beginning with great geniuses all the way to mediocre bards in the gallery? Isn't it true that every being who is at a higher level of development, who is older and more mature, is dependent in a thousand different ways on beings who are less well developed, and doesn't this dependence permeate us through and through, to our very core and to the extent that we can say: the elder is created by the younger? When we write, don't we have to accommodate the reader? Just as when we speak—don't we depend on the person we're addressing? Are we not mortally in love with youth? Are we not obliged then, at every moment, to ingratiate ourselves with beings who are below us, to tune in with them, to surrender, be it to their power or to their charms—and isn't this painful violence that's being committed on our person by some half-enlightened, inferior being the most seminal of all violence? Thus far, however, and contrary to all your rhetoric, you have only been able to hide your head in the sand, and your scholarly and didactic mentality, suffused with conceit, has made you unaware of this matter. In reality you're constantly being violated, yet you pretend that nothing is happening—because you, oh mature ones, keep company solely with other mature ones, and your maturity is so mature that it can only chum up with maturity!

If you were, however, less concerned with Art or the edifying and perfecting of others and more with your own pitiful selves, you would never acquiesce to such a terrible violation of the self; a poet, instead of creating poems for another poet, would feel that he's being suffused and created by forces from below, forces of which, thus far, he had not even been aware. He would realize that only by accepting them would he be able to free himself of them; and he would do his best to show, in his style, in his artistic as well as everyday attitude and form, a clear link with all that's inferior to him. He would then feel not only like a Father, but like a Father and a Son: he would write not solely like a wise, refined and mature one, but rather like a Wise One who benefits from stupidity, like a Refined One who profits from being tirelessly brutalized, and like a Mature One who is being ceaselessly rejuvenated. And if, upon leaving his writing desk, he were to run into that youth or that lowbrow he would no longer pat him condescendingly on the back like a preacher or a pedagogue, but instead he would wail and roar in holy trembling, and perhaps even fall to his knees! Instead of fleeing from immaturity and shutting himself within the ambit of the sublime, he would realize that a universal style is one that knows how to embrace lovingly those not quite developed. And this would finally lead all of you to a form that would pant with creativity and be filled with poetry, so much so that the whole bunch of you would transform yourselves into powerful geniuses.

Take note then, what hope I send your way with such an individually personal concept—and what perspectives! But, for this idea to be a hundred percent creative and definitive, you must take yet another step forward—but this step must be so bold and resolute, so limitless in its possibilities and destructive in its consequences, that my lips will mention it only softly and from a distance. Here it is: the time has come, the hour has struck on the clock of history—make an effort to overcome form, to liberate yourselves from it. Stop identifying yourselves with that which delimits you. You, artists, try to avoid all expression of yourselves. Don't trust your own words. Be on guard against all your beliefs and do not trust your feelings. Back away from what you are on the outside and tremble with fear at any self-manifestation, just as a little bird trembles at the sight of a snake.

I don't know, truly, whether such things should pass my lips this day, but the stipulation—that an individual be well defined, immutable in his ideas, absolute in his pronouncements, unwavering in his ideology, firm in his tastes, responsible for his words and deeds, fixed once and for all in his ways—is flawed. Consider more closely the

Preface to "The Child Runs Deep in Filidor"

chimerical nature of such a stipulation. Our element is unending immaturity. What we think, feel today will unavoidably be silliness to our great grandchildren. It is better then that we should acknowledge today that portion of silliness which time will reveal . . . and the force that impels you to a premature definition is not, as you think, a totally human force. We shall soon realize that the most important is not: to die for ideas, styles, theses, slogans, beliefs; and also not: to solidify and enclose ourselves in them; but something different, it is this: to step back a pace and secure a distance from everything that unendingly happens to us.

A Retreat. I have a hunch (but I don't know whether my lips should confess it now) that the time for a Universal Retreat is at hand. The son of earth will henceforth understand that he is not expressing himself in harmony with his deepest being but always in accordance with some artificial form painfully thrust upon him from without, either by people or by circumstances. He will then dread that form of his and feel ashamed of it, much as he had thus far idolized and flaunted it. We will soon fear our persons and our personalities, because it will become apparent that they are by no means truly our own. And instead of roaring: "I believe in this—I feel it—that's how I am—I'm ready to defend it," we will say in all humility: "Maybe I believe in it—maybe I feel it—I happened to say it, to do it, or to think it." The bard will scorn his own song. The leader will shudder at his own command. The high priest will stand in terror of the altar, and the mother will instill in her son not only principles but also ways of escaping them so that they do not smother him.

It will be a long and arduous road. For nowadays individuals as well as whole nations are quite good at managing their psychological life, and they are not strangers to creating styles, beliefs, principles, ideals, and feelings at will and with their immediate interests in mind; yet they do not know how to live without adhering to a style; and we still don't know how to defend the depths of our freshness against the demon of order. Great discoveries are indispensable—powerful blows struck by the soft human hand at the steel armor of Form, as well as unparalleled cunning and great integrity of thought and an extreme sharpening of intelligence—so that man may break loose from his rigidity and reconcile within himself form with the formless, law with anarchy, maturity with sacred and eternal immaturity. But before this happens, tell me: in your opinion, are Anjou pears better than Bosc pears? Do you like to snack on them while comfortably s i t t i n g in wicker chairs on the porch, or do you prefer to abandon yourselves to this activity in the shade of a tree while a fresh and gentle breeze is cooling your body parts? And I ask you this in all seriousness and with total responsibility for my words, and likewise with the greatest respect for all your parts without exception, because I know that you are a part of Humanity, of which I am also a part, and that you partly take part in the part of something which is also a part and of which I am also in part a part, together with all the particles and parts of parts, of parts, of parts, of parts, of parts, of parts, of parts, of parts, of parts, of parts, of parts . . . Help! Oh, confounded parts! Oh, bloodthirsty, nightmarish parts, you've grabbed me once again, is there no escaping you, hah, where can I find shelter, what am I to do? oh, that's enough; enough, enough, let's finish this part of the book, let's swiftly move on to another part, and I swear that in the next chapter there will be no more particles, because I'll shake myself free of them and cast them off, and I'll dump them outside while inside I remain (in part at least) without parts.

5 The Child Runs Deep
in Filidor

The Prince of all the most gloriously renowned synthesists of all time was without a doubt Dr. Professor of Synthetology at the University of Leyden, the High Filidor, born in the southern environs of Annam. He acted in the pompous spirit of High Synthesis mainly by addition + infinity, and, in emergencies, also with the aid of multiplication + infinity. He was a man of goodly size, quite obese, with a windblown beard and the face of a prophet in spectacles. But, in the natural order of things and in keeping with the Newtonian principle of action and reaction, a spiritual phenomenon of such magnitude could not remain unchallenged and therefore, as a counter-phenomenon, an equally illustrious Analyst was born in Colombo, and, having obtained a doctorate and a Professor's chair in the department of High Analysis at Columbia University, he soon climbed to the highest echelons of a scientific career. He was a lean, small-boned, smoothly shaven man with the face of a skeptic in spectacles, and his only inner mission was the pursuit and ruination of the illustrious Filidor.

The Analyst's method was decomposition, and his specialty was to decompose a person into parts by means of calculation in general, and by filliping noses in particular. He would fillip a nose and thus activate it to a life of its own, whereupon, to the horror of its owner, the nose would move spontaneously in every direction. The Analyst often practiced his art while riding a streetcar, especially if he was bored. And so, following the voice of his innermost calling, he set out in pursuit of Filidor and, in a small town in Spain, he even managed to secure for himself the genteel title of anti-Filidor, which made him very proud indeed. When Filidor found out that he was being pursued he set out, needless to say, in pursuit of anti-Filidor, and, since pride wouldn't let either of them admit that he was not only the pursuer but also the pursued, the two scientists chased each other for a long time to no avail. And therefore, when Filidor was in Bremen, for example, anti-Filidor sped from The Hague to Bremen, unwilling or unable to accept the fact that Filidor, at the same time and with the same goal in mind, was boarding the express from Bremen to The Hague. The collision, at breakneck speed, of the two scientists—a catastrophe ranking in magnitude among the greatest railroad catastrophes—took place quite accidentally on the premises of a classy restaurant in the Hotel Bristol in Warsaw. Filidor, train schedule in hand and accompanied by Mrs. Professor Filidor, was just at that moment studying the best connections, when anti-Filidor, straight from the train and out of breath, rushed into the restaurant with his anlytical traveling companion, Flora Gente from Messina, on his arm. We, i.e., the three assistants here present, Drs. Teofil Poklewski, Teodor Roklewski, and I, realizing the gravity of the situation, immediately began taking notes.

Anti-Filidor walked up to our table and silently looked daggers at the Professor, who rose to his feet. At first they tried to apply spiritual pressure. The Analyst pressed coolly from below, the Synthetist responded from above, with a gaze charged with defiant dignity. When the duel of looks gave no definitive result, the two spiritual enemies began a duel of words. The Doctor and master of Analysis declared:

"Noodles!"

The Synthetologue responded:

"One noodle!"

The anti-Filidor roared:

"Noodles, noodles, namely a mixture of flour, eggs, and water!"

Filidor retorted instantly:

"Noodle, namely the higher being of the Noodle, the highest Noodle himself!"

His eyes flashed lightning, his beard fluttered, it was clear that he had scored a victory. The Professor of High Analysis backed off a few steps in helpless fury, but he quickly seized on a dreadfully brainy concept, namely—physical weakling that he was compared to Filidor—he went for Filidor's wife, beloved above all else by the old and revered Professor. The course of events, as stated in the official Record, continued thus:

1. Mrs. Professor Filidor is buxom, fat, quite majestic, she sits, says nothing, concentrates.

2. Professor Dr. anti-Filidor, his brainy plan in mind, placed himself opposite Mrs. Professor, and began to observe her with a look that stripped her of all her clothing. Mrs. Filidor shook with cold and in shame. Dr. Professor Filidor silently covered her with a traveling rug and cast a withering glance full of the utmost disdain at the arrogant man. He revealed thereby a trace of anxiety.

3. Whereupon anti-Filidor said quietly: "The ear, the ear!" and he burst out with a derisive laugh. Under the effect of these words the ear instantly came into focus and became lewd. Filidor ordered his wife to pull her hat over her ears; however, this was of little use because, just then, anti-Filidor muttered, as if to himself: "There are two holes in the nose," thereby laying bare the nostrils in the venerable Mrs. Professor's nose in a manner most shameless, as well as analytical. Since there was no way in which her nostrils could be covered, the situation became grave indeed.

4. The Professor from Leyden threatened to call the police. The scale of victory was clearly beginning to tilt to the Colombo side. The master of Analysis said brainily:

"Fingers, the fingers of your hand, five fingers."

Unfortunately, Mrs. Professor's obesity was not sufficient to obviate this fact, which suddenly stood before those gathered in its full, unparalleled vividness, namely the presence of her fingers. There they were, five on each side. Mrs. Filidor, totally defiled, tried with waning strength to pull on her gloves, but—it's simply unbelievable—the doctor from Colombo made a spot analysis of her urine and roared victoriously:

"H_2OC_4, TPS, a few leucocytes, and albumin!"

Everyone rose. Dr. Professor anti-Filidor took his leave with his paramour, who burst out in vulgar laughter, while Professor Filidor, with the help of the undersigned, immediately took his wife to the hospital.

Signed:

T. Poklewski, T. Roklewski, and Anton Świstak

Assistants

The following morning Roklewski, Poklewski, and I, together with the Professor, met at Mrs. Filidor's sickbed. The woman's decomposition continued all too predictably. Bitten into by anti-Filidor's analytic tooth, she was losing her internal cohesion. From time to time she moaned numbly: I the leg, I the ear, my leg, my ear, finger, head, leg—as if saying goodbye to her body parts, which had already began to move autonomously. Her whole being was in agony. We all focused on a search for immediate measures to save her. But there were no such measures. After consulting with Docent S. Łopatkin, who arrived by plane from Moscow at 7:40 A.M., we agreed once again that it was crucial to apply the most drastically synthetic scientific methods. But there were no such methods. Filidor concentrated all his faculties to such a degree that we took a step back, whereupon he said:

"A slap in the face! A slap in the face, and a sharp one at that—of all body parts it's the face—a slap in the face is the only thing that can restore my wife's good name and resynthesize all those scattered elements in the most honorable manner of slapping and smacking. To work, away!"

However, it was no easy matter to find the world-renowned Analyst in the city. Not until that evening did he let us catch up with him in a high-class bar. In a state of sober drunkenness he downed one bottle after another, and the more he drank the more sober he became, and his analytical mistress likewise. Actually they were more drunk with sobriety than with alcohol. As we entered, the waiters, white as sheets, were hiding behind the counter like cowards while the couple silently gave themselves over to various ill-defined, cold-blooded orgies. We laid our plans. The Professor was to feign an attack with his right hand to the Analyst's left cheek, after which he was to deliver a slap with his left to the Analyst's right cheek, while we—i.e., the Doctor Assistants of Warsaw University, Poklewski, Roklewski, and I, as well as Docent S. Łopatkin—were to proceed forthwith with writing our report. The plan was simple, the action uncomplicated. But the Professor's raised hand fell to his side. We, the witnesses, stood aghast. There was no cheek! There was, I repeat, no cheek to be slapped, only two little roses, and something like a wreath of little doves!

With demonic cleverness anti-Filidor had foreseen and forestalled Filidor's plans. That sober Bacchus had tattooed two little roses and a vignette of little doves on each cheek! As a result, the cheeks, and thereby the slap in the face intended by Filidor, lost all meaning, let alone any higher meaning. Because indeed—a slap delivered at the roses and the little doves would no longer be a slap in the face—it would be more like hitting wallpaper. Since we could not allow a widely respected pedagogue and educator of youth to become the object of ridicule by pounding wallpaper because his wife was sick, we strongly advised him against an action that he would later regret.

"You dog!" roared the old man. "You despicable, oh, you despicable, despicable dog!"

"You heap of things!" replied the Analyst with a dreadful, analytical disdain. "I too am a heap. If you wish—kick me in the abdomen. You won't be kicking m e in the abdomen, you'll be kicking my abdomen—nothing more. You wanted to attack my cheeks by slapping them, didn't you? You can attack my cheek but not me. There is no me. No me at all. No me!"

"I'll get at you yet! God willing, I'll get at you!"

"For the time being my cheeks are slap-proof!" anti-Filidor smirked. Flora Gente, sitting next to him, burst out laughing, the cosmic doctor of analysis cast a lascivious look at her and then departed. Flora Gente, however, remained. She sat on a high stool and looked at us with the spent eyes of a totally analyzed parrot and cow. At once, that is at 8:40 A.M., we proceeded—Professor Filidor, the two medics, Docent Łopatkin, and I—to our conference; Docent Łopatkin, as usual, wielded the pen. The conference took the following course.

All Three Doctors of Law

Let it be known that we see no possibility of settling the conflict honorably, and we advise the Right Honorable Professor to ignore the insult, as coming from an individual unable to render honorable satisfaction.

Professor Dr. Filidor

How can I ignore it while my wife lies dying?

Docent S. Łopatkin

Your wife is beyond saving.

Dr. Filidor

Don't say it, don't say it! Oh, a slap in the face, that's the only remedy. But there's no chance of a slap. No cheeks. There's no means of godly synthesis. There's no honor! There's no God! Yet—there are cheeks! There does exist a slap in the face! There is God! Honor! Synthesis!

The Child Runs Deep in Filidor

I

I see that logical thinking is failing you, Professor. Either there are cheeks, or there are not.

Filidor

You forget, gentlemen, that there are still my two cheeks. There are no cheeks of his, but mine are still here. We can still play the card of my two untouched cheeks. Gentlemen, try to understand my thinking—I can't slap him in the face, but he can slap me—and whether it's me him or he me makes no difference, it will still be a Slap in the Face and it will still be Synthesis!

"All well and good! But how are we to make him slap you, Professor?!"

"How to make him slap you, Professor?!"

"How to make him slap you, Professor?!!"

"Gentlemen," the brilliant thinker answered with concentration, "he has cheeks, and so do I. The principle is that of analogy, and I will therefore act not so much logically as analogically. There is more certainty *per analogiam,* because nature is ruled to some extent by analogy. If he is the king of Analysis, then I am the king of Synthesis. If he has cheeks, I too have cheeks. If I have my wife, he has his mistress. If he has analyzed my wife, I'll synthesize his mistress, and I will thus wrench from him the slap in the face which he is so loath to give me! Since I can't slap him in the face I'll provoke him, I'll make him slap my face." And without further ado he beckoned to Flora Gente.

We fell silent. She came up to us, all her body parts in motion; she squinted at me with one eye and at the Professor with the other, she bared her teeth toward Stefan Łopatkin, and she thrust her bosom toward Roklewski, while wiggling her behind in the direction of Poklewski. The resulting impression was such that the Docent whispered:

"Are you really going to take on with your synthesis these fifty disparate pieces, this soulless, for-hire combination of $(dp + pd)$ to the nth power?"

It was the universal Synthetologue's attribute never to lose hope. He invited Flora Gente to our table, treated her to a glass of Cinzano, and, to test her, he began synthetically:

"The soul, the soul."

She answered in a similar but slightly different vein, she answered with part of something.

"I!" the Professor said earnestly, searchingly, and in the hope of awakening her dissipated self. "I!"

She replied:

"Oh, 'you,' very good, five zlotys."

"Unity!" heatedly exclaimed the Professor. "Higher Unity! The One!"

"It's all one to me," she said indifferently, "whether it's an old man or a child."

We breathlessly watched this hellish analyst of the night whom anti-Filidor had trained as he pleased, perhaps he had even raised her for himself since her childhood.

The Creator of Synthetic Science, however, would not desist. A period of great stress and strain followed. He read her the first two chants from *Spirit King*, and for this she demanded ten zlotys. He had a long and inspired conversation with her about Almighty Love, the Love which embraces and unites us all, for which she took eleven zlotys. He read to her two run-of-the-mill novels by the leading female authors on the subject of revival through Love, for which she charged a hundred and fifty zlotys, and she wouldn't be talked down one whit. When, however, he tried to awaken her dignity, she demanded no less, no more than fifty-two zlotys.

"One has to pay for kinkiness, you old fogey," she said, "but it's tax-free."

And letting loose her dumb owl eyes, she remained impassive, expenses grew, while somewhere downtown anti-Filidor laughed up his sleeve at the hopelessness of these efforts and measures . . .

At a conference in which Dr. Lopatkin and the three Docents took part, the illustrious researcher reported his defeat in the following words:

"This has cost me, in all, a few hundred zlotys, I truly don't see any way of synthesizing her, I tried all higher Unities in vain—Humanity for example, but she keeps turning everything into money and giving back the change. Humanity priced at forty-two zlotys ceases to be a Unity. I really don't know what to do. Meanwhile, my wife is at the hospital losing what remains of her inner cohesion. Her leg sets off for a walk round the room, and after a nap—my wife, not the leg, of course—must hold on to it with her hands, but her hands don't want to do it, what a terrible anarchy, what a terrible free-for-all.

Dr. of Medicine T. Poklewski

Meanwhile, anti-Filidor is spreading rumors that you, Professor, are a disagreeable maniac.

Docent Łopatkin

However, could you possibly get through to her by means of money? Since she changes e v e r y t h i n g into money couldn't you work on her with money? I'm sorry, I'm not quite sure what I mean, but there is something like this in nature—for example, I once had, as a patient, a woman who suffered from shyness, I couldn't treat her with audacity because she could not assimilate audacity, so I gave her such a dose of shyness that she couldn't stand it any longer, and therefore, because she couldn't, she became audacious, all of a sudden she became exceedingly audacious. The best method *per se* is to turn the sleeve and its lining inside out, be that as it may. Be that as it may. You'd have to synthesize her with money, however, I admit, I don't see how . . .

Filidor

Money, money . . . Yet money is always a number, a sum, it has nothing in common with Unity, actually only the grosz is indivisible, but the grosz isn't going to impress her. Unless . . . unless . . . gentlemen, what if I gave her a sum that would spin her head? Spin her head? Gentlemen . . . enough to spin her head?

We fell silent, Filidor jumped to his feet, his black beard fluttering. He succumbed to one of those manic states to which a genius succumbs regularly every seven years. He sold two of his townhouses and a villa in the suburbs, and then he changed the sum of 850,000 zlotys thus obtained into single zlotys. Poklewski watched this in wonder, this shallow physician from the provinces had never been able to understand genius, he never understood and never would. And in the meantime the philosopher, self-assured, issued a sarcastic invitation to anti-Filidor, who, responding to sarcasm with sarcasm, arrived at nine-thirty sharp in the lounge of the restaurant Alkazar, where the decisive experiment was to take place. The scientists did not shake hands, and the master of Analysis broke into a dry and malicious laughter:

"Well, go for it, sir, go for it! My girl isn't so eager to compose as your wife is to decompose, I'm quite sure on that score."

And he too was gradually falling into a hypomanic state. Dr. Poklewski held the pen. Łopatkin held the paper.

Professor Filidor approached the matter at first by placing on the table only a single zloty. Gente didn't react. He placed a second zloty, nothing, he added a third, again nothing, but at four zlotys she said:

"Ooh, four zlotys."

At five she yawned, and at six she coolly said:

"Now there, little old man, you're off into the clouds again?"

Not until ninety-seven did we note the first signs of surprise, and at hundred and fifteen her eyes, hitherto wandering between Dr. Poklewski, the Docent, and myself, were now beginning, ever so slightly, to synthesize on the money.

At one hundred thousand Filidor breathed heavily, anti-Filidor became somewhat anxious, while the courtesan, heterogeneous up to this point, showed some signs of concentration. She was riveted as she watched the growing heap, which by now was no longer merely a heap, and although she tried to count, her arithmetic didn't quite add up. The sum ceased to be a mere sum, it was becoming something unfathomable, unthinkable, something more than a sum, expanding the brain with its enormity, equal to the enormity of the Heavens. Flora let go a hollow groan. The Analyst lunged to rescue her, but both doctors held him back with all their force—he begged her in vain to break up the whole into hundreds or five hundreds, but the whole would not be split up. When the triumphant high priest of logarithmic knowledge dispensed everything he had and sealed the heap, or rather the enormity, this mount, this Mount Sinai of cash, with one single, indivisible grosz, it was as if a God had entered the courtesan, she rose to her feet and displayed all the synthetic symptoms—crying, sighing, smiling, pondering, and she said:

"This is me, gentlemen. This is me. This is my higher self."

Filidor shouted in triumph, and then anti-Filidor, with a cry of horror, tore away from the medics' arms and slapped Filidor in the face.

The shot was a thunderbolt—it was the lightning of synthesis torn from analytic entrails, shattering the murky darkness. The Docent and the medics, highly moved, congratulated the Professor thus defiled at last, while his sworn enemy writhed by the wall and groaned in torment. But once the course was set on the path of honor, no amount of howling could stop it, because the affair, thus far not one of honor, now rolled onto the customary tracks of honor.

Professor Dr. G. L. Filidor from Leyden nominated two seconds in the persons of Doc. Łopatkin and myself—Professor Dr. P. T. Momsen with the genteel title of anti-Filidor nominated two seconds in the persons of both his assistants—Filidor's seconds honorably called out anti-Filidor's seconds, while the latter called out Filidor's seconds. At each of these honorable steps synthesis grew. The Colombian writhed as if on hot coals. The Leydenian, however, smiling and in silence, stroked his long beard. While in the city hospital the sick Mrs. Professor began to unite her parts, with a barely audible voice she demanded milk, and her physicians took heart. Honor peeked from behind the clouds and sweetly smiled on people. The final encounter would take place the following Tuesday morning at seven sharp.

Dr. Roklewski was to hold the pen, Docent Łopatkin the pistols, Poklewski was to hold the paper, and I the coats. The undefeatable combatant from under the sign of Synthesis entertained no doubts. I remember what he told me the previous morning.

"My son," he said, "he can be felled just as I can, but whoever falls, my spirit will be victorious, for this is not about death but about the quality of death, and the quality of death will be synthetic. If he falls he will pay tribute to Synthesis—if he kills me he will kill me in a synthetic mode. Thus my victory will continue beyond the grave."

Thus, deeply moved and wanting to celebrate the more splendidly his moment of glory, he invited the two ladies, i.e., his wife and Flora, to watch from the sidelines, in the role of ordinary attendants. Yet ill forebodings gnawed at me. I dreaded something—but what was it? I had no idea, the fear of not knowing tormented me all night, and not until I was on the field did I realize why. The morning was picture-perfect, bright and clear. The spiritual opponents stood opposite each other, Filidor bowed to anti-Filidor, anti-Filidor bowed to Filidor. It was then that I realized what I had been dreading. It was symmetry—the situation was symmetrical, and therein lay its strength, but also its weakness.

The situation was such that each of Filidor's moves had to correspond to each of anti-Filidor's analogous moves, and Filidor had the first move. If Filidor bowed, anti-Filidor also would have to bow. If Filidor fired, anti-Filidor also would have to fire. And everything, I stress, had to occur along the axis that led through both combatants, which was the axis of the entire situation. Well now! What will happen if anti-Filidor ducks to the side? If he jumps aside? What if he plays a prank and somehow escapes the iron laws of symmetry as well as analogy? Indeed, what passions and treacheries might lurk in anti-Filidor's brainy head? I was fighting with my thoughts when suddenly Professor Filidor raised his pistol and aimed concentrically at his opponent's heart and fired. He fired and missed. He missed. Then, in his turn, the Analyst raised his pistol and aimed at his opponent's heart. Yes, yes, we were almost ready to proclaim victory. Yes, yes, it seemed that since the other had synthetically fired at the heart, this one must also fire at the heart. It seemed there was no other solution, there was no side wicket for the intellect. But suddenly, in the blink of an eye and with the greatest effort, the Analyst uttered a squeak, whined, deviated slightly to the side, led the barrel of the pistol away from the axis and shot to the side, at what?—at the little finger of Mrs. Professor Filidor, who stood nearby with Flora Gente. The shot was masterful! The finger fell off. Mrs. Filidor, surprised, lifted her hand to her lips. While we, the seconds, momentarily lost our composure and gave a shout of admiration.

Then something terrible happened. The High Professor of Synthesis could not contain himself. Fascinated by the Analyst's masterful aim, by symmetry, bewildered by our cry of admiration, also veered his aim to one side and shot at the little finger of Flora Gente's hand, then laughed briefly, dryly, gutturally. Gente lifted her hand to her lips, we gave a shout of admiration.

The Analyst then fired again, knocking off another of Mrs. Professor's fingers, and she lifted her hand to her lips—we gave a shout of admiration, a quarter of a second later, the Synthetist's shot, fired with unerring certainty from a distance of seventeen meters, knocked off Flora Gente's analogous finger. Gente lifted her hand to her lips, we gave a shout of admiration. And on it went. The firing continued nonstop, fast and furious and as glorious as glory itself, and fingers, ears, noses, teeth fell like leaves tossed by the wind while we, the seconds, could hardly keep up with our shouts torn from within us by the lightning marksmanship. Both ladies were shorn bare of all their natural appendages and protrusions, they didn't fall dead simply because they too could not keep up, but anyway, I think they were delighted—being exposed to such marksmanship. Finally the bullets ran out. With the last shot the master from Colombo pierced the apex of Mrs. Professor Filidor's lung, and the master from Leyden immediately responded by piercing the apex of Flora Gente's lung, once more we gave a shout of admiration, and silence fell. Both torsos died and slid to the ground—the duelists looked at each other.

Now what? They looked at each other, and neither knew—what now? Actually what? There were no more bullets. In any case both corpses already lay on the ground. There was nothing to do. It was almost ten o'clock. Actually Analysis had won, but so what? Absolutely nothing. Synthesis could have won equally well, and there would have been nothing to that, either. Filidor picked up a stone and threw it at a sparrow, but he missed and the sparrow flew away. The sun began to scorch us, anti-Filidor picked up a clod and threw it at a tree stump—he hit it. In the meantime a hen chanced Filidor's way, he aimed at it, hit it, the hen ran away and hid in the bushes. The scientists left their positions and departed—each in his own direction.

By evening anti-Filidor was in Jeziorna, Filidor in Vaver. One hunted for crows by a haystack, the other found an out-of-the-way lamppost and aimed at it from a distance of fifty paces.

And so they wandered around the world aiming with whatever they could at whatever they could. They sang songs, but they liked breaking windows best, they also liked to stand on a balcony and spit upon the hats of passersby, even more so if they were able to target some fat cats riding by in a carriage. Filidor became so good at it that he could spit at somebody on a balcony from the sidewalk. Anti-Filidor could extinguish a candle by throwing a box of matches at the flame. But best of all they liked to hunt frogs with a BB gun or to hunt sparrows with a bow and arrow, or else they threw pieces of paper and blades of grass from a bridge onto the water. But their greatest delight was to buy a child's balloon and run after it through fields and forests—hey, ho! and watch it burst with a bang as if shot with an invisible bullet.

The Child Runs Deep in Filidor

And whenever anyone from the world of science reminisced with them about their splendid past, their spiritual battles, about Analysis and Synthesis and their glory irretrievably lost, they would reply dreamily:

"Yes, yes, I remember that duel . . . the pop-popping was great!"

"But Professor," I exclaimed, and Roklewski, who in the meantime had married and started a family on Krucza Street, joined in, "but Professor, you talk like a child!"

To which the old man gone childish replied:

"The child runs deep in everything."

6 Seduction and Further Driving Me into Youth

At the very moment when the terrible psychophysical rape of Syphon by Kneadus reached its climax the door opened and the *deus ex machina*, Pimko—ever, and every inch his most infallible self—entered the classroom.

"Oh, good, I see you're playing ball, children, little ballie!" he exclaimed, though we were not playing ball, there wasn't even any little ballie around. "Little ballie, you're playing ballie, oh, how nicely you're throwing the ballie to each other, and see how nicely one of you is catching it!" And noticing the feverish-red blotches on my otherwise pale and fear-shrunken face, he added: "Oh, what rosy little cheeks! School seems to agree with you, Joey, and so does playing ballie. Come along now," he said, "I'll take you to your lodgings at Mrs. Youngblood's, I've already settled the whole matter with her over the phone. I found lodgings for you at the Youngbloods'. It would be most inappropriate, at your age, to have an apartment of your own downtown. As of today—your place is at Mrs. Youngblood's."

He then led the way and, to kindle my interest, told me what he knew about Mr. Youngblood, a construction design engineer, and about Mrs. Youngblood, the Mrs. Engineer. "It's a modern house-hold," he remarked, "modern and naturalistic, favoring the trends, and foreign to my ideology. Now, Joey, I've noticed an affectation in you, a posturing, you're still trying to pass for an adult—well, the Youngbloods will cure you of this unpleasant shortcoming, they'll teach you how to behave naturally. But—I forgot to tell you—there's also a young daughter, Miss Zuta Youngblood, a schoolgirl," he added under his breath, clasping my hand and giving me that ped-agogical squint from behind his spectacles. "The schoolgirl," he said, "she's modern too. Hmm, it's not the best company, and fraught with danger . . . but on the other hand there is nothing like a modern schoolgirl to lure one to youth . . . she'll inspire you with young-blooded patriotism, I can assure you."

Streetcars rolled by. There were flowerpots on windowsills. Some fellow threw a plum pit at Pimko from a balcony, but missed.

What? What was this? A schoolgirl? In an instant I grasped Pimko's plan—he wanted to use the schoolgirl to imprison me in youth, once and for all. He figured that if I fell in love with a young schoolgirl I would no longer want to be an adult. At home, and in school—not a moment's letup, not a chance to bolt through a crack. There wasn't a minute to lose. I hurriedly bit his finger and took to my heels. I saw an adult, a woman, standing on a corner, so it was toward her I sped—my face contorted, stunned, and terror stricken—the farther from Pimko and his horrible schoolgirl the better. Like lightning, the Great Belittler was upon me in a bound or two and caught me by the collar.

"To the schoolgirl!" he shouted, "to the schoolgirl! To youth! To the Youngbloods!"

He shoved me into a horse-drawn cab and had us driven to the schoolgirl, and so we trotted through busy streets full of people, vehicles, and birdies' songs.

"Let's go, let's go, why are you looking back, there's no one behind you, I'm the only one beside you."

Clasping my hand and drooling at the thought of where we were going, he purred:

"To the schoolgirl, to the modern schoolgirl! Trust the schoolgirl to enamor him with youth! Trust the Youngbloods to belittle him! Trust them to deal him the perfect pupa! Giddy-up, giddy-up, giddy-up!" he shouted until the horse began kicking, and the cabdriver, settling himself on the coach-box, turned his back on Pimko with the boundless disdain of the common man. Yet Pimko sat there in a manner most absolute.

However, at the threshold of a cheap little house in Staszyc or Lubecki, one of the suburbs inhabited by the intelligentsia, he seemed to waver and slump, and—oh, marvel of marvels!—he lost some of his absolutism.

"Joey," he whispered, quivering and shaking his head. "I'm making a great sacrifice for you. I'm doing this solely for the sake of your youth. It's entirely for the sake of your youth that I'm risking an encounter with a modern schoolgirl. Ooh-hoo, a schoolgirl, a modern schoolgirl!"

And he kissed my cheek, trying to secure my goodwill out of fear, it seemed, and, at the same time, as if kissing me goodbye. When we got out of the cab, and, tapping the ground with his cane and greatly vexed, he proceeded to cite and recite, to declaim aphorisms and to propound his thoughts, opinions, and ideas, all of the best quality, most classically prof-like, yet as if he were an ailing prof whose very existence was being threatened. He dropped the names of some of his literary friends, who were unfamiliar to me, and I heard him softly quoting their favorable opinions of him, and in turn expressing his favorable opinion of them. Three times he signed his name with a pencil on a wall, "T. Pimko," as if he were Antaeus drawing strength from his signature. I looked at the teacher with surprise. What was this? Could it be that he too was scared of the modern schoolgirl? Or was he just pretending? Why on earth would such a seasoned prof be scared of a schoolgirl? But just then the maid

Seduction and Further Driving Me into Youth

opened the door, and we went in—the professor rather timidly, without his usual air of superiority, and I with my face crumpled up like a dishrag, pale, stunned, and stupefied. Pimko tapped the floor with his cane and asked: "Are Mr. and Mrs. Youngblood home?" At that moment an inside door opened and a schoolgirl came toward us. Modern indeed.

Sixteen years old, in a skirt, sweater, and sneakers, athletic looking, easygoing, smooth, limber, agile, and impudent! The sight of her made my spirit and my face freeze in fear. I understood at a glance—here was a powerful presence, probably more powerful than Pimko himself, and equally absolute in her way, even more so than Syphon. She reminded me of someone—but who, who?—ah, she reminded me of Kopyrda! Remember Kopyrda? Just like him but tougher, similar in type but more intense, a perfect schoolgirl in her schoolgirlishness, and absolutely modern in her modernity. And doubly young—first by age and secondly by modernity—it was youth multiplied by youth. I was as frightened as someone who comes upon a presence stronger than oneself, moreover, my fear intensified when I saw that it was the prof who was scared of her, rather than she of the prof, that he was somewhat unsure of himself while exchanging greetings with this modern schoolgirl.

"Greetings, young lady," he called out half-cheerily and affecting refinement. "Miss Zuta is not at the beach? On the Vistula? Is Mommy home? How's the water in the swimming pool, eh? Cold? That's good for you! In the olden days I myself used to swim in cold water!"

What was this? I heard in Pimko's voice old age wheedling up to youth with athletics, obsequious old age—I took a step back. The schoolgirl didn't answer Pimko—just looked—she placed between her teeth a small wrench which she had held in her right hand, she extended her left hand with an unceremonious indifference, as if he were not Pimko . . . This disconcerted the professor, he didn't know what to do with the youthful left hand stretched out to him, so he finally clasped it in both his hands. I bowed. She took the wrench from between her teeth and said, matter-of-factly:

"Mother isn't in, she should be back soon. Please come in . . ."

And she led us into a modern livingroom, took her place by a window, while we took our seats on a sofa.

"Mommy is probably at a committee meeting," the professor attempted small talk.

The modern one said:

"I don't know."

The walls were painted pale blue, the curtains were cream colored, a radio stood on a little shelf, the cute furniture was contemporary, consistently modern, clean, smooth, simple, with two built-in closets and a little table. The schoolgirl stood at the window, unmindful of anyone's presence in the room, and she picked at her skin, which was peeling off her sunburned shoulders. As far as she was concerned we were not there—she could not care less about Pimko—and minutes passed. Pimko sat, crossed his legs, folded his hands, and twiddled his thumbs, just like someone who's being ignored. He stirred in his seat, cleared his throat a couple of times, and coughed, hoping to keep the conversation going, but the modern one turned toward the window, her back to us, and continued picking at her skin. He didn't say a word, he merely sat, yet his sitting thus—without conversation—seemed incomplete, imperfect. I rubbed my eyes. What was going on? Something most certainly was—but what? Was it Pimko's imperious yet incomplete sitting? An abandoned prof? A prof? The incompleteness was clamoring for completion—like those nagging gaps when one thing is ending and another has not yet began. And a void opens up in one's head. I suddenly saw the prof's old age showing. I hadn't noticed until now that the professor was over fifty, never before had this dawned on me, as if the absolute prof were an eternal and timeless being. Is he old or is he a professor? How so— old or a professor? Why not an old professor? No, that's not the point, it's that something is brewing here (they were in cahoots against me—there was no doubt about that). O God, why is he sitting? Why had he come here to sit beside me with the schoolgirl? His sitting was all the more painful because I sat t o g e t h e r w i t h h i m. If I had been standing it wouldn't have been so terrible. But getting up was tremendously difficult, and, strictly speaking, there was no reason to get up. And that isn't even the point—but rather why does he sit with this schoolgirl, why sit agedly with a young schoolgirl? Have pity! But there is no pity. Why does he sit with the schoolgirl? Why is his old age not just a simple old age, rather than a schoolgirl old age? How so—old age with a schoolgirl? What is the meaning of—a schoolgirl old age? Suddenly things became horrible, and yet I couldn't run away. A schoolgirl old age—a young-old old age—these were the incomplete, defective, hideous formulas galloping through my brain. And suddenly I heard singing in the room. I couldn't believe my ears. The prof was singing an aria to the schoolgirl. Startled, I came to my senses. No, not singing, he was humming—hurt by the schoolgirl's indifference, and to stress her inappropriate behavior, her bad manners and brashness, Pimko hummed a few bars from an operetta. Was he really singing? Yes, she had forced the granddaddy to sing! Was this the same awesome, absolute, crafty Pimko, become this granddaddy, abandoned on the sofa, and forced to sing for the schoolgirl?

I felt very weak. After the many ordeals of this morning, since the moment the ghost visited me, my facial muscles had had no chance to relax, my face was burning as if I had spent a sleepless night riding on a train. But now the train seemed to be coming to a stop. Pimko was singing. I was embarrassed at having surrendered for so long to a harmless little old man to whom an ordinary schoolgirl paid no attention whatsoever. My face was imperceptibly returning to normal, I made myself more comfortable in my seat, and I soon regained all my equilibrium, and—oh, joy of joys!—I regained the "thirty-year-old" I had lost. I decided to leave, calm and collected, ignoring all protests, but the professor caught my hand—he seemed quite different now. He had aged, softened, he looked awkward and forlorn, pitiful.

"Joey," he whispered in my ear, "don't follow the example of this modern girl, this new species from the postwar era of athletics and jazz bands! Custom and tradition gone wild since the war! No culture! No respect for one's elders! This new generation's thirst for pleasure! I'm beginning to worry that the atmosphere here won't be right for you. Promise that you won't let this unbridled girl influence you. You're both alike," he went on as if in a fever, "you have a lot in common, I know, I know, actually, you're also a modern boy, and I brought you to this modern girl quite unnecessarily!"

I looked at him as if he'd gone crazy. What? I and my thirty-year-old had something in common with this modern schoolgirl? Pimko seemed downright stupid. And yet he went on warning me against the schoolgirl.

"These are new times!" he continued, "you young ones, you present-day generation. You scorn your elders, and right off the bat you're on a first-name basis with each other. No respect, no reverence for the past, just dancing, kayaking, America, impulse of the moment, *carpe diem*, oh, you young ones!"

And he went on, fast and furious, flattering my supposed youth and modernity—whereas we were the modern youth, whereas for us it's only legs, whereas whatever else—meanwhile Miss Youngblood stood there, indifferent to everything, picking at her skin, unaware of what was brewing behind her back.

I understood at last what he was up to—he wanted, quite simply, to make me fall in love with the schoolgirl. His scheme was as follows: he would draw me into the girl, so to speak, in one fell swoop, hand me over—from one cute little hand to another—so that I couldn't escape. He was inculcating me with an ideal, and he was quite sure that once I had acquired this paradigm of youth, as Syphon and Kneadus had done, I would remain imprisoned forever. The professor didn't care much what kind of a boy I would become, as long as I never again crept out of boyhood. If he succeeded, right then and there, in making me fall in love, and if he inculcated me with the paradigm of the ideal modern boy, he would then be able to walk away in peace, to embrace his numerous, sundry pursuits, no longer having to personally hold me prisoner to belittlement. And here was a paradox: Pimko, who ostensibly cherished his superiority above all else, had now deigned to play the humiliating role of an old-fashioned good soul shocked by the modern generation of young women in order to lure me to the schoolgirl. By using his fuddy-duddy, avuncular indignation he was uniting us against himself, and, by means of old age and antiquated ways, he wanted to make me fall in love with youth and modernity. But Pimko had yet another, no less important, goal in mind. To make me fall in love was not enough—he wanted me to bond with her in the most immature way, it would not have served his designs for me to simply fall in love with her, no, he wanted me to become infatuated with that particularly trashy and disgusting young-old, modern-antiquated poetry born of the union of the prewar fuddy-duddy and the postwar schoolgirl. Obviously, the prof wished to participate, however indirectly, in my enchantment. Although utterly stupid, it was all ingeniously conceived, and therefore, imagining that I was totally free of Pimko, I listened to his inept old-uncle flatteries. Stupid me! I didn't know that only stupid poetry can really entangle you!

And out of nothing evolved a monstrous configuration, a horridly poetic cast of characters: there under the window the could-not-care-less, modern schoolgirl, here on the sofa the fuddy-duddy professor bemoaning postwar barbarism, and I, between the two of them, hemmed in by the young-old poetry. God help me! What about my thirty-year-old?! I must leave, leave as fast as I can! But the world seemed to have collapsed and reorganized itself on new principles, the thirty-year-old grew pale again and out-of-date, while the modern one, there by the window, grew ever more alluring. And the accursed Pimko would not let up.

"Legs," he egged me on to modernity, "legs, I know you, I know your athletics, I know the ways of the new Americanized generation, you prefer legs to hands, legs are the most important thing to you, the calves of your legs! The finer, spiritual things in life mean nothing to you, your calves are the thing. Athletics! The calves of your legs, legs," he went on flattering me, fast and furious, "it's the calves of your legs, it's your calves, calves, calves!"

And just as he had earlier, during their lunch hour, insinuated the problem of innocence to the formalists—which had incensed them and boosted their immaturity a hundredfold—he was now making an issue of my modern legs. And there I was, listening and lapping it all up—his linking the calves of my legs with those of the new generation—and coming to feel the cruelty of youth toward old calves! And there was also a kind of leg camaraderie with the schoolgirl, plus a clandestine, voluptuous collusion of legs, plus leg patriotism, plus the impudence of young legs, plus leg poetry, plus youngblooded pride in the calf of the leg, and a cult of the calf of the leg. Oh, what a fiendish body part! I needn't add that all this was happening quietly behind the schoolgirl's back while she stood by the window on those contemporary legs of hers, picking at her skin, suspecting nothing.

I would have managed, nonetheless, to break free from those calves, but the door suddenly opened and someone new appeared in the room; and the entrance of this new and unfamiliar personage was my final undoing. It was Mrs. Youngblood, a rather obese woman, but intelligent and civic-minded, with a keen and alert expression, also a member of a committee for rescuing infants or perhaps for combating the scourge of child-beggary in the capital. Pimko quickly rose from the sofa, all smiles and refinement, as if nothing had been going on—the old-guard professor from the prewar Polish Galicia.

"Ah, my dear lady! Bless your heart—you're always overworked, always active, just back from a committee meeting, no doubt. Well,

I've brought you my Joey, whom you have so graciously accepted under your care, here he is—this is Joey, this youth here—Joey, pay your respects to Madame, my child."

What's this? Pimko had switched again and resumed his indulgent and condescending tone. Pay my respects to the old woman, I, a juvenile again? And with all due reverence? I simply had to—the Youngblood woman extended her small, plump hand, and with fleeting surprise glanced at my face as it was swinging back and forth between thirty and seventeen.

"How old is the boy?" I heard her ask Pimko as she was taking him aside, and the professor good-naturedly replied:

"Seventeen, seventeen, my dear lady, he turned seventeen in April, looks older than his age, he may be posturing a bit, pretending to be an adult, but a heart of gold, hmm, hmm!"

"Ah, posturing, is he," the Youngblood woman said.

Instead of protesting I sat down again, I just sat on the sofa, riveted. The stupidity of this insinuation precluded any explanation. And I began to suffer terribly, because Pimko pulled Mrs. Youngblood to the window, right where the schoolgirl was standing, and the two of them proceeded to chat confidentially, from time to time glancing in my direction. Once in a while the trite prof would deliberately, yet as if by chance, project his voice. What torture! Because I heard him unite me with himself in relation to the Youngblood woman—as he had united me before with the schoolgirl against himself—he was now uniting me with himself. As if it weren't enough to present me as a poser who was pretending to be mature and blasé, he now emoted about my attachment to him, extolled the virtues of my mind and heart ("his only shortcoming is that he postures a bit—but it will pass"), and since he talked with a sort of senile tenderness and with the voice of an old-fashioned, typical prof, it followed that I too was old-fashioned and far from modern! And he contrived a devilish situation: here am I, sitting on the sofa, having to pretend that I haven't heard anything, and there is the schoolgirl standing by the window and hearing it all or not, I don't know which, and there is Pimko in a corner shaking his head, coughing now and then, and emoting about me, titillating the tastes and trends of the *avant-garde* Mrs. Engineer. Oh, only a person who fully appreciates what it's like to enter a relationship with a stranger you've just met, what an incredibly risky process that is, full of traps and treachery, can grasp my helplessness in relation to Pimko's accord with Mrs. Youngblood. He had led me into the Youngbloods' home under false pretenses, and, if that were not enough, he was now deliberately raising his voice so that I could hear how falsely he had led me there—oh, how treacherously he had led me into the Youngbloods', and the Youngbloods into me!

No wonder Mrs. Youngblood looked at me with pity and exasperation. Pimko-dimko's sickly-sweet prattling must have fed her annoyance, and besides, today's enterprising engineers' wives, fired up about group action and emancipation, despise any artificiality and affectation in young people, and they particularly can't stand their posing as adults. Progressive as they are, with all their energies geared toward the future, they hold a cult of youth more ardently than it has ever been held by anyone before, and nothing annoys them more than a boy messing up his tender years with posing. Worse still, not only do they dislike it, they actually like their dislike, because it gives them a sense of how progressive and modern they themselves are—they're always ready to give their dislikes a free rein. Mrs. Engineer didn't have to be told twice—this fat woman could have actually picked any other basis for her relationship with me, and not necessarily predicated it on the formula of modernity versus the old-fashioned, yet it was all contingent on the first chord—the first chord we choose ourselves, the rest is merely a consequence. But Pimko drew his old pedagogical bow across her modern string, and she took up the tune in no time.

"Oh, I don't like that," she said with a grimace, "not one bit! A young old man, blasé and probably not athletic either! I can't stand artificiality. That's what your outdated methods lead to, and what a contrast, my dear Professor, with my Zuta—she's frank, easygoing, natural."

When I heard this I lost any remaining confidence in the efficacy of protest, she wouldn't have believed that I was an adult anyway, because she now fancied herself and her daughter in relation to me— as an old-fashioned boy, brought up in the old ways. And when a mother fancies you with her daughter, that's it, you must be just what her daughter needs. I could have protested of course, who says I couldn't—I could have risen to my feet at any moment, walked up to them, and—no matter how difficult it would have been—made it abundantly clear that I was not seventeen but thirty. I could have— yet I couldn't because I didn't want to, the only thing I wanted was to prove that I was not an old-fashioned boy! That's all I felt like doing! I was furious that the schoolgirl had heard Pimko's prattling, and that she might form a negative opinion of me. This overshadowed the issue of my thirty-year-old, which now had paled! This is what burned me up now, what stung me, hurt me! I sat on the sofa unable to shout that he was deliberately lying—so, I make myself more comfortable, stretch my legs, try to sit modernly, look relaxed and daring, and I mutely cry out that it's all untrue, because I'm not like that, I'm quite different, oh, legs, calves, calves! I bend forward, I look bright and natural, with my whole posture I mutely belie everything—should the schoolgirl turn around, let her see me—but suddenly I hear the Youngblood woman say quietly to Pimko:

"You're right, such morbid mannerisms, just look at him—he's constantly striking poses."

I could not budge. If I changed my pose, it would be obvious that I had heard her, and she would perceive it as yet another mannerism, from now on everything I did would be a mannerism. Whereupon the schoolgirl turns from the window, looks me over as I sit there unable to revert to something more natural, and I see her unfriendly look, which makes it even more difficult to change my position. I also see the girl's cutting, young-blooded hostility welling up—a pure, whiplike hostility. And it wells up to such a degree that her mother feels obliged to interrupt her conversation and ask her daughter *en camarade*, buddy-buddy fashion:

"Why do you look at him like that, Zuta?"

The schoolgirl does not take her eyes off me, and, loyal to her mother—she's all loyalty now, she's loyal, frank, and direct—puckers her cute little lips and spits out:

"He's been eavesdropping all this time. He's heard everything."

Oh! That was razor-sharp! . . . I wanted to protest, yet I couldn't. The Youngblood woman lowered her voice and, savoring the girl's outburst, said to the professor:

"Nowadays our girls are exceptionally sensitive about loyalty and naturalness—they're quite crazy on that point. That's the new generation. The morality of the Great War. We're all children of the Great War, we and our children." She was obviously relishing it all. "It's the new generation," she repeated.

"Look how her pretty little eyes darkened," the little old man said good-naturedly.

"Pretty little eyes? My daughter doesn't have 'pretty little eyes,' Professor, she has eyes. We all have—eyes. Zuta, keep your eyes still."

The girl switched off her facial expression and shrugged her shoulders in repudiation of her mother. Pimko was shocked, and remarked to Mrs. Youngblood as an aside:

"Do you consider this to be proper behavior? . . . In my time a young person wouldn't dare shrug her shoulders . . . and at her mother too!"

But the Youngblood woman was ready for him, this was up her alley, and she let him have it with vigor:

"It's the era, Professor, the era! You don't know the contemporary generation. Profound changes are afoot. A great revolution in customs and traditions, this is a wind that demolishes, these are subterranean upheavals and we're riding upon them. It's the era! We have to build anew! Demolish everything that's old in this country of ours, leave only the new, demolish Kraków!"

"Kraków?!" Pimko exclaimed.

Whereupon the schoolgirl, who thus far had been rather contemptuously listening to the dispute of the old folk, chose an opportune moment to kick me, from the side, she gave me a quick, concise kick in the leg, on the sly, with impudence and hatred, not changing her bodily stance or facial expression one bit. Having kicked me she withdrew her leg and continued to stand impassively, indifferent to what Pimko and Mrs. Youngblood were talking about. While the mother was constantly at her daughter, the daughter was avoiding her mother—with an air of superiority, just because she was the younger of the two.

"She kicked him!" the professor exclaimed. "Did you see that, Mrs. Youngblood. We're just chatting here, while she's kicking him. What wildness, what audacity, what nerve of the unbridled postwar generation. She kicked him with that leg of hers!"

"Zuta, keep your legs still! Don't worry, Professor, it's nothing," she laughed, "it won't do your Joey any harm. Worse things happened at the front during the Great War. Even I, as a nurse in the trenches, have been kicked by common soldiers many times."

She lit a cigarette.

"In my time," Pimko said, "young ladies . . . and what would Norwid say to this?"

"Who's Norwid?" the schoolgirl asked.

She did it perfectly—she asked the question with the sporty ignorance of the young generation, with the amazement of the Era, matter-of-factly and without unduly involving herself in the question, and that's that, just to give him a taste of her sporty ignorance.

"She has not heard of Norwid!" he exclaimed.

The Youngblood woman smiled.

"It's the era, Professor, the era!"

The atmosphere became very pleasant indeed. The schoolgirl

tossed her ignorance of Norwid to Pimko, Pimko tossed his shock at her ignorance of Norwid back to the schoolgirl, and the mother laughed within the Era. I alone sat there, excluded from the company, and I could not—I could not speak up, nor comprehend how the roles had been reversed, how this old relic, with legs a thousandfold worse than mine, was now in cahoots with the modern one against me, and how I had become a counterpoint to their melody. Oh, Pimko, you devil incarnate! As I sat there silently, kicked, I must have looked angry and sullen, because Pimko said to me in a kindly voice:

"Why are you so quiet, Joey? When in company, one ought to say something . . . are you cross with Miss Zuta by any chance?"

"Ha, he's miffed!" the sportsgirl jeered.

"Zuta, apologize to the young man," Mrs. Engineer said forcefully. "You've offended him, but you young man, don't be cross with my daughter, you shouldn't be so touchy. Zuta will apologize, of course, but on the other hand we're posturing a bit, aren't we, and that's the truth. Be more natural, look lively, just watch me and Zuta—well, we'll break this young man of his habits, rest assured, Professor. We'll teach him a lesson."

"I think that in this respect his stay here will do him good. Well, Joey, uncloud your little brow."

And so each one of these pronouncements finally and—it seemed—irrevocably determined the order of things, defined and settled them. Pimko and Mrs. Youngblood briefly discussed the financial arrangements, then Pimko kissed me on the forehead.

"Good luck, my boy, goodbye, Joey. Be good now, don't cry, don't cry, I'll visit you here every Sunday, and at school I won't let you out of my sight either. Greetings, my dear lady, goodbye, goodbye, Miss Zuta, shame, you be good to Joey!"

He left, but one could still hear him from the stairs, coughing now and then, clearing his throat: "Ough, ough, hem, hem, ough, ough! Eh, eh, eh!" I set off to protest and explain. But Mrs. Youngblood

Seduction and Further Driving Me into Youth

steered me to a small, modern, cheerless cubbyhole just off the parlor, the parlor that (as it turned out) also served as Miss Youngblood's room.

"Here you are," she said, "your room. The bathroom is next door. Breakfast is at seven. Your things are here—the maid has brought them in."

And before I had a chance to stammer "thank you," she was gone to her committee meeting to combat the un-European scourge of child-beggary in the capital. I was left all alone. I sat on a chair. Everything was quiet. There was buzzing in my head. I sat in these new circumstances, in my new room. After being with so many people since this morning, I suddenly found myself in total isolation, only the schoolgirl was moving about and puttering in the parlor next door. No, no, this was not solitude—this was solitude with a schoolgirl.

7 Love

And again I wanted to break out in protests and explanations. I had to do something. I could not let myself become entrenched in this situation forever. Any delay threatened to make it permanent. Rather than sorting and folding my things, which the maid had brought in on Pimko's command, I sat stiffly in my chair.

"Now," I told myself, "now is my only chance to explain myself, to clarify things, to make myself understood. Pimko has gone. Mrs. Youngblood is out. The schoolgirl is here alone. Don't delay, because time weighs heavily on everything and solidifies it, go now, go at once, explain everything, show Zuta your true colors, because tomorrow will be too late. Show her, show yourself to her,"—oh, how desperately I wanted to do just that, I was seized by a desire to show her. All well and good, but show her—what? That I'm an adult, a thirty-year-old? No, no, forever no, at this moment I had no wish to make my way out of youth and admit that I was a thirty-year-old; my world had collapsed, I no longer saw the world except as a marvelous world through the eyes of this modern schoolgirl—sports, agility, arrogance, legs, calves of legs, wantonness, dancing, boating, kayaking—these were the new pillars of my reality! Yes, yes—I wanted to appear modern! The ghost that had visited me this morning, Syphon, Kneadus, Pimko, the duel—I pushed aside everything that had happened—I was only concerned with the schoolgirl's thoughts about me, whether she had believed Pimko that I wasn't modern, and just a poser; all I had to do was go to her right now, to present myself as modern and unaffected, to make her realize that Pimko had lied about me, that in reality I was quite different, that I was like her, her contemporary in age and era, that the calves of our legs made us kith and kin . . .

To appear before her, yes—but under what pretext? How was I to explain anything when I hardly knew her—a stranger to me in social terms—even though, in her mind, I was already at her beck and call? As far as I was concerned reaching her at a deeper level of reality would be extremely difficult—I could reach her only through trifling details, I could knock on her door and merely ask when supper is served. The kick she had dealt me made the task no easier—it was a parenthetical kick, delivered without the participation of her face, and in fact I felt deprived of a face that would go with it. I sat on the chair like a caged animal, like a horse on a lead held at a distance with a whip, and I rubbed my hands—how could I, under what pretext could I take things in hand with the Youngblood girl and within myself?

Suddenly the telephone rang, and I heard the schoolgirl's footsteps.

I stood up, carefully opened the door to the hallway, and looked around—no one was there, the house seemed empty, it was twilight, but I could hear her making plans with her girlfriend on the phone, for seven at the coffee shop, she would be there, also Leo and Babe (they had their nicknames, their own expressions and appellations). "You'll be there, seven sharp, sure, yeah, no, fine, my leg hurts, I've pulled a ligament, he's an idiot, a photo, oh, be sure to come, yeah, you'll come, I'll be there, it's all a lark, for sure." These words, spoken under her breath by a modern one to another modern one, into the receiver and unaware of anyone standing by, moved me deeply. "This is their own language," I thought to myself, "their own modern language!" It then occurred to me that—immobilized as she was by the telephone, her lips busy talking, her eyes roaming around—the girl would be more accessible and receptive to my designs. I could appear before her without any explanations, just show up—without any comments.

I quickly straightened my collar and tie, licked my hair flat to show off my part, because I knew that in these circumstances a straight line on the side of one's head was not devoid of meaning. The line, God knows why, was something modern. As I crossed the dining room I picked up a toothpick from the table, and I appeared before her (the phone was in an anteroom), emerging nonchalantly on the threshold, and, leaning with my shoulder against the door, I stood there. I quietly bent forward with my entire being, still chewing on the toothpick. A modern toothpick. Don't think that it was easy to stand there, a toothpick in my mouth pretending that I was at ease while everything within me was still paralyzed, to be aggressive while inwardly remaining deathly passive.

In the meantime Miss Youngblood was talking to her girlfriend.

"No, not necessarily, hell, sure, go with her, no, not with him, the photo, what fun, I'm sorry—wait a minute."

She put down the receiver and asked me:

"Do you want to make a phone call?"

She said this in a sociable, cool tone, quite as if it wasn't me she had kicked. I shook my head. I wanted her to realize that I was here for no other reason than: "it's just you and me, I have the right to stand in the door while you're making a phone call, I'm your comrade in modernity and your contemporary, and, do understand, Miss Youngblood, that any explanations between us are superfluous, that I can join you, standing on no ceremony, it's as simple as that." I was risking a great deal because, had she asked for any explanations, I would have been hard pressed to explain anything, and this horribly artificial situation would have immediately forced me to retreat. But what if she were to receive and accept me, to silently agree with me?— a naturalness I hardly dared dream of! And then I'd be one with her, and truly modern. "Oh, Kneadus, Kneadus," I anxiously thought to myself as I remembered his horribly contorted face after his initial smiles. It's easier with a woman though, I must admit. The otherness of our bodies created better possibilities.

But the Youngblood girl, the receiver to her ear, did not look at me, she talked for a long time (time began to threaten me again and weigh heavily), then finally she said:

"Fine, at seven sharp, for sure, the movies, bye," and hung up.

She rose and went to her room. I took the toothpick out of my mouth and went to my room. There was a little stool to one side near a closet by the wall, not for sitting, but rather to be used as a night table—I sat stiffly on this stool and rubbed my hands. She had ignored me—she didn't even jeer at me. Well and good, but having started something, I couldn't just let it go, I had to resolve it somehow while Mrs. Youngblood was still out of the house, "try again," I thought to myself, "because after your hapless performance she will truly, once and for all, take you for a poser, in any case your pose seems to be solidifying, intensifying by the minute, why are you sitting here to one side, by the wall, why are you rubbing your hands? Surely, rubbing your hands in your room, while sitting on this stool, is the antithesis of modernity, it's so old-fashioned. O God!"

I calmed down and listened to what was happening on the other side of the wall. The Youngblood girl moved about in her room like all girls do when they're at home. And while moving, she was bound to, at the same time, settle herself more and more firmly in her opinion of me as a poser. This was terrible—to feel pushed out, and to just sit while she was thinking God knows what about me—but how was I to accost her, to accost her a second time, what was I supposed to do? I had no more pretexts—and even if I had any I couldn't use them, because the whole issue had become too intimate for mere pretexts.

Meanwhile, dusk was falling, and solitude—that false solitude when one is alone and yet not alone in a painful spiritual relationship with another human being who is on the other side of the wall, yet alone enough that things like rubbing one's hands, fingers cramping and similar other symptoms, seem ridiculous—thus the dusk and that false solitude made my head spin, it blinded me and removed all vestiges of reality, plunging me into the night. Oh, how night has a way of tearing into our day! Alone in my room, sitting on the little stool, all too aimless in my activity, I couldn't bear it any longer. States which we live through and share openly with someone else are not a threat but, without a partner they become unbearable. Solitude forces one outward. Therefore, after so much torture, I opened the door again and, emerging from my solitude blind as a bat, appeared on the threshold. As I stood there I realized once more that I didn't know how to grapple with her, how to, so to speak, lay hands on her— she continued to be totally separate and closed off—what a hellish thing, that precise and clear-cut contour of the human form, that cold demarcation line—the form!

Bending over, her foot resting on a stool, she was polishing her shoe with a soft suede cloth. There was something classical about it, and it seemed to me that the girl was not so much interested in the shine of her shoe as in trying, with the use of her leg and her calf, to secretly perfect her type and to keep up that solid, modern style. This encouraged me because I thought that the modern one, caught in the act with her leg, would be more gracious and less formal. I went toward her—I stood near her, no more than one or two steps away, and, not looking at her, drawing back my gaze, I silently placed myself at her disposal—to this day I remember perfectly—I walk toward her, I stand a step away, right on the border of her space, I withdraw all my senses so that I can come even closer, and I wait. What for? To avoid surprising her. This time no toothpick, no particular pose. Let her accept me or reject me, I tried to be totally passive, neutral.

She removed her leg from the stool and straightened herself up . . .

"You have some . . . business with me?" she asked hesitantly, looking askance, like a human being who is being crowded by another human being for no good reason; and now that she stood up, the tension between us rose. I sensed that she would have preferred to move away. But she couldn't because I stood too close to her.

Did I have any business with her?

"No," I answered softly.

She let her arms drop by her side. She frowned.

"You're posing then?" she said defensively, just in case.

"No," I persisted, whispering, "no."

There was a small table next to me. Further on—a radiator. A brush and a penknife lay on the table. Dusk was falling—the evanescent light between night and day gradually blurred all boundaries, as well as that ominous demarcation line between us, and, thus shrouded in the veil of dusk, I felt sincere, sincere to my utmost, eager and ready for the schoolgirl.

I wasn't faking. If she had realized that I wasn't faking now, it would have meant that it was my affected behavior in Pimko's presence that was the fake. Why did I think that a young woman isn't supposed to refuse a man who insists on her consent? Did I think that the schoolgirl would, under the cover of darkness, succumb to the temptation of considering me useful? And why not opt for my being friendly and useful? Why wouldn't she rather host an American-style colleague than an old-fashioned, soured, and disgruntled faker? Why not play her melody upon me now, at this hour of dusk—I'm here, I'm offering myself—oh, play, play your melody upon me, that modern melody that everyone is humming in cafés, on beaches, and in dance halls, the pure melody of universal youth dressed in tennis pants. Strum upon me the modernity of those tennis pants. Won't you?

Surprised by my being so close to her, the Youngblood girl sat on the table, and, with a kind of bodily whimsy she pressed her hands against the edge—her face, vacillating between surprise and amusement, emerged from the dusk—and I thought that she had seated herself as if to play . . . That's how American girls are wont to sit and dangle their legs over the side of a boat. And the mere fact that she sat down made me tingle all over, her behavior indicated at least a tacit agreement to prolong the situation. She seemed to have settled herself for the duration, come what may. My heart pounding, I watched her set in motion some of her charms. She cocked her cute little head—she impatiently wiggled her little leg—she pouted her little mouth—while her large eyes, her modern-girl eyes, turned cautiously aside, toward the dining room, to check whether the housemaid was there. Because what would the housemaid say if she saw us, almost total strangers, in this odd configuration? Would she think us too affected? Or too natural?

But this is the kind of risk that girls like to take, those girls of the dusky hour who show what they can do only under the cloak of dusk. I sensed that I had conquered the schoolgirl with affectation's wild naturalness. I stuck my hands into my jacket pockets. Straining toward her, taking in her every breath, I was totally with her, quietly yet fervently, with all my might—I was so amiable, oh, so amiable . . . Time was now on my side. Every second, while intensifying the affectation, intensified the naturalness. I expected her to suddenly say something to me, as if we had known each other for ages, something about her leg, that it was hurting her because she had pulled a ligament:

"My leg hurts, I've pulled a ligament . . . You drink whisky, don't you, Annabelle . . ."

She was just about to say it, her lips began to move—when suddenly she came up with something completely different, almost in spite of herself—and in a formal tone she asked:

"What can I do for you?"

I took a step back while she—tickled pink by what she had just said, yet losing none of the dash and style of a young, modern girl sitting on a table and dangling her legs, indeed, looking even more stylish—she repeated with emphasis, her interest was cold and formal:

"What can I do for you?"

And, sensing that those words detracted nothing from her own self—on the contrary, they imparted to her a sharpness, an unsentimental matter-of-factness, even added to the general effect—she looked at me as if I were a madman and asked again:

"What can I do for you?"

I turned around and walked away, but my shoulders, in their retreat, must have annoyed her even more, because from behind the door I heard her say:

"What a clown!"

Rebuffed, shoved away, I sat on my little stool by the wall, totally exhausted.

"It's all over," I whispered, "she's ruined it all. But why? Something must have cut her to the quick—she'd rather ride roughshod over me than ride with me. Hello, my little stool, here by the wall, but it's high time to unpack my things, my suitcase is still in the center of the room, there are no towels."

I meekly sat on the stool, it was almost dark, I began folding my underwear and placing it in the drawer—I must do it now, school is tomorrow—I didn't turn on the light, it wasn't worth it really, just for me. I felt wretched and pitiful but that was all right, I only wished to move no more, to sit down and to keep sitting, to desire nothing, nothing ever.

But after a few minutes of sitting it became obvious that, regardless of all the exhaustion and wretchedness, I must become active again. "Is there no rest?" I wondered. Now, for the third time, I'd have to go into her room and be the clown again so that she would know that I had been clowning all along, and that it was I who was making fun of her and not the other way around. *Tout est perdu sauf l'honeur*—as

Francis the First had said. Therefore, regardless of my wretchedness and fatigue, I got up and began to get ready. My preparations took a rather long time. Finally I half-opened the door, first inserting into her room only my head. What blinding intensity of light!—she had lit her lamp. I closed my eyes. An impatient remark reached my ears:

"Please don't come in without knocking."

Moving my head in the gap of the door, my eyes still closed, I replied:

"Your obedient servant, at your feet."

I opened the door fully and now entered *in toto*, ambling in, waggishly, oh, the ambling of a human wretch! Remembering the old maxim that anger detracts from beauty, I made up my mind to make her mad. I hoped she'd get exasperated while I, maintaining composure behind a clown's mask, would then have the upper hand. She exclaimed:

"Your manners are terrible!"

The words, coming as they did from those modern lips, surprised me, especially since they rang true—as if good manners were the ultimate court of appeal of the wild and unruly postwar schoolgirls. Those modern ones were masters at juggling in turn good and bad manners. I felt like a yokel. It was too late to retreat—the world goes on existing solely because it is always too late to retreat. I bowed and replied:

"At your feet, your ladyship."

She rose and turned toward the door. What disaster! If she goes out and leaves me, together with my crassness—all will be lost! I lunged forward and blocked her way. She stopped.

"What do you want?"

She looked worried.

And I, imprisoned be the consequence of my movement and unable to retreat, began bearing down on her. And onto her, like a madman, a clown, a poser, an ape, onto this young miss, I, a Baroque formalist and a prankster, with dumb arrogance—she retreats behind the table—I amble toward her, like an ape, and with my finger pointing which way she's supposed to go, I push on toward her, like a drunkard, like a fiendish cad, a bandit—she's at the wall, I follow her. But, damn it!—while I'm on her heels, hideously, like a monster, all a-goggle, I see that—c o n f r o n t e d   w i t h   t h i s   m a d m a n s h e   l o s e s   n o n e   o f   h e r   b e a u t y—while I become in-human, she—a slight figure by the wall, bent over, pale, her hands by her side, her arms slightly bent at the elbows, her pupils di-lated, panting as if I had thrown her against the wall—she's ex-tremely quiet, tense with danger, hostile, incredibly beautiful—like a film star—modern, poetic, artistic, and fear, instead of marring her beauty, adorns her even more! One moment more. I'm getting closer, and surely some resolution needs now to follow—it passes through my mind that this is the end, that I must catch her by that little face of hers—I am in love, in love! . . . when suddenly there's screaming in the hallway. It's Kneadus attacking the housemaid. We didn't hear the doorbell ring. He had come to visit me in my new quarters and, finding himself alone with the housemaid in the hall-way, wanted to force himself on her.

Since his duel with Syphon, Kneadus could not be rid of his horrible face-pulling, he was so hellishly entangled that he couldn't contain his monstrous behavior. When he saw the housemaid he couldn't help behaving in the most coarse and brutal way possible. The girl raised hell. Kneadus kicked her in the belly and walked into the room, a half-bottle of vodka under his arm.

"Ah, so you're here!" he yelled. "Hi, Joey, old pal! I'm here to pay you a visit. I've brought some vodka and sausage! Ho, ho, ho, that's quite a mug you've got on! But don't worry, mine's no better!

> Let a mug hit a mug in the mug!
> That's our fate! That's our fate!
> Hit your mug in the teeth,
> Lest you hang from a tree!

What a mess—did that Syphon make you look like this?! Hey, who's that slip by the wall? Greetings, ma'am!"

"I've fallen in love, Kneadus, I've fallen in love . . ."

To which Kneadus replied with the wisdom of a drunkard:

"So that's why you've got this mug for a face? That's my buddy, Joey! Well, that's quite a mug your beloved has stuck on you. If you could only see yourself. But never mind, never mind, mine's quite a sight too. That's my buddy! But let's go, let's go, don't even bother with her, show me your 'suite,' bring some bread so we can have it with the sausage—I've brought a bottle to drown our sorrows! Stop fretting, Joey! Let's have a drink, buddy, let's shoot the breeze, shoot our mugs off about whatever, it'll do us good! This is my third bottle today. It'll do us good. Greetings, your ladyship . . . *bon jour* . . . *au revoir* . . . Good evening! *Allons, allons!*"

Once again I turned to the modern one. I wanted to say something, to explain—to say the one word that would save me—but there was no such word, then Kneadus caught me by the arm and we headed toward my room, reeling, drunk not with alcohol but with those mugs of ours. I burst into tears and told him everything, absolutely everything about the schoolgirl. He heard me out tenderly, like a father, and then intoned:

> Hey the mug
> On a tree
> Like a chickadee!

Drink, drink up, why aren't you drinking? Wet your whistle! Kiss that little bottle, give it a smooch!"

His face looked terrible, horribly coarse and vulgar, and he ate the sausage from a greasy piece of paper, shoving it into his gaping mouth.

"Kneadus," I exclaimed, "I want to be free! Free!"

"Free of your mug? Shit."

"No, free of the schoolgirl! After all, Kneadus, I'm thirty years old, not a day younger! Thirty!"

He looked at me in surprise, my words must have conveyed real pain. But then he burst out laughing.

"Hey, what drivel! Thirty years old! What an idiot, you're off your rocker, what a moron (and he used a few expressions that I won't repeat). Thirty! Hey, know what?" he took another swig from the bottle and spat, "I know this doll of yours from somewhere. I know her by sight. Kopyrda's after her."

"Who's after her?"

"Kopyrda. The one from our class. He's taken a fancy to her because he's also—modern. Tell you what, if she's truly modern it's a bummer, you won't get anywhere with her! This modern one will take up only with other modern ones, only with her own kind. Well, well, if this modern one stuck this mug on you, you won't get back on your feet that easily. That's worse than Syphon. Never mind, old boy, everyone has some kind of an ideal that's stuck to his person, like a block of wood on Ash Wednesday.* Drink up, drink up, have a swig! Do you think I'm free? I've turned my mug into a dishrag, and the farmhand still plagues me."

"But you've raped Syphon, haven't you?"

"So what? I've raped him, but my mug is still the same. Look," he said in disbelief, "we're quite a pair, me with my farmhand and you with your schoolgirl. Have another swig of vodka! Hey, hey, oh, the farmhand," he suddenly waxed sentimental, "hey, hey, the farmhand! Joey, oh, how I want to run to my farmhand. Hey-ho to the meadows, hey-ho to the fields, oh, let's run away, let's run," he kept muttering, "to the farmhand . . . to the farmhand . . ."

---

*Block of wood on Ash Wednesday—allegedly a custom according to which a bachelor who failed to become engaged by the beginning of Lent continues to have a small block of wood attached to him on Ash Wednesday (personal communication).

But I was not in the least concerned with his farmhand. The modern one was the only one on my mind! All at once I was seized with jealousy—oh, so Kopyrda is after her! But if he's "after her," and not "with her," it may mean that they don't even know each other . . . I did not dare ask. And so we sat with our mugs, on two separate tracks, each with his own thoughts, taking a swig from the bottle now and then. Kneadus rose unsteadily.

"I have to go," he said under his breath, "the old woman might come back any minute. I'll go through the kitchen," he mumbled. "I'll look in on the housemaid. You've got yourself quite a housemaid there, not bad, not bad at all . . . Still, it's not the same as a farmhand, but at least she's lower class. Maybe she has a farmhand for a brother. Ech, old boy—a farmhand . . . a farmhand . . ."

He left. And I was left with the schoolgirl. The moon cast a pale light on flecks of dust that filled the air in great multitudes, swaying to and fro.

8 Fruit Compote

And next morning there's school again, and Syphon, Kneadus, Hopek, Mizdral, Gałkiewicz and *accusativus cum infinitivo*, Ashface, bards, and the daily general impotence—boring, boring, boring! And the same grind again! And the bard bards again, the teacher—to earn his keep—babbles about the bard, the students suffer prostrate under their desks, the toe in one's shoe keeps twirling like a top, and Peter Piper picked a peck of pickled peppers, and Peter Piper pickled a peck of peppers, and Bard the Piper picked a peck of pickled peppers, boring, boring! And again boredom oppresses us, and under the pressure of the boredom, the bard, and the teacher, that which is real slowly turns into a world of ideals, oh, let me dream, let me—no one knows anymore what is real and what doesn't even exist, what is truth and what is illusion, what one feels or doesn't feel, what is natural behavior and what is affectation or make-believe, and, what s h o u l d b e becomes confused with what inexorably i s, one disqualifying the other, one depriving the other of all *raison d'etre*, oh, what a great schooling in unreality! And so I too dreamt about my ideal, for five solid hours a day, my mug expanding in this emptiness like a balloon, without impediment—because, in this unreal, imaginary world, there was nothing that could return it to normal. I too had my unreality—the modern schoolgirl. I was in love. I had my daydream, the doleful lover and aspirant that I was. After my unsuccessful attempts to win my beloved—such as by jeering at her—a great sorrow came over me, I knew all was lost.

Like rosary beads, a string of monotonous days ensued. I was trapped. What can I say about those days—all identical images of one another? In the morning I went to school, and after school I returned to the Youngbloods' for dinner. I was no longer interested in running away, nor in explaining anything, nor in protesting—on the contrary, I took pleasure in becoming a schoolboy because, as a schoolboy, I would, after all, be closer to the schoolgirl than as an independent young man. Hey, hey! I almost forgot about my erstwhile "thirty-year-old." The teachers grew to like me, Principal Piórkowski patted my pupa, and during ideological debates I too shouted, my cheeks flushed: "Modernity! Hooray for the modern boy! Hooray for the modern girl!" Which made Kopyrda laugh. Remember Kopyrda—the one and only modern boy in the entire school? I wanted to be in league with him, I tried to befriend him and to extract from him the secret of his relationship with the Youngblood girl—but he brushed me off, treating me with even greater disdain than he treated the others, as if sensing that I had been rebuffed by his sister-in-kind, the modern schoolgirl. On the whole, the ruthlessness with which the students persecuted any species of youth other than their own was amazing, sticklers for cleanliness hated the unclean, modern ones were repulsed by the old-fashioned, and so on. And so on and on! And on!

What else can I say? Syphon died. Raped through the ears, he could not recover, he could not by any manner or means rid himself of those hostile elements which had been forced into his ears. He agonized in vain, he tried for hours on end to forget those words of initiation that had been forced upon him. He felt nothing but disgust for his tainted self and walked around with a foul taste, growing more and more pale each day, burping constantly, spitting, choking, wheezing, coughing, unable to do anything, until finally, one afternoon, feeling totally worthless, he hanged himself from a coat rack. This caused a great uproar, there were even press releases. Nonetheless, it was of little use to Kneadus, Syphon's death didn't improve the condition of his mug one bit. Syphon died, so what? The faces that Kneadus had pulled during the duel still stuck to him—it's not easy to be rid of a grimace, a face is not made of rubber, once it is distorted it does not easily return to its former shape. And so he walked around with a face so ugly that even his friends, Hopek and Mizdral, avoided him whenever they could. And the more monstrous he looked, the more—of course—he panted after the farmhand; and the more he panted, the more hideous—of course—his mug became. Misery brought us closer, he was panting for the farmhand, I for the schoolgirl, and so time passed slowly in this joint panting, and, as if a rash were covering our faces, reality became unattainable and inaccessible to us. He told me that he stood a chance of seducing the Youngbloods' housemaid—the other night, while soused, he forced a kiss on her as he was going out through the kitchen, but this did not satisfy him in the least.

"It's not the same thing," he kept saying, "not the same. To steal a kiss from a hussy? It's true the hussy's a bare-footed country girl and, as I found out, she does have a farmhand for a brother, but so what, shit, damn, crap (and other expressions which I won't repeat), a sister is not the same as a brother, a housemaid is not a farmhand. I go to her in the evenings when that Mrs. Youngblood of yours is at her committee meetings, I wag my tongue, I shoot off my mouth, I even talk like a peasant, but still she won't take me for one of her own."

And so his world was shaping itself—the housemaid taking second place, the farmhand first place. But my world had moved—lock, stock, and barrel—from school to the Youngbloods' home.

With a mother's perspicacity the Youngblood woman soon noticed that I was infatuated with her daughter. I need not add that the engineer's wife—duly excited by Pimko to begin with—became even more excited by this discovery. An old-fashioned and affected boy, unable to hide his admiration for the schoolgirl's modern attributes, was like a tongue with which she could sense and relish all her daughter's charms, and, indirectly—her own. And so I became a tongue to the fat woman, and the more old-fashioned, insincere, and affected I became the more they developed a sense of modernity, sincerity, and simplicity. And thus the two infantile realities—modern, old-fashioned—stimulating each other, chafing and exciting each other with a thousand of the strangest electric shocks, cumulated and rose into a world that became more and more fragmentary and green. And the upshot of it was that the old Youngblood woman began to strut before me like a peacock, flaunting and showing off her modernity, which was purely and simply a surrogate for youth. At mealtimes, whenever we found time, there were conversations about Moral Freedom, the Era, Revolutionary Upheavals, about Postwar Times, etc., that went on endlessly, and the old woman was thrilled that the Era was making her younger than the boy who was younger by age. She turned herself into a young woman, and she turned me into a little old man.

"So how goes it, our young little old man?" she would ask, "our rotten egg?"

And with the sophistication of the intelligent, modern engineer's wife that she was, she tormented me with her vitality, and with her experience of life, and with the fact that she knew what life was all about, and with having been kicked during the first World War while a nurse in the trenches, and with her enthusiasm, and with her wide horizons, and with the liberalism of the Avant-garde, Active, and Bold woman, and also with her modern ways, daily baths, and with what had thus far been a covert activity—her now overt visits to the toilet. Strange, strange things! Pimko came to visit me from time to time. The old teacher delighted in my pupa. "What a pupa," he purred, "unsurpassed!" and he seized every opportunity to flatter the Youngblood woman by exaggerating his old-fashioned pedagogical genre, and he continued to be utterly shocked by the modern school-girl. I noticed that elsewhere, as at school with Mr. Piórkowski, for example, Pimko didn't present himself as particularly old, nor did he adhere to those old-fashioned principles, and I couldn't quite grasp whether it was the Youngbloods who elicited his old-fashioned ways, or—on the contrary—it was he who elicited the Youngbloods' mo-dernity, or whether—in the final analysis—they played off each other for some higher rhyme or reason. I don't know to this day whether Pimko, otherwise the absolute prof, was forced by Miss Young-blood's postwar unruliness into becoming one of those prewar spe-cies of prof, or whether he provoked her unruliness by purposefully adopting the mien of an unhappy, inept, and kindly granddaddy. Who created whom—did the modern schoolgirl create the grand-daddy, or did the granddaddy create the modern schoolgirl? A rather useless and sterile question. But how strangely whole worlds can crystallize between two people's calves.

One way or another, they both thrived—he as the pedagogue of bygone views and principles, Zuta as the unbridled youth—and gradually his visits became longer, he devoted less attention to me and concentrated more on the modern one. Need I tell you?—I was jealous of Pimko. I suffered terribly as I watched the two of them fulfilling each other, concurring in everything, rhyming little lyrics and together creating spicy little old-new poetry, and it was horrible to watch how this antique of a man—his calves a thousandfold in-ferior to mine—was more in synchrony with this modern girl than I was. Norwid in particular became the pretext for a thousand frolics, the kindly Pimko couldn't acquiesce to her ignorance of the subject, it offended his most sacred sentiments, while she preferred pole-vaulting—he constantly expressed indignation, she laughed, he'd recommend something, she'd have none of it, he entreated her, she'd just hop and skip—and on and on and on! I admired the wisdom and maturity with which the prof, while not for a moment ceasing to be a prof and always acting on the principle of a prof, was nevertheless able to derive pleasure from the modern schoolgirl by means of contrast and antithesis, how he excited her schoolgirlishness with his "prof" while she incited him with her schoolgirlishness to be the prof. I was terribly jealous—after all, I too incited her antithetically and was in turn excited by her—but, O my God, I didn't want to be old-fashioned with her, I wanted to be modern!

Oh, what torment, torment, torment! I could not, I just could not set myself free. All my efforts came to naught. My derision—I spared her none in my thoughts—brought no results, in fact, what does cheap derision behind someone's back accomplish? Anyway, all the derision was nothing but homage. Because deep within the derision lurked a poisonous desire to please her—and deriding her probably served no other purpose than to adorn myself with the peacock feathers of derision—and was simply the result of her negation of me. But the derision turned against me and made my mug look even uglier and more horrible. And I dared not deride her openly—she would just have shrugged her shoulders. Because a girl, similar in this to everyone else, will never be intimidated by someone who derides her just because he's been refused admission . . . And the only effect that my clownish attack on her had, that time in her room, was that from then on she was on guard against me, she ignored me—she ignored me as befits a modern schoolgirl, realizing perfectly well how much in love I was with her modern charms. She therefore intensified those charms with the refined cruelty of a magpie, though carefully avoiding any hint of coquetry that might make her dependent on me. She became, just to please herself, more wild and impudent, more bold, harsh, lithe, sporty, leggy, and she promptly let herself be carried away by her own modern charms. She would sit down to dinner, oh, so mature in her immaturity, so self-assured, indifferent, and self-contained, while I sat there for her, for her, I sat there for her alone, and I couldn't miss a single second of sitting for her, I was within her, she enclosed me within herself, my derision and all, her likes and dislikes meant the world to me, and I could like myself only as much as she liked me. What torture—to be totally stuck within a modern schoolgirl. And never, not even once, did I catch her letting go of that modern style in the slightest, never providing me with a chink through which I could escape to freedom, to bolt!

This was precisely what captivated me—the maturity and autonomy of her youth, the self-assurance of her style. While we in school had our blackheads, constantly broke out in pimples and ideals, while our movements were gawky and each step was a gaffe—her *exterieur* was entrancingly polished. Youth, for her, was not a transitional age—for this modern one, youth was the only time befitting a human being—s h e d i s d a i n e d m a t u r i t y, i m m a t u r i t y w a s h e r m a t u r i t y—she had no time for beards, mustaches, wet nurses, mothers with children—and this was the source of her magical power. Her youth had no need of ideals, it was in and of itself an ideal. No wonder that, tormented by idealistic youth, I too thirsted for that ideal youth, like a mushroom for rain. But she didn't want me! She put the screws to my mug! And with every passing day she tightened the screws so that my mug looked more and more horrible.

By God—how she tortured that "beauty" of mine! Oh, I know no greater cruelty than that of one human being putting the screws to the mug of another. No holds barred, just shove it into the ridiculous, the grotesque, make a sham of it, because the ugliness of one man sustains the beauty of another, and oh, believe me, dealing someone the pupa is nothing compared to putting the screws to someone's mug! I was finally at my wits' end, and I began to dream up wild schemes in which I physically destroyed the schoolgirl. To disfigure that little face of hers. To put out of shape that nose of hers, to cut it off. But if the example of Kneadus and Syphon served any purpose it was to show that brute force isn't much good, no, the soul has little use for the nose, the soul is set free by spiritual mastery alone. But what could I do when my soul was stuck inside her, when I was within her and she was hemming me in. Is it possible to extricate oneself from someone, under one's own power, when that person is one's only support, the only contact you have, when that person's style dominates you completely? No, not under your own power, that's impossible, totally out of the question. Unless a third person helps you from the sidelines, offers you at least the tip of his finger. But who could help me? Kneadus, who never visited the Youngbloods (except in their kitchen, on the sly) and was never a party to my association with the schoolgirl? Mr. Youngblood, Mrs. Youngblood, or Pimko?—they were the schoolgirl's sworn allies. Or finally, a housemaid for hire, a creature without a voice? All the while my mug became more and more horrible, and the more horrible it became the more the two Youngblood women hardened in their modern style and tightened the screws on my mug. Oh, style—the tool of tyranny! Oh, damnation! But the two hags miscalculated! Because the time came when, quite by chance and thanks to Mr. Youngblood (yes, Mr. Youngblood), the trammels of their style loosened, and little by little I regained my power. And then I went on the offensive, full steam ahead. Forward and away, giddy-up, giddy-up, ride roughshod over style, over the modern schoolgirl's beauty!

A strange thing—I owe my liberation to the engineer because, were it not for the engineer, I would have been imprisoned forever, but he unwittingly brought about a small shift, and the schoolgirl suddenly found herself inside me and not I inside her, yes, the engineer pulled his daughter inside me, and I'll be grateful to him until the day I die. I remember how it started. I remember that day—I come home from school for dinner. The Youngbloods are already at the table, the housemaid brings potato soup, the schoolgirl also sits there—she sits perfectly, with her slightly Bolshevik *physique-kultur*, in sneakers. She didn't eat much soup that day—instead she gulped a glass of water and followed it with a slice of bread, she stayed away from the soup—a watered-down mush, warm and too effortless, definitely bad for her type—and she probably wanted to go hungry as long as possible, at least until the meat dish, because a hungry modern girl is more classy than a satiated modern girl. Mrs. Youngblood also ate very little soup, and she didn't ask how my day went at school. Why didn't she ask? Because she didn't go for those motherly questions, she was generally a bit disgusted with "mother," she disliked "mother." She preferred "sister."

"Here you are, Victor, have some salt," she said in the tone of a true and faithful comrade and a reader of H. G. Wells, as she passed the salt to her husband, and, with her gaze turned partly into the future, partly into space, a gaze emphasizing the humanitarian revolt of a human being who combats the infamy of social ills, injustice, and injury, she added:

"Capital punishment is obsolete."

Whereupon Mr. Youngblood, that man of Europe, an engineer and enlightened urban planner who studied in Paris, whence he brought that dark, European flair—that man then, casual in his attire, sporting new yellow buckskin shoes that looked very striking on him, wearing horn-rimmed glasses and his collar *à la* poet Słowacki—a robust pacifist devoid of prejudices, an admirer of scientifically organized work, and given to telling scientific jokes and anecdotes, and cabaret jokes, took the salt and said:

"Thank you, Joanna."

And, in the tone of an enlightened pacifist, but with a hint of the engineering student's voice, he added:

"In Brazil they dump whole barrels of salt in water, while we pay six groszes per gramme. Oh, those politicians! We are the experts. The world needs reorganizing. League of Nations."

Whereupon the Youngblood woman took a deep breath and,

envisioning a better tomorrow and Żeromski's glass houses of the future—referring to the tradition of struggle of yesterday's Poland and striving for the Poland of tomorrow—she said sensibly:

"Zuta, who was that boy who walked you home from school today? You don't have to answer if you don't want to. You know I'm not one to pressure or embarrass you in any way."

The Youngblood girl nonchalantly ate a piece of bread.

"I don't know," she replied.

"You don't know?" the mother asked pleasantly.

"He accosted me," said the schoolgirl.

"Accosted you?" Mr. Youngblood asked.

It was just an offhand question. But the very fact that he asked it loaded the issue and may have created the impression of outdated fatherly disapproval. That's why the Youngblood woman intervened.

"And what's so strange about that?" she exclaimed with what seemed excessive cheekiness. "He accosted her—big deal! Let him! Zuta, did you make a date with him? Great! Perhaps you'd like to go kayaking with him—for the whole day? Or maybe you'd like to go away for the weekend and not come back at night? Don't come back then," she said obligingly, "go ahead and stay overnight! And maybe you'd like to go without any money, maybe you'd like him to pay for you, or maybe you'd rather pay for him, so he'd be on your keep—in that case I'll give you some money. But on the other hand, I'm sure you'll both manage without money, eh?" she exclaimed harshly, insisting with her whole body, it seemed. Indeed, the engineer's wife overshot the mark a bit, but the daughter deftly staved off her mother, who was trying, all too obviously, to live vicariously through her daughter.

"Yes, yes, Mother," the girl dismissed her, and declined a second helping of meat patties because ground meat did not agree with her—it was too mushy and somehow too easy on her. The modern girl was wary of her parents, she never let them get too close to her.

But the engineer had already caught his wife's drift. And since she had insinuated that he disapproved of the fact that his daughter had been accosted, he was eager, in his turn, to show his mettle. They thus went on catching each other's drift. And he exclaimed:

"Of course there's nothing wrong with it! Zuta, if you want to have an illegitimate child, be my guest! And what's wrong with that?! The cult of virginity is no more! We—designer-engineers of the new social reality—repudiate the old-time hayseeds' cult of virginity!"

He took a gulp of water and, sensing that he may have gone too far, broke off. However, the Youngblood woman picked up the drift again and began, indirectly, in a vague sort of way, to egg on her daughter to have an illegitimate child, she expressed her liberalism, talked about conditions in America, quoted Benjamin Barr Lindsay, and under-scored contemporary youth's unique ease in this matter, etc., etc. . . . This suddenly turned into the Youngbloods' favorite hobbyhorse. When one of them got off, sensing that he or she had gone too far, the other mounted it again and sped on. It was all the more strange, because, as I've said before, they all (including Mr. Youngblood) didn't like the idea of mother, of child. But please understand that they mounted the idea not from a mother's side but from a school-girl's side, nor from the child's side—they didn't care about the child, only about its illegitimacy. And especially the Youngblood woman wanted to move to the forefront of history through her daughter's illegitimate child, to have the child conceived casually, easily, boldly, impudently, in the bushes, on a sports trip with her contemporary, just as they describe it in modern love stories, etc. Actually, just talking about it and egging on the schoolgirl was enough to produce the flavor they desired. And they reveled in it all the more, be-cause they sensed my impotence in relation to the girl—indeed, thus far I had been unable to defend myself against the charms of the seventeen-year-old in the bushes.

But they overlooked the fact that on this particular day I was too depleted to feel any jealousy. Indeed—for two weeks straight they had been putting the screws to my mug until finally my mug became so awful that there was nothing left with which I could be jealous. I suspected that the boy Mrs. Youngblood had mentioned was probably Kopyrda, but what of it, so what—there was nothing but grief and sadness—sadness and misery—misery and great weariness, and resignation. So instead of thinking my thoughts in sky-blue-green colors, giving them a fresh and bold form, I opted for the puny and the miserable: "Well, a child is a child," I thought to myself, and I imagined labor, wet nurses, illnesses, exudative skin rashes, child-related messiness and living expenses, and I thought that an infant, with its milk and baby warmth, would destroy the girl, turning her into a lubberly, warm little mommy. I therefore leaned toward Miss Youngblood, and miserably, as if speaking to myself, I said:

"Mommy . . ."

And I said it warmly, mawkishly, with great sadness, and I infused the word with all the sickly-sweet-mommy warmth that they, with their harsh, brisk, girlish, and youthful vision of the world, wouldn't even consider. Why did I say it? Well, just so, for no particular reason. The girl was, like all girls, first and foremost, an aesthete, good looks were her main assignment, whereas, by matching her type with the warm, emotional, and somewhat sloppy-negligée expression "Mommy," I was creating something disgustingly slovenly and indecorous. I hoped she'd have a fit. Yet I knew she would duck me and that the ugliness would be mine again, because the way things were between us, anything I attempted against her would stick fast to me, as if I were spitting into the wind.

But lo and behold—Mr. Youngblood giggled!

His guttural giggle surprised him, and, embarrassed, he grabbed the tablecloth—he went on giggling, his eyes bulged, he choked and roared into the tablecloth, horribly, mechanically, in spite of himself. I was astounded! What was it that had so tickled his nervous system? The expression "Mommy"? He must have been amused by the contrast between his "girl" and my "Mommy," something clicked, cabaret humor perhaps, or perhaps my sad and doleful voice had led him

Fruit Compote

to humanity's backyard. He had the capacity, common to all engineers, of being easily tickled by *szmonces*, and my phrase had indeed the flavor of a *szmonces*.* And the more he had reveled, a moment ago, in the idea of an illegitimate child, the more he now giggled. His glasses fell off his nose.

"Victor," Mrs. Youngblood said.

But I stepped on the gas:

"Mommy, Mommy . . ."

"I'm sorry, I'm sorry," he giggled, "I'm sorry, so sorry . . . But just imagine it! So help me! I'm sorry . . ."

The girl bent over her plate, and I suddenly saw, almost physically, that through her father's giggling, my words had touched her—so after all I did touch her, she was now touched—yes, yes, I was not mistaken, her father's laughter (aside, as it were) had changed things around, it had extricated me from the schoolgirl. I could finally touch her! I sat quiet as a mouse.

Her parents also noticed it and ran to her rescue.

"Victor, I'm surprised at you," the Youngblood woman said with displeasure, "our little old man's remarks aren't in the least witty. It's a pose, nothing more!"

The engineer finally controlled his laughter.

"You think I was laughing at this, do you? Never on my life, I didn't even hear it—it's something I've just remembered . . ."

But their efforts only served to involve the schoolgirl even more. Although I didn't quite understand what was happening I repeated "Mommy, Mommy" a couple of times in the same sleepy, puny little voice, and, by repeating it, the word must have gained new strength because the engineer giggled again, briefly, then laughed with a jerky, guttural, choking laughter. And it must have all appeared funny to him because he suddenly burst into unrestrained laughter, stuffing his mouth with a napkin.

---

*Szmonces—a Jewish quip. Pronounced "shmontzes."

"Stop butting in!" the Youngblood woman shouted at me angrily, but her anger served to involve the daughter even more, because the girl shrugged her shoulders.

"Oh, let it be, Mother," she remarked with apparent indifference, but this too drew her in. Strange as it seemed—the configuration between us changed so radically that every single word drew them in more and more. Actually, it was all rather nice. I felt I had regained my potency in relation to the girl. Yet it no longer made any difference to me. I also felt I had regained my potency because of my very indifference, yet if I were to make the mistake, even for a split second, of substituting triumph for my former sadness and grief, my potency would be instantly annihilated, because it was actually a strange superpotency woven into the canvas of a blatant and long-suffering impotency. Therefore, to affirm my misery and to underscore my indifference, and how unworthy I was of everything, I began to dabble in my fruit compote, tossing into it bread crumbs, bits of rubbish, bread pellets, and stirring it with my spoon. I still had my ugly mug, so what, this was good enough for me—"shit, what do I care," I thought sleepily, adding a little salt, pepper, and a couple of toothpicks, "oh, so what, I'll eat it all as long as it fills me, makes no difference . . ." It was as if I were lying in a ditch, little birdies flying about . . . stirring with my spoon I felt warm and cozy.

"Well, young man? . . . Well, young man? . . . Why is our young man dabbling in his compote?"

Mrs. Youngblood asked this softly yet anxiously. I lifted my inept gaze from the compote.

"I . . . just, it's all the same to me . . ." I whispered, calm and slime in my voice. And I proceeded to eat the pap; and the pap didn't really make the slightest difference to my spirit. It's hard to describe the effect this had on the Youngbloods, I didn't expect such a powerful effect. For the third time the engineer giggled uncontrollably with that cabaret giggle, with that backyard, backside giggle of his. The girl bent over her plate and ate the compote in silence, with decorum and restraint, even with heroism. Mrs. Engineer turned pale—she stared at me as if hypnotized, bug-eyed, she was obviously afraid of me. Afraid!

"It's just a pose! A pose!" she kept mumbling. "Don't eat that . . . I forbid you! Zuta! Victor—Zuta! Victor! Zuta! Zuta! Victor—stop him, tell him to stop! Oh . . ."

But I went on eating, because why shouldn't I? I'll eat it all, I'd eat a dead rat, it's all the same to me . . . "Hey, Kneadus," I thought to myself, "this is good, good . . . It's good . . . So what, what of it, anything to stuff my mug with, so what, what of it, so what . . ."

"Zuta!" screeched the Youngblood woman. To a mother, the sight of her daughter's admirer eating everything in sight was unbearable. But then the schoolgirl, who had just finished her compote, stood up from the table and left. Mrs. Youngblood followed her. Mr. Youngblood also left, giggling convulsively and stuffing his mouth with a napkin. It wasn't clear whether they'd finished dinner or whether they were fleeing. But I knew—they fled! I ran after them! Yippee-yeay! On with it, attack, catch, and thrash them, chase, pursue, on their heels, nab and crush them, choke them, choke and badger them, don't let up! Were they afraid? Scare them even more! Were they fleeing? Chase them, then! But be calm, tread softly, softly, softly, like a beggar and a wretch, don't change the beggar into a conqueror, remember it was the beggar who led you to conquest. They were afraid that I might fix the girl's brain like I had fixed the compote. Ha, now I knew how to get at her style! I would stuff her brain, her intellect, with anything I could lay my hands on, then scramble it up, mince it and stir it, by fair means or foul! But keep calm, keep calm . . .

Who would ever believe that Mr. Youngblood's subterranean giggling would restore my ability to resist them? My thoughts and deeds acquired claws again. I hadn't yet won the game, no. But at least I could act. I knew what line to follow. The fruit compote made it all clear to me. Just as I had messed up the compote by changing in into a dissolute pap, so I could destroy the schoolgirl's modernity by introducing into it foreign and heterogeneous elements, scrambling everything up for all it was worth. Giddy-up, giddy-up, giddy-up, ride roughshod over modern style, over the modern schoolgirl's beauty! But quietly, quietly . . .

9 Peeping and Further Incursion into Modernity

I quietly went into my room and lay down on my bed. I had to devise a plan of action. I trembled, and sweat poured off me as I realized that in this pilgrimage of mine I was descending, through a sequence of defeats, to the very bottom of hell. Nothing that is really tasty can be really awful (as the word "tasty" indicates), and only that which has bad taste is truly inedible. With envy, I was reminiscing about those beautiful, romantic, classical crimes, the rapes and gouging of eyes in poetry and prose—herring with jam, that I know are awful, unlike those wonderful and beautiful crimes in Shakespeare. So don't talk to me, don't, about those rhymed agonies we swallow as easily as oysters, don't talk about the candy of disgrace, about the chocolate cream of horror, the little cakes of wretchedness, about the lollipops of suffering and sweetmeats of despair. So why does this busybody of a woman, who uses her finger to tear at the most bloody social ills, death by starvation of a worker's family of six, why, I ask, does she not dare, with the same finger, to pick her ear in public? Because this would have been much more dreadful. Death from starvation, or the death of a million in war—this can be eaten, even relished—yet there still exist in this world combinations that are not edible, that make us vomit, that are bad, discordant, repulsive, and repellent, oh, even satanic, and these the human organism rejects. And yet our first and foremost task is to relish, we must relish, relish, let the husband, wife, and children lie dying, let our heart be torn to shreds, as long as it's done tastefully, yes, tastefully! Indeed, that which I was about to undertake in the name of Maturity, and in order to free myself from the schoolgirl's spell, would be an anti-culinary and a counter-palatable activity, something the gullet finds quite revolting!

Anyway, I didn't delude myself—my success at lunch was rather dubious, it mainly affected the parents, the girl escaped unharmed, she remained distant and unattainable. How could I defile her modern style from a distance? How was I to pull her into the orbit of my activity? And, in addition to the psychological distance, there was also the physical distance—she saw me only during lunch and dinner. How could I break her down, pierce her mentally from a distance, that is, when I was not with her, when she was alone? "Perhaps," I went on with my lame thinking, "by peeping and eavesdropping." The Youngbloods had paved the way for me because they had perceived me, from the first moment of our encounter, as an eavesdropper and a Peeping Tom. "And who knows," I thought, drowsy but hopeful, "perhaps if I put my eye to the keyhole I'll immediately see in her something repugnant, many a beauty in her own room behaves repulsively till one splits one's sides." But then again there was the danger that some schoolgirls, impressed with their own charms and well disciplined in style, are as much on their guard in solitude as they are in public. Hence, instead of ugliness I could equally well behold beauty, and beauty beheld in solitude is even more lethal. I remembered walking unexpectedly into her room and finding the schoolgirl, the shoe cloth by her leg, in a very stylish posture—yes, but on the other hand, the very fact of peeping would despoil and pierce her, because while we act hideously and peep at a beauty, something from our gaze settles on that beauty.

I reasoned this as if in a fever—I finally dragged myself off the bed and directed myself toward the keyhole. However, before I put my eye to the hole I looked out the window—it was a beautiful autumn day, bright and clear, and, in the street brightened by autumn, Kneadus was creeping toward the kitchen door. He was apparently making his way to the housemaid. Pigeons flew in the bright sunshine and over the roof of a neighboring house, then flocked together, the horn of a car sounded in the distance, a nursemaid played with a child on the sidewalk, windowpanes bathed in the setting sun. A beggar stood in front of the house, an old, bedraggled beggar, one of those burly, hairy, bearded duffers who hang around church doors. The sight of the bearded man gave me an idea—I went sleepily and sluggishly out to the street and to a nearby square where I broke off a green twig.

"Listen, old fellow," I said, "here's fifty groszes. I'll give you one zloty this evening, but you must put this twig between your teeth and remain with it until nightfall."

The bearded man stuck the greenery in his mouth. I blessed the money that wins allies and returned to my room. I put my eye to the keyhole. The schoolgirl was moving about, as girls are wont to do in their rooms. She shifted things in her drawers, took out a notebook, placed it on a table, I saw her face in profile—the face of a typical schoolgirl looking at a notebook.

I went on peeping like a miserable wretch from four in the afternoon till six (while the beggar continuously held the twig in his mouth), I waited in vain for any sign of anxiety that may have resulted from the defeat sustained at lunch, such as biting her lip or wrinkling her forehead. But no. As if nothing had changed. As if I did not exist. As if nothing had disturbed her schoolgirlishness. Time passed, her schoolgirlishness became more and more cruel and cold, more and more indifferent, remote, and it seemed unlikely that there was any possible way to sully the schoolgirl, who behaved the same way in solitude as she did in public. As if nothing had happened at lunch. At about six o'clock the door to the girl's room opened suddenly, cunningly—Mrs. Engineer stood on the threshold.

"Are you working?" she asked with relief, scrutinizing her daughter. "Are you working?"

"I'm doing my German," the schoolgirl replied.

The mother breathed more easily.

"You're working—that's good. Keep working, keep working."

She stroked the girl's head, reassured. Had she too expected that her daughter might come apart? Zuta impatiently drew back her cute little head. The mother wanted to say something, opened her mouth and closed it—she checked herself. She cast around a suspicious eye.

"Work! Work! Work!" she went on nervously. "Keep busy—work hard. And this evening sneak out to a dance—sneak out to a dance—sneak out to a dance. Come back late, fall asleep like a log . . ."

"Don't bother me, Mother!" Zuta exclaimed harshly. "I don't have time!"

Her mother looked at her, trying to conceal her admiration. The schoolgirl's harshness reassured her completely. She realized that her daughter hadn't gone to pieces at lunchtime. But the schoolgirl's brutal sharpness grabbed me by the throat. The sharpness was aimed directly at herself, and nothing pains us to the same degree as watching our beloved when she's not only inexorably sharp toward us but also, in our absence, as if in advance, is hardening herself. And with this her manifestation was painfully imprinted with the girl's brutality. After Mrs. Youngblood's departure she brought her profile back to the notebook and, self-sufficient, detached, and brutal, resumed her lessons.

I felt that I could no longer allow the girl to manifest herself in solitude, and unless I could establish contact between her and my peeping, things would take a tragic turn. Instead of defiling her, I was delighting in her person, instead of catching her by the throat, she was catching me by the throat. I swallowed my saliva loudly, right next to the door, so that she would hear me and realize that I was peeping. She shuddered but didn't turn her head—which was clear evidence that she had heard me—and she tucked her cute little head between her shoulders, as if wounded. But her profile instantly ceased to exist in and of itself, and therefore, all at once and quite remarkably, its beguiling manifestation breathed its last. The girl with the peeped-at profile fought long and hard in silence, and the fight consisted of her not batting an eye. She continued to move her pen on paper, and she behaved as if no one were peeping at her.

But lo and behold, after a few minutes the keyhole itself, as if looking at her with my eye, began to bother her—and in order to proclaim her independence and affirm her indifference she sniffled loudly, she sniffled coarsely and repulsively as if to say: "See, I don't care a hoot, I can sniffle too." That's how girls show their greatest disdain. And that's exactly what I was waiting for. When she made the tactical error of sniffling, I too sniffled near the door, I sniffled obviously, but not too loudly, as if I couldn't help it, as if her sniffling were contagious. The girl became quiet as a mouse—the nasal duet was unacceptable to her—but her nose, once set in action, began to annoy her, and after a brief struggle she was forced to take out her handkerchief and blow her nose, and then at longer intervals she sniffled nervously, inconspicuously, which I went on repeating near the door, sniffle by sniffle. I congratulated myself on my success in so easily seizing that nose of hers, the girl's nose was infinitely less modern than the girl's legs and easier to conquer. By highlighting the nose and wresting it from her I took an enormous step forward. If only I could make the Youngblood girl catch a nervous cold, if only I could make her modernity catch a cold.

And yet, after all that sniffling, she couldn't simply get up and cover the keyhole with a piece of cloth—this would have been tantamount to admitting that the sniffling was a sign of anxiety. But shush, let us sniffle wretchedly, hopelessly, let us conceal our hope! I underestimated, however, the girl's skill and craft. Suddenly, with a wide sweep of her hand—with her whole forearm—she wiped her nose from ear to ear, and this bold, sporty, feisty, and amusing gesture changed the situation to her advantage and adorned the sniffling with charm. She grabbed me by the throat. At the same time—I barely managed to jump away from the keyhole—cunningly, unexpectedly, Mrs. Youngblood stepped into my room.

"What is our young man doing?" she asked suspiciously when she saw me vacillating in the middle of the room. "Why is our young man . . . standing here? Why isn't our young man doing his lessons? Doesn't our young man participate in sports? You have to get busy with something," she cried out in rage. She was afraid for her daughter. She sniffed some vague design on her daughter in my ill-defined stance in the middle of the room. I made no move to clarify anything, I continued to stand listlessly and awkwardly, arrested in motion, till the Youngblood woman turned sideways. She then saw the beggar in front of the house.

"What's this, he's got . . . ? Why the twig . . . in his mouth?"

"Who?"

"The beggar. What's the meaning of this?"

"I don't know. He stuck it in and he's holding it."

"You have talked to him, young man. I saw it through the window."

"Well yes, I did."

She scurried over my face with her eyes. She swung like a pendulum. She suspected that the twig had a hidden meaning, a message of hostility and malice toward her daughter. But she had no idea what associations I had in mind, she had no way of knowing that for me the twig in the mouth had become an attribute of modernity. Her suspicion that it was I who told the bearded fellow to hold the greenery between his teeth was such nonsense that it could not be put into words. She surveyed my mind with mistrust, suspecting that it had fallen prey to a whim, and she left. Giddy-up, follow her! Hit her! Hold her! In swift pursuit! She's the prisoner of my fantasy! The prey of my whim! Quiet, quiet! I jumped back to the keyhole. As events

developed, I found it more and more difficult to maintain my origi-
nally hopeless and miserable posture—the fight heated me up, mon-
key spitefulness gained the upper hand over exhaustion and resignation. The schoolgirl had disappeared. Having heard voices on the
other side of the wall she realized that I was no longer watching her,
and this enabled her to escape the trap. She went downtown. Will she
notice the twig in the beggar's face, will she guess for whose benefit
the bearded man is holding it? Even if she didn't guess—the twig in
the bearded man's mouth, the acrid, green bitterness in the beggar's
mouth, would have to weaken her, because it would have been too
much at odds with her modern perception of the world. Dusk was
falling. Street lamps bathed the city in violet. The caretaker's little
son was returning from the corner market. In the clear and limpid
air, trees were losing their leaves. A small airplane whirred above
the houses. The front door slammed, announcing the Youngblood
woman's departure. Mrs. Engineer, anxious, ruffled, sensing something bad in the air, went to her committee meeting to fortify herself
with a breath of something civic-minded, worldly, and mature.

Madam Chair

Dear ladies, on today's agenda we have the plague of abandoned
infants.

Mrs. Youngblood

Where are the funds coming from?

Dusk was falling, and the beggar was still under the window with
the young greenery, like a discordant note. I was all alone in the
apartment. A Sherlock Holmes situation began to evolve in the
empty rooms, some kind of a detective plot was developing here as I
stood in the semi-darkness, looking for the continuation of this
happily begun adventure. Since the two of them had fled I decided to
trespass their rooms, perhaps I'd succeed in reaching them through
that small part of their aura which they had left behind. In the
Youngbloods' bedroom—a bright, cramped, clean, and frugally furnished room—there was the scent of soap and bathrobe, the sweetish

warmth of the intelligentsia, modern, orderly, yet at the same time smelling of nail clippings, gas heaters, and pajamas. I stood in the center of the room for a long while, breathing in its ambience, examining its elements, and searching for some distasteful essence, something with which to contaminate it all.

On the face of it I couldn't find fault with anything. Cleanliness, order, sunlight, thrift, and simplicity—and the scent of cosmetics was even better than in old-fashioned bedrooms. And I didn't know why the modern engineer's bathrobe, his pajamas, face cloth, shaving cream, his slippers, his wife's Vichy lozenges and rubberized sports gear, the bright little yellow curtain in a modern window pointed to something disgusting. Standardization perhaps? Philistinism? Bourgeois narrow-mindedness? No, that wasn't it, no—then what? I stood there unable to discover the formula for my disgust, because there was no word, no gesture or act with which I could catch that distasteful essence and call it my own—and then my eyes fell on a book lying open on a bedside table. It was Chaplin's memoirs, opened to the page on which he tells how H. G. Wells had danced before him a solo of his own arrangement. "... Then H. G. Wells magnificently dances a fantastic dance." An English writer's solo dance helped me to catch that distaste, as if on a fishing line. Here was an appropriate commentary! This room was W e l l s himself dancing solo for C h a p l i n. Because who was Wells in his dance?—a Utopian. This old modern man thought that he was free to express his joy and to dance, he insisted on his right to joy and harmony ... he pranced with a vision of the world as it was to be thousands of years hence, he pranced solo, overtaking our time, he danced conceptually because he thought he had the right to ... And what was this bedroom?—a Utopia. Where was there any room for those gasps and moans that a man lets out in his sleep? Where was there room for his better half's obesity? Where was there any room for Youngblood's beard, a beard actually shaven off but nonetheless existing *in potentia*? After all, the engineer h a d a b e a r d even though he threw it into the sink every day with the

Peeping and Further Incursion into Modernity

shaving cream—and this room was c l e a n s h a v e n. In times gone by, the soughing forest was mankind's bedroom, but where was the room for soughs, for the darkness and blackness of the forest in this bright room amid the towels? How stingy was this cleanliness—and cramped—light blue, incompatible with the color of earth and of a human being! And the engineer and his wife seemed to me just as dreadful in this room as Wells in the dance of his own invention in front of Chaplin.

But not until I abandoned myself to my solo dance—not until then did my thoughts acquire flesh and become action, ridiculing everything around me and drawing out a foul taste. I danced—and my prancing without a partner, in emptiness and in silence, swelled with frenzy, oh, give me courage! When I finished dancing around the Youngbloods' towels, pajamas, shaving cream, beds, and sports gear I retreated quickly, closing the door behind me. I had filled their modern interior with dancing! But onward, onward, now to the schoolgirl's room, now dance and spoil everything there!

But Miss Youngblood's room, actually a parlor where she slept and did her lessons, was infinitely more difficult to turn into something distasteful. The mere fact that the girl didn't have her own room and merely slept in the hallway gave off delightful and intoxicating meanings. There was in it the great transiency of our century, the schoolgirl's nomadic life and something like *carpe diem* that linked up, through mysterious transfigurations, with the sleek, automobile-engendered nature of present-day youth. One would suppose that she falls asleep instantly, as soon as she lays her little head (not just head; schoolgirls had eyes—but they still had "little heads") on her pillow, and this in turn brought to mind the speed and intensity of contemporary life. Moreover, in the absence of a bedroom, *sensu stricto,* it was impossible for me to do again what I had done in the Youngbloods' bedroom. The schoolgirl actually slept in public, not in private, she had no private life at night, and this hard public life united her with Europe, America, with Hitler,

Mussolini, and Stalin, with labor camps, flag waving, hotels, railroad stations, giving her an immensely wide scope, eliminating the need for a room of her own. Her bedsheets, stashed in the hideaway sofa, had an auxiliary character, they could at most be an accessory to sleep. There was no dressing table. The schoolgirl looked at herself in a wall mirror. She had no little hand mirror. By her sofa there was a small black table, such as any schoolgirl might have, on which lay books and notebooks. On the notebooks—a nailfile, on the window-sill—a penknife, a cheap pen for six zlotys, an apple, a sports pro-gram, photographs of Fred Astaire and Ginger Rogers, a pack of opium-laced cigarettes, a toothbrush, a tennis shoe with a flower in it, a carnation, discarded inadvertently. And that was all. How mod-est, yet how powerful!

I stopped by the carnation in silence—I couldn't help but admire the schoolgirl! What skill! By tossing the flower into the shoe she killed two partridges with one stone—she spiced love with sports, and she seasoned sports with love! She had tossed the flower into a sweaty tennis shoe rather than into an ordinary shoe because she knew that flowers aren't hurt by athlete's sweat alone. By associating athletic sweat with the flower she was imposing a favorable connec-tion with her sweat in general, she made it into something flowerlike and sporty. Oh, masterful girl! While the old-fashioned, naive, and ordinary girls grew azaleas in flowerpots, she had tossed a flower into a shoe, and a sports shoe at that! And—oh, the rascal—she surely did it unconsciously, inadvertently!

I wondered what to do with this conundrum! Should I throw the flower into the sink? Stick it into the bearded beggar's trap? Yet these mechanical and artificial measures would merely help to circumvent the real difficulty, no, the flower had to be destroyed right where it was, not by physical violence but by psychological violence. The bearded man, the green twig in the thicket of his beard, stood true and steadfast under the window, a fly buzzed on the windowpane, and from the kitchen came the housemaid's tedious clamor as Kneadus tried to prevail upon her to be his farmhand, somewhere in the distance a streetcar squealed around a bend in the tracks—I stood among those strains and stresses, smiling dubiously—the fly buzzed louder. I caught it, tore off its legs and wings, I turned it into a suffering, dolorous, frightful, and metaphysical little ball, not quite round, but most definitely abysmal, I p l a c e d it in the flower, and softly lay both inside the shoe. The sweat that at this moment covered my brow had more power than the flowerlike tennis-shoe sweat. It was as if I had set the devil on the modern girl! The fly, through its numb and dumb suffering, vitiated the shoe, the flower, the apple, the cigarettes, the schoolgirl's entire household, while I stood there with an evil little smile, listening to what was now going on in the room and within me, studying the ambiance, I and a madman, we were like two peas in a pod—and I thought that it's not only little boys who drown cats and torture little birds, big boys sometimes also torture, just for the sake of ceasing to be schoolgirls' boys, just to get the better of their schoolgirl, yes, the schoolgirl! Wasn't this why Trocki tortured? Or Torquemada? What was the nature of Torquemada's schoolgirl? Quietly, quietly.

The bearded man, decked in greenery, stood at his post—the fly suffered mutely in what was now a Chinese, a Byzantine shoe—my dance was still taking place in the Youngbloods' bedroom—I now began to rummage through the modern one's belongings. I reached into the built-in closet where she kept her underwear, but her underwear fell short of my hope. Her modern panties didn't bespoil the girl, her panties were just panties—no more domestic than sea shanties. However, in a drawer that I pried open with a knife—there were stacks of letters, the schoolgirl's love letters! I pounced on them while the bearded fellow, the fly, and the dance continued their work, unceasingly.

Oh, what pandemonium in the modern schoolgirl's life! What substance this drawer contained! Only then did I realize what awesome mysteries are lorded over by contemporary schoolgirls, and what effect it would have if one of them chose to reveal the secrets entrusted to her. But, like a stone cast in the water, everything sinks into those girls, they are too good-looking, too beautiful to tell . . . and those who don't have beauty as their handicap don't receive such letters . . . It's a wondrous thing that only those constrained by beauty have access to certain essences of man's psychology. Oh, a girl, that receptacle of shame, under beauty's lock and key! It was here, to this sanctuary, that man, whether young or old, brought such things that, rather than have publicized, he would probably prefer to die three times and be roasted over a slow fire . . . And the face of this century—the face of the twentieth century, the century of all centuries gone mad, lurked ambiguously like Silenus in the thicket . . .

There were, among other letters, love letters from pupils in our school, as unpleasant, irritating, irksome, awkward, puerile, deplorable, shameful, and embarrassing as any ever beheld by History—either ancient or medieval. And if some fellow (of the same age as these pupils) from Syria, Babylon, Greece, or medieval Poland, or even a simple pauper from the time of King Sigismund Augustus, ever read them, he'd certainly blush, he might even bash their faces. Oh what horrible cacophonies they emitted! What falsehoods rasped in their love songs! It was as if Nature herself, in her boundless disdain for those wretches, for those stuffed coxcombs, had silenced them in relation to the Girl, unwilling to let the race of those formalists procreate and multiply. And only the letters that out of fear expressed nothing were bearable: *Zuta with Marysia and Olek to the tennis court, tomorrow, give me a call, Heniek*. Only those were not degrading . . . I found Mizdral's and Hopek's letters, two each, their contents vulgar, their form coarse, and aspiring to maturity with incredible hubris. They swarmed like moths to a flame, knowing full well that they would burn . . .

Although the college students' letters were no less timorous, their fear was more deftly disguised. One could see how each student trembled and suffered as he put pen to paper, how watchful he was as he weighed his words in order not to tumble down an incline straight into his own immaturity, down to the calves of his legs. That was why I never found any reference whatsoever to those calves, instead there was a great deal about emotion, about public affairs and social issues, about making a living, bridge playing, and horse racing, even about changing the country's political system. Student politicos in particular, those loudmouths from the "college life," hid their calves with the utmost skill and care as they systematically sent the schoolgirl their programs, appeals, and ideological declarations. *Dear Miss Zuta, perhaps you would like to become acquainted with our program*—they wrote, but in those programs there was nothing clearly stated about the calves of their legs either, unless occasionally there was a *lapsus linguae* when, for example, instead of "onward, don't lag behind," they wrote "onward, don't leg behind." Also some citizens from the town of Lemno made a typo, and instead of "we—Lemnites" wrote "we—Legnites." Aside from these two instances, the calves of their legs never made any appearance. Similarly in magazines, which were otherwise rather lascivious and with the help of which old aunts, writing articles for the press on the subject of "the jazzband era," tried to bond spiritually with the schoolgirl and to restrain her on her downward course to ruin, the calves were very strictly camouflaged. When reading all this, one had the impression that it had nothing to do with the calves of legs.

Furthermore—whole stacks of those minor and now commonplace little volumes of verse, no fewer than three or four hundred, lay scattered about at the bottom of the drawer, and actually—one had to admit—were neither opened nor read by the said schoolgirl. They were furnished with dedications in a personal tone, upright, sincere, honest, that exhorted the girl most vigorously to read their poems, compelled her to read them, censured her in most elaborate and murderous phrases for not reading them, while others extolled and praised her to high heaven for reading them or threatened to exclude her from cultural society for not reading them and demanded that she read them for the sake of the poet's loneliness, the poet's work, the poet's mission, the poet's role, the poet's suffering, the poet's originality, the poet's calling, and even for the sake of the poet's soul. Strangely enough, even in this context there was no mention of the calves of legs. And stranger still, there wasn't an ounce of calves in the titles of these little collections. Only Pale Dawns and Dawning Dawns, and New Dawns, and New Dawning, and Era of Struggle, and Struggle in the Era, and Troublesome Era, and Young Era, and Youth on the Watch, and Youth's Watchfulness, and Struggling Youth, and Youth Advancing, and Youth at a Standstill, and Hey, the Young! and Bitterness of Youth, and Eyes of Youth, and Lips of Youth, and Young Springtime, and My Springtime, and Springtime and I, and Springtime Rhythms, and Machine-gun Rhythm, and Fire a Salute, and Semaphores, and Antennae, Propellers and My Kiss, and My Precious, and My Yearnings, and My Eyes, and My Lips (not a whit about calves of legs anywhere), and everything was written in a poetic tone, in delicate assonance, or without delicate assonance and in bold metaphors, or else with a subterranean melody of words. And yet, almost nothing about calves, or very little, disproportion-ately very little. The authors deftly and with great poetic skill hid behind Beauty, Perfection of Craft, behind Inner Logic of Composi-tion; behind Ironclad Sequence of Associations, or behind Aware-ness of Social Class, Struggle, Dawning of History, and other similar, objective, anti-leg matters. But it was clearly visible at the outset that the little poems, in their convoluted, forced, and useless art, were nothing but a complicated code, and that there must have been a real and not a trifling reason which made those numerous, scrawny, minor-league dreamers compose such odd charades. Therefore, af-ter a moment's profound reflection, I managed to translate the sub-stance of the following stanza into comprehensible language:

Horizons burst like flasks
a green blotch swells high in the clouds
I move back to the shadow of the pine—
and there:
with greedy gulps I drink
                    my diurnal springtime
My Translation
Calves of legs, calves, calves
Calves of legs, calves, calves, calves
Calves of legs, calves, calves, calves, calves—
The calf of my leg:
the calf of my leg, calf, calf,
                    calves, calves, calves.

Furthermore—it was here that the schoolgirl's real pandemonium
began: behind these letters there was a heap of confidential letters
from judges, attorneys, public prosecutors, pharmacists, business-
men, urban and rural citizens, doctors and such—from those high
and mighty who had always impressed me so! I stood there astonished while the fly suffered in silence. Did these men, pretense
notwithstanding, socialize with the schoolgirl? "Unbelievable," I
went on repeating, "unbelievable!" Were they so oppressed by their
Maturity that, unbeknownst to their wives and children, they had to
send long letters to a modern schoolgirl? And here, of course, there
was even less about calves of legs, on the contrary, each one of them
explained in detail his reasons for the "exchange of thoughts," that he
felt that "Miss Zuta" would understand him, that she wouldn't mis-
construe etc., etc. They then went on and paid homage to the modern one in words that were long-winded yet servile, imploring her, in
between the lines, to deign dream about them, in secret, of course.
And each one, not mentioning the calves of his legs, not even once,
underlined and emphasized to the utmost his modern boyishness.

A public prosecutor:

Even though gowned, I am nothing but a messenger boy. I am well disciplined. I do as I'm told. I have no opinions of my own. It's the chief justice's prerogative to rebuke me. He recently called me an ignoramus.

A politico was assuring her:

I'm a just a boy, a purely political boy, a history-making boy.

A noncommissioned officer with an exceptionally sensuous and lyrical soul wrote as follows:

I am bound by blind obedience. I must lay down my life on command. I'm a slave. Indeed—our leaders call us "boys," regardless of our age. Don't believe my birth certificate, that's a purely extraneous detail, my wife and children are mere appendages, I am no knight in shining armor, just a military boy, with a boy's blind and faithful soul, and in the barracks I'm just a dog, a dog!

A landowning citizen:

I've gone bankrupt, my wife has taken on housecleaning, my children have gone to the dogs—I'm no citizen, I'm a boy in exile. Secretly, I'm in a state of bliss.

Nevertheless, calves of legs were not mentioned *en toutes lettres*, not even once. In their postscripts they begged the schoolgirl for secrecy, pointing out that their careers would be ruined forever if a single word of these confidences were to become public.

This is for You alone. Keep it to yourself. Don't tell anyone!

Unbelievable! These letters made me finally realize the extent of the modern schoolgirl's power. Where wasn't it present? Inside whose head were the calves of her legs not stuck? And, as I thought about it all, my legs also trembled, and I would have danced in honor of those aging Boys of the twentieth century who had been drilled and driven, egged on and flogged with a whip, when suddenly, at the bottom of the drawer, I noticed a large envelope from the school superintendent's office, addressed quite obviously in Pimko's handwriting! The letter was dry and blunt.

I will no longer tolerate, Pimko wrote, *your disregard and out-rageous ignorance of matters pertaining to the school curriculum.*

I summon you to present yourself in my study—at the superinten-dent's office, the day after tomorrow, Friday at 4:30 P.M., the objective being explanation, lecturing, and tutoring you on Norwid, to fill this gap in your education.

Please note that I am summoning you legally, formally, officially, and with all due civility, as your professor and educator, but, in case of any recalcitrance on your part, I shall write a letter to the dean of girls suggesting your dismissal from school.

I wish to point out that I can no longer tolerate the said gap and, as your Professor, I have a right not to. Please comply.

T. Pimko, Ph.D. and Professor Honoris Causa
Warsaw . . .

So that's how far it has gone between them? He was threatening her, was he? Really? She had wooed and courted him with her igno-rance until she forced the prof to show his claws. Pimko, unable to make a date with the schoolgirl as Pimko, was summoning her in his capacity as professor of middle and higher education. He was no longer satisfied with frolicking with her only in her home, under her parents' eyes—he was now taking advantage of the authority of his status, he wanted to force Norwid on the girl by entirely legitimate means. Since he could not do it in any other way, he was going to use Norwid so that he could play a prominent part in her life. I was astonished as I held his letter in my hand, I stood over the pile of papers not knowing whether the revelation was, for me, bad news or good. However, under his letter there was in the drawer yet another sheet of paper—torn out of a notebook, a few sentences in pencil— and I recognized Kopyrda's handwriting! Yes, it was Kopyrda's, no doubt about it, it was Kopyrda's, no one else's! I feverishly grabbed the note. It was concise, crumpled up, careless—which meant that it had been tossed through the window.

I forgot to give you my address (here followed Kopyrda's address). *If you want me, I want you too. Let me know. H. K.*

Kopyrda! Remember Kopyrda? Oh, I instantly understood it all! My hunch had been right! Kopyrda was the strange boy who had accosted the schoolgirl, he was the subject of conversation at lunchtime! Kopyrda had tossed the note through her window as he passed by a little while ago. He had accosted the girl in the street, and now, lo and behold, he was enlarging on his proposition—how daring, and modern at that! "If you want me, I want you too"—he went straight to the point, propositioning her tersely, matter-of-factly . . . He saw her in the street, was drawn to her sexually and . . . he started talking to her—and now he tossed in the note as he passed under her window, not standing on ceremony, according to youth's new customs . . . Kopyrda! And she—she didn't even know his last name, because he hadn't introduced himself to her . . .

Something caught me by the throat.

And there was also Pimko, old Pimko, who, like a true gentleman, was openly, legally, formally, and officially coercing her with his professorship. "You must, you must satisfy me through Norwid, because I am your lord and master, your Professor, you are my slave—you, a schoolgirl! . . ." The other one had the right to her as her modern brother and her contemporary, while this one had his right as an educator at the high-school level, a licensed pedagogue . . .

Something caught me by the throat again. All the confessions of the citizens, the attorneys' moans, and the ridiculous, poetic charades were nothing in the face of these two letters. These two were the harbingers of calamity and defeat. The threat, the real danger was that the girl was about to submit to Pimko and to Kopyrda without any feelings, on the strength of custom alone, just because they each had a right—modern and private in one case, old-fashioned and public in the other. Yet this intensified her charm immensely . . . and neither my dancing nor my working on the fly would have saved me, she would have choked me with her charms. What if she lets Kopyrda lay her—calmly, unsentimentally, physically, in the modern way . . . Or what if, obeying the prof's orders, she goes to Pimko . . . Is she the kind of girl who goes to an old man just because she's a schoolgirl? . . . Is she the kind of girl who goes to bed with a young man just because she's modern? . . .

Oh, this cult, this obedience, the girl's slavery just because she is a schoolgirl and because she's modern! Addressing her so harshly and tersely they both knew what they were doing, they knew that the girl would, f o r   t h i s   v e r y   r e a s o n, be ready to accede . . . The experienced Pimko surely did not expect her to be scared by his threats, on the contrary—he counted on her being charmed by the idea of submitting, under duress, to an old man—almost as charming as submitting to a young man simply because he spoke to her in a modern tongue. Oh, this was slavery to the point of self-effacement for the sake of style, what o b e d i e n c e on the girl's part! I knew that the unavoidable was about to happen . . . And then . . . what would I do, where would I take shelter . . . how would I protect myself . . . against this incoming tide and freshet? Yet note how strange it all was. They were both actually destroying the Young-blood girl's modern charms: Pimko wanted to annihilate her sporty ignorance of poetry, and in Kopyrda's case—worse still, it could end up with—mommy. Yet the actual moment of her (possibly) being destroyed enhanced her charms a hundredfold. Why had I looked in her drawer? Ignorance is bliss. If only I had remained ignorant—I could have continued my activity against the schoolgirl as planned. But now I knew it all—and this weakened me terribly.

These were the penetrating, piercing secrets of the seventeen-year-old's private life, the demonic contents of the schoolgirl's drawer. Poetry . . . How to contaminate it? How to spoil it for oneself? The fly continued to suffer, immobile, voiceless. The bearded man continued to chew the twig. Holding these letters in my hand, I wondered what course of action to take, what to do next, how was I to cope with the inevitable yet frightful surge of charm, beauty, enchantment, longing . . .

Finally, in all my madness, an idea for a plot dawned on me—it was so bizarre that until I began to carry it out, it seemed unreal. I tore a sheet out of a notebook. I took a pencil and, in the Youngblood girl's clear, sprawling handwriting, I wrote:

Tomorrow, Thursday, at 12 midnight, knock on the verandah window, I'll let you in. Z.

I placed it in an envelope. I addressed it to Kopyrda. And I wrote a second, identical letter:

Tomorrow, Thursday, after 12 midnight, knock on the verandah window, I'll let you in. Z.

I addressed it to Pimko. The plan was this: Pimko, having received such a terse, informal little note in response to his professorial letter, will lose his head. It will be like a knock on the old man's head. He'll imagine that the schoolgirl wants to have a *sensu stricto* date with him. The sheer audacity, cynicism, moral depravity, demonic quality of it all—considering his age, social class, and upbringing—will intoxicate him like hashish. He won't be able to maintain his role as a professor—he won't be able to persist in his legality and openness. Secretly and illegally he'll make haste to the window, and he'll knock. He will then run into Kopyrda.

What then? I didn't know. But I knew that I'd scream, wake up the family, drag the whole matter into the open, that by using Kopyrda I would ridicule Pimko, and by using Pimko I would ridicule Kopyrda—we would then see what the wooing would look like out in the open, what would then be left of those charms!

10 Legs on the Loose
and New Entrapment

Next morning, after a stormy night tormented by dreams, I jumped out of bed at the crack of dawn. Not to school, however. I hid behind a coat rack in a small vestibule that separated the kitchen from the bathroom. Following a relentless call to battle, I decided to attack the Youngbloods psychologically, in the bathroom. Hail, pupa! Hail, queen! I needed to muster all my resources and energize my spirit for the final encounter with Pimko and with Kopyrda. I trembled, sweating—yet a struggle for life and death cannot choose its means, I could not afford to lose my trump card. Catch your enemy in the bathroom. Look at him and see what he's like then! Look him over and remember him! When his attire falls off, and with it, like an autumn leaf, all his glitter and pretense of chic, swank, and pizzazz, your spirit can pounce on him like a lion pounces on a lamb. You mustn't overlook anything that might arouse and energize you, thus enabling you to overpower the enemy, the goal sanctifies the means, so fight, fight, fight above all, fight using the latest methods available, nothing but fight! That's what the wisdom of nations has always proclaimed. The entire household was asleep as I lay in wait. No murmurs came from the girl's room, she slept without rustling while Mr. Youngblood, the engineer, in his light-blue bedroom, snored like an official from the provinces or some other dunce . . .

The housemaid begins puttering around the kitchen, sleepy voices are waking, the family is getting up for their morning ablutions and other rituals. I strained all my senses. My spirit gone wild, I was like a wild civilized animal in a *Kulturkampf*. The cock crowed. The first to appear was the Youngblood woman in her pale gray dressing gown and slippers, her hair brushed down a bit. She walked calmly, her head raised, her face lit with a particular wisdom, I'd say, the wisdom of plumbing. She even walked with a certain reverence in the name of sacred naturalness and simplicity, and in the name of rational morning hygiene. Before she entered the bathroom, she veered into the john for a minute where, her brow raised high, she vanished—wisely, consciously, intelligently, and with culture—like a woman who knows better than to be ashamed of her natural functions. S h e c a m e   o u t   m o r e   p r o u d   t h a n   s h e   w e n t   i n, as if—strengthened, made brighter, made human, she emerged as if from a Greek temple! I then understood that she had also entered it as if it were a temple. It was indeed a temple from which modern Mrs. Engineers and Mrs. Attorneys ladled up their power! Every day she came out of this place better, more cultured, wielding high the banner of progress, here was the source of the intelligence and the naturalness with which she tormented me. Enough said. She crossed over into the bathroom. The cock crowed.

And then Mr. Youngblood ran up at a trot, in his robe, clearing his throat noisily and hawking, all done briskly, not to be late for the office, with his newspaper, to save time, glasses on his nose, towel round his neck, cleaning his fingernails with a fingernail, clapping his slippers, and whimsically flashing his bare soles. Noticing the door to the john he giggled with his backyard, backside giggle, same as yesterday, then he sashayed into the john like an engineer and a working member of the intelligentsia, coy, jocular, amazingly witty.

Legs on the Loose and New Entrapment

He lingered there a long time, smoked a cigarette and sang the *carioca,* but he came out thoroughly demoralized, a typical intelligentsia yokel, his mug so facetiously cretinlike, so disgustingly gross and offensively muttonlike that I would have pounced on that mug of his had I not forcibly restrained myself.* What a strange thing— the toilet had worked on his wife constructively, whereas on him it seemed to work destructively, even though he was a construction design engineer.

"Hurry up!" he called lasciviously to his wife, who was washing herself in the bathroom. "Hurry up, old girl! Vicky is in a hurry to get to the office!"

It was the visit to the toilet that made him call himself Vicky, in the diminutive, he then left, towel in hand. I cautiously peeked into the bathroom through a chink in the frosted glass. Mrs. Engineer, naked, was wiping her thigh with a bath towel, while her face, of darker complexion, sharp and wise-looking, hung over the fatty-white, calf-like, innocent, hopeless calf of her leg like a vulture over a calf. And here was a terrible antithesis, it seemed that the eagle was helplessly circling, unable to seize the calf that was bleating to high heaven: this was Mrs. Engineer Youngblood, hygienically and intelligently beholding her old woman's hunk of a leg. She jumped. She assumed a position for aerobics, hands on her hips, and she made a half-turn with her torso from right to left, inhaling and exhaling. Then from left to right, exhaling and inhaling! She thrust one leg up—her foot was petite and pink. Then the other leg with the other foot! She set off into sit-ups! She executed twelve sit-ups in front of the mirror, breathing through her nose—one, two, three, four, so that her boobs clapped and even my legs twitched, and I was tempted to begin a cultural, hellish prance. But instead, I jumped behind the coat rack. The schoolgirl was approaching with light steps, I lay in ambush as in a jungle, all set for a psychological pounce, gone bestial . . .

*A very popular tune in the 1930s from the film *Carioca.*

inhumanly, more than inhumanly bestial . . . Now or never, nab her right out of sleep, while she's still warm and untidy, disheveled, I'll destroy her beauty within me, her cheap, schoolgirl charms! We'll see whether Kopyrda or Pimko can save her from annihilation!

She walked whistling, she looked funny in her pajamas, a towel round her neck—all with a quick, precise motion, all action. One moment and she was in the bathroom, and I pounced on her with my eyes from my hiding place. Now, now or never, now, when she's her weakest, her most sloppy self!—but she was so quick that no sloppiness could cling fast to her. She stepped into the bathtub—turned on the cold shower. She shook her curls, her well-proportioned nudity trembled, ducking and splashing in the stream of water. Ha! So it wasn't I who caught her, it was she who caught me by the throat! The girl, unforced by anyone, first thing in the morning, before breakfast, took a cold shower and subjected her body to spasms and twitches so that she could, with a youthful splashing on an empty stomach, regain her daytime beauty!

In spite of myself I had to admire the discipline that was involved in the girl's good looks! With all swiftness, precision, and dexterity she managed to dodge that most difficult transition—between night and day—and she floated like a butterfly on motion's wings. And if that weren't enough—she subjected her body to cold water, to a sharp and youthful splashing, instinctively sensing that a dose of sharpness would annihilate anything slovenly. When all is said and done—what could harm a girl vigorously puffing in cold water? When she turned off the faucet and stood naked, dripping with water, panting, she began as if anew, as if the other had never been. Hey!—if instead of cold water she had used soap and warm water, it would have served no purpose. Only cold water could, by gushing, force oblivion.

I crept out of the vestibule like a sleaze. I dragged my despicable self back to my room, convinced that further peeping would accomplish nothing, on the contrary, it might prove disastrous. Damn it, damn—

yet another defeat, at the very bottom of intelligentsia hell I was still suffering defeat. Biting my fingers until they bled, I swore to deny the Youngbloods victory, to go on driving and energizing myself, and I wrote in pencil on the bathroom wall: *Veni, vidi, vici.* Let them know I had seen them, let them feel that they've been seen! Their enemy is not asleep, he lies in ambush. Energize, vitalize! I went to school, nothing new there, Ashface, the bard, Mizdral, Hopek and *accusativus cum infinitivo,* Gałkiewicz, faces, mugs, pupas, the toe in my shoe, and the daily universal impotence, boring, boring, boring! As I had expected, my letter left no mark on Kopyrda's face, he seemed to wiggle his legs a little more, but I wasn't sure, I could have been imagining it. My schoolmates, however, looked at me in disgust, Kneadus even asked:

"For God's sake, what sort of a mess have you got yourself into?"

Indeed, after all this dynamizing and energizing, my mug became so dumb that I didn't really know which end was up, but never mind, forget it, soon it would be night, it was the night that mattered most, I awaited the night in trembling, the night would settle it all, the night would decide. Perhaps the night would bring a turning point. Will Pimko yield to the temptation? Will the seasoned, double-barreled prof be thrown off balance by the girl's sensuous letter? Everything depended on it. Let Pimko lose his balance, I prayed, lose his head, but suddenly, terrified by the mug, the pupa, by my letter, by Pimko, by what had been and what was yet to be, I tried to make a run for it, I kept jumping to my feet in the classroom, like a complete idiot—then I sat down again—because where would I run, backward, forward, to the left or right, from my own mug, from my own pupa? Shut up, shut up, there's no escape! The night will decide.

During lunch nothing noteworthy happened. The schoolgirl and Mrs. Engineer were tight-lipped, not throwing about their modernity, as they usually did. They were scared. They must have felt my energy and vitality. I noticed that the Youngblood woman sat stiffly in her chair, with the dignity of someone whose sitting was under surveillance, funny, this gave her a matronly air, I had not expected this effect. In any case there was no doubt that she had read my inscription on the wall. I watched her keenly, and I made the remark, in a miserable, sleazy, and detached tone, that I was noted for an exceptionally sharp and piercing vision, which is able to go right through a face and exit on the other side . . . She pretended not to hear me, while the engineer burst into giggles in spite of himself, and he went on giggling for a long time, mechanically. As a result of recent events Mr. Younblood manifested—if my eyes did not mislead me—a tendency to messiness, he spread butter on large slices of bread and stuck huge pieces into his mouth, making smacking noises as he chewed.

After lunch I tried peeping at the schoolgirl from four until six o'clock—to no avail, however, because not once did she come into the perimeter of my vision. She must have been on her guard. I also noticed that the Youngblood woman was spying on me, because she walked into my room several times with some lame excuse, she even suggested, rather artlessly, that she would treat me to the movies. Their anxiety grew, they felt threatened, they scented enemy and danger, although they didn't know what was threatening them, nor what I was up to—they caught the scent and were demoralized by it, its shapelessness provoked anxiety that, in turn, gave them nothing concrete to hold on to. And they couldn't even talk among themselves about the danger, because their words sank into a shapeless and ill-defined darkness. Groping her way, Mrs. Engineer tried to organize some sort of defense, and, as I found out, she spent the whole afternoon reading Bertrand Russell and gave her husband Wells to read. But Mr. Youngblood declared that he preferred reading the yearbook of "The Warsaw Figaro" and Boy Żeleński's *Words*, and from time to time I heard him burst out laughing. All in all, they couldn't settle down. Finally, Mrs. Youngblood decided to busy herself with household bills, thus retreating to the solid ground of fiscal realism, while the engineer hung around the house, sat down on one piece of furniture, then on another, all the while humming rather frivolous tunes. It bothered them that I sat in my room, not showing any signs of life. I therefore tried all the more to keep silent. Quiet, quiet, quiet, every so often the silence mounted in intensity and the buzzing of a fly sounded like the blowing of a horn, shapelessness seeped into the silence, creating murky swamps. Around seven o'clock I saw Kneadus slipping between the fence posts toward the housemaid, signaling in the direction of the kitchen window.

By evening, Mrs. Engineer also began flitting from one chair to another, and the engineer had a few nips in the pantry. They couldn't find the right form nor space for themselves, they couldn't sit still, they kept sitting down and jumping back up as if prodded with a hot poker, and they walked hither and thither tense and wrought up, as if pursued from behind. Their reality, under the powerful stimulus of my action, was swept off its course, it bubbled and spilled over, roared and groaned numbly, while the dark, absurd elements of ugliness, of disgust and sordidness became more and more tangible and grew on their rising anxiety as if on yeast. Mrs. Engineer could hardly sit at dinner, all her concentration having gone into her face and upper regions, while Mr. Youngblood, on the contrary, came to the table wearing just his vest without a jacket, he tucked the napkin under his chin and, buttering thick slices of bread that he had gnawed off, he told quasi-intellectual jokes and giggled. The awareness that he had been spied upon tumbled him into vulgar infantilism, he totally attuned to what I saw in him, he became a petty, coquettish, amused little engineer—a jolly, cuddlesome, spoiled little engineer. He also kept winking at me and sending me witty, knowing little signals to which—of course—I didn't respond, and I sat looking pale and miserable. The girl sat tight-lipped, indifferent, she ignored everything with truly girlish heroism, one could swear she knew nothing—oh, I was frightened as I watched that heroism, which only enhanced her beauty! But night will give the verdict, night will decide, and if both Pimko and Kopyrda default, the modern girl will most certainly be victorious, and nothing will save me from slavery.

Night was coming, and with it the decisive encounter. I couldn't foresee what would happen, there was no set program, all I knew was that I had to act in unison with each disfiguring, absurd, murky, grotesque, and disharmonious element that would emerge, with each destructive component—and I was steeped in a rancid, sickly terror, compared to which the powerful fear of being murdered is a mere trifle. After eleven o'clock the schoolgirl went to bed. Earlier in the day I had used a chisel to widen the angle of sight through the slit in the door, and now I could see that part of the room which, so far, had been inaccessible to my vision. She quickly undressed and turned off the light, but instead of going to sleep she tossed and turned on the hard mattress. She lit a lamp, picked up an English crime novel from her bedside table, and I could tell that she was forcing herself to read. The modern one looked attentively into space as if visually trying to decipher the danger, to guess its shape and see at last the configuration of horror, to realistically understand what was brewing against her. She didn't know that the danger had neither shape nor sense—senseless, shapeless, and lawless, a murky, jumbled-up, elemental force devoid of style was endangering her modern shape, and that was all.

I heard raised voices coming from Mr. and Mrs. Engineer's bedroom. I quickly ran to their door. The engineer, in his underwear, all a-giggle, cabaret-style, was again telling anecdotes aimed at having the distinct flavor of the intelligentsia.

"That's enough!" The Youngblood woman rubbed her hands. "Enough, enough! Stop it!"

"Wait, wait, Joannie—just a little more . . . I'll soon stop!"

"I'm no Joannie. I am Joanna. Take off those underpants, or put on your pants."

"Panties!"

"Shut up!"

"Panties, shmanties, hee, hee, hee, panties!"

"Shut up, I tell you . . ."

"Panties, pants . . ."

"Shut up!" she abruptly switched off the lamp.

"Switch it on, old girl!"

"I'm no old girl . . . I can't bear to look at you! Why did I ever fall in love with you? What's the matter with you? What's the matter with us? Get hold of yourself. We're surely marching together to the New Days ahead! We are the champions of Modern Times!"

"Sure, sure, you fat fish—hee, hee, hee—you're my dish. Fatty, creamy, yet so dreamy. But his heart has ceased to thump, 'cause she's turned into a frump . . ."*

"What's this? Victor! What are you saying?"

"Vicky is so cheery! Vicky's having fun! Vicky frisks at a trot!"

"What are you saying, Victor? The death penalty!" she exclaimed, "the death penalty! Our Era! Culture and progress! Our aspirations! Our transports! Victor! oh, not so fatty, not so racy, not so diminutive either . . . What has entangled you? Zuta? Oh, this is so hard! Something's wrong! Something fateful is in the air! Treachery . . ."

"Treachy-reachy-rie," Mr. Youngblood said.

"Victor! Stop using diminutives! Stop it!"

"Treachy-letchy-rie, Vicky says . . ."

"Victor!"

They broke into a free-for-all!

"The light," the Youngblood woman panted, "Victor! The light! Switch it on! Let go of me!"

"Wait!" he panted and giggled, "wait, let me smack you, let me give you a smack in the scruff of your neckie!"

"Never! Let go, or I'll bite you!"

*Based on excerpts from Boy Żeleński's *Words*.

Legs on the Loose and New Entrapment

"I'll smack you, smack you in the little scruff of your neckie, your scruffie, your little scruffie . . ."

And he suddenly spat out all the bedroom love diminutives, beginning with sweetie-pie all the way to little pussy . . . I retreated in fear. Even though I lacked none of my own disgusting jargon, I couldn't bear this. The hellish b e l i t t l e m e n t that had so powerfully affected my fate was now making their life miserable. This was the little engineer's devilish excess, oh, it's horrible when a petty engineer takes the bit between his teeth, what are these times we live in? I heard a smack. Did he hit her in her little scruffie or slap her in the face?

It was dark in the girl's room. Was she asleep? All was quiet in her room, and I imagined her sleeping with her arm over her head, halfway under the covers, all worn out. Suddenly she groaned. She groaned but not in her sleep. She moved abruptly, anxiously on her couch. I knew she was huddling up and that her wide-open eyes were fearfully searching in the darkness. Had the modern schoolgirl become so sensitized that my gaze could strike her in the darkness through the keyhole? Her groan was incredibly beautiful, torn out of the depths of night—as if the girl's ill-boding fate itself had groaned, calling for help in vain.

I heard her groan again, numbly, desperately. Had she sensed that at this very moment her father, depraved by me, was smacking her mother? Had she become aware of the odiousness that was besetting her on all sides? I thought I saw her in the semi-darkness, wringing her hands and gnawing on her forearm until it hurt. As if she wanted to grab with her teeth the beauty within. The depravity surrounding her and lurking from all corners excited her charms. What treasures, what charms she possessed! The first treasure—the girl. The second treasure—the schoolgirl. The third treasure—modern. And it was all locked up in her like a nut within a shell, but she couldn't reach her arsenal, even though she felt my heinous gaze, and knew that a spurned admirer would naturally want to befoul, ruin, destroy, and psychologically deface her girlish beauty.

And I was not at all surprised that the girl, sensing the threat that I secretly wished her to become ugly, went berserk. She jumped out of bed. She threw off her nightshirt. She pranced all over the room. She no longer cared that I was spying on her, indeed, she seemed to be challenging me to a fight. Her legs nimbly and lightly lifted her body, her hands fluttered in the air. She tucked her little head this way and that. She enfolded her head in her arms. She shook her curls. She lay on the floor, then rose again. She sobbed, she laughed, she sang softly. She jumped on the table, from the table onto the couch. She seemed scared to stop even for a moment as if chased by rats and mice, as if eager for the lightness of her movement to lift her above all horror. She no longer knew what to hold on to. She finally grabbed a belt and began whipping her back with all her might, anything to subject herself to youthful pain . . . Something caught me by the throat! Oh, how her beauty tormented her, drove her to do things, hurled and threw her about, rolled her around! I stood dead still by the keyhole, my mug absurd and loathsome, equally split between rapture and hate. The schoolgirl, hurled about by her beauty, turned into a hellion. All the while I adored her and hated her, I quivered with delight, my mug spasmodically expanding and contracting like stretched gutta-percha, my God, so this is where love of beauty will drive us!

Midnight struck in the dining room. There was a quiet knocking on the window. Three times. I froze in fear. The whole thing was about to begin. Kopyrda, Kopyrda was here! The schoolgirl stopped jumping about. The knocking repeated, insistent, quiet. She went to the window and pulled back the blind slightly. She stared . . .

"Is that you? . . ." a whisper came from the porch in the night's silence.

She pulled on the string of the blind. Moonlight poured into the room. I saw her standing in her nightshirt now, tense, watchful . . .

"What do you want?" she asked.

I admired her command of the situation, the magpie that she was! Because this was a surprise—she hadn't expected Kopyrda to arrive at her window. Another girl in her place, an old-fashioned one, would have gone on with trite questions and exclamations: "I beg your pardon! What's the meaning of this? What do you want at this hour?" But this modern one sensed instinctively that to show surprise would have ruined it . . . that it would be more beautiful without surprise . . . Oh, mistress of the situation! She leaned out the window unceremoniously, cordially, like a good sport.

"What do you want?" resting her chin on her arms, she repeated in the subdued tone of a young female.

Since he had addressed her informally, she replied in kind. And I admired the unbelievably abrupt transition in style—from jumping up and down into sociability! Who would have guessed that only a moment ago she had been jumping and throwing herself about? Modern though he was himself, Kopyrda was somewhat put off by the schoolgirl's remarkable matter-of-factness. Yet he immediately tuned in to her tone and, boyishly, nonchalantly, with his hands in his pockets, he said:

"Let me in."

"What for?"

He whistled and said rudely:

"Don't you know? Let me in!"

He seemed excited, and his voice trembled slightly, but he tried to hide his excitement. All the while I shuddered at the thought that he might spill the whole thing about the letter. Luckily, talking a lot or being terribly surprised wouldn't be in keeping with the modern way, they had to pretend that it all went without saying. Nonchalance, brutality, terseness, disdain—this was poetry, just as sighing, moaning, and mandolins would have been to lovers of yore. He knew that the only way to possess the girl would be with disdain, that without disdain—nothing doing. His face was in the vines that were creeping up the wall, and with a hint of sensuous, modern sentimentalism in his voice he added longingly, emphatically, numbly:

"You wanted it!"

She made a move to close the window. But suddenly—as if this move actually provoked her to do the opposite—she stopped . . . She tightened her lips. She stood still for a second, only her eyes moving from side to side, slowly. The expression that came over her face was . . . an expression of supermodern cynicism . . . And the schoolgirl, excited by the expression of cynicism, by eyes and lips in the moonlight, in the window, suddenly leaned out halfway, and with her palm—nothing humorous in her gesture—she tousled his hair.

"Come in!" she whispered.

Kopyrda showed no surprise. This was no time to show surprise at her or at himself. The slightest hesitancy would have ruined everything. He had to act as if the reality that they were creating between them were something ordinary, everyday. Oh, what a master! And so he acted accordingly. He clambered onto the windowsill and jumped to the floor of her room exactly as if he were in the habit of clambering every night to visit a newly met schoolgirl. Once in the room he laughed softly, just to be on the safe side. She, however, took him by the hair, pulled back his head and with her lips devoured his lips!

The devil, the devil of it! What if she's still a virgin?! What if the girl is still a virgin?! What if she's a virgin, and she's about to give herself without ceremony to the first man who knocks on her window. The devil of it, the devil! Something caught me by the throat. Because, if she were an ordinary tart and a slut, well, no harm done, but if she's a virgin, then—I must admit—this modern one was able to elicit incredibly wild beauty from within herself and from Kopyrda. To be able—so impudently and quietly, so brutally and effortlessly—to grab the boy by the hair—and to grab me by the throat . . . Ha! She knew I was peeping through the keyhole, and she stopped at nothing as long as she was victorious through her beauty. I was shaken. If only it were he who grabbed her by the hair—but it was she who grabbed him by the hair! Hey, you young ladies, marrying with pomp and after much ado, you trite ones, who allow a stolen kiss, look how this modern one goes after love and how she treats her own self! She threw Kopyrda onto the couch. I was shaken again. No holds barred! The seventeen-year-old obviously played her beauty as her trump card. I prayed that Pimko would arrive—if Pimko lets me down I'm lost, never, never will I be free of this modern one's wild charms. She was choking me, strangling me, yet all along it was I—I was the one, when all was said and done, who wanted to strangle her, to conquer her!

Her girlhood in full bloom, she and Kopyrda meanwhile went on hugging each other on the couch, and, with his help, she was about to reach the climax of her charms. Casually, slapdash, lustfully, and without love, without any respect for herself, just to grab me by the throat with her wild, schoolgirl poetry. The devil of it, the devil, she was winning, winning, winning!

At last there was a godsend knock on the window. They stopped hugging. At last! Pimko was coming to the rescue. This was to be the final reckoning. Will Pimko manage to spoil her beauty and her charms—or will he enhance it all? That's what I was thinking as I was preparing my mug behind the door to intervene. For the moment Pimko's knocking brought relief because they had to stop their orgy and frenzy, and Kopyrda whispered:

"Someone's knocking."

The schoolgirl jumped to her feet from the couch. They listened, wondering whether they could resume their frenzy. More knocking.

"Who is it?" she asked.

There was ardent puffing and huffing at the window:

"Zuta, dear!"

She pulled back the blind slightly, signaling to Kopyrda to step back. But before she could say anything Pimko frantically clambered into the room. He was afraid of being seen at the window.

"Zuta, dear!" he whispered passionately, carnally, "little Zuta! Oh, my schoolgirl! Oh, little one! Call me by my first name! You're my colleague! I'm your colleague!" My letter must have gone to his head. The double-barreled and trite prof's lips were painfully contorted with poetry. "Yes, by my first name, Zuta, dear! Will anyone see us? Where's Mama?" But the danger was intoxicating him even further. "Look at her . . . such a little one, so young . . . yet so insolent . . . with no regard for age or status . . . How could you . . . how dare you . . . toward me? Do you find me exciting? Call me by my first name! Yes, yes! Tell me what you fancy in me."

Ha, ha, ha, ha, ha, what a lustful pedagogue!

"What do you want? What's the matter with you, sir? . . ." she stammered. The other matter, with Kopyrda, was over, it came to naught.

"Someone's here!" exclaimed Pimko in the semi-darkness.

Silence was the only response. Kopyrda was mum. The modern one stood between the two of them in her nightshirt, senselessly, playing the little la-di-da.

Whereupon I screamed from behind the door:

"Thieves! Thieves!"

Pimko twirled around a couple of times as if pulled by a string, then ran for cover to the closet. Kopyrda tried to jump out the window, but he didn't make it and hid in the other closet. I ran into the room as I was, just in my shirt and underpants. I caught them! Red-handed! Behind me the Youngbloods, he—still smacking her, she—being smacked.

"Thieves?!" he shouted like a bourgeois, dime-a-dozen little engineer, barefoot, in his underpants, his sense of ownership riding high.

"Someone came in through the window!" I exclaimed. I turned on the light. The schoolgirl lay under her comforter, pretending to be asleep.

"What happened?" she asked half-asleep, her style perfect, deceitful.

"Yet another intrigue!" exclaimed the Youngblood woman, in her nightgown, casting a basilisk glance at me, her hair a mess, dark blotches on her cheeks.

"Intrigue?" I exclaimed, picking Kopyrda's suspenders up off the floor. "What intrigue?"

"Suspenders," the little engineer said numbly.

"They're mine!" the Youngblood girl exclaimed insolently. The girl's insolence had a soothing effect, but of course no one believed her!

I jerked open the closet door, and Kopyrda's lower body appeared to those assembled—a pair of lean legs in pressed flannel pants, wearing lightweight sport shoes. His upper body was wrapped in dresses hanging in the closet.

"Aah . . . Zuta!" the Youngblood woman was the first to speak.

The schoolgirl tucked her cute little head under the covers, only her legs and the mop of her hair showing. How skillfully she played it! Another girl in her place would have mumbled something under her breath, would have looked for excuses. But this one just stuck out her naked legs, moving her legs to and fro and playing on the situation—with her legs, with her movement and charm—as on a flute. Her parents looked at each other.

"Zuta," Mr. Youngblood said.

And they both began laughing. All the smacking, vulgarity, and vileness left them, and a strange beauty set in. The parents—amused, animated, thrilled, quite at ease, and laughing indulgently—looked at the girl's body while she went on fussing and timidly hiding her pretty little head. Kopyrda, realizing that he need not fear the strict principles of yore, came out of the closet and stood smiling, jacket in hand, a nice, fair-haired modern boy, caught in the act with the parents' girl. The Youngblood woman squinted at me maliciously. She was triumphant. I must have been jinxed. I wanted to dishonor the girl, yet the modern boy had not dishonored her at all! To make me feel totally superfluous, she asked:

"And what are you, young man, doing here? Our young man shouldn't be concerned with all this!"

Thus far I had deliberately refrained from opening the closet where Pimko was hiding. My intent was to let the situation stabilize until it reached the fullness of the young and modern style. I now opened the closet in silence. Pimko, crouching, had hidden himself between the dresses—only a pair of legs, a professorial pair of legs in crumpled trousers was visible, and those legs stood in the closet, incredible, crazy, tacked on . . .

The effect knocked them out of their socks, bowled them over. The laughter died on the Youngbloods' lips. The whole situation shook as if struck from the side by a murderer's knife. Idiotic indeed.

"What is this?" whispered Mrs. Youngblood, her face paling.

From behind the dresses came a little cough and a conventional tittering with which Pimko prepared his entrance into the room. Since he knew that in a moment he would appear foolish, he was ushering in his tomfoolery with foolish laughter. The tittering from behind the girl's dresses was so cabaretlike that Mr. Youngblood chuckled once and got stuck . . . Pimko stepped out of the closet and bowed, feeling foolish outwardly, miserable inwardly . . . I felt a vindictive, furious sadism inwardly, but outwardly—I burst out laughing. My revenge dissolved in laughter.

But the Youngbloods were dumbfounded. Two men, one in each closet! What's more, in one of them—an old man. If there were two young ones! Or, for that matter, two old ones. But no, one young and one old. An old man, and Pimko to boot. The situation had no axis— no diagonals—no commentary could be found to fit the situation. They automatically looked at the girl, but the schoolgirl played possum under the covers.

Suddenly Pimko, wanting to clarify the situation, cleared his throat, grinned pleadingly, and began to explain something about a letter . . . that Miss Zuta had written to him . . . that it was just about Norwid . . . but that Miss Zuta wanted it to be informal . . . informal . . . on first-name basis . . . with him . . . that's all he wanted too . . . Well, I've never heard anything so obscene and at the same time so idiotic in my whole life, the little old man's secret and private ravings were impossible to understand in a situation so clearly illuminated by the ceiling lamp, but no one wanted to understand him anyway, so no one understood. Pimko saw that no one wanted to, but he'd gone too far already—the prof thrown off balance as a prof was utterly lost, I couldn't believe that it was the same absolute and seasoned double-barreled man who had once dealt me the pupa. As he was drowning in the sticky mess of his explanations, his ineffectiveness evoked pity, and I would have pounced on him, but I gave up. Pimko's dark and murky ravings pushed the engineer into officialdom—and this was stronger than the legitimate distrust the engineer would have felt for me in this situation. He exclaimed:

"What are you doing here, sir, at this hour, may I ask?"

This in turn dictated the tone to Pimko. For a brief moment he was back to form.

"Do not raise your voice, sir."

To which Mr. Youngblood replied:

"What? What? You dare correct me in my own house?"

But Mrs. Engineer looked out the window and squeaked. The bearded face, twig in mouth, appeared above the railing. I had totally forgotten about the beggar! I ordered him to stand with the twig today as well, but I forgot to give him the zloty. The bearded man steadfastly stood until nightfall, and when he saw us in the illuminated window he showed his "face for hire" and, decked in greenery, reminded me to pay him! The face slid between us as if on a platter.

"What does this man want?" exclaimed Mrs. Engineer. The sight of a ghost wouldn't have had a greater impact. Pimko and Mr. Youngblood fell silent.

The wretch, who for a moment became the center of attention, moved the twig as if it were his mustache, he didn't know what to say. So he said:

"A favor for the beggar."

"Give him something," Mrs. Engineer dropped her hands and spread her fingers wide. "Give him something," she screamed hysterically, "so he'll go away . . ."

The engineer fumbled for change in his pockets but didn't find any. Pimko, clutching at every possible activity, quickly took out his wallet, and, perhaps reckoning that, in the general confusion, Mr. Youngblood would accept the change from him, which of course would make further hostilities rather difficult—but Mr. Youngblood did not accept. Petty accounting tore in through the window and raged among people. As for me, I stood there with my mug, carefully watching the unfolding of events, ready to jump, but actually I watched it all as if through a magnifying glass. Oh, whatever happened to my revenge, and to my messing up their lives, and to the roar of wrenched reality, and to style bursting open, and to my frenzy atop all the wreckage? The farce slowly began to wear me out. I thought about irrelevant things, for example—where does Kopyrda buy his ties, is Mrs. Engineer fond of cats, how much does it cost them to live here?

All this time Kopyrda stood with his hands in his pockets. This modern boy didn't come up to me, his face showed no signs of recognizing me—he was already too annoyed by Pimko being coupled with the girl to say hello to a schoolmate dressed in nothing but underwear—neither coupling suited him in the least. When the Youngbloods and Pimko began looking for change, Kopyrda slowly turned toward the door—I opened my mouth to shout, but Pimko, noticing Kopyrda's maneuver, quickly put away his wallet and followed him. Suddenly, when the engineer saw them both absconding so swiftly, he bounded after them like a cat after a mouse.

"I beg your pardon!" he exclaimed, "you're not getting off scot-free!"

Kopyrda and Pimko stood still. Kopyrda, now infuriated by being coupled with Pimko, moved away from him; Pimko, however, under the momentum of Kopyrda's movement, automatically moved closer to him—and so they stood like two brothers—one younger . . . one older . . .

Mrs. Engineer, totally unnerved, grabbed the engineer by the arm.

"Don't make a scene! Don't make a scene!" Which of course provoked him to make a scene.

"Forgive me!" he roared, "but I am her father, aren't I! And I ask you—how and with what in mind did you two gentlemen find yourselves in my daughter's bedroom? What is the meaning of this? What is this?"

Suddenly he looked at me and fell silent, terror creeping over his cheeks, he realized this was grist for my mill, the mill of scandal, and—he would have stopped talking, he would have—but having started it . . . he repeated once more:

"What is the meaning of this?" softly, just to round things off, secretly pleading that the issue go no further . . .

There was silence because no one could answer him. Everyone had his own understandable rationale, but the whole made no sense. In the silence the nonsense was stifling. And suddenly the girl's hollow, hopeless sobs came from under the covers. Oh, how masterful! She sobbed, sticking her naked calves from under the covers, her calves which, as she sobbed, slid out more and more from under the covers, and the crying of an underage girl united Pimko, Kopyrda, and her parents, and threaded them on a string of demonism. The whole matter, as if cut with a knife, ceased to be funny and nonsensical, it made sense again, a modern yet murky, black, dramatic, and tragic sense. Kopyrda, Pimko, and the Youngbloods felt better—while I, caught by the throat, felt worse.

"You have . . . d e f i l e d her," the mother whispered. "Don't cry, don't cry, child . . ."

"Congratulations, Professor!" the engineer exclaimed furiously. "You'll answer to me for this!"

Pimko, it seemed, breathed a sigh of relief. Even this felt better than not having been placed anywhere at all. So they've d e f i l e d her. The situation turned to the girl's advantage.

"Police!" I exclaimed, "we must call the police!"

This was a risky step, because police and an underage girl had for a long time formed a rounded, beautiful, and grim whole—and so the Youngbloods proudly raised their heads—though my goal was to scare Pimko. He paled, cleared his throat, and coughed.

"Police," the mother repeated, savoring the image of police standing over the girl's naked legs, "police, police . . ."

"Please do believe me," the professor stammered, "please believe me, all of you . . . There's some mistake here, I'm being accused falsely . . ."

"Yes!" I exclaimed. "I'm a witness. I saw it through my window! The professor walked into the garden to relieve himself. Miss Zuta looked out the window, the professor said 'hello,' and then came the usual way through the door, which Miss Zuta opened for him!"

Pimko broke down in fear of the police. Despicably, like a coward, he clutched at this explanation, regardless of its sickening and shameful meaning.

"Yes, that's right, I had the urge, I stepped into the garden, I forgot that this is where you live—and Miss Zuta happened to look out the window, so I pretended, hee, hee, hee, I pretended that I came to visit . . . You understand . . . in this drastic situation . . . it's a *quid pro quo, a quid pro quo*," he kept repeating.

It struck those assembled as vile and revolting. The girl pulled her legs under the covers. Kopyrda pretended not to hear, the Youngblood woman turned her back to Pimko, but, realizing that she had turned her back to him, she quickly turned to face him. Mr. Youngblood blinked—ha, they had again fallen into the throes of that deadly part, vulgarity returned full steam, I watched its return with interest, and how it was bowling them over; was it the same part in which I had recently been wallowing, yes, the same part perhaps—except that this time it was strictly between them. The Youngblood girl gave no sign of life under the covers. And Mr. Youngblood giggled—who knows what tickled him—maybe Pimko's *quid pro quo* brought back memories of a cabaret under that name that had existed in Warsaw—he then burst into that ultimate giggle of a petty engineer, that backside, ghastly, pantomime giggle—he exploded and—furious at Pimko for his own giggling—he jumped toward him, and, with a swift, arrogant, little engineer's slap, he whacked him in the mug. He whacked—he froze, panting, his arm still in the air. He turned serious. Rigid. I brought my jacket and my shoes from my room and began to dress slowly, not letting the scene out of my sight.

Having received the slap in the face, something gurgled in Pimko's throat, corked him up—yet I was convinced that deep down he was grateful for the slap, it somehow defined him.

"You shall pay for this," he said coldly, visibly relieved. He bowed toward the engineer, the engineer bowed toward him. Eagerly taking advantage of the bowing, Pimko turned to the door. Kopyrda quickly joined in the bowing and followed Pimko, in the hope of also slipping out . . . Mr. Youngblood sprang up. "What? There are consequences to be faced here, a duel, while this scoundrel Kopyrda wants to leave as if nothing had happened and to shirk all responsibility!" And so punch him in the snoot too! The engineer jumped toward him with his arm outstretched, but in a split second he realized that he couldn't very well slap a sniveling brat in the face, a schoolboy, a whippersnapper, his arm followed an awkward twist and, unable to counteract the momentum he g r a b b e d Kopyrda, instead of hitting him he g r a b b e d him by the chin. This illegal hold infuriated Kopyrda more than if he had been slapped in the face, and what's more, the false move—a foul after a long quarter-of-an-hour's nonsense—released his most primitive instincts. God knows what had hatched in his head—that the engineer caught him on purpose, "if you me, I you"—some such thought must have gripped him, therefore, according to a law that one might call "the law of the diagonal," he bent down and swept the engineer below the knee. Mr. Youngblood came down with a thud, whereupon Kopyrda bit his left flank, he hung on to him with his teeth and wouldn't let go—he then lifted his face, madly sweeping the room with his eyes from one end to the other and biting into Mr. Youngblood's flank.

I was tying my tie and putting on my jacket, but I stopped, intrigued. I had never seen anything like it. Mrs. Engineer rushed to her husband's rescue, she caught Kopyrda by the leg and pulled on it with all her might. They all swirled and tumbled down in a heap. What's more, Pimko, who stood a step from the swirling heap suddenly did something exceedingly strange, almost beyond telling. Had the prof finally given up? Had he surrendered? Had he run out of determination to keep standing while others lay? Did lying down seem no worse to him than standing on his legs? Suffice it to say that he voluntarily lay down on his back in a corner and raised his four paws in a gesture of complete helplessness. I tied my tie. I wasn't moved even when the girl threw off her covers, sprang up sobbing, and proceeded to jump up and down around the Youngbloods, who were rolling about with Kopyrda, as if she were a referee at a boxing match, pleading through her tears:

"Mommy! Daddy!"

The engineer, stupefied by the rolling about and looking for a handhold, unwittingly grabbed her leg above the ankle. She fell. The four of them rolled on the ground quietly, as if in church, because shame wouldn't let them do it otherwise. At one point I saw the mother biting her daughter, Kopyrda pulling Mrs. Youngblood, the engineer pushing Kopyrda, then Miss Youngblood's calf flashed on top of her mother's head.

At the same time the professor in the corner began to display an ever stronger predilection for swarming—lying on his back, all fours extended upward, he definitely began to gravitate in their direction and oscillate (seemingly without moving) toward them, doubtless the swarming and rolling about became for him the only viable solution. He couldn't get up, and why should he?—yet he couldn't lie on his back any longer. Just to get some sort of hold would be enough, and when the family and Kopyrda rolled closer—he caught Mr. Youngblood in the vicinity of the liver and was pulled into the vortex. I finished packing the most essential things into a small suitcase and put on my hat. I was weary of it all. Farewell, oh modern one, farewell Youngbloods and Kopyrda, farewell Pimko—no, not farewell, because how could I say farewell to something that didn't exist anymore. I was departing with a light heart. Oh, how sweet, how sweet it is to shake the dust off my shoes and depart, leaving nothing behind, no, not depart, just go . . . Was it so that Pimko, the classic prof, had dealt me the pupa, that I had been a pupil at the school, a modern boy with a modern girl, that I had been the dancing one in the bedroom, the one pulling wings off a fly, the one peeping in the bathroom, tra la la . . . ? That I had been the one with the pupa, with the mug, with the leg, tra la la . . . ? No, it was all gone, I was neither young nor old, neither modern nor old-fashioned, neither the pupil nor the boy, neither mature nor immature, I was neither this nor that, I was nothing . . . To depart and go, to go and depart and carry no memories. Oh, blithe indifference! No memories! When everything dies within you, and no one has yet had time to beget you again. Oh, it is worth living for death, to know that all has died within us, that it is no more, that all is empty and barren, all quiet and pure—and as I departed it seemed to me that I was going not alone but with myself—and right next to me, or maybe within me or around me, walked someone identical and cognate, mine—within me, mine—with me, and there was no love between us, no hate, no lust, no revulsion, no ugliness, no beauty, no laughter, no body parts,

no feeling nor anything mechanical, nothing, nothing, nothing . . .
But only for one hundredth of a second. Because as I was crossing
the kitchen, feeling my way in the semi-darkness, someone called
softly from the servants' quarters:

"Joey, Joey . . ."

It was Kneadus sitting on the servant girl, hurriedly putting on his
shoes.

"I'm here. Are you leaving? Wait, I'll go with you."

His whisper struck me from the side, and I stopped as if a bullet
had hit me. I couldn't see his mug distinctly in the darkness, but
judging by his voice it must have looked horrible. The servant girl
breathed heavily.

"Shhh . . . be quiet. Let's go." He climbed off the servant girl.
"Here, this way . . . Careful—here's a basket."

We found ourselves in the street.

It was getting light. Little houses, trees, railings stretched in orderly fashion as if on a string—and the air, limpid near the ground,
thickening above into a desperate mist. Asphalt. Space. Dew. Emptiness. Next to me Kneadus buttoning his pants. I tried to avoid looking at him. From the open windows of the villa—a pale electric light
and a continuous shoving of bodies rolling about. A piercing chill, a
sleepless cold as if on a train; I began to shiver, my teeth chattered.
Through the open window Kneadus heard the Youngbloods shoving
and asked:

"What's that? Is someone getting a massage?"

I didn't answer, and he, noticing the small suitcase in my hand,
asked:

"Are you running away?"

I lowered my head. I knew he'd catch me, he'd have to catch me
because there were just the two of us, next to each other. But I
couldn't move away from him without a reason. So he moved closer,
and with his hand he took me by the hand.

"Are you running away? I'll run away too. We'll go together. I've raped the servant girl. But that's not it, that's not it . . . A farmhand, a farmhand! Let's run away to the countryside—if you want to. To the countryside we'll go. There are farmhands there! Out in the countryside! We'll go together, do you want to? To the farmhand, Joey, to the farmhand, the farmhand!" he went on repeating frantically. I held my head straight and stiff, not looking at him.

"Kneadus, what good is your farmhand to me?"

But as soon as I began walking he went with me, and I went with him—we went together.

11 Preface to "The Child Runs Deep in Filibert"

And again a preface . . . and I'm a captive to a preface, I can't do without a preface, I must have a preface, because the law of symmetry requires that the story in which the child runs deep in Filidor should have a corresponding story in which the child runs deep in Filibert, while the preface to Filidor requires a corresponding preface to Filibert. Even if I want to I can't, I can't, and I can't avoid the ironclad laws of symmetry and analogy. But it's high time to interrupt, to cease, to emerge from the greenery if only for a moment, to come back to my senses and peer from under the weight of a billion little sprouts, buds, and leaves so that no one can say that I've gone crazy, totally blah, blah. And before I move any further on the road of second-rate, intermediate, not-quite-human horrors, I have to clarify, rationalize, substantiate, explain, and systematize, I have to draw out the primary thought from which all other thoughts in this book originate, and to reveal the primeval torment of all torments herein mentioned and brought into relief. And I must introduce a hierarchy of torments as well as a hierarchy of thoughts, and provide analytic, synthetic, and philosophical comments on this work so that the reader will know where the head is, where the legs, the nose, where the heel is, so that I'm not accused of being unaware of my own goals, of not marching straight and stiffly forward like the greatest writers of omnitime, but that I've senselessly gone bonkers. But which of the torments is the chief and fundamental one? Where is this book's primeval torment? Where are you, oh, primeval mother of all torments? The longer I probe, study, and digest these things, the clearer it becomes that the chief, basic torment, as I see it, is simply the torment of bad form, of bad *exterieur*, or, in other words, it's the torment of platitude, grimace, face, mug—yes, that's the source, the wellspring, the beginning, and it's from here that all other suffering, frenzy, and torture flow harmoniously, without exception. Or perhaps one should really say that the chief, basic torment is nothing other than the suffering that comes from our being constricted by another human being, from the fact that we are strangled and stifled by a tight, narrow, stiff notion of ourselves that is held by another human being. Or, perhaps at the base of this book is the major and murderous torment of the

not-quite-human greenery, of little sprouts, leaves, and buds

or the torment of development and not-quite-development,

or maybe the suffering of not-quite-shaping, not-quite-forming,

or the torment of our inner self being created by others,

or the torment of physical and psychological rape

the suffering of driving, interpersonal tensions

the biased and unclarified torment of psychological bias

the lateral torture of psychological wrenching, twisting, and miscuing

the unceasing torment of betrayal, the torment of falsehood

the mechanical agony of mechanism and automatism

the symmetrical torment of analogy, and the analogous torment of symmetry

the analytical torment of synthesis, and the synthetic torment of analysis or maybe the agony of parts of the body and the disruption of the hierarchy of its individual organs

or the suffering of gentle infantilism

of the pupa, of pedagogy, of formalists and educators

of inconsolable innocence and naiveté

of departure from reality

of phantasm, illusion, musings, idle notions, and nonsense

of higher idealism

of lower, shabby, hole-in-the-corner idealism

of daydreaming on the sidelines

or maybe of the very odd torment of pettiness and belittlement

the torment of contending

the torment of aspiring

the torment of apprenticeship

or perhaps simply the torture of pulling oneself up by one's boot-straps and straining beyond one's ability, and hence the torture of inability, general and particular

the agony of giving oneself airs, and of blowing one's own horn

the pain of humiliating others

the torment of superior and inferior poetry

or the torture of the dull psychological impasse

the devious torture of craftiness, evasiveness, and of foul play

or rather the torture of the age in its particular and general sense

the torment of the old-fashioned

the torment of modernity

the suffering resulting from the emergence of new social strata

the torment of the semi-intelligent

the torment of the nonintelligent

the torture of the intelligent

or maybe simply the torment of petty-intelligent indecency

the pain of stupidity

of wisdom

of ugliness

of beauty, of attractiveness and charm

or maybe the torture of cutthroat logic, and of consistency in foolishness

the anguish of reciting

the despair of imitating

the boring torture of boredom, and of talking in circles

or perhaps the hypomanic torment of hypomania

the ineffable torture of ineffability

the aching lack of sublimation

of pain in the finger

in the fingernail

of toothache

of earache

the torture of horrifying interrelation, interdependence, and dependence, of interpenetration of all torments and of all parts, and the torment of one hundred and fifty-six thousand, three hundred and twenty-four and a half other tortures, not counting women and children, as an old French author of the sixteenth century would have said.

Which of those tortures is to be the basic primeval torture, which part is the integral, by which of its parts is one to seize this book, and what should one pick from the above parts and torments? Oh, accursed parts, will I ever be free of you, oh, what an abundance of parts, what an abundance of torments! Where is the chief, primeval mother, and should the basis for the torment be metaphysical or physical, sociological or psychological? And yet I must, I must and I cannot not, because the world at large is about to consider me unconscious of my goals and to think that I've lost my bearings. But perhaps, in this case, it would be more rational to develop and bring out the genesis of the work with words, and not on the basis of torments, but in the face of, with regard to, in relation to that it arose:

in relation to pedagogues and schoolboys

in the face of half-witted wise guys

with reference to deep or high-level beings

with regard to the leading writers of contemporary national literature, and the most polished, structured, and rigid representatives of
the world of criticism

in the face of schoolgirls

in relation to the mature, and to men of the world

in interdependence with men of fashion, dandies, narcissists,
aesthetes, haughty spirits, and men about town

with regard to those experienced in life

in bondage to cultural aunts

in relation to urban citizens

in the face of the country citizenry

with reference to petty physicians in the provinces, engineers and
civil servants of narrow horizons

with reference to high-level civil servants, physicians and lawyers
of wide horizons

in relation to ancestral and other kinds of aristocracy

in the face of the rabble.

It's also possible, however, that my work was conceived out of
torment from associating with an actual person, for example, with
the distinctly repulsive Mr. XY, or with Mr. Z, whom I hold in
utmost contempt, and NN, who bores and wearies me—oh, the
terrible torment of associating with them! And—it's possible—that
the motive and goal for writing this book is solely to show these
gentlemen my disdain for them, to agitate, irritate, and enrage them,
and to get them out of my way. In this case the motive would seem to
be clear-cut, personal, and aimed at the individual.

But perhaps my work came from imitating masterworks?

From inability to create a normal work?

From dreams?

From complexes?

Or perhaps from memories of my childhood?

and perhaps because I began writing and so it happened to come out

From anxiety disorder?

From obsessive-compulsive disorder?

Perhaps from a bubble?

From a pinch of something?

From a part?

From a particle?

From thin air?

One would also need to establish, proclaim, and define whether the work is a novel, a memoir, a parody, a lampoon, a variation on a fantasy, or a study of some kind—and what prevails in it: humor, irony, or some deeper meaning, sarcasm, persiflage, invective, rubbish, *pur nonsens, pur claptrapism,* and more, whether it's simply a pose, pretense, make-believe, bunkum, artificiality, paucity of wit, anemia of emotion, atrophy of imagination, subversion of order, and ruination of the mind. Yet the sum of these possibilities, torments, definitions, and parts is so limitless, so unfathomable and inexhaustible that one must say, with the greatest responsibility for one's words and after the most scrupulous consideration, that we know nothing, chirp, chirp, little chickie; and consequently, whoever would like to better understand, to gain deeper insight, I invite him to read "The Child Runs Deep in Filibert," because my answer to all these tormenting questions lies in its hidden symbolism. Because Filibert, positioned conclusively and in analogy with Filidor, conceals within its strange unity the final, secret meaning of this work. And having thus revealed it, there is nothing to stop one from venturing somewhat deeper, into the thicket of those separate and tedious parts.

12 The Child Runs Deep
in Filibert

At the end of the eighteenth century a peasant in Paris had a child, and this child had a child, then this child had a child, which had a child; and this last child played a tennis match as the world champion on the court of the illustrious Paris Racing Club, in an atmosphere of great excitement and to the accompaniment of unceasing and thunderous applause. However (oh, how incredibly treacherous life can be!), a certain colonel of the *Zouaves,* sitting in the crowd on the side bleachers, suddenly became envious of the two champions' impeccable and thrilling game, and wishing to show off in front of the six thousand spectators (and especially in front of his fiancée, sitting next to him) unexpectedly fired his pistol and hit the ball in midair.* The ball burst and fell to the ground while the champions, so suddenly deprived of their object, continued to swing their rackets in empty space; however, realizing the nonsense of their movements now that the ball was gone, they pounced on each other with their claws. A thunderous applause rose from the spectators.

Zouaves—the name given to certain infantry regiments in the French Army, first raised in Algeria in 1831 (Encyclopaedia Britannica, vol. 23, 1970).

And this surely would have been the end. But something else happened—the colonel, in his excitement, forgot or did not take into consideration (oh, how careful one must be!) the spectators sitting on the other side of the court, on the so-called sunny side of the stands. He thought, God knows why, that the bullet, having punctured the ball, would have spent itself; however, in its further trajectory it unfortunately struck a ship owner in the neck. Blood spurted from a ruptured artery. The wife of the wounded man, on first impulse, wanted to pounce on the colonel and snatch the pistol from him, but since she couldn't (she was trapped in the crowd), she simply slapped the mug of her neighbor on her right. And she did it because she couldn't vent her agitation in any other way, and because, in the deepest recesses of her inner self and motivated by purely feminine logic she thought that, as a woman, she was at liberty to do so, and why not? Not so, as it turned out (oh, how unceasingly one must take everything into account), because the man was a latent epileptic who, due to the psychological shock of the slap in the face, went into a seizure and erupted like a geyser in jerks and convulsions. The hapless woman found herself between two men, one spurting blood, the other foam. A thunderous applause rose from the spectators.

Whereupon a gentleman sitting nearby suddenly panicked and jumped on the head of the lady seated below, she in turn took off and, carrying him on her back at full speed, bounded into the center of the court. A thunderous applause rose from the spectators. And this surely would have been the end. But something else happened (oh, how one must always anticipate everything!)—a modest pensioner from Toulouse, a man given to dreaming in secret, sat relaxing not far off, and, for a long time and at every public event, he had been dreaming of jumping onto the heads of people sitting below him, yet, by sheer willpower, he had thus far restrained himself. Now, carried away by the example, he instantly mounted a woman sitting below him, and she (a minor office clerk from Tangiers),

The Child Runs Deep in Filibert

surmising that these must be proper city manners and quite the thing to do—also carried him on her back, taking pains to make her movements appear totally relaxed.

Whereupon the more sophisticated sector of the public began to applaud tactfully so as to cover up the gaffe in front of the delegates from foreign consulates and embassies who had thronged to the match. But this led to yet another misunderstanding, because the less sophisticated sector mistook the applause for a sign of approval, and they too mounted their ladies. The foreigners showed increasing astonishment. So what could the more sophisticated sector of the company do? As if nothing had happened, they too mounted their ladies.

And this almost certainly would have been the end. But then a certain marquis de Filiberthe, sitting in the grandstand with his wife and her family, was suddenly roused by the gentleman within and stepped into the center of the court in his light-colored summer suit and, pale yet determined, he coolly asked if anyone, and if so who, wished to insult his wife, the marquise de Filiberthe? And he threw into the crowd a bunch of visiting cards inscribed: Phillipe Hertal de Filiberthe. (Oh, how terribly careful we must be! How difficult and treacherous life is, and how unpredictable!) Dead silence ensued.

And suddenly no fewer than thirty-six gentlemen began riding up at a slow canter, bareback on their elegantly and ornately dressed women—thoroughbred and slim at the fetlocks—to insult the marquise de Filiberthe and to feel themselves roused by the gentleman within, just as her husband the marquis himself had been roused by the gentleman within. Panic-stricken, the marquise miscarried—and a child's whimpering was heard at the marquis' feet and under the hooves of the trampling women. The marquis—so unexpectedly made aware of the child that ran deep in him, and realizing, just at that moment when he was acting singly and as a gentleman mature within himself, how sustained and replenished he had been by the child—was overcome with embarrassment and went home—while a thunderous applause rose from the spectators.

The Child Runs Deep in Filibert

13 The Farmhand, or Captive Again

And so we're off, Kneadus and I, in search of the farmhand. The villa had disappeared around the corner with whatever remained of the Youngbloods tumbling and rolling about as we had left them, and ahead of us lay the long stretch of Filtrowa Street, a shining ribbon. The sun rose, a yellow ball, we're eating breakfast at a drugstore, the city is awakening, it's eight o'clock, we move on, I with my small suitcase, Kneadus with a walking stick. Little birds chirp on trees. Onward, onward! Kneadus stomps briskly, hope carries him into the future, his hope heartens me, his captive! "Let's go to the outskirts of the city, to the outskirts," he keeps repeating. "We'll find ourselves a swell farmhand there, that's where we'll find him!" The farmhand paints the morning in bright and pleasant colors, it's nice, it's great fun to walk through the city in search of a farmhand! What will become of me? What will they do with me? Under what circumstances? I know nothing, I stomp briskly behind Kneadus, my lord and master, I can't torture myself nor be sad because I'm in a good mood! In this neighborhood the entrances to buildings are few and far between, and the air in them reeks of janitors and their families. Kneadus peeks into each doorway, but a janitor is a far cry from a farmhand, isn't a janitor just a peasant in a flowerpot? Here and there we run into a janitor's son, but Kneadus is not satisfied, because isn't a janitor's son actually a farmhand in a cage, a farmhand caged in a stairwell? "There's no wind here," he declares. "In these doorways there are only drafts, and I don't fancy a farmhand in drafts, for me a farmhand lives where the wind blows free."

We pass nannies and nursemaids pushing infants in squeaking baby carriages. Wearing their mistresses' discarded dresses, they walk on heels bent out of shape, giving us the glad eye. Two gold teeth, wheeling someone else's child, in tatters, Rudolph Valentino in their heads. We pass executives, office workers with briefcases under their arms hurrying to their daily tasks, but they're all of *papier mâché*, very Slavic and bureaucratic, their cuffs and cufflinks like emblems of their egos, each has his own watch chain, these husbands of wives and employers of nursemaids. Above them the great Sky. We pass young la-di-das wearing coats in Warsaw chic, some skinny and swift, others sluggish and soft, their heads stuck into their very own hats, and, without much to differentiate them, they catch up and pass one another, Kneadus won't even deign to look, and I'm thoroughly bored, I begin to yawn. "To the outskirts," he exclaims, "there we'll find a farmhand, nothing doing here, it's all so cheap, they're a dime a dozen, intelligentsia cows and horses, attorneys' wives and nannies, their husbands are like cab horses. Damn them all, cows and mules! Look how educated and yet how stupid they are! All overdressed, damn it, and so vulgar! It's the pupa, the damn pupa again!" At the end of Wawelska Street we see some municipal buildings planned on a grander scale, their formidable appearance passes as nourishment for the masses of hungry and exhausted employees. The buildings remind us of school, so we quicken our pace. On Narutowicz Square, where the students' dormitory is located, we run into bands of students, bleary-eyed from lack of sleep, their trousers frayed, their hair unkempt, hurrying to a lecture or waiting for a streetcar. Their noses in their lecture notes, they eat hard-boiled eggs, shove the eggshells into their pockets, and breathe the dust of the big city. "Pah, these are ex-farmhands!" he exclaimed. "They're all sons of peasants studying to become intelligentsia! To hell with ex-farmhands! I hate ex-farmhands! They still wipe their noses with their fingers, and already they're studying their lecture notes! Learning in a peasant! A peasant turned lawyer or physician! Just look how their heads are swollen with Latin terms, look at their stubby fingers! How unfortunate," fumed Kneadus, "that's just as bad as if they'd become monks! Oh, so many good, first-rate farmhands, but nothing doing, they've changed their garb, they've been murdered, killed! To the outskirts of the city, to the outskirts, there's wind there, the air blows free!" We turn into Grojecka Street, dust, soot, noise, and stench, no more brownstone buildings, only tenement houses and preposterous carts with Jewish goods and chattels, carts full of vegetables, goose down, milk, cabbage, grain, hay, scrap metal, and debris, they fill the street with their jingling, clanging, and banging. On top of every cart sits a peasant or a Jew, wobbling—either a city peasant or a country Jew—I don't know which is better. We actually venture farther into the inferior regions, the immature outskirts of the city, and there are more decayed teeth, more ears stuffed with wads of cotton wool, fingers bound in rags, hair smeared with grease, hiccups, blackheads, cabbage, and a pervasive musty stench. Diapers dry in the windows. Radios rattle on without a break, educational talk whirrs, and numerous Pimkos, with a voice that's either artificially naive and warm, or gruff or cheery, educate the soul of drugstore owners, lecturing them on their responsibilities and teaching them to love Kościuszko. Grocers relish reading tabloids that describe the life of the upper classes, and their wives, scratching themselves on the back, relive their previous night with Marlene Dietrich. Pedagogical activity is in full swing, innumerable female delegates bustle among the populace, teaching and lecturing, persuading and developing, awakening and generating civic-mindedness with an *ad hoc* simplicity pasted on their faces. Here a group of streetcar conductors' wives dances in a circle, singing and smiling and promoting joy of life under the direction of a person delegated for this purpose, an especially cheerful wag from the intelligentsia, there horse-cab drivers sing canticles, thus creating a strange sense of innocence. Somewhere else, ex-farmgirls are learning to discover the beauty of a sunset. And tens of conceptualists, dogmatists, demagogues, and agitators shape and reshape people, sowing their ideas, opinions, doctrines, concepts—all specially prepared and simplified for the "little ones." "The mug, the mug everywhere," said Kneadus abruptly, "just like in school! No wonder disease eats them alive, poverty chokes them, no wonder this motley crew is being choked and eaten alive. Who the devil fixed them like this—I'm sure if someone hadn't put them up to it, they wouldn't have spawned all this ugliness, abomination, and filth, it sticks out a mile, why doesn't it stick out of a peasant, even though he never washes himself! Who, I ask, has turned this good and respectable proletariat into such a factory? Who has taught them this filth and quirkiness? Oh, Sodom and Gomorrah—we'll never find a farmhand here. Let's go on, on. When will the wind finally blow?" But there is no wind, only stagnation, human beings wallowing in their humanity like fish in a pond. The stench hits the sky, and still the farmhand is nowhere to be seen. Lonely seamstresses get skinny, petty hairdressers grow plump in cheap luxury, minor craftsmen's stomachs growl, unemployed female servants on their short, fat legs spout vile language, artificial phrases, pretentious accents, and the pharmacist's wife—her stomach growling—lords it over the washerwoman, the washerwoman preens herself on spiked heels. Feet that are actually bare yet shod in dainty shoes, feet that seem odd when clad in shoes, likewise their heads in hats, bodies from the country or some village in gents' and ladies' outfits. "What a mug," said Kneadus, "nothing sincere, nothing natural, everything copied, trashy, fake, bogus." And the farmhand is still nowhere to be seen. Finally we come upon a journeyman, not bad, a nice, fair-haired, well-proportioned man, but unfortunately already enlightened about social class and echoing Marx. "What a mug," said Kneadus, "what a philosopher!" Yet another one—a typical rogue, knife between his teeth, a smart aleck from these seedy outskirts—seemed for a moment to be the longed-for farmhand, but unfortunately he wore a bowler hat. Another type we approached on a street corner seemed to suit Kneadus to a "T," but, alas, he used the expression "whereas." "Yet another mug," Kneadus whispered furiously, "he's no good. Onward, onward," he repeated feverishly, "all this is trash. Just like in our school. The outskirts are taking lessons from the city. Damn it, the lower classes are actually at grade-school level. These fellows are just entry-level pupils, that's probably why their noses are still dripping. Devil take all that mangy, scabby lot, will we ever escape school? Nothing but the mug. Oh, the mug, mug, mug! Onward, onward!" We move on, on, small wooden houses, mothers delousing their daughters, daughters—their mothers, children wading in gutters, workers returning from work, the great one and only word resounds from on high and from below, the entire street is full of it by now, it's transforming itself into a real hymn of the proletariat, it resounds with challenge and arrogance, it is hurled with passion into space and provides at least an illusion of life and power. "Look at them!" Kneadus marveled, "look how they puff themselves up, just like we do in school. That won't cure the pupa, that great and classical pupa, which has been stuck on these sniveling brats. It's terrible that there's no one nowadays who isn't still at the age of immaturity. Onward—there's no farmhand here!" And just as he finished saying these words a breeze blew gently on our cheeks, there were no more houses, streets, gutters, sewers, hairdressers, windows, workers, wives, mothers and daughters, vermin, cabbage, stuffy air, cramped spaces, dust, proprietors, artisans, shoes, blouses, hats, heels, streetcars, shops, vegetables, smart alecks, shop signs, blackheads, stuff, glances, hair, eyebrows, lips, sidewalks, bellies, tools, organs, hiccups, knees, elbows, windowpanes, shouts,

The Farmhand, or Captive Again

sniveling, spitting, throat clearing, conversations, children, clatter. We came to the city limits. Ahead of us—fields, forests. A highway.

Kneadus started singing:

> "Hey, hey, a forest green
> Hey, hey, a forest green!

Pick up a stick. Cut a branch for yourself. In the fields—that's where we'll find a farmhand! I can already see him in my mind's eye. Not bad, that farmhand!"

I sang:

> "Hey, hey, a forest green
> Hey, hey, a forest green!"

Yet I couldn't take another step forward. The song died on my lips. Space. On the horizon—a cow. Earth. In the distance a goose flies by. The sky is enormous. In the mist the horizon is blue-gray. I stopped at the city limits, and I felt that I couldn't continue without the herd and its works, without the human among humans. I caught Kneadus by the hand. "Don't go there, Kneadus, let's turn back, don't leave the city, Kneadus." Among unfamiliar bushes and grasses I shook like a leaf in the wind, I felt deprived of people, and the deformities inflicted upon me by them seemed nonsensical and unjustified without them. Kneadus also hesitated, but the prospect of finding a farmhand overcame his fear. "Onward!" he called, brandishing his stick. "I won't go alone! You must come with me! Let's go, let's go!" The wind came up, trees swayed, leaves rustled, and one leaf especially—at the top of a tree and ruthlessly exposed to space—terrified me. A bird soared high above. A dog bolted from the city and tore across the black fields. Yet Kneadus moved boldly down a path along the highway—and I followed him, as if in a boat under way to the open sea. Land disappears, and so do the chimneys and spires, we're alone. Silence, one can almost hear the cold and slippery stones sticking out of the ground. I move on, I no longer know anything, the wind blows in my ears, I sway to the rhythm of walking . . . Nature. I don't want nature, people are nature for me, Kneadus, let's turn back, I prefer crowds in a movie house to ozone in the fields. Who said that in relation to nature man becomes small? On the contrary, I grow and assume gigantic proportions, yet I weaken, I feel naked, as if served up on a platter of huge fields of nature in all my human unnaturalness, oh, where did my forest disappear, my thicket of eyes and lips, of words, glances, faces, smiles, and grimaces? A different forest approaches, a forest of evergreens, below which a hare scampers and a caterpillar crawls. Yet here, as if out of spite, not a village in sight, the road passes through fields and forests. I don't know how many hours we trudged awkwardly across the fields, stiffly, as if on a tightrope—there was nothing else we could do, because standing would tire us even more, and we could neither sit nor lie on the damp, cold earth. We passed a couple of villages, but they looked dead—boarded-up cottages with empty eye sockets. There was no more traffic on the highway. How long were we to tramp through this emptiness?

"What's the meaning of this?" asked Kneadus. "Has plague descended on the peasants? Are they all dead? If this continues we'll never find the farmhand."

Finally, coming upon yet another deserted village, we began knocking on the doors of the cottages. Ferocious barking answered us, as if a pack of wild dogs, from huge mastiffs to small mongrels, were sharpening their teeth to attack us. "What is this?" Kneadus asked. "Where do all these dogs come from? Why are there no peasants here? Pinch me, I must be dreaming . . ." His words hardly had time to dissolve in the limpid air, when, from a nearby potato pit, a peasant's head popped up and immediately hid again, and when we came closer, ferocious barking came from the hollow. "Damn it," Kneadus said, "dogs again? Where's the peasant?" We walked round the pit (in the meantime outright howling came from the cottages), and we flushed out the peasant and his wife with little quadruplets whom she had been nursing with one almost dried-up breast (since the other had long been useless), barking desperately and furiously. They broke into a run, but Kneadus sprang and caught the peasant. The latter was so emaciated and skinny that he fell to the ground and moaned: "Oh, lordie, lord, have me'cy on us, let us be, leave us alone, oh, sire!" "Look, mister," said Kneadus, "what's the matter with you? Why are you hiding from us?" At the sound of the word "mister," the barking in the cottages and down the paths by the fences redoubled, and the poor little peasant turned white as a sheet. "Oh, have me'cy, sire, I'm no mister, le' me be!" "Citizen," Kneadus replied in a conciliatory tone, "are you crazy? Why are you barking, you and your wife? We have good intentions." At the sound of "citizen," the barking tripled, and the peasant woman broke out wailing: "Have pity, sire, he's no citizen! They've sent us some Yententions again, damn them!" "Friend," Kneadus said, "what's the matter? We're not going to hurt you. We want nothing but your good." "Friend!" exclaimed the peasant, terrified. "He wants our good!" screamed the woman. "We're no human folk, we're just dogs, we're dogs! Woof! Woof!" Suddenly the baby at the breast barked, the peasant woman looked around and, realizing that there were only two of us, growled and bit me in the belly. I tore my belly out of the hag's teeth! But now from behind the fences all the villagers appeared, barking and growling: "Get 'em, boys! Don't be scared! Bite 'em! Snap! Snap! Set the dogsss on them! Git those yententions! Git those yentelligentsias! Sock it to 'em, sock 'em, set dogsss on 'em, cats too, cats! Ksss...Ksss..." Thus setting upon us and hounding us, they came closer—what's worse, to draw attention away from themselves, or to spur themselves on, they brought real dogs on ropes, and the dogs stood on their haunches, jumping, saliva dribbling from their snouts, barking ferociously. Our situation became critical, even more from the psychological standpoint than the physical. It was six o'clock in the evening. It was getting dark, the sun was behind the clouds, it was beginning to drizzle, while we—in an unfamiliar territory, a cold, fine rain falling—were faced with a huge number of peasants pretending to be dogs so they could dodge the all-encompassing activity of the city intelligentsia. Their children could no longer speak but barked on all fours, their parents encouraging them: "Barkie, barkie, sonny, little Spot, so they'll leave you in peace, barkie, barkie, Spottie-dog." This was the first time I had ever observed a whole village hurriedly transforming itself into dogs on the strength of the law of mimicry and out of fear of humanization, too intensely applied. And it was impossible to defend ourselves because it's one thing to defend yourself from one dog or one peasant, but quite another to defend yourself from growling, barking peasantry wanting to bite you. Kneadus drops the stick out of his hand. I look vacuously at the slippery, mysterious turf ahead of me, where I'm about to give up the ghost, and under such feigned circumstances. Farewell my body parts. Farewell my mug, and farewell, too, my docile pupa!

And we surely would have been, on this very spot, devoured in some unknown manner, when suddenly everything changes, the horn of a car resounds, a car drives into the crowd and stops, my aunt Hurlecka, née Lin, sees me and calls out:

"Joey! What are you doing here, child?"

Unaware of the danger and as usual not noticing anything, my aunt, swathed in shawls, gets out of the car and, her arms outstretched, rushes to kiss me. Oh, no! It's auntie! Auntie! Where can I hide from her? I would prefer to be devoured than to be hitched to Auntie on this great road of my life. This auntie has known me since I was a child, she has preserved the memory of my little pants! She's seen me kicking my little legs in my crib. So she runs up to me, kisses me on the forehead, the peasants stop barking and burst out laughing, the whole village shakes and roars—they realize I'm not some all-powerful city official, I'm just auntie's little boy! Confusion takes over. Kneadus takes off his hat while auntie presents him her hand to be kissed.

The Farmhand, or Captive Again

"Joey, is this your friend? My pleasure."

Kneadus kisses auntie's hand. I kiss auntie's hand. My aunt asks if we aren't cold, where are we going, where from, what for, when, with whom, why?" I reply we're on a hike.

"On a hike? But my children, who has let you out in such damp weather? Get into the car, we'll go to my place, to Bolimov. Your uncle will be delighted."

It's no use protesting. My auntie won't hear of any protests. On this great road of mine, in the mizzly, spattering drizzle, among rising mists—we are here with auntie. We get into the car. The chauffeur sounds the horn, the car starts, the peasants roar with laughter, the car, strung on the line of telephone poles, gathers speed—we're off. While my auntie: "Well, Joey, aren't you glad, here I am, your second cousin's cousin's aunt twice removed, my mother was your mother's second cousin twice removed. Your dear departed mama! Dear Cesia! It's so many years since I've seen you. It's four years now since the Franks' wedding. I remember how you played in the sand— remember the sand? What did these people here want from you? Oh, how they scare me! Today's peasantry is most uninteresting. Germs everywhere, don't drink unboiled water, don't let unpeeled fruit pass your lips unless it has been washed in hot water. Please wrap this shawl around you or you'll hurt my feelings, and have your friend take the other shawl, no, no, don't be cross, I could be your friend's mother. I'm sure his mama is worrying at home." The driver honks the horn. The car hums, the wind hums, my aunt hums, utility poles and trees rush by, puny cottages, small towns like puddles rush by, birch and alder groves, clusters of firs rush by, the vehicle carries us swiftly over potholes, we bounce in our seats. While my auntie: "Not too fast, Felix, not too fast. Do you remember uncle Frank? Krysia's getting married. Little Ann had whooping cough. Henio's been drafted into the army. You look pale and haggard, if you have a toothache I have an aspirin here. And how's your schoolwork— good? You probably have talent for history because your departed mother had an amazing gift for history. You've inherited it from your mother. Also her blue eyes, your father's nose, your chin, however, is typical of the Pifczyckis. And do you remember how you cried when they took that apple core from you, you stuck your little finger in your mouth and cried: 'Tia, tia, tia, here, appie, appie, here!' (Oh, accursed aunt!) Wait, wait, how many years ago was that—twenty, twenty-eight, yes, it was nineteen hundred and . . . of course, I used to go to Vichy then and had bought a green trunk, yes, yes, that would make you thirty now . . . Thirty . . . yes, of course—thirty, to be exact. Wrap that shawl round you, my child, one can't be too careful of the draft."

"Thirty?" asked Kneadus.

"Thirty," said my aunt. "He turned thirty on St. Peter's and St. Paul's! He's four and a half years younger than Terenia, and Terenia is six weeks older than Zosia, Alfred's daughter. The Henryks were married in February."

"But Mrs. Halecka, he goes to our school, same grade as me!"

"That's right, it must have been February because it was five months before my trip to Mentona, and it was freezing weather. Helenka died in June. Thirty. Mama was returning from Podole. Thirty. Exactly two years after Bolek's diphtheria. The ball in Mogilczany—thirty. Would you like some candy? Joey, would you like some candy? Your auntie always has candy—remember how you'd stretch out your little arm and call: 'Candy, auntie! Candy!' I still carry the same kind of candy, take some, take it, it's good for a cough. Cover yourself up, child."

The chauffeur honks. The car speeds on. Utility poles and trees speed by, also cottages, pieces of fences, pieces of checkered fields, pieces of woods and meadows, pieces of unfamiliar places. Flatlands. It's seven o'clock. It's dark, the chauffeur lets out beams of electricity, my aunt turns on the light inside and offers me my childhood candy. Kneadus, surprised, sucks on a piece of candy, my aunt also sucks on one, paper bag in hand. We're all sucking. 'If I'm thirty years old, woman, I'm thirty—don't you understand that?' No, she doesn't understand. She's too good. Too kind-hearted. It's nothing but kindness. I'm drowning in auntie's kindness, I'm sucking on her sweet candy, and according to her—I'm still two years old, and anyway, do I exist for her? I don't, my hair is uncle Edward's, my nose is my father's, my eyes are my mother's, my chin belongs to the Pifczyckis, I'm a collection of the family's body parts. Auntie sinks into the family and tucks the shawl around me. A calf runs onto the road and stands, its legs spread out, the chauffeur sounds the horn like an archangel, but the calf doesn't want to give way, the car stops and the chauffeur pushes the calf off the road—we speed on while auntie tells how I used to draw letters with my finger on a windowpane when I was ten years old. She remembers things I don't remember, she knows me as I've never known myself, but she's too good, I can't kill her—God knew what he was doing when he swathed in kindness every aunt's knowledge of embarrassing, amusing details of one's tear-filled, long-gone childhood. We speed on, we enter a huge forest lit only by our headlights, fragments of trees flash by, and, from my memory—fragments of the past, the area here is evil and menacing. We are so far from everything! Where are we?! A huge stretch of brutal, black countryside, slippery from rain, dripping with water, surrounds our box, while within auntie prattles on about my fingers, that I once cut my finger and probably still carry a scar while Kneadus, a farmhand in his head, puzzles over my thirty-year-old. It has started to really rain. The car turns onto a side road, up and down through a sandy stretch, one more turn and dogs jump out, tough and ferocious mastiffs, the night watchman runs out, chases them away—they growl, bark, and whimper—a servant runs out onto the porch, another servant behind him. We get out of the car.

Countryside. The wind tears at the trees and the clouds. In the night the hazy outline of a large building appears, it's not unfamiliar to me—I know it—because I've been here before, a long time ago. Auntie is afraid of the damp, the servants lift her under her armpits and help her into the hallway. The chauffeur lugs in heavy suitcases. An old butler with sideburns takes off auntie's coat. A chambermaid takes off my coat. A young valet takes off Kneadus' coat. Little dogs sniff us, I know it all, though I don't remember it . . . it was here I was born and spent the first ten years of my life.

"I brought you visitors," auntie calls out. "Konstanty dear, this is Ladislas' son, Ziggie dear—your cousin! Zosia! Joey—your cousin. This is Joey, the departed Cesia's son. Joey—your uncle, Kostie— Joey."

Shaking hands, kissing on the cheeks, bumping into body parts, making declarations of joy and hospitality, they take us to the living room, seat us on old Biedermeiers, inquire about my health, "are you well?"—I inquire about their health in turn, and conversation about various illnesses unfolds, gets hold of us, and won't let go. Auntie has a heart condition, uncle Konstanty has rheumatism, Zosia recently succumbed to anemia and she's prone to colds, her tonsils are not up to snuff, there's a lack of means for definitive treatment. Zygmunt is also prone to colds and had an awful bout with his ear as well, he was exposed to drafts a month ago when autumn brought with it winds and damp weather. That's enough—it seemed unhealthy to have to listen, immediately on arrival, to all the illnesses the family has had, but as soon as the conversation waned: "Sophie, parle," auntie whispered, and Zosia, to keep the conversation going, to the detriment of her charms, pulled out other illnesses. Sciatica, rheumatism, arthritis, aches in the bones, gout, coughs and colds, tonsillitis, flu, cancer and neurodermatitis, toothache, tooth fillings, lazy bowels, neurasthenia, liver, kidneys, Carlsbad, Professor Kalitowicz, and Dr. Pistak. It almost stopped at Pistak, but no, to keep the conversation going, my aunt brings up Dr. Vistak, that his hearing is superior to Pistak's, and back to Vistak, Pistak, percussion, diseases of the ear, of the throat, respiratory diseases, heart valve insufficiency, consultations, gallstones, chronic dyspepsia, asthenia, and blood cells. I couldn't forgive myself for having asked about their health. And yet I couldn't have not asked about their health. Zosia especially was worn out by the topic, and I saw how it pained her to expose her own scrofula, just to keep the conversation going, but it would have been bad manners to treat the newly arrived young men to silence. Was this the usual mechanism, was this how they always caught anyone who arrived in the countryside, was it never with anybody that they began in the countryside, other than through illnesses? It was a calamity for the landed gentry that age-honored good manners required them to establish relations from a rheumy reference point, and that's why they always looked so pale and rheumy in the light of an oil lamp, little dogs on their laps. Oh, countryside! Countryside! The old country manor! Age-old laws and age-old mysteries! How different from those of city thoroughfares and the crowds on Marszałkowska Street.

It was only my aunt who, out of kindness and without being forced, wallowed in my uncle's subfebrile states and bloody diarrhea. The chambermaid, red-faced, wearing a little apron, came in and turned up the lamp. Kneadus, saying little, was impressed with the abundance of servants and with the family's two richly embroidered sashes from Słuck. There was great nobility in all this—but I didn't know whether my uncle also remembered me as a child. They treated us somewhat like children, but they treated themselves similarly, in a kindergarten style inherited from their ancestors. I had some vague recollection of playing under a scratched table, and the fringe of a worn-out sofa standing in a corner loomed out of the distant past. Did I chew on it, eat it, braid it—or more likely dip it in a little tumbler and smear it—with what, when? Or maybe I stuck it in my nose? My aunt sat on a sofa according to the old school—erect, bosom thrust forward, head slightly back, Zosia sat slumped and sickened by the conversation, her fingers intertwined, Zygmunt, his elbows on the arm rests, stared at the tips of his shoes, while my uncle, tugging at a dachshund, stared at an autumn fly traversing the white and immense ceiling. Outside the wind blew hard, the trees in front of the house rustled with a few remaining fragile leaves, the shutters creaked, inside the air moved slightly—and I was overcome by a premonition of a totally new and hypertrophied manifestation of the mug. The dogs howled. And when will I howl? That I would howl was a given. The gentry's strange and unreal customs of being pampered and mollycoddled by something, hypertrophied in an unimaginable vacuum, their languor and softness, fussiness, politeness, refinement, pride, tenderness, nicety, and lurking quirkiness in each and every word—filled me with mistrust and anxiety. But what was more dangerous—a solitary late-fall fly on the ceiling, an aunt with her memories of childhood, Kneadus and his farmhand, illnesses, the fringe on a sofa, or the whole lot, bunched up and lumped onto the tip of a small spike? Anticipating the unavoidable mug, I sat quietly on my ancestral Biedermeier, a memento inherited from my forebears, while my aunt sat on hers and, to keep the conversation going, began groaning about drafts, that they're a terrible thing for one's bones at this time of the year. Zosia, an ordinary young woman, not in any way different from other young women of which there are thousands in our country manors, burst out laughing in an attempt to keep the conversation going—and everyone burst out laughing with a laughter of sociable, polite bewilderment—and they stopped laughing . . . For whom did they laugh, perchance, for whom?

But uncle Konstanty, who was tall and lean, effete, balding, with a long, thin nose, gaunt fingers, thin lips and delicate nostrils, highly polished manners, experienced in life, reclined in his chair with extraordinary ease and nonchalant elegance, and rested his feet, clad in suede shoes, upon the table.

"Drafts," he said, "yes, we had them. But they're gone now."

The fly buzzed.

"Kostie," auntie exclaimed tenderly, "stop fretting." And she gave him a piece of candy.

But he fretted anyway and yawned—he opened his mouth wide,

The Farmhand, or Captive Again

till I saw his farthest cigarette-stained yellowish teeth, and he bla-
tantly yawned twice more with the utmost nonchalance.

"Tereperepumpum," he mumbled, "a dog once danced in a backyard, and a she-cat laughed so hard!"

He pulled out a silver cigarette case and tapped it with his fingers,
but it fell to the floor. He didn't pick it up, he yawned again—at
whom did he yawn? For whom did he yawn? His family accompanied his actions in silence, sitting on their Biedermeiers. Francis,
the old servant, entered.

"Dinner is served," he announced; he wore a frock coat.

"Dinner," auntie said.

"Dinner," Zosia said.

"Dinner," Zygmunt said.

"My cigarette case," my uncle said. The servant picked it up—we
moved to the dining room, which was in the style of Henry IV, old
portraits hung on the walls, in a corner a samovar was hissing.
They served baked ham in a crust, and canned peas. Conversation
sounded again. "Dig in," Konstanty said, helping himself to a little
mustard and some horseradish (but against whom did he do this?),
"there's nothing better than ham baked in a crust, if properly prepared. Simon's is the only place where you can get good ham, the
only place, tereperepumpum, is Simon's! Let's have a drink. A jigger."

"Let's have a swig," Zygmunt said, and my uncle asked: "Do you
remember the ham they served before the war on Erywańska Street?"
"Ham is hard to digest," auntie answered. "Zosia, why so little, no
appetite again?" Zosia answered, but no one listened because she
obviously did it just to say something. Konstanty ate rather loudly,
though with style, punctiliously; working his fingers over his plate he
would take a rasher, add some mustard or horseradish, maybe salt or
pepper, butter a slice of toast, and shove the ham into his gaping
mouth—once he even spat out a piece of it because he didn't like it.
The valet immediately removed it. Against whom did he spit it out?
Against whom did he butter the toast? Auntie ate kind-heartedly,

rather copiously but a thin slice at a time, Zosia was shoving it in, Zygmunt ate listlessly, while the servants waited on us t i p t o e i n g. Suddenly Kneadus stopped eating, his fork halfway to his mouth, and he froze, his gaze darkened, his mug turned ashen-gray, his lips parted, and a most beautiful mandolin smile blossomed on his horrible mug. A smile of welcome, of greeting, hail, so you're here, I'm here too—he rested his hands on the table and leaned forward, his upper lip rose as if to sob; but he didn't sob, he just leaned farther. He had spotted a farmhand! A farmhand was in the room! The valet! The valet was the farmhand! I had no doubt—the valet serving the ham and peas was the farmhand of his dreams.

A farmhand! Kneadus' age, no more than eighteen, neither short nor tall, neither ugly nor handsome—fair-haired but not blond. He bustled and waited on us barefoot, a napkin slung over his left arm, no collar, his shirt buttoned at the neck with a stud, a farmhand's usual Sunday best. He had a mug all right—but his mug wasn't anything like Kneadus' awful mug, it was not an artificially created mug, but a natural, rough-hewn, ordinary peasant mug. It was not a face that had turned into a mug, but a mug that had never ever had the honor of being a face—his mug was as dumb as a leg! He wasn't worthy of having a respectable face, just as he wasn't worthy of being called blond and handsome—a valet unworthy of being a butler! Without gloves and barefoot, he changed the smart set's plates, which surprised no one—a young man not worthy of a frock coat. A farmhand! . . . What bad luck had brought him here, to my aunt's and uncle's house? "Here we go," I thought, chewing the ham that now tasted like rubber, "it's starting . . ." But to keep the conversation going they began to urge us to eat, I had to try some of the pear compote—and again there was a round of small pretzels with tea, I had to say "thank you," eat candied plums that stuck in my throat, and auntie kept apologizing for such a modest dinner.

"Tereperepumpum," said uncle Konstanty, who sprawled at the table and, opening his mouth wide, lazily tossed in a plummie,

The Farmhand, or Captive Again

which he had picked up with two fingers. "Eat up! Eat up! To your hearts' content, my dears!" He swallowed it, smacked his lips—and said, as if with a deliberate display of satiety:

"Tomorrow I'll lay off six grooms, without pay, because I have no money!"

"Oh, Kostie!" auntie exclaimed, all heart. But he replied.

"Cheese-e-oh, please."

Against whom did he say that? The servants waited on us t i p t o e i n g. Kneadus stared, he drank with his eyes that uncontorted peasant's mug, meadowy and dumb, he imbibed it as if it were the one and only drink in the whole world. The valet tripped under that onerous and distracted stare, almost spilling tea on auntie's head. Old Francis lightly boxed his ear.

"Oh, Francis," auntie said kindly.

"He better watch out!" my uncle mumbled, and he took out a cigarette. The valet sprang to him with a light. My uncle let out a cloud of smoke through his thin lips, cousin Zygmunt let another cloud pass between his equally thin lips, and we moved to the living room, where everyone sat on his or her priceless Biedermeier. The pricelessness filled us with terrible luxury from below. Foul weather howled outside the windows; cousin Zygmunt, mildly animated, suggested:

"A little game of bridge, perhaps?"

But Kneadus didn't know how to play, so Zygmunt fell silent and just sat there. Zosia mentioned something about the weather, that it often rains in the fall, auntie asked me about auntie Jadzia. The conversation was petering out—my uncle crossed his legs, raised his head, and looked at the ceiling where a listless fly wandered to and fro—and he yawned, showing us his palate and a row of cigarette-stained, yellowish teeth. Zygmunt silently busied himself with slow leg-wagging as he tracked glints of light across the tip of his shoe, auntie and Zosia sat with their hands in their laps, a little pinscher sat on a table and watched Zygmunt's leg, while Kneadus sat in the shadow, his head resting on his palm, and he was awfully quiet. Then auntie perked up, ordered the servants to prepare the guest room, to place hot-water bottles in our beds, and to bring us a small dish of nuts and fruit preserves as a nightcap. My uncle, on hearing this, said casually that he too would like some, whereupon the servants swiftly obliged. We ate, though we were already full—we couldn't refuse, it was all on a tray, ready to be eaten, and also because they kept insisting and inviting us to eat. Kneadus declined over and over, he definitely didn't want any fruit preserves, and I had an idea why—because of the farmhand—but, out of the kindness of her heart auntie spooned him a double portion, and she offered me candy from a small bag. It's all so sweet, all too sweet, sickly-sweet, but with a dessert plate in front of me, I can't say no, I'm nauseous, my childhood, auntie, short pants, family, the fly, the pinscher, the farmhand, Kneadus, my full stomach, it's stuffy here, the weather is foul outside the window, glut and excess of everything, it's all too much, dreadful wealth, the Biedermeier satiates me from below. But I can't get up and say goodnight, not without saying something first . . . we finally try, but they stop us, inviting us to eat more. Against whom does uncle Konstanty stuff one more strawberry between his sugared and weary lips? Suddenly Zosia sneezes, and this gives us an out. Goodbyes, bows, thanks, bumping into body parts. The chambermaid leads us up wooden, winding stairs that I seem to remember . . . Behind us walks a servant with nuts and fruit preserves on a tray. It's stifling and warm. I burp, the fruit preserves repeat in my mouth. Kneadus also burps. The country manor . . .

When the door closed behind the chambermaid he asked:

"Did you see that?"

He sat down and hid his face in his hands.

"You're talking about the valet?" I replied, feigning indifference. I quickly pulled down the blind—the lit window in the dark expanses of the wooded grounds was scaring me.

The Farmhand, or Captive Again

"I have to talk to him. I'll go down! Or, no—ring for him! He's surely assigned to serve us. Ring twice."

"What for?" I tried to dissuade him. "There can be complications. Remember that these are my aunt and uncle . . . Kneadus!" I exclaimed, "don't ring, tell me first what you want with him?"

He pressed the bell.

"Damn it!" he growled, "as if the fruit preserves weren't enough, they've left us apples and pears. Hide them in the closet. Throw away the hot-water bottles. I don't want him to see it all . . ."

He was furious with the kind of fury behind which lurks the fear of one's fate, the fury of the most intimate human affairs.

"Joey," he trembled as he whispered warmly, sincerely, "Joey, did you see that, he's got a real mug—not one of those rigged-up ones, this is an ordinary mug! A mug without any face-pulling! A classic farmhand, I won't find a better one anywhere. Help me! I can't manage it all by myself!"

"Calm down! What do you want to do?"

"I don't know, I don't know. If I become friends with him . . . if I succeed in fra . . . fra . . . fraternizing with him . . ." he admitted, embarrassed, "to frater . . . nize! Socia . . . lize! I must do it! Help me!"

The valet entered the room.

"At yer service," he said.

He stood in the door, waiting for orders, so Kneadus ordered him to pour some water into a washbowl. The valet poured the water and again stood still—so Kneadus ordered him to open a casement, and when the fellow did that and stood still Kneadus ordered him to hang a towel on a peg; when he did that, Kneadus ordered him to put his jacket on a hanger—but these orders tortured Kneadus terribly. He ordered, the farmhand carried everything out without a murmur—these orders, however, became more and more like a bad dream, oh, to order one's farmhand about instead of fraternizing with him—to order him about with lordly capriciousness, to go through a whole night of lordly fantasies in an ordering frenzy! Finally, not knowing what else to command, having run out of things to command, he ordered him to bring out the hot-water bottles and apples hidden in the closet, and he whispered to me, totally broken:

"You try. I can't."

I slowly took off my jacket, and I sat on the edge of my bed, dangling my legs—a position more conducive to gabbing with a farmhand. I asked him slowly, out of boredom:

"What's your name?"

"Valek," he replied, and it was obvious that this wasn't just an informal name, it agreed with him—as if he were unworthy of the formal 'Valenty' or of a last name. Kneadus shuddered.

"How long have you been in service here?"

"About a month, sire."

"And where were you employed before that?"

"In the stables, sire."

"Do you like it here?"

"Yes, sire."

"Bring us some warm water."

"Very good, sire."

When he left, Kneadus had tears in his eyes. He cried his heart out. Tears trickled down his haggard face. "Did you hear that? Did you hear that? Valek! He doesn't even have a last name! Oh, it all fits perfectly! Did you see his mug? A mug without any artifice, just an ordinary mug! Joey, if he won't fra . . . fraternize with me, I don't know what I'll do!" He was working himself into a rage, he reproached me for having ordered the valet to fetch hot water, and he could not forgive himself for having ordered Valek, while at a loss for other commands, to bring out the hot-water bottles we had hidden in the closet. "He probably never uses hot water, let alone water in bottles for his bed. He probably never washes himself. And yet he's not dirty. Joey, did you notice he doesn't wash, and yet he's not dirty—his dirt seems harmless, it's not disgusting! Hey-ho, look at our filth, our filth . . ."

In this guest room of an old country manor his passion was erupting with a mighty force. He wiped away his tears—the valet returned with the water. This time Kneadus followed my line of questioning:

"How old are you?" he asked looking straight ahead.

"Eeeh . . . how should I know, sire."

Kneadus was flabbergasted. The valet didn't know! He didn't know how old he was! A heavenly farmhand indeed, free of ridiculous appendages! Under the pretext of wanting to wash his hands he went closer to the farmhand and, controlling his trembling, he said:

"You're probably my age."

But this was not a question. It left the valet some leeway to respond. Fra . . . ternization was supposed to begin. The valet replied:

"Very good, sir."

Whereupon Kneadus returned to the unavoidable questioning:

"Do you know how to read and write?"

"Ee . . . why no! sire."

"You have a family?"

"I have a sister, sire."

"And what does your sister do?"

"She milks the cows, sire."

He stood there, while Kneadus focused on him—it seemed there was no other way except through questioning and giving orders, commands or questions. So he sat down again and commanded:

"Take off my shoes."

I sat down too. The room was long and narrow, not easy for the three of us to move about. The huge, grim house stood in the wet and murky wooded grounds. The wind seemed to have let up, but this was worse—a sharp wind would have felt better. Kneadus stuck out his leg, the farmhand knelt, and, his mug lowered, he bent over the leg while Kneadus' mug hovered feudally above him, pale and horrible, hardened in commands, no longer knowing what to ask. I asked out of the blue:

"Does the squire ever slap you in the mug?"

The valet suddenly brightened and called out cheerfully, like a true peasant:

"Oh, yes sir, in the mug! Jee, yeah, in the mug!"

As soon as he said that, I sprang up, I swung my arm and smacked him in the left cheek as hard as I could. In the quiet of the night the sound was like a pistol shot. The fellow clutched his mug but instantly dropped his hand and stood up.

"Wow, that was a good slap, sire!" he whispered all agog with admiration.

"Get out!" I shouted.

He went out.

"What on earth did you do that for?!" Kneadus said, wringing his hands. "I wanted to shake hands with him! Go hand in hand with him! Then our mugs, and everything else, would have been equal. Yet see what you've done with your hand, you hit him in the mug! And I stuck my leg into his hands! To unlace my shoe," he moaned, "my shoe! Why did you slap him?!"

I had no idea why. It happened as if a spring had been released, I shouted "get out" because I had hit him, but why did I hit him? There was a knock at the door—and cousin Zygmunt, candle in hand, in slippers and trousers, appeared on the threshold.

"Did someone fire a shot?" he asked. "I thought I heard a shot from a Browning?"

"I shot your Valek in the snoot."

"You shot him in the snoot?"

"He filched my cigarette."

I preferred him to hear it from me, in my version, than tomorrow morning from the servants. Zygmunt was slightly surprised, but, like a good host, he laughed and said:

"Great. That'll teach him! But—you hit him in the mug, just like that?" he asked in disbelief. I laughed, while Kneadus cast me a look which I'll never forget, a look of one betrayed, and he went to the bathroom, or so I thought. My cousin's gaze followed him. "Your friend seems to disapprove—eh?" he observed with slight irony, "he's indignant? Typical bourgeois!" "Bourgeois!" I said, what else could I say? "Bourgeois," he said, "a guy like Valek will respect you like his lord and master if you hit him in the snoot. You have to know the likes of them! They love it!"

"They love it!" I said. "They love it, love it, ha, ha, ha! They love it!" I couldn't believe that this was my cousin who, until now, had treated me with reserve, now his apathy was gone, his eyes were shining, he liked my slapping Valek's mug, and he now liked me; a pure bred young master surfaced from within an indolent and bored student, as if he had just breathed through his nostrils the aroma of forests and of common folk. He placed the candle on the windowsill and sat at the foot of the bed with a cigarette. "They love it," he said, "they love it! You may slap them, but you must tip them too—I don't go for slapping without tipping. In times past, my father and uncle Severyn used to hit the doorman at the Grand Hotel in the snoot." "And our uncle Eustachy," I said, "once hit his barber in the snoot." "No one hit the snoot as well as grandma Evelina, but that belongs to the past. Well, Toby Patz got drunk and smacked a train conductor in the snoot. Do you know Pavel Patz, he's very unaffected." I replied that I knew a few of the Patz men, all extremely natural and unpretentious, but thus far I hadn't met Toby. I said I knew that Harry Pitwicki once broke a window at the Club Cockatoo with a waiter's snoot. "I only bashed a ticket collector in the snoot on one occasion," Ziggie said. "Do you know the Pipowskis? The Mrs. is a fanatical snob, but she has extremely good taste. We may go partridge hunting tomorrow." (Where was Kneadus? Where did he go? Why isn't he back?) In the meantime my cousin showed no inclination to leave, the slap in Valek's face brought us closer, like a shot of vodka, and, while smoking his cigarette he chatted about face-bashing, about partridges, about Mrs. Pipowska, about unpretentiousness, about Tacyanki and Colombina, about Toby and Harry, how one had to be savvy about life, realistic, he talked about the agricultural school, and about the dough I'll earn when I'm done studying. I responded in a similar vein. So he's back with the same stuff again. So I'm back with the same. So he's back with snoot-bashing, that one has to know when, with whom, and for how much, so I'm back with it's better to box an ear than to punch someone in the jaw. But in all of this there was something unreal, and I tried a few times to interject into our talk that all this doesn't happen anymore, it's no longer acceptable, nowadays no one bashes anyone, that's gone, perhaps it never was, it's a legend, a squire's imagination. Yet I couldn't, oh, how sweet this chatting, the squirely imagination has grabbed us and won't let us go, we hold forth like one young master to another! "Sometimes it's a good thing—mug slapping!" "In the snoot—it's good for you! Nothing like hitting a guy in the snoot! Well, it's time for me to go," he finally said, "I've stayed too long already . . . We'll see each other from time to time in Warsaw. I'll introduce you to Toby Patz. Look—it's almost midnight. Your friend's been in the bathroom a long time . . . maybe he's sick. Goodnight."

He hugged me.

"Goodnight, Joey."

"Goodnight, Ziggie," I replied.

Why wasn't Kneadus back? I wiped sweat off my brow. Why this conversation with my cousin? I looked out the casement, it had stopped raining, I could see no farther than fifty paces, here and there in the thick of night I guessed at the shapes of trees—but their shapes seemed darker than darkness itself and even less defined. Behind this veil the wooded grounds, secret and who knows what else besides, woven through and through by tracts of desolate fields, dripped with moisture. Unable to make out what was before my eyes, looking, yet unable to see anything except shapes, darker than the night, I closed the window and retreated into the back of the

The Farmhand, or Captive Again

room. There had been no need for it all. No need to hit the farm-hand. No need for the chat. Here the snoot-hitting was like a shot of vodka, quite different from the democratic, dry face-slapping in the city. What the hell is a servant's snoot in an old country manor? It was terrible that, by slapping him in the face, I had brought the valet's mug to the surface and, to top it all off, I had lied about him to the young master. Where was Kneadus?

He returned at about one in the morning; he didn't come in right away but peeked through the half-open door to see if I was asleep—he slipped in as if returning from some nocturnal carousal and quickly turned down the lamp wick. He undressed hurriedly. When he leaned over the lamp I noticed that his mug had undergone a sordid transformation—it was puffed up, swollen on the left side, and it looked like a little apple, a little stewed apple, and everything about him came out like mush. What a hellish b e l i t t l e m e n t! It again appeared in my life, this time on my friend's face! He's turned into a horrible coxcomb—that's what popped into my head—a hor-rible coxcomb. What gigantic force had fixed him like this? He an-swered my question in a voice that was a bit too thin and squeaky:

"I was in the pantry. I frater . . . ternized with the farmhand. He hit me in the mug."

"The valet hit you in the mug?" I couldn't believe my ears.

"He did," he joyfully assured me, but with a joy that was artificial and still too feeble. "We're brothers. I was finally able to communi-cate with him." But he said this like a *Sonntagsjäger,* like a city official bragging about drinking at a country wedding. He'd been man-handled with a crushing, devastating force—but his attitude toward that force was insincere. I pressed him with questions, and he grudg-ingly revealed, hiding his face in the shadow:

"I ordered him."

"What?!" my blood boiled, "what do you mean? You ordered him to hit you in the face?! He'll think you're crazy! Congratulations! Wait till my aunt and uncle hear about this!"

"It's your fault," he said grimly and tersely, "you shouldn't have hit him. You started it. You fancied yourself a lordship! I had to take it from him, because you gave it to him . . . Without it there would be no equality, and I wouldn't be able to fra . . . ter . . ."

He turned off the light and spewed out in broken sentences the whole story of his desperate endeavors. He found the farmhand in the pantry cleaning his masters' shoes, and he sat next to him, whereupon the valet stood up. *Da capo*, again—he tried to make conversation, to put the fellow at ease, make him open up and be friends, but his words, even as they left his lips, deteriorated into a sickening and senseless pastorale. The farmhand did his best to answer him, but it was obvious that it was beginning to bore Valek, and he didn't understand what this crazy lordship wanted from him. Kneadus finally became entangled in cheap verbosity derived from the French Revolution and from the Bill of Rights, he went on to explain that all men are equal and, under this pretext, demanded that the valet shake hands with him—but the latter flatly refused. "My hand's not fit fer your lo'dship." Kneadus then had the preposterous idea that if he succeeded in forcing the farmhand to slap him in the mug, the ice would be broken. "Hit me in the snoot," he implored, unmindful of anything, "in the snoot!" and bending over, he bared his face to the valet's hand. The valet, however, went on refusing: "Ee," he said, "why should I hit your lo'dship?" Kneadus begged and begged, until finally he yelled: "Slap me, damn it, do as I tell you! What the devil is the matter with you?!" At that instant he saw stars, smash, bang—the farmhand had whacked him in the mug! "Once more," Kneadus yelled, "once more, damn it!" Crash, bang, stars again. He opened his eyes and saw the valet standing in front of him with his hands, ready to carry out his orders! But a slap in the face that is given in answer to a command is not a true slap in the face—no more than pouring water into the washbowl or taking off his shoes—and a blush of embarrassment covered the blush from the slapping. "More, more," the martyr whispered, so that the farmhand would at last fra . . . ternize with him by way of his face. And again—crash, bang, stars—oh, this mug-pounding in an empty pantry, among wet dishrags, over a tub of hot water!

Fortunately, this son of the peasantry found his lordship's whims amusing. He probably reached the conclusion that his lordship had gone soft in the head (and nothing emboldens the rabble like their lordships' mental illness), and he proceeded to make fun, peasant style, which created a kinship of sorts. Soon enough the farmhand was fraternizing to such a degree that he was poking Kneadus in the ribs and finagling small change from him.

"Gimme, mister, for some smokes!"

But this wasn't it at all, it was hostile, unbrotherly, and unfriendly, full of peasant style mockery, lethal, far from the desired fraternization. Yet Kneadus put up with it, he preferred the valet to abuse him, rather than to abuse the valet as if he were his lord and master. A kitchen maid, Marcy, came out of the kitchen with a wet rag to wash the floor and began to marvel at the shenanigans:

"Jesus A'mighty! This really is somethin'!"

The house was asleep—and so they could, with impunity, indulge in frolicking with his lordship who was paying them a visit in the pantry, to laugh at him with their peasant, rustic superlaugh. Kneadus himself helped them along and laughed with them. But gradually, while ridiculing Kneadus, they began also to laugh at their own master and mistress. "That's them ohright! They do notin', they're fer ever doin' notin' but stuffin' and stuffin' 'emselves till they bust! They stuff 'emselves, get sick, lie around, walk about their rooms, talkin' about somethin'. An' how they gobble! O Mother o' Jesus! I wouldn't eat half that much, even though 'am just a simple bastard. There's dinner, and afternoon tea, candy, and fruit preserves, eggs 'n onions for brunch. Their lo'dships eat like pigs and gorge 'emselves with sweets, then—bellies up they lie about and get sick from it all. An' during a hunt the squire clambered up the gamekeeper! Up the gamekeeper he clambered! Vincenty, the gamekeeper, was standin' behind him with a spare shotgun, the squire shot at a boar, the boar bounded toward him, so the squire dropped the shotgun and clambered up Vincenty—Marcy, be quiet—up Vincenty he clambered! 'Cause there was no tree close by, he clambered up Vincenty! Later the squire gave him a zloty an' told him not to breathe a word of it, or it'll cost him his job." "O Jesus! Oh, for chrissakes stop it, me belly aches from laughin'!" Marcy grabbed her belly. "An' the young lady promenades, lookin' around—goes for walks. The Mr. and Mrs. promenade, lookin' around. His lo'dship Zygmunt keeps lookin' at me, only I'm kind 'a below him—he pinched me once, but nothin' doin'! He kept lookin', an' lookin' around so nobody's watchin' us till I got a belly ache from laughin', an' I run away! So later he gave me a zloty, told me not to tell nobody, but nobody, he said he was drunk!" "Drunk, me foot!" the farmhand butted in. "Other girls won't have nothin' to do with him either, 'cause he's for ever lookin' round. So he's got that hag in the village, Josie, the widah, an' he keeps meetin' up with her in the bushes by the pond, but he made her swear she'd never blab on him to nobody, but nobody—oh, yeah, I bet!" "Hee, hee, hee, hee! Shush, Valek, darlin'! Their lo'dships are very proper-like! Very delicate-like!" "Oh, yeah, delicate, you have to wipe their noses, they can't do nothin' fer the'selves. 'Gimme this, hand me that, fetch me t'other,' you have to hold their coats for 'em, they won't put 'em on the'selves. When ah first came here—ah felt kinda strange. If anybody got to groomin' and accommodatin' me like that, ah'd rather sink into the ground—honest. I have to put lotions on the squire of evenin's." "A'n I have to knead the young lady," squeaked the girl, "knead the young lady wit' my hands, 'cause she's flabby-like. The Mr. and Mrs. are so soft, and their little hands! Hee, hee, hee, what soft little hands they have!" "O Jesus! They promenade, they gorge the'selves, they parley Francey, and git bored." "Shush, Valek, darlin'! That's loose talk, the squire's lady's kind!" "Oh, yeah, kind, she puts the squeeze on us folk—so she's got to be kind! The stomachs in the village are growlin'

The Farmhand, or Captive Again

wit' hunger. Them put the squeeze on us. Yes, siree, everybody works for 'em, the squire goes into the fields just to watch 'em slavin' away."

"An' the squire's lady's afraid of the cows. She's afraid of the cows!!! Their lo'dships are conversin'! Their lo'dships walk about and converse—hee, hee, hee—their lo'dships' skin is so white-like! . . ." The wench went on clamoring and marveling, the farmhand prattled in wonderment, gloating, when suddenly Francis walked in . . .

"Francis walked in?" I interrupted Kneadus. "The butler?"

"Yes, Francis! The devil himself brought him," Kneadus squeaked. "Marcy's clamor must have wakened him. He didn't dare say anything to me, of course, but he scolded Marcy and the farmhand—that this was no time for jabbering, scram, to work, he told them that the hour was late and the dishes weren't done. They took off. What a mean lackey!"

"Did he hear anything?"

"I don't know—maybe he did. He's so commonplace—a flunky with sideburns and a stiff collar. A peasant with sideburns—a traitor. A traitor and an informer. If he heard anything—he's sure to tell on us. And we had such a good time gabbing."

"There will be hell to pay . . ." I said softly.

But he whined, raising his voice to a treble.

"Traitors! And you too—you're a traitor! You're all traitors, traitors . . ."

I couldn't fall asleep for a long time. Above the ceiling, in the attic, martens or rats scurried around making a racket, I heard their squeaks, sudden jumps, running and chasing, awful screeches of animals tense with wildness. The roof dripped with water. Dogs howled like so many automatons, and our room with its shades drawn tightly was a box of darkness. Kneadus lay on the other bed awake, I lay supine on mine, also awake, my hands under my head, my gaze fixed on the ceiling—we were both watchful as our inaudible breathing indicated. What was he doing under the cover of darkness—yes what, since he wasn't asleep he must have been doing something—and I was doing something too. Someone who is not asleep is active, cannot be inactive. Hence he must have been active. I too was active. What was he thinking about? What was he longing for in his squeaky, high-pitched state, tense and taut as if seized by claws. I was asking God to let him sleep, so that he wouldn't be so silent, but more open, less secretive—he'd relax, loosen up . . .

A night of torture! I didn't know what to do! Run away at the crack of dawn? I was sure that Francis, the old servant, would tell my aunt and uncle about the mug-slapping and Kneadus' palaver with the farmhand. And then the infernal dance would begin, and discord, deceit, devil on the loose, and the mug, the mug would come into its own again! And the pupa! Is this why I escaped from the Young-bloods? We had awakened the beast! We had released the servants' impudence! That terrible night, as I lay sleepless on my bed, I finally grasped the mystery of a country manor, of squires and landed gentry in general, the mystery whose manifold and murky symptoms had, from the very first moment, filled me with foreboding of the mug and its terrifying business! It was their servants who were the mystery. Ragtag peasantry was the gentry's mystery. Against whom did my uncle yawn, or shove one more sweet strawberry into his mouth? Against the ragtag peasantry, against his own servants! Why didn't he pick up his cigarette case? So that the servants would pick it up for him. Why did he extend civilities to us with a school-boy's zeal, so much politeness and consideration, so much style and *bon ton?* In order to draw the line between himself and the servants and, by opposing the servants, to preserve patrician custom. And everything, no matter what the gentry did, was done with regard to and in the face of servants, in relation to house servants and to farmhands.

Could it have been otherwise? Those of us living in the city didn't even feel like lords of the manor, we dressed, spoke and gestured the same way as the proletariat, and a myriad of imperceptible semi-tones united us with the proletariat—going down the rungs of society to the shopkeeper, the street car conductor, the cabdriver, one could inconspicuously go down all they way to the garbage collector; but here in the country, lordliness towered like a lonely poplar in all its nakedness. Here at the manor there was no intermediary between the squire and his servant, the estate manager lived in the farm outbuildings, the priest lived at the refectory. My uncle's proud, ancestral lordliness sprouted directly out of the rabble undergrowth, it was from the rabble that it drew its vital juices. In the city, services were provided in a roundabout way, in a discretionary manner— each to each, a little at a time—while here the squire had an actual, personal yokel, who, when the squire raised his leg, would clean his shoe . . . And my uncle and auntie certainly didn't know what was said about them in the pantry—how they looked in the yokels' eyes. They knew—but they wouldn't let this knowledge loose, they stifled it, strangled it, pushed it into the cellars of their brain.

Oh, to be seen through the eyes of your yokel! To be watched and tattled about by a yokel! To be constantly refracted by the boorish prism of a servant who has access to your rooms, who hears your conversations, who watches your behavior, who is allowed to serve coffee at your table or at your bedside—to be the subject of coarse, fallow, insipid kitchen prattle, and never be able to explain yourself on an equal footing. Truly, it is only through servants like the butler, coachman, chambermaid, that one can discover the core of country gentry. Without the butler you will not know the squire. Without the chambermaid you will not fathom the mettle of the squire's lady nor the pitch of her lofty aspirations, and you will know the squire's son through the country wench. Oh, I finally understood the cause of their strange anxiety and constraint, which struck everyone coming from the city to visit a country manor. It was the rabble that scared the gentry. It was the rabble that constrained them. The rabble had them in their pocket. Here was—the real cause. Here was—their perpetual, secret festering. Here was—their subterranean, life and death pain, seasoned with all the possible venoms of their struggles, concealed and subterranean. A hundredfold worse than mere financial disputes, because it was a struggle dictated by otherness and estrangement—otherness of body and estrangement of spirit. Their souls, in the midst of peasant souls, were in the woods; their lordly and delicate bodies, in the midst of yokels' bodies, were in the jungle. Their hands were repulsed by the yokel paws, their legs hated yokel legs, their faces hated the mugs, their eyes—the yokels' eyeballs, their little fingers—the rabble's stubby fingers, the situation smacked all the more of humiliation because they were constantly touched and groomed by them, as the farmhand had said, pampered and rubbed down with creams . . . To have in one's own home and near you nothing but dissimilar, foreign body parts!—because indeed, within the radius of many kilometers there were only peasant limbs, peasant speech " 'course, darlin'," "I ain't," "you was," "chrissake," "mommy-luv," "daddy-luv," and only the parish priest and the manager in the farm buildings were the squires' kinsmen. But the manager merely had a position, and the priest actually wore a skirt. Wasn't it loneliness then, that gave rise to the rapacious hospitality with which they clung to us after supper—with us they felt more at ease. We were their allies. Yet Kneadus betrayed their lordly faces with the farmhand's peasant mug.

The perverse fact that the valet had hit Kneadus' face—the face, no less, of his lordship's guest and a young sir himself—must bear equally perverse consequences. The time-honored hierarchy was based on the supremacy of lordly parts, and it was a system of intense and feudal hierarchy, in which his lordship's hand was level with the servant's mug, and his leg was at the peasant's midriff. This was archaic hierarchy. An ancient system, canon and law. It was the mystical clasp holding his lordship's and the yokel's body parts together, sanctified by centuries of custom, and it was solely in this configuration that their lordships could touch and make contact with the yokels. Hence the magic of mug-slapping. Hence Valek's almost religious worship of mug-slapping. Hence Zygmunt's lordly revelry. Nowadays, of course, they slapped no more (although Valek did admit sometimes getting it from my uncle), yet the potential for a slap in the face was always there, and that's what sustained them in their lordliness. And now, didn't the yokel's paw unceremoniously mate with his lordship's face?

And now the servants were proudly raising their heads. On went the kitchen tittle-tattle. On went the peasantry, emboldened and corrupted by familiarity with the body parts, openly denigrating their lordships, the yokels' criticism was on the rise—what will happen, what will transpire when this penetrates to my aunt and uncle, and his lordship's face stands face to face with the peasant's lumpish mug?

14 Mug on the Loose and New Entrapment

And indeed, next morning after breakfast my aunt took me aside. It was a brisk, sunny morning, the earth was damp and black, copses of trees trailing their cerulean autumn foliage stood in the huge courtyard; under the trees peaceable hens scratched and pecked at the ground. Time stood still at that morning hour, and golden streaks of sunlight lay on the floor of the smoking room. Docile dogs wandered about here and there. Equally docile pigeons cooed. My aunt, however, was inwardly billowing like a heavy sea.

"My dear child," she said, "please explain . . . Francis told me that your friend is apparently hobnobbing with the servants in the kitchen. Is he some kind of an agitator?"

"He's a theoretician," Zygmunt said. "Don't worry, Mother—he's a theorist of life! He arrived here to the countryside with his theories— a democrat from the city!"

He was still cheerful and somewhat foppish after last night.

"Ziggie, my dear, he's no theoretician, he's a practitioner! Apparently, Francis says, he shook hands with Valek!"

Fortunately, the old butler hadn't told everything, and, as far as I could tell, my uncle hadn't been informed of what had happened. I pretended that I hadn't heard either, I chuckled (oh, how often life makes us chuckle), I said something about Kneadus' leftist ideology, and so, for the time being, the whole affair came to nothing. Of course no one talked with Kneadus about it. We played *King*—a card game Zosia had suggested, it would have been rude to refuse—and the game held us in its grip until dinner. Zosia, Zygmunt, Kneadus, and I, all of us bored yet laughing, laid out the cards on the green felt, higher denominations on lower, by color, hearts were trump. Zygmunt played with precision—an austere game, as if he were at his club, a cigarette between his lips—he threw his cards horizontally, aiming accurately at the stack, and his white fingers picked up the tricks with a snapping sound. Kneadus licked his fingers, kneaded the cards, and I noticed that he was embarrassed, playing such a lordly game as *King,* he repeatedly looked at the door, wondering whether the farmhand saw this—he would have preferred to sit on the floor and play *Dummie.* Above all I feared dinnertime because I was almost certain that Kneadus would not be able to handle an encounter at the table with the farmhand—my fears turned out to be justified.

We were served *bigos* as an appetizer, then clear tomato soup, veal cutlets, pears in vanilla sauce—all prepared with the cook's coarse fingers, while the servants waited on us t i p t o e i n g—Francis in white gloves, the farmhand barefoot, a napkin over his arm.* Kneadus looked pale and, his eyes downcast, ate the fine, carefully chosen dishes that Valek placed before him, miserable that the farmhand was feeding him such delicacies. To make matters worse, my aunt, in an attempt to gently make Kneadus aware of the impropriety of his excesses in the pantry, treated him with extreme politeness, she asked him about family matters and about his departed father. Forced to

---

Bigos—a Polish dish traditionally served after a hunt and consisting of sauerkraut stewed with pieces of meat. Pronounced "beegos."

turn well-rounded phrases Kneadus was in torment, speaking to her softly so that the farmhand wouldn't overhear, not daring to look in Valek's direction. And perhaps that's why, when dessert was served, instead of answering my aunt, he lost himself in longing, a meek smile on his squeaky-thin mug—the dessert spoon idling in his hand. I couldn't nudge him because I was sitting on the far side of the table. My aunt fell silent, while the farmhand burst into an embarrassed, peasant guffaw, as peasants are wont to do when their lo'dships are lookin' at us, and he covered his mouth with his hand. The butler boxed his ear. Right at this moment my uncle lit a cigarette and was inhaling the smoke. Did he see what had just happened? It was so obvious that I was afraid he would tell Kneadus to leave the table.

But instead, Konstanty let the smoke out through his nose rather than his mouth!

"Wine!" he exclaimed, "wine! Oh, let us have wine!"

All of a sudden his spirits seemed to rise, he sprawled on his chair and drummed on the table with his fingers.

"Wine! Tell them, Francis, to bring that 'granny Henry' from the cellar—we'll have a sip! Valek, coffee—black! Cigars! Let's light up a cigar—to hell with cigarettes!"

And, drinking to Kneadus, he began to reminisce about days gone by when he used to go pheasant hunting with Prince Severyn. And, drinking especially to Kneadus and to no one else, he went on talking about a barber at the Bristol Hotel, the best barber he'd ever encountered. He became lively, excited, while the servants doubled their attention and, with their peasant fingers, swiftly filled our glasses with wine. Kneadus, looking like a corpse, a glass in his hand, drank to my uncle Konstanty, he was in torment, not knowing why he deserved such unexpected attention, but he had to imbibe the old, delicate, fusty wine with its fine bouquet right in Valek's presence. I too wondered about my uncle's unexpected reaction. After dinner he took me by the arm and led me to the smoking room.

"Your friend," he said in his most aristocratic tone and with experience in his voice, "he's a pede . . . pede . . . Hmm . . . He's after Valek! Did you notice that? Ho, ho. Well, let's hope the ladies don't get wind of this. Prince Severyn also had his moments!"

He stretched his long legs. Oh, he delivered this with a truly aristocratic and masterful skill! With that lordly finesse to which four hundred waiters, seventy barbers, thirty jockeys, and the same number of maitre d's had contributed, oh, with what pleasure did he bring into relief a *bon vivant's*, *a grand seigneur's* peppery, restaurant knowledge of life! This is how truly high-bred lordliness, when it hears of something like sexual perversion or intemperance, displays its masculine knowledge of life, which it has learned from waiters and barbers. My uncle's peppery, restaurant wisdom infuriated me, I was like a dog maddened by a cat, I was shaken by the cynical simplicity with which he offered such a facile and lordly interpretation of the incident. I forgot all my fears. Out of sheer spite I told him everything! May God forgive me—impelled by his restaurant maturity I tumbled into greenery, and I resolved to treat him to a dish that was more undercooked than any of those he'd ever eaten in a restaurant.

"It's not at all what you think, uncle," I replied innocently, "he was just fra . . . ternizing."

"Fraternizing?" Konstanty said, surprised, "what do you mean—fraternizing? What do you mean by 'fraternizing'?" Thus unsaddled, he looked at me askance.

"Fra . . . ternizing," I replied, "he wanted to fra . . . ternize."

"Fraternize with Valek? How do you mean—fraternize? Perhaps you mean—stir up the servants? An agitator? Bolshevism—eh?"

"No, fraternizing like one young fellow with another."

My uncle stood up and shook the ashes from his cigar—he fell silent, searching for words.

"Fraternizing," he repeated, "he's fraternizing with peasantry, eh?" He tried to give it a name, to make it passable in a worldly, social, experiential sense, because a purely boyish fraternization was unacceptable, he felt that he wouldn't have been served this in a good restaurant. He was highly irritated by my following Kneadus' example and pronouncing "fra . . . ternizing" with a touch of a shy and embarrassed stammer. This floored him totally.

"He's fraternizing with peasantry?" he asked gingerly.

To which I replied: "No, he's fraternizing with the boy."

"Fraternizing with the boy? Which means what? He wants to play ball with him, or what?"

"No. To be his buddy, like a boy—they're fraternizing like one boy with another boy." My uncle's face turned red, probably for the first time since he started shaving, oh, that *à rebour* blush of a grown up man about town in relation to a naive youth!—he pulled out his watch, looked at it, and wound it up, searching all the while for a scientific, political, economic, or medical term in which he could box up, under lock and key, this sentimentally slippery matter. "A perversion, is it? Eh? Some complex? He's fra . . . ternizing? Maybe he's a socialist, a member of the Polish Socialist Party? A democrat, eh? He's fra . . . ternizing? *Mais qu'est que c'est* fra . . . ternizing? *Comment* fra . . . ternizing? *Fraternité, quoi, egalité, liberté?*" He began in French, yet he was not being truculent, but rather like someone who is hiding and literally "running for recourse" to the French language. He was helpless in relation to the young fellow. He lit his cigarette and put it out again, he crossed his legs, stroked his moustache.

"He's fraternizing? *What is that** fra . . . ternizing? Damn it! Prince Severyn . . ."

I went on gently and doggedly repeating "fra . . . ternizing," and I wouldn't have passed up for anything the green, soft naiveté that I was smearing all over my dear uncle.

"Kostie," auntie said kind-heartedly, as she stood on the threshold

*In English in the original text.

with a bag of candies in her hand, "don't be upset, he's probably fraternizing in Christ, fraternizing in brotherly love."

"No!" I answered stubbornly. "No! He fra . . . ternizes nakedly, without anything!"

"So he's a pervert after all!" Konstanty exclaimed.

"Not at all. He fraternizes without anything, and without perversion. He fraternizes like a boy."

"A boy? A boy? But what does it mean? *Pardon, mais qu'est-ce que c'est*—boy," he played dumb, "as a boy with Valek? In my house—with Valek? With my lackey?" He got mad and pressed the bell. "I'll show you the boy!"

The valet ran into the room. My uncle went up to him, his arm drawn back, and he might have given him a swift smack in the mug without even having to wind up, but he stopped halfway, disoriented, tottering inwardly, and he couldn't hit him, he could not make connection with Valek's mug under these circumstances. To hit the boy just because he was a boy? To hit him because he was "fraternizing"? It was out of the question. And Konstanty, who would have hit him for spilling coffee, dropped his arm.

"Out!" he yelled.

"Kostie!" exclaimed auntie, all heart, "Kostie!"

"It's no use," I said. "On the contrary, punching the valet in the snoot will only encourage Kneadus to fra . . . ternize. If someone gets it in the snoot—Kneadus loves him all the more."

My uncle blinked as though he were brushing a caterpillar off his waistcoat but said nothing; attacked by ironic naiveté from below, this virtuoso of drawing-room and restaurant irony behaved like a fencing master who is being accosted by a duck. The worldly country squire proved childishly naive when faced with naiveté. What's more interesting—in spite of his knowledge and experience of life, it didn't occur to him that I could be on Kneadus' and Valek's side against him, and that I could enjoy his lordly fits and spasms—it was characteristic of him to hold fast to the loyalty of the higher social class, which did not allow treason in its own circles. Old Francis came in wearing his coattails, shaved, with sideburns, and he stood in the center of the room.

Konstanty, somewhat ruffled, resumed his nonchalant attitude.

"What is it, my dear Francis?" he graciously asked, but in his voice there was a lord's regard for an old, seasoned servant, as there would be for an old, dry Hungarian wine. "What's on your mind, Francis?" The old servant looked at me, but my uncle waved his hand. "You can speak up."

"Did your lordship talk to Valek?"

"Ah, yes I did, I did, my dear Francis."

"I just wanted to be sure that your lordship had talked to him. If it were me, your lordship, I wouldn't have kept him another minute! I would have thrown him out on his face. He got too familiar with your lordships! People are already gabbing, your lordship!"

Three wenches ran through the courtyard, their bare legs flashing. A lame dog ran after them, barking. Zygmunt slipped out into the smoking room.

"They're gabbing?" uncle Konstanty asked. "What are they saying?"

"Their gabbing about your lordships!"

"They're gabbing about us?"

Fortunately the old servant didn't want to say anything more.

"They're gabbing about your lordships," he said. "Valek got familiar with the young master who has just arrived, so now, begging your pardon, sir, they're gabbing about your lordships without any respect. Mostly Valek and the wenches in the kitchen. I myself heard them gabbing with the young master till late at night, they gabbed about everything. They're gabbing for all their worth, anything they can think of! They're gabbing, it's terrible! I'd kick the scoundrel out on his face, your lordship, this very second."

The distinguished-looking servant blushed like a peony, all crimson, oh, the blush of an old butler! The lordship's soft and delicate blush answered him. His lord- and ladyship sat without a murmur—it wouldn't do to ask questions—maybe the butler would add something himself—their lordships hung on his words—but he didn't add anything.

"All right, all right, my dear Francis," uncle Konstanty finally said, "you may leave."

And the servant left just as he had come.

"They're gabbing about their lordships," he had said, and they didn't find out anything more. My uncle satisfied himself with a sour remark in auntie's direction: "You're too lax with the servants, my sweet, why are they so undisciplined? What drivel!" With that they turned to other matters, and, long after the servant had gone, they exchanged banalities and trivialities like: "where is Zosia?" and "has the mail arrived?" and they trivialized the whole affair to hide that Francis' insinuation had struck their weak spot. After almost a quarter of an hour of trivializing, Konstanty stretched himself, yawned, and unhurriedly crossed the parquet floor to the living room. I suspected that he was looking for Kneadus. He must have a talk with him, he felt the pressure of an inner need to have things immediately explained and clarified, he could no longer endure these murky waters. Auntie followed him.

Kneadus, however, was not in the living room, Zosia was the only one there, sitting with a textbook on practical vegetable farming on her lap, looking at the wall, at a fly—he was neither in the dining room nor in the study. The entire farmstead dozed in after-dinner silence, the fly buzzed, outside the hens circled on the withered lawns and pecked at the ground, the little pinscher nudged the mutt and nipped at his tail. My uncle, Zygmunt, and auntie cautiously dispersed through the house, each on his own, searching for Kneadus. It would have been below them to admit that they were looking for him. However, the sight of their lordships being released into what seemed a nonchalant, slow yet persistent motion was more menacing than the hottest pursuit, and I searched my mind for a way to avert the row that was swelling, like an abscess, on the horizon. But they seemed beyond reach. They had closed themselves off. I could no longer talk with them about it. As I crossed the dining room I noticed that my aunt stopped at the door to the butler's pantry, through which one could usually hear the clamor in the kitchen, the maids chattering and squealing as they washed the dishes. Pensive yet watchful, she stood with the look of the mistress of the house eavesdropping on her servants, and her usual kindliness had disappeared without a trace. When she saw me she coughed and walked away. At the same time, my uncle strayed through the courtyard in the direction of the kitchen and stood near a window, but when one of the kitchen maids stuck her head out the window, he shouted: "Zieliński! Tell Nowak to patch up that drainpipe!" and he slowly strolled down an avenue of hornbeams, gardener Zieliński following him, cap in hand. Zygmunt came up to me and took me by the arm.

"I don't know if you have a taste for an old, slightly overripe, peasant crone—I myself fancy a crone—Toby Patz started this fad—I love a crone—once in a while, I must admit, I love a crone—*j'aime parfois une simple* 'crone,' I love a crone, damn it! I love a crone! Tra la li, la li, la, I love an ordinary crone, must be a bit on the old side!"

Ah, yes—he was worried that the servants had tattled about his old woman, about the widah Josie, with whom he was cavorting in the bushes by the lake; and now he was hiding behind the quirkiness of a fad, dragging the young Patz into it. I didn't answer him because I realized that once released into action, nothing could hold back their lordships from quirkiness, the star of madness had again arisen in my firmament, and I remembered all my adventures since that day when Pimko had dealt me the pupa—this one seemed to be the worst. I went with Zygmunt to the courtyard where my uncle soon appeared at our end of the lane of hornbeams with gardener Zieliński following him, cap in hand.

"What lovely weather!" he exclaimed in the limpid air, "it's dry at last."

The weather was indeed wonderful, blue skies in the background, trees dripping with rusty-golden foliage, the pinscher and the mutt excited and shoving one another. No sign of Kneadus. Auntie arrived with two mushrooms on her palm, displaying them from a distance, smiling gently and benevolently. We gathered in front of the porch, and, since not one of us wanted to admit that we were all looking for Kneadus, an unusual gentleness and politeness supervened. Auntie, all heart, asked if anyone was cold. Jackdaws sat on trees. Little peasant urchins, their grimy fingers stuck in their mouths, sat on the gate of the barnyard and gawked at their lordships walking to and fro, and they gabbed about somethin' until Zygmunt stomped his foot and chased them away; but they soon began gawkin' through the railing, so he chased them away once more; whereupon gardener Zieliński drove them away with rocks—they took off, but they gawked again from near the well until finally Zygmunt gave up, while Konstanty ordered the servants to bring apples, then showed off eating them, scattering the peels. He ate against those peasant kiddies.

"Tereperepumpum," he murmured.

Still no Kneadus, yet not a word was said, even though everyone desired some sort of confrontation, some explanation. If this was a pursuit, it was an extremely sluggish pursuit, perfectly nonchalant, almost immobile, and hence—even more threatening. Lordliness was in pursuit of Kneadus, but the lords and ladies hardly budged. Nevertheless, dallying in the courtyard seemed pointless, especially since the kiddies were still gawkin' through the railings, so Zygmunt suggested that we have a look in the barn.

"Let's walk over to the barnyard," he said, and we slowly sauntered in that direction, uncle Konstanty with the gardener behind him, cap in hand—while the urchins moved their gawkin' from the railings to the vicinity of the granary. It was muddy beyond the gate, geese attacked us, the foreman pounced on them; a lame dog bared its teeth and growled, the night watchman rushed out to chase it away. The dogs chained near the stables began to howl and growl, incited by the strangeness of our attire—indeed, I was wearing a gray city suit, collar and tie, dress shoes, my uncle wore a tweed coat, auntie had on a black cape trimmed with fur over her shoulders and a boat-shaped hat, Zygmunt wore Scottish socks and knickers. It was indeed the Way of the Cross, slow, the hardest road I had ever traveled; you'll hear some day about my adventures in the prairies and among the Africans, but no African could compare to the peregrination through the Bolimov barnyard. No place more exotic than this one. Nowhere else—more noxious poisons. Nowhere else had such unhealthy phantasms, and flowers, orchids, bloomed under one's feet—nowhere so many Oriental butterflies, oh! no downy hummingbird will ever equal in its exoticism a goose that has never been touched by hands. Oh, because here nothing had ever been touched by our hands, the grooms near the barn—untouched, the wenches by the granary—untouched, untouched were the cattle and the fowl, and the pitchforks, and the whipple-trees, chains, leather straps, and flour sacks. Neither wild poultry nor mustangs nor wild wenches nor wild pigs. At most the grooms' mugs may have been touched by my uncle's hand, and auntie's hand was touched by the grooms who planted on it their peasant kisses of allegiance. Otherwise—nothing, nothing, and again nothing—all unfamiliar and never experienced by us! We were walking, flat on our heels, when cows were driven in through the gate, the huge herd goaded and prodded by ten-year-old boys, totally filled the barnyard, and we found ourselves among those beasts, unfamiliar and never experienced by us.

"*Attention!*" auntie exclaimed. "*Attention, laissez les passer!*"

"Atasionlesaypasay! Atasionlesaypasay!" aped the peasant kiddies by the granary, but the night watchman and the foreman moved swiftly and chased away the little urchins as well as the cows. The wenches by the barn—never experienced by us—burst into a folk

Mug on the Loose and New Entrapment

ditty: "Hey, hey-ho!" but we couldn't catch the lyrics. Maybe they sang about the young master? But the most unpleasant aspect of this situation was that their lordships seemed to be looked after by the peasants, and even though they actually lorded over the peasants and exploited them, it seemed to an outsider that the peasants coddled them, as if their lordships were the yokels' little darlings—and the foreman, as auntie's slave, carried her across a puddle, and yet it seemed that he was coddling her. Their lordships sucked the peasantry dry of their finances, but besides the fiscal sucking they carried on an infantile kind of sucking, they sucked not only their blood but also their sweet milk, and no matter how harshly and mercilessly my uncle swore at the grooms, no matter how much, like a mommy, auntie let them kiss her hands with matriarchal kindliness—neither matriarchal nor patriarchal kindliness, nor the severest of commands could quell the impression that the squire was actually the peasantry's little son, and the squire's lady—their little daughter. For indeed, the local peasantry had not yet been kneaded by the intelligentsia, unlike the rabble on the outskirts of the city who tried to escape from us by turning into dogs; here the peasantry were primeval and intact, secure within themselves, so that, even passing them from afar, we felt their power to be like that of hundred thousand rampant work horses.

By the chicken coop the housekeeper shoved feed into the gullet of an already fat turkey, satiating it beyond its limits, honoring the lordly tastes, and preparing a tasty dish for their lordships. By the forge the tail of a team-colt was being cut for fashion's sake, while Zygmunt patted its rump, checked its teeth, because a horse was one of those few things that a young master was allowed to touch, and the wenches—unfamiliar to us and sucked dry—sang for him even louder: "Hey, hey-ho, hey, hey-ho, hey-ho!" But the thought of the crone ruined his foppery, and, dejected, he let go of the horse's neck and mistrustfully looked at the wenches, wondering whether they were laughing at him. An old, gnarly peasant, also unfamiliar and a bit sucked dry, walked up to auntie and kissed her on the permitted body part. Our cortege finally reached the far end of the barn. Beyond the barn—a road, checkerboard fields, a wide expanse. From far, far away another sucked-dry peasant spotted us and stopped for a while by his plow but immediately hit the horse with a whip. The damp earth did not allow sitting down nor continuing to sit. To their lordships' right little hand—stubble fields, crests of earth, fallow land, and peatbogs, to their left little hand—an evergreen forest, coniferous greenery. No sign of Kneadus. A wild native hen pecked in a field of oats.

Suddenly, a few hundred steps from us, Kneadus emerged from the forest—not alone—the valet was by his side. He hadn't noticed us—he saw nothing of the world around him, he was all passion, all-ears, all-agog with the farmhand. He twirled, jumped up and down like a pretentious jackass, every now and then grabbing the farmhand's hand and looking into his eyes. The farmhand jeered at Kneadus for all his worth with a peasantlike, bucolic superchuckle, and unceremoniously slapped him on his back. They walked skirting the edge of the copse, Kneadus with the farmhand—or rather, the farmhand with Kneadus by his side! Kneadus, all passion, kept reaching into his pocket and shoving something into the farmhand's hand, money, most likely, while the farmhand kept unceremoniously poking him in the ribs.

"They're drunk!" auntie whispered . . .

No, not drunk. The ball of the sun, slowly descending in the west, illuminated and brought everything into relief. And, in the setting sun, the farmhand slapped Kneadus on the cheek . . .

A shout from Zygmunt, like a whiplash:

"Valek!"

The valet took to his heels and headed into the forest. Kneadus stopped in his tracks, all magic gone. We began to walk toward him, cutting across a stubble field, and he walked toward us. But Konstanty didn't want to settle things in the middle of the field because the peasant kiddies were still gawkin' from the barn, and the sucked-dry peasant was still plowing.

"Let's have a walk in the forest," he suggested, suddenly becoming exceptionally polite, and we entered the dark grove directly from the fields. Silence. The showdown was to take place among firs, densely set—we stood in tight proximity to each other, very close indeed. Uncle Konstanty shook inwardly, but he doubled his politeness.

"I notice that Valek's company suits you," he began with subtle irony.

Pale with hatred, Kneadus replied in a squeaky voice:

"Yes, it suits me . . ."

Tucked into a prickly fir, his mug screened by branches, like a fox in a battue—two paces from him auntie stood among the branches of a little conifer, also my uncle, and Zygmunt . . . My uncle, however, approached the subject in an icy manner with barely perceptible sarcasm.

"You, sir, are apparently fra . . . ternizing with Valek?"

A hateful and furious squeak:

"Yes, I'm fra . . . ternizing!"

"Kostie," Auntie kindly remarked, "let's go. It's damp here."

"This grove is rather dense. We should cut every third tree," Zygmunt said to his father.

"I'm fra . . . ternizing!" Kneadus whimpered. I had no idea they would subject him to such torture. Is this why they sidled into the grove—to pretend to be deaf? Is this why they pursued him, so that, having seized him, they could give vent to their disdain? How about the explanations? How about a showdown? They perfidiously reversed roles, they weren't s e t t l i n g w i t h h i m a t a l l—they were haughty, and in such a hurry to show him their disdain that they gave up on clarifications. They made everything look trivial. They were snubbing him. They hardly noticed him—oh, their lordships, furious and despicable!

"And you, sir, scrambled up the gamekeeper!" Kneadus exclaimed, "you scrambled up the gamekeeper because you were afraid of the boar! I know all about it! Everybody's talking! Tereperepumpum! Tereperepumpum," he said, aping my uncle, in his fury he lost any remaining self-control.

Konstanty tightened his lips and—silence fell.

"Valek will be kicked out on his ass!" Zygmunt said coldly to his father.

"Yes, Valek will be dismissed," uncle Konstanty took up coldly. "I'm sorry, but I'm not in the habit of putting up with demoralized servants."

They were taking revenge on Valek! Oh, perfidious and despicable lordships, they wouldn't even respond to Kneadus and were sacking Valek instead—they struck at Kneadus through Valek. Didn't old Francis do the same when, in the butler's pantry, he didn't say a word to Kneadus, but gave hell to Valek and the wench instead? The fir trembled, and I was about to jump at their throats—when suddenly the gamekeeper, in a green, short, close-fitting jacket, his shotgun over his shoulder, emerged out of the thicket, close to us, and saluted us with all due formality.

"Clamber up him, you!" Kneadus exclaimed. "You there, clamber up him, a boar's coming! A boar!!! . . . The crone, Josie the crone!" he hurled at Zygmunt, and took off into the woods like a madman. I dashed after him. "Kneadus, Kneadus!" I shouted in vain, the firs whipped and lashed my face! I absolutely did not want him to be alone in the forest. I jumped over ravines and hollows, burrows, crevices, roots. From the grove we ran into a thick forest, he doubled his speed and ran, he ran like a crazed boar!

I suddenly saw Zosia, who was taking a walk through the woods and, bored, was picking mushrooms among the mosses. We were heading toward her, and I was scared that in his madness he might harm her. "Run!" I screamed. My voice must have sounded urgent, for she took to her heels—and Kneadus, realizing she was running away, began to chase her, and to catch up with her! With a final sprint I tried to reach him just as he almost caught up with her—luckily he tripped on a root and fell in a small clearing. I ran up to him.

"What do you want?" he growled, pressing his face against the mosses, "what do you want?"

"Come home!"

"Yer lo'dships!" he spat the words through his teeth, "yer lo'dships! Go away, go! You're too—a lo'dship!"

"No, no!"

"Oh yeah? You's yer lo'dship too! Yer lo'dship!"

"Come home, Kneadus—stop it! This is bound to lead to disaster! We have to stop it, end it—there must be some other way!"

"Yer lo'dship! Yer lo'dships, damn it! They won't let oop! They're curs! O Jesus! They're twistin' ya round too!"

"Cut it out, this isn't your language! Why do you talk like this? Why to me?"

"He's moin, moin . . . Ah won't let 'em! He's moin! Leave him alone! They wanna throw Valek out! Throw him out! Ah won't let 'em—he's moin—ah won't let 'em! . . ."

"Come home!"

What an inglorious homecoming! He moaned and groaned, he mooned in sylvan lamentation—"oh, woe's me, oh, woe's me!" The wenches by the barn and the grooms scratched their heads and marveled at the young master wailing in their tongue. It was dusk by the time we crept in through the back porch; I told him to wait in our room upstairs while I went to talk things over with uncle Konstanty. I ran into Zygmunt in the smoking room where, hands in his pockets, he walked from one side of the room to the other. The young master was fuming within but was stiff without. I learned from his dry account that Zosia ran back from the forest barely alive and, it seemed, caught a cold, auntie was taking the girl's temperature. Valek, who was back in the kitchen, was forbidden entry to the rooms, and early tomorrow morning he would be sacked and kicked out. Zygmunt noted, moreover, that he was not holding me responsible for "Mr. Kneadalski's" disgraceful behavior, and, in his opinion, I should be more careful in the choice of my friends. He regretted that he would no longer have the pleasure of my company, but he did not think that any further stay in Bolimov would be pleasant for us. Tomorrow morning at nine o'clock there is a train that goes to Warsaw, the coachman has been given his orders. As for supper, we would surely prefer to eat in our room upstairs, Francis has already been duly instructed. Zygmunt informed me of all this in a tone that allowed for no discussion, semi-officially, and in his role as the son of his parents.

"As for me," he said through his teeth, "I will respond in my own way. I will, forthwith, take the liberty of punishing Mr. Kneadalski for insulting my father and my sister. I belong to the fraternity Astoria."

That's how he spat out the threat of a slap in the face! I knew what he was up to. He wanted to discredit the face that had been hit in the mug by peasantry, he wanted, by hitting it, to remove it from the list of lordly and honorable faces.

Fortunately, uncle Konstanty heard these threats as he came into the room.

"What do you mean by 'Mr. Kneadalski'?" he exclaimed. "Who is it you want to slap in the face, my dear Zygmunt? A callow, school-age whippersnapper? Spank the brat's pupa instead!"—and Zygmunt blushed and faltered in his honorable undertaking. After hearing my uncle's words he couldn't slap the face, he, a twenty-two-year-old, really couldn't honorably hit the green youth, barely eighteen years old, especially since the "eighteen-year-old" aspect had been underscored and brought into relief. The worst of it was that Kneadus was actually at a transitional age, and, while their lordships could consider him a mere pup, to the peasantry, which matures earlier, he was a fully fledged lordship, his face had for them the full value of a lord's countenance. How was it then—a face good enough for Valek to hit as a lord's face, but not good enough to give their lordships satisfaction? Zygmunt looked at his father with fury for this injustice of nature. However, Konstanty wouldn't even entertain the thought that Kneadus was anything but a brat, Konstanty, who at dinnertime drank to Kneadus like a fellow traveler on homoerotic terrain, was now denying all commonality with him, and treated him like a green youth, a brat, and used his age to trivialize him! His pride wouldn't let him behave otherwise! His race was in revolt, his race! This lord whom History, in its merciless progression, was depriving of his estates and of his power, had remained after all a thoroughbred in body and soul, but particularly in body! He could endure agricultural reform and legal and political equalization in a general sense, but his blood boiled at the thought of personal and physical equality, at fra . . . ternization of his person. At this point equalization encroached upon the most murky recesses of his person—into the primeval backwoods of race, which were guarded by an instinctual, hateful reflex, by disgust, horror, and abomination! Let them take away his estate! Let them introduce reforms! But don't expect his lordship's hand to seek out the farmhand's hand, let not his noble cheeks seek out the boorish hand. To strive toward peasantry out of sheer longing for them, how can that be? Isn't that betrayal of one's race—this adulation of servants, this naive and downright adulation of a servant's body parts, movements, and utterances, this love of a yokel's very existence? And what would be the position of a lord whose servant was the subject of such flagrant tribute from another lord—no, no, Kneadus wasn't even a lord, he was an ordinary green youth and a sniveling brat! These were bratty excesses resulting from Bolshevik propaganda.

"I can see that Bolshevik trends hold sway among the school youth," he spoke as if Kneadus were a revolutionary schoolboy and not a lover of another race. "Spank his pupa!" he laughed, "spank him!"

And suddenly shuffling and squealing came through the half-open casement from the bushes by the kitchen. It was a warm evening, Saturday . . . Farmhands from outlying cottages were visiting the kitchen wenches and necking . . . Konstanty stuck his head out the window.

"Who's there?" he shouted. "Off with you, I forbid you to be there!"

Someone darted into the thicket. Someone laughed. A stone spun in hard under the window. And someone beyond the bushes, in a voice changed intentionally, shrieked to high heaven:

> A wagtail, a wagtail wags on a tree
> Who's slapped in the mug, who can it be?
> His lo'dship, hee, hee!

And once more someone squeaked and laughed! The peasantry got wind of everything. They knew what had happened. The kitchen wenches had spilled the woid to the farmhands. It was to be expected, yet the squire's nerves couldn't stand the impudence with which they were singing under his windows. He stopped trifling, red blotches appeared on his cheeks, and, without a word, he took out a pistol. Fortunately, auntie appeared in the nick of time.

"Kostie, dear," she called out with kindliness, wasting no time on questions, "Kostie, put it down! Put it down! Put it down, I beg you, I hate loaded weapons, if you want to have it by your side, at least unload it!"

And, just as a moment ago he had trivialized Zygmunt's threats, so auntie was now trivializing him. She kissed him—he was being kissed while holding a pistol in his hand—she adjusted his tie, thus totally invalidating the pistol, she closed the casement because of drafts, and with other similar actions she tirelessly belittled and itsy-bitsied everything. She cast onto the balance of events the rotundity of her person, aglow with a gentle, motherly warmth, which swathed her like a wad of cotton wool. She took me aside and furtively gave me some candy that she kept in a small bag.

"Oh, you rascals, you," she whispered with a kindly reproach, "what mischief you've created! Zosia is sick, your uncle is upset, oh dear, this love affair with the peasantry! You need to know how to treat the servants, you can't hobnob with them, you need to know them—these people are like children, ignorant and immature. Your aunt and uncle Stas' son Kiki also went through a phase when he blindly idealized the peasantry," she added, scrutinizing my face, "you even look like him, yes, here, at the corners of your nose. Well, I'm not cross with you, but don't come down for supper because your uncle doesn't wish it, I'll send up a little dish of fruit preserves as a consolation—and do you remember how our former butler, Ladislas, gave you a thrashing because you called him a slob? What a mean man, that Ladislas! I'm still shaking when I think of it! I dismissed him on the spot. Imagine hitting such a little angel! My little treasure! My all and everything! My thousandfold darling!"

In a sudden surge of mawkishness she kissed me and again gave me candy. I quickly walked away with the candy of my childhood in my mouth, and, as I did so, I heard her ask Zygmunt to take her pulse, and the young master took her wrist and, looking at his watch, took her pulse—he took the pulse of his mother who, having slumped into a sofa, gazed into space. As I was returning upstairs with the candy, I had a feeling of unreality, because in relation to this woman everyone became unreal, she had a strange knack for melting people with her kindness, of dunking them in illnesses and confusing them with other people's body parts—was it out of her fear of the servants, by any chance? "She's good so she can put the squeeze on us"—I remembered Valek saying. "She puts the squeeze on us, so why shouldn't she be kindly?" The situation was becoming dangerous. They trivialized each other, my uncle out of pride, auntie out of fear, thanks to all of which there had been no shooting thus far— neither had Zygmunt hit Kneadus, nor had my uncle fired his pistol. I was anticipating our departure with joy.

I found Kneadus on the floor, his head tucked between his arms—

he now gave himself to covering his head, wrapping and enfolding it in his arms, he didn't move, and with his head tucked in, he plaintively sang of youth and meadows.

"Hey-a, hey," he mumbled, "hoy, hoy, hoy-a hoy!" and other words without rhyme or reason, words gray and coarse like the earth, green like a young hazel tree, peasantlike, rustic and callow. He lost all sense of shame. Even when Francis came in with our supper he didn't stop his lamentation, nor his quiet, pastoral moans; he had reached the point where he was no longer ashamed of longing for the servants in their presence, nor sighing for the valet in front of the old butler. Never before had I seen anyone from the intelligentsia sink so low. Francis didn't look his way, but his hands shook with disgust when he placed our tray on the table, and he slammed the door as he left. Kneadus didn't take a single bite, he was inconsolable—something in him went on a-chattin', a-croakin', a-longin' and yearnin', in mist envelopin', he scuffled and tussled, he groaned, some kin'a laws deducin' . . . Now and then a pure and simple vulgar fury would catch him by the throat. He blamed my aunt and uncle for his debacle with the farmhand, it was their lo'dships' fault, yes, their lo'dships', if it weren't for their interference and meddling, he surely would have fra . . . ternized! Why did they stand in his way? Why sack Valek? I tried in vain to convince him that we had to leave the next day.

"Ah'm not leavin', ah tell ya, ah'm not leavin', ah tell ya! Let 'em leave, if they wanna! Here's Valek, here's me too. Wit' Valek! Wit' me very own Valek, hey, hey-ho, ho, wit' me farmhand!"

I couldn't communicate with him, lost as he was in the farmhand, all earthly considerations having gone by the boards. When he finally understood that it was impossible for us to stay, in terror he begged me not to leave the farmhand behind.

"Ah'm not leavin' wit'out Valek! Ah'm not leavin' Valek to 'em! Let's take him—ah'll work for our livin', for our home—ah'll drop dead before ah leave this Valek of moin! For chrissake, Joey, not wi'out Valek! If they throw us outa' the estate, ah'll find me a place in the village, at the crone's," he added with venom, "ah'll settle in wit' the crone! How about that?! They won't chase me outa' the village! Anyone has the roit to live in the village!"

I had no idea what to do with this conundrum. It was not outside the realm of possibility that he would move in with Zygmunt's hapless crone, the *widah*, as the valet had called her, and he would harass the manor and humiliate my aunt and uncle, and squeal on the secrets of the manor in this vulgar tongue—a traitor and an informer—and a laughingstock for the yokels!

Suddenly, in the courtyard just outside the window, we heard a tremendous slap in the face. Everything jangled, the dogs barked as one. We pressed our noses to the windows. On the porch, in the light coming from the house, uncle Konstanty stood with a rifle, gazing into darkness. He brought the weapon up to his cheek and fired again—the bang sounded in the night like a rocket. It rang out into the distance over the dark reaches of the land. The dogs ran riot.

"He's shootin' at the fa'mhand!" Kneadus clutched at me, "he's aimin' at the fa'mhand!"

Konstanty was firing warning shots. Had the farm servants sung something more? Or did he fire because his nerves gave out, or because he'd been primed to shoot from the moment he took his pistol from the drawer in the smoking room? Who knows what went on inside him? Did this act of terror arise from haughtiness and pride? The angered lord was announcing with a boom far away and down the most distant roads, to the lone willows along country lanes, that he stands guard, fully armed. Auntie ran onto the porch and quickly offered him candy, she flung a scarf around his neck and pulled him into the house. But the boom had already spread beyond recall. When the dogs on the estate calmed down for a moment, I heard the faraway response of the dogs in the village, and for a moment I imagined the peasants' excitement—the farmhands, the wenches, and the peasants asking each other "what's goin' on, why are they shootin' at the manor? Is it his lo'dship shootin'? Why's he shootin'?" Then the tittle-tattle about the mug-slapping, that the young master Kneadus got it in the snoot from Valek amplifying from one mouth to another, provoked by the resounding and vainglorious firing of the rifle. I couldn't contain my anxiety. I decided to run away that very moment, I feared the night, here, in this country manor, its subterranean forces unleashed and full of noxious vapors. Run! Run away at once! But Kneadus wouldn't go without Valek. Therefore, to speed things up, I agreed to take the farmhand with us. He was going to be dismissed anyway. We finally decided to wait until everyone in the house was asleep, then I would go to the valet and persuade him to run away—order him if need be! I would return with him to Kneadus, and then the three of us would decide how to get out to the fields. The dogs knew Valek. We would spend the rest of the night in a field, then take the train to the city. To the city, on the double! To the city, where man is smaller, better settled among people, and more like other people. Minutes dragged into eternity. We packed our belongings and counted our money, and we wrapped the supper we had hardly touched in a handkerchief.

After midnight, having checked through our window that all the rooms were in darkness, I took off my shoes and went through a small hallway, barefoot—making sure that I reached the pantry as quietly as possible. When Kneadus shut the door it cut off any remaining light, and I began my venture, my secretive incursion into the sleeping house, I realized how mad my undertaking was, how crazy my goal—penetrating space to kidnap some farmhand. Isn't it action that, in the final analysis, reveals all the madness of madness? I advanced step by step, the floor creaked, rats gnawed and squealed in the timbers above the ceiling. In the room behind me was Kneadus, gone rustic; below me on the first floor were my uncle, auntie, Zygmunt, and Zosia, to whose servant I was proceeding soundlessly and barefoot; ahead of me in the butler's pantry was the said servant, the object of all these endeavors. I had to be very careful. If someone

Mug on the Loose and New Entrapment

were to spot me in the hallway, in the darkness, how would I explain the meaning of this escapade? How do we find ourselves on these tortuous and abnormal roads? Normality is a tightrope-walker above the abyss of abnormality. How much potential madness is contained in the everyday order of things—you never know when and how the course of events will lead you to kidnap a farmhand and take to the fields. It's Zosia that I should be kidnapping. If anyone, it should be Zosia, kidnapping Zosia from a country manor would be the normal and correct thing to do, if anyone it was Zosia, Zosia, and not this stupid, idiotic farmhand. And in the semi-darkness of this little hallway the temptation to kidnap Zosia seized me, a crystal-clear and simple kidnapping of Zosia, oh yes, it was crystal-clear—kidnap Zosia!

Hey, to kidnap Zosia! To kidnap Zosia in a mature, lordly fashion, just as had been done many times of yore. I had to fend off that thought, convince myself how unsound it was—and yet, the farther I fought my way over the treacherous floorboards the more tempting normality seemed, the simple and natural kidnapping as opposed to this convoluted kidnapping. I tripped over a hole—there was a hole under my toes, a hole in the floor. Why was the hole there? It seemed familiar. Hello, hello—this is my hole, I made this hole years ago! My uncle had given me a little hatchet for my birthday, and it was with this hatchet that I had chopped the hole. Auntie had rushed in. She stood right here, yelling at me, I remembered as if it were yesterday—the loose fragments of her scolding, the snatches of her shouting—and I—hack! I hacked her leg from below with my little hatchet! "Oh, oh!" she screamed. Her scream was still here—I stood as if the scene had caught me by the leg, the scene which was no more, and yet it was here, at this very spot. I had hacked her in the leg. I now clearly saw in the darkness how I had hacked her, God knows why, in spite of myself, mechanically, and I heard her screams. She screamed and jumped. My actions now were mixing and intertwining with my actions of the past, of the long-gone past, and suddenly I began to shiver, my jaws clenched. I could have chopped off her leg, for God's sake, had I swung harder, luckily I didn't have the strength, oh, blessed weakness. But now I did have the strength. Perhaps, instead of going to the farmhand, I should go to auntie's bedroom and hack her with an ax? Begone, begone childishness. Childishness? But, as God is my witness, the farmhand was also childishness, if I was going to the farmhand I could equally well have gone and hacked auntie, one was as good as the other—hack, hack! Oh, childishness. I carefully felt the floor with my foot, because any loud creaking could have betrayed me, and I thought that I felt the floor as if I were a child, as if I now walked it as a child. Oh, childishness. The childishness latched on to me in three different ways, I could have handled one way, but there were three. The first was the childishness of the pursuit of the valet—the farmhand. The second was the childishness of what I had lived through here, years ago. The third was the childishness of lordliness, because now, as a lord, I was also a child. Oh, there are places on this earth and in life that are more childish or less childish, but a country manor is probably the most childish place of all. Here the lords of the manor and the peasantry entrap and hold onto each other in childishness, here everyone is a child to everyone else. Walking barefoot farther and farther and concealed by blackness, I strode as if into a lordly past, into my own childhood, while a sensuous, carnal, infantile, and unpredictable world was enfolding me, pulling on me and sucking me in. Blind actions. Automatic reflexes. Atavistic instincts. Lordly-childish fancy. I walked as if into the anachronism of a gigantic slap in the face, which was simultaneously a tradition of many centuries and an infantile smack, and it liberated, in one fell swoop, the lord and the child.

I finally touched the banister, down which I used to slide in yesteryear, delighting in the gravitational downslide—from the top to the very bottom! An *Infante,* an infant—a king, a child, a lord-child full speed ahead, oh, if only I were to hack auntie now, she'd never get up—and I was terrified of my own strength, of my claws and talons, of my punches, frightened of the man within the child. What was I doing here, on these stairs, why and where was I going? And it again dawned on me that kidnapping Zosia was the only acceptable reason for this foray, the only manly solution, the only place for a man to be . . . To kidnap Zosia! Kidnap Zosia like a man! I kept driving the thought away but it went on pestering me . . . buzzing within me.

I went downstairs and stopped in a hallway. Dead silence—nothing stirred anywhere, they had retired at the usual hour, auntie had surely ordered everyone to bed by now, and tucked them into their comforters. However, their rest was unlikely a rest, under their comforters everyone wove their own canvas out of the day's events. In the kitchen it was also quiet, but light seeped through a crack in the pantry door, Valek was polishing shoes, and I saw no animation on his mug, it was its usual self. I slipped in slowly, closed the door behind me, placed my finger on my lips and, with extreme caution, whispering into his ear, I began my exhortations. He was to pick up his cap right now, drop everything and come with us, we were going to Warsaw. This was a terrible role to play, I would have preferred anything to this stupid coaxing, and whispering it too. Especially since he put up a resistance. I told him that their lordships were about to sack him, that he'd be better off if he ran away, far, far away, to Warsaw, with Kneadus who would pay for his keep—but he didn't understand, he couldn't grasp this.

"What's this runnin' away for," he kept saying with an instinctual mistrust of all lordly whims, and I was again assailed by the thought that Zosia would have accepted it more easily, that whispering with Zosia in the middle of the night would have made more sense. Time was running short for more lengthy exhortations. I smacked him in the mug and gave him an order, he then obeyed—but I smacked him through a dishrag. Through a dishrag I smacked him in the mug, I had to place a dishrag on his mug and smack him through it to avoid making a noise—oh, oh!—in the dead of night I was slapping a farmhand through a dishrag. He obeyed, though the dishrag put some doubts in his mind, because the peasantry does not like deviations from the norm.

"Come on, damn it," I ordered him and went out into the hallway, he followed me. Where were the stairs? It was pitch dark.

Down the hall a door creaked and I heard my uncle's voice:

"Who's there?"

I quickly caught the valet by the arm and pushed him into the dining room. We crouched behind the door. Konstanty approached slowly and entered the room, he walked right by me.

"Who's there?" he repeated, quietly, not to make a fool of himself in case no one was there. Having thrown out the question he followed it deeper into the interior of the dining room. He stopped. He had no matches, and the darkness was impenetrable. He turned around, but after a few steps he stood still—instantly and perfectly still—did he sense, in the darkness, a whiff of the farmhand's specific, peasant odor, did his lordship's delicate skin sense the paws and the mug? He was so close that he could have reached us with his hand, yet this was exactly what told him to keep his hands by his side, he was too close, the closeness had caught him in its trap. He didn't move and, slowly at first, then more and more quickly, his immobility froze into a state of alarm. I don't think he was a coward, although people said he clambered up the gamekeeper out of fear—no, the reason he couldn't move was not that he was afraid, but he was afraid because he couldn't move—once he put on the brakes and stood silent, every passing second, for purely logistic reasons, made any movement increasingly difficult. Terror had been locked inside him for a long time, but it only now emerged to conspire against him, and his lordship's thin little bones stuck in his throat. Not a peep out of the farmhand. And so the three of us stood just a few feet apart. Our skin crawled, our hair stood on end. I was not about to interrupt this. I figured that he would finally regain control and leave, thus letting us leave and escape upstairs through the hallway, but it didn't occur to me that the growing fear would paralyze him—for now I was sure that an inner shift and reversal had taken place, he was no longer afraid because he couldn't move, he couldn't move because he was afraid. I sensed the grave terror on his face, concentration, seriousness beyond belief . . . and I in turn began to fear—not him, but his fear. If we were to retreat or make the slightest move he could have pounced on us and grabbed us. If he had the pistol, he could have fired—but no, we were too close for him to shoot, he could have physically but not mentally—because one needs to precede a shot with an inner, mental shot, and there wasn't enough distance for this. But he could have pounced on us and used his hands. He didn't know what lurked in front of him, and into what trouble he'd be shoving his hands. We knew his form—he didn't know ours. I wanted to come out, I wanted to say "uncle" or something like that. But after so many seconds, or even minutes, I couldn't, it was too late—because how was I to explain our silence? I wanted to laugh, as if someone were tickling me. Here was proliferation. And expansion. Everything was expanding in blackness. Inflating and widening, yet at the same time shrinking and straining, evading something, and some kind of winnowing, general and particular, a coagulating tension and a tensing coagulation, a dangling by a fine thread, as well as transformation into something, transmutation, and furthermore—a falling into some cumulative, towering system, and as if on a narrow little plank raised six stories up, together with the excitement of all organs. And tickling. We heard slippers shuffling in the hallway, yet we felt too impotent to budge and so we did not budge. It was Zygmunt approaching in his slippers.

"Is anyone here?" he asked on the threshold.

He took another step and repeated: "Is anyone here?" and fell silent, he froze, sensing something was afoot. He knew that his father was somewhere here, since he must have heard Konstanty's footsteps and questions—so why didn't his father say something? Archaic fears and anxieties had corked up the father, ha, ha, ha, and so he couldn't, he couldn't because he was frightened! And the father's fear corked up the son. All the fear that had been generated thus far petrified Zygmunt, and he fell silent, as if forever. Perhaps at first he felt unclear, but soon the unclearness clarified itself into fear and grew upon itself. *Da capo*—winnowing, distending, magnifying, raising to the 101st power, proliferating and stretching, mollifying and caressing, straining, intently listening to a monotone, piling up and suspending—endlessly, endlessly going up and under—all the while Zygmunt standing a few steps away. Choking, unable to swallow and damming up, holding on to one's head, falling and breaking apart, prolonged disentangling, summing up, pushing out and leading up to, changing and intensifying, intensifying . . . One minute? One hour? What was going to happen? Universes soared through my brain. I recalled: it was here, long ago, that I lurked to scare my nanny—at this very spot—and I almost laughed. Shush! Why laugh? That's enough, cut it out, stop it, what will happen if my childishness is finally disclosed, what if, after all this time, they discover me with the valet—it would be strange, and inexplicable—but oh, with Zosia, to be with Zosia, to hold my breath with Zosia rather than with the farmhand! With Zosia it wouldn't be childish! I suddenly took a bold step, I slipped behind the drapes, quite sure that the other men wouldn't dare move. Indeed, they didn't dare. In the darkness, besides fear, there was now an awkwardness, what's more, it would have been awkward for them to interrupt, perhaps they intended to, they thought about it, but they didn't know how to do it. I'm talking here about their silence. For I interrupted mine by moving. It's possible that they thought about the logistics, they looked for excuses and pretexts, some outer justification, and, what's worse, each one of them hampered the other by his presence, and both those thinkers stood there, unable to stop, to cut short, while the pushing out and disentangling continued unbroken. Having regained my ability to move I decided to catch the farmhand, pull him along and make a quick exit into the hallway, but before I could carry out my decision—light, light!—a gleam on the floor, a creaking and a shuf-fling, it was Francis, Francis had arrived with a light, there was the outline of my uncle's leg coming to light, into light, out into the open!! Fortunately for me, I was behind the drapes! But their old servant brought to light everything that was happening in the dark! And they all stepped out: my uncle, Zygmunt, the valet—they all had to step out! My uncle, his hair roughed up a bit, only a step from the valet, both facing each other—and Zygmunt stuck farther back in the room, like a post.

"Is someone walking about?" asked the butler with a somewhat plaintive voice, lighting up the room with a small paraffin lamp; but he asked this after the fact, merely to justify his arrival. He obviously saw them as if on the palm of his hand.

Konstanty moved. What did Francis think, seeing him close to the valet? Why were they standing next to each other? Konstanty couldn't step back right away, and yet, by a slight movement, he widened the space between them; he took a step to one side.

"What are you doing here?" Konstanty exclaimed, transforming his fear into anger.

The valet didn't answer. He couldn't find an answer. He had no problem standing, but he couldn't find his tongue. He was alone with their lordships. The silence of the son of the common people and his inability to explain things cast a shadow of suspicion. Francis looked at my uncle—their lordships here with Valek in the darkness? Was the squire also hobnobbing with the common people?—the old servant stood erect, lamp in hand, slowly turning red and shining like the sun's afterglow at dusk.

"Valek!" exclaimed Zygmunt.

All those exclamations were ill-timed, they came either too soon or too late, and I crouched behind the drapes.

"I heard someone walking about," Zygmunt began, confused and looking right and left, "I heard someone walking. Walking. What are you doing here? What are you up to? Speak up! What do you want here? Answer me!!! Answer me, damn it!!!" He ranted on in great confusion.

"It's obvious what," answered the butler after a long and deadly silence, inflamed, "it's obvious, your lordship."

He stroked his sideburns.

"The table silver is in the drawer. And tomorrow your lordships were going to release him from his duties. So he figured . . . he'd filch it."

Filch it! Valek had wanted to steal the silver! They found a rationalization—he wanted to steal, and they caught him at it. Everyone, Valek included, felt better, and, behind the drapes, I too breathed more easily. Konstanty moved away from the valet and sat on a chair by the table. He regained his customary lordly relationship with the farmhand, as well as his self-assurance. The farmhand had wanted to steal!

"Come here," said Konstanty, "come here, I tell you . . . Closer, closer . . ." He was no longer afraid of closeness and obviously relished the fact that he was no longer afraid. "Closer," he repeated, "closer," as Valek approached him with mistrust, dragging his feet, "come on, closer," until the farmhand almost touched him, then he drew back his fist and, still sitting, punched him in the snoot, *Mane, Tekel, Fares!*[*] "I'll teach you to steal!" Oh, the bliss of a punch by the lamplight, after all the fear in the darkness, oh, to punch the mug that scared you, to punch within the well-defined notion of thievery! Oh, the bliss of a normal relation after so many abnormal relations! Zygmunt, following his father's example, punched Valek's teeth as if they were the hanging gardens of Semiramis! He punched them with a bang and a whack! Behind the drapes I tensely coiled myself as if upon a spool.

"Ah wasn't stealin'!" the farmhand said catching his breath.

---

[*]*Mane, Tekel, Fares* is the writing on the wall that appeared during Baltasar's feast, foretelling the doom of Babylon.

That's exactly what they were waiting for. It enabled them to exploit the excuse of thievery to its limits. "You weren't stealing?" said Konstanty, and, stretching from his chair he again smacked him in the snoot. "You weren't stealing?" said the young lordship, and, as he stood there, he too hit him in the snoot with a brisk and succinct whack. They pounced on him. "You weren't stealing? You weren't stealing?"—and asking this question over and over again, unremittingly, they went on smacking him, searching for his mug with their hands and, having found it, hitting it again, briskly, as if releasing a spring, or with a sweep and a crash! He covered himself with his arms, but they knew how to get at him! For a long while they could reach only his mug, but I felt their scope would widen; indeed, his lordship managed to break the barrier, he caught Valek by the hair and, having caught him by the hair, banged his noodle on the counter of the sideboard.

"I'll teach you to steal! I'll teach you to steal! . . ."

Ha, and so it began! Oh, accursed billowing night! Accursed darkness that magnified, darkness that unleashed all, were it not for immersion in darkness this would never have happened. A sediment of darkness spread over it. Kostie the squire went on a rampage. Under the guise of thievery he gave the farmhand a thrashing: for the fear, for the terror, for the blushing, for the fra . . . ternizing with Kneadus, for everything he had suffered. "This is mine! Mine!" he repeated, hitting him against drawers, against edges, against ornaments and moldings. "It's mine, damn you!" And the "mine" slowly changed its meaning, it was no longer clear whether he meant the silver and the flatware or his own body and soul, his hair, his customs, his hands, his lordliness, his refinement, his race and culture, he no longer banged him against a drawer, he banged him in space, without any pretexts! It seemed that by thrashing and sacking the farmhand he was enforcing his own self, not the silver nor his estate, but himself. It was his own self that he was enforcing! What terror! Terror! To terrorize, to enforce oneself upon the farmhand lest he dare fra . . . ternize again, no more prattlin' or marvelin', the valet must accept their lordships as the godhead! With his lordly, dainty little hand the squire was pounding his own being into that snoot! That's how a turkey would pound a turkey into a sparrow! A foxterrier pound the cult of a foxterrier into a mongrel! An owl—into a jay! A buffalo—into a dog! I rubbed my eyes behind the drapes, I wanted to scream, cry for help, but I couldn't. Francis, meanwhile, lit everything from the side with his small paraffin lamp. Auntie! Auntie! Did my eyes mislead me, or did I see auntie standing in the door of the smoking room, candy in hand. Hope swept through me, I thought my aunt might save the situation, smooth things over—neutralize them. But no! She lifted her arms as if to scream, but instead of screaming she smiled without rhyme or reason, she waved it all aside, made a nondescript gesture or two, and retreated into the smoking room. She pretended not to be there, she didn't take in what she had seen, didn't assimilate it, the dose was too potent—and she vanished into herself and into the interior of the room, or rather, she flowed back so mistily that I doubted whether she had ever been there. Konstanty's energy would leave him momentarily—then he would resume enforcing—while Zygmunt kept jumping in from the side, also enforcing himself on the farmhand, enforcing and enforcing, limited only by the reach of his arm. When my uncle let up, Zygmunt let the farmhand have it, and he enforced himself with all his power, roar and uproar! And through their clenched jaws they let fly breathless words such as:

"So I climbed up the gamekeeper! On the gamekeeper I climbed! And you, you, you fancy fra . . . ternizing!"

"So I love the oldie, do I?!"

And they beat him, once and for all driving it into him and enforcing it. They enforced it while following all the rules, never hitting his legs nor his back, it was always his mug that they bashed, smashed, beat with their hands! They weren't fighting with him— they weren't fighting him—it was only his mug they hit! And this they were permitted to do. It was their age-old, officially sanctioned right. While old Francis went on shining his light and, when their hands grew weak, tactfully suggesting:

"Your honorable lordhips will teach him not to steal! Your honorable lordships will teach him a lesson!"

They finally stopped. They sat down. The farmhand was catching his breath, blood oozed from his ear, his head and his mug were beaten to a pulp. They offered each other cigarettes, the old butler jumped to with a match. They were through, it seemed. But Zygmunt let out a circle of smoke.

"Give us the *starka*," he exclaimed, "serve up the oldie!"*

Have they gone mad? How was he supposed to serve up the oldie? The farmhand blinked with his bloodied eyes.

"But she's in the village, your lo'dship!"

I wiped my brow. They didn't mean the peasant, the shy old Josie, but the old, mature, delicious, and lordly rye vodka *oldie*, which was right there in the pantry, in a bottle! And when the valet finally understood and sprang to the cupboard, took out the bottle and the glasses and filled them, Zygmunt and his father clinked their shot glasses and each downed a shot of the noble, dry vodka. Then another! Then a third and a fourth!

"We'll teach him a lesson! We'll drill him all right!"

And it all began again, all over again . . . until I wondered whether my senses were misleading me. For nothing misleads us as much as our senses. Could this be real? Hidden behind the drapes, barefoot, I wasn't sure whether I was looking at the truth or the continuation of darkness—I was barefoot, can one see the truth, barefoot? Take off your shoes, hide behind drapes, and look! Look, while barefoot! What grotesque kitsch! Drinking up one glass after another of the mature, dry *oldie*, they began to train the farmhand to become a mature lackey. "Fetch me this, fetch me that!" they shouted. "Glasses!

Starka—from "stara," meaning old, and denoting mature rye vodka.

Napkins! Bread and rolls! Appetizers! Ham! Set the table! Wait on us!" The farmhand scurried and ran around like a top. And they ate in front of him and relished their food, they drank and feasted—they forced down the food, they forced down the lordly spread. "Their lo'dships are drinkin'!" exclaimed Konstanty downing a glass of the *oldie*. "Their lo'dships are eatin'!" seconded Zygmunt. "Ah'm eatin' what's moin! Ah'm drinkin what's moin! It's moin what ah'm drinkin'! It's moin what ah'm eatin'! Moin, not yaus! Moin! Know who's the boss here!" they shouted, and, pushing their persons right under his nose they enforced themselves with all their characteristics, so that he wouldn't dare criticize, nor question, to the end of his days, nor marvel, nor scoff, nor sneer, so that he'd accept the whole thing in and of itself. *Ding an sich!* And they shouted: "What the lord sayeth, the servant obeyeth!" and they spat out commands, there was no end to the commands, and the farmhand went on and on, carrying them out! "Kiss my leg!" he kissed. "Make your bows! On your knees!" he fell to his knees, while Francis, as if with a trumpet, marked the beat:

"Your honorable lordships are drilling him! Your honorable lordships are teaching him!"

They drilled him! By the light of a small paraffin lamp, at the table stained with *oldie*! All above board, because they were training a peasant farmhand to be a lackey. I wanted to exclaim: "that's enough, enough," but I couldn't. I was ashamed to let on that I saw it all. I wasn't even sure it was as I saw it, or whether I was imagining it, how much of this kitsch was my own ugly creation unfolding before me, perhaps if I had my shoes on I wouldn't have seen it at all. And I was scared that the gaze of yet some other person might encompass me in this scene, and as part of the scene. I shrank under the blows that fell on the farmhand's mug, I choked with dread and despair, yet I wanted to laugh, and I laughed in spite of myself like someone whose foot is being tickled, oh, Zosia, if only Zosia were here, to kidnap Zosia, to run away with Zosia like an adult man! In the meantime

Mug on the Loose and New Entrapment

they went on drilling, drilling the immature boy, in a mature and lordly fashion, with elegance, even with wit, with pizzazz, sitting by the table, sprawled over the chairs and sipping the dry *oldie*.

Kneadus appeared at the door!

"Let'm go! Let'm go!"

It wasn't a scream. It was a throaty squeak. He went for my uncle! I suddenly saw that everything was in full view! Out there! There was a crowd outside the window. Farmhands, wenches, grooms, men and womenfolk, housekeepers, estate servants, house servants—everyone was looking in! The curtains hadn't been drawn. The uproar in the dead of night had called them here! They had watched with respect the way their lordships were drivin' Valek—how they were teachin', drillin', and trainin' him to be a lackey.

"Watch out, Kneadus!" I shouted. Too late. Konstanty found time to turn away from Kneadus in disdain and once again smack the valet in the snoot. Kneadus sprang forward and caught the farmhand in his arms, hugging him.

"He's moin! Ah won't let ya! Let'm go!" he squealed, "let'm go! Ah won't let ya!"

"You sniveling brat!" Konstanty shrieked, "I'll spank you! I'll spank your pupa! You'll get it in the pupa, you sniveling brat!" He and Zygmunt pounced on him. When they heard Kneadus' boyish squealing their lordships went berserk. To trivialize him through the pupa! To deprive fra . . . ternization of all meaning, to spank his pupa in front of Valek and in front of all the rabble outside the window!

"Ee-ho, ee-ho ee-ho!" squeaked Kneadus, cowering awkwardly. He then leapt behind the farmhand. And the latter, as if fraternizing with Kneadus had restored his daring and arrogance toward their lordships, abandoned all formality and smashed Konstanty in the snoot.

"What are ya buttin' in for?" he exclaimed rudely.

The mystic clasp broke! The servant's hand fell on the lordly countenance. Crash, bang, and stars in front of Konstanty's eyes. He was unprepared for this and went sprawling. Immaturity spilled every-where. Crash of a broken window. Darkness. A well-aimed rock broke the lamp. Windows let go—the peasants had forced them open and slowly began crawling in, in the darkness the place became thick with peasant body parts. The air was stifling, as in an unventilated manager's office. Hands and feet—no, the rabble doesn't have feet—paws, a huge number of paws, all solid and heavy. The peasants, encouraged by the unique immaturity of the whole scene, lost all respect and manifested a desire to fra . . . ternize. I heard Zygmunt squeak, my uncle squeaked—I think the peasants somehow dragged them into their midst and began to take them in hand, rather slowly and clumsily, but I didn't see it because it was dark . . . I jumped out from behind the drapes. Auntie! Auntie! I suddenly remembered auntie. I run barefoot to the smoking room, grab auntie, who lay on the sofa playing possum, and I pull her heave-ho, push her into the heap, to mix her in with the heap.

"My child, what are you doing, child?" she pleaded and kicked, and offered me candy, but I, just like a child, pull and pull, pull her into the heap, push her into it, they've got her, they're holding on to her! My aunt is in the heap! She's in the heap! I dashed through the rooms. Not to flee—but just to run, to run, nothing but run full speed ahead, run, egging myself on and stomping my bare footsies! I dashed onto the porch! The moon sailed from behind the clouds, yet it was not the moon, it was the pupa. A pupa of tremendous size atop the trees. A child's pupa atop the world. And the pupa. Nothing but the pupa. Over there they are tumbling in a heap, and here it's the pupa. Little leaves on the bushes are trembling in a light breeze. And here it's the pupa.

Deadly despair caught me in its grip. I was totally infantilized. Run, but where? Back to the manor? There was nothing there—just slapping, smacking, and tumbling in a heap. Where do I turn, what do I do, where am I in this world? Where do I put myself? I was all alone, even worse than alone, because I had become like a child. I couldn't be alone for long, not connected to anything. I ran down the road jumping over dry sticks like a grasshopper. I was seeking a connection with something, a new if temporary order, so that I wouldn't stick out in space any longer. A shadow broke away from a tree. Zosia! She grabbed me!

"What happened down there?" she asked. "Have the peasants attacked my father?"

I grabbed her.

"Let's run away!" I said.

Together we ran through fields and meadows into an unknown expanse, and she was as if the kidnapped, and I as if the kidnapper. We ran down a path across the fields until we were out of breath. We spent the rest of the night in a tiny meadow by a pond's edge, buried in bulrushes, shivering with cold, our teeth chattering. Grasshoppers shrilled. At dawn another pupa, red, and a hundredfold more magnificent, made its appearance on the horizon and filled the world with its rays, causing all objects to cast elongated shadows.

We didn't know what to do. I could neither explain nor express in any way what had happened at the manor because I was ashamed, I couldn't find the right words. She probably guessed more or less what had happened, because she too was ashamed and couldn't express it either. She sat among the reeds by the water, coughing a little because of the damp air that was coming from the rushes. I counted my money—I had about fifty zlotys and some small change. Theoretically speaking, we could have walked on foot to one of the nearby estates and asked for help. Yet how were we to present the whole situation, put it into words for the people at the estate, I would have been too ashamed to speak, I would rather have spent the rest of my life in the bulrushes than to speak of it. Never! It was better to assume that I had kidnapped her, that we were running away from her parents' home, this would have been much more mature-easier to accept. Going on with this line of reasoning, I wouldn't have had to clarify or explain anything to Zosia, because a woman will always accept that she's being loved. Under this pretext we could slip away to the railroad station, take a train to Warsaw, and begin a new life in secrecy from everyone—and the kidnapping would have justified such secrecy.

So I pressed a kiss on both her cheeks, and I confessed my passion for her, I began to apologize that I had kidnapped her, and to explain that her family would never have consented to a union with me because my financial situation wasn't good enough, I told her I had fallen in love with her at first sight, and that I had sensed immediately that she felt the same for me.

"There was no other way than to kidnap you, Zosia," I said, "and for us to run away together."

She was a little surprised at first, but, after I had been proposing to her for a quarter of an hour, she began to make little faces, look coyly at me because I looked coyly at her, and twirl her fingers. She forgot all about the peasants and the anarchy at the estate, and she soon believed that I had kidnapped her. This flattered her enormously because, until now, she had only done needlework, studied, or sat and gawked, or spent time being bored, or taken walks, or looked out the window, or played the piano, or done charitable work at *United Front,* or taken exams in vegetable cultivation, or flirted and danced while music played, or gone to spas, or conversed and looked through windowpanes into the far yonder. Not until now did she entertain any hope that someone would turn up who would possess her. And now, there was someone like that, someone who had actually kidnapped her! So she mustered all her talents for love, and she fell in love with me—because I had fallen in love with her.

In the meantime the pupa rose and fired a billion glistening rays over a world that was only a substitute world, made of cardboard, touched up in green, lit from above with a burning glare. Avoiding human settlements, we slipped along out-of-the-way paths toward the railroad station, and it was a long way—about fifteen miles. She walked and I walked, I walked and she walked, and together we kept on walking under the rays of the merciless, brilliant, blazing, infantile, and infantilizing pupa. Grasshoppers hopped. Crickets buzzed in the grass. Birdies sat on trees or flew about. At the sight of any human being we would make a detour or hide in the bushes by the road. Zosia, however, assured me that she knew the way, because she had gone this way a thousand times before, either by carriage or cabriolet, or by buggy or on sleds. The heat was getting to us. Fortunately, we were able to refresh ourselves with milk, secretly sucking dry a cow that was standing by the roadside. And we walked again. All this time, because of my declaration of love, I had to keep talking love and to show consideration, for example, by helping her to negotiate planks tossed across streams, chasing away flies, inquiring whether she was tired—and many such considerations and favors. She in turn did likewise: she inquired, chased away flies, and showed consideration. I was terribly tired, oh, just to reach Warsaw, to be free of her, to begin living again. I wanted to use her merely as a pretext and a guise under which I could get away from that heap at the estate with some semblance of maturity, and to arrive in Warsaw where I could, after a while, set myself up. But in the meantime I had to show interest in her and generally carry on an intimate conversation with her like two people who delight in each other, and Zosia, as mentioned above, touched by my emotion, became more and more proactive herself. And the pupa, incredibly scorching and towering at the altitude of a billion cubic miles, ravaged the valleys of this world.

She was a young lady from the country, raised by her mother and my aunt, Mrs. Hurlecka, née Lin, and by servants—thus far she had dabbled in self-education and studied at the College of Gardening and taken courses at the School of Business, or dabbled in making jams, or dabbled at skinning currants for preserves, or developed her heart and mind, or sat around a bit, also worked as office help, or played the piano just a tad, or walked around a little and said something, but most of all she waited and waited, she waited for the one who would come, fall in love with her, and kidnap her. She was a great expert at waiting, she was gentle, passive, timid, and that's why she suffered from bad teeth, for she was exceptionally well-suited to a dentist's waiting room, and her teeth knew it. And now, when the long-awaited man appeared on the scene and kidnapped her, when that festive day finally dawned, she began to work at it intensely, to show off and display, to bring to light all her trump cards and exhibit them, pulling little faces, smiling, jumping up and down, rolling her eyes, laughing with her teeth and with the joy of life, gesticulating or humming melodies under her breath to display her musical sophistication (because she played the piano a little and could render the Moonlight Sonata). Moreover, she brought forward and displayed body parts that were attractive, hiding those that were not. And I had to look and gaze and pretend that I was taken by it, and take it all in . . . All the while the fiery and exalted pupa dominated the world from the boundless blue skies, glorying, shining, glistening, baking and burning, drying up the herbs and grasses. Since Zosia knew that one is happy when in love, she was happy—and she gazed with a bright, luminous gaze, and I too had to gaze. And she whispered:

"I so wish that all people could be as content and happy as we are—and if they're good, they will be happy."

Or else:

"We're young, we love each other . . . the world belongs to us!" and she would snuggle up to me, so I had to snuggle up to her.

Since she was convinced that I loved her, she opened up and began to confide in me, and talk sincerely and intimately as she had never done before. Until now she was frightened of people because she had been brought up by aunt Hurlecka, née Lin (now totally lost in that heap), and by servants in aristocratic isolation, she had never confided in anyone for fear of being criticized or found wanting, she was somehow left incomplete, ill-defined, unresolved, lacking inner checks and balances and therefore unsure of the impression she was creating. She badly needed kindness, she couldn't live without it, she could only talk to someone who'd be in advance, *a priori,* kindly and warmly disposed toward her . . . And now, realizing that I loved her, and thinking that she had acquired a warm, an unquestioning admirer who would *a priori* accept with love anything she said because he loved her, she began to confide and unbosom herself, she told me of her joys and sorrows, of her tastes and fancies, her enthusiasms, illusions, and disappointments, her transports of joy, her emotions, memories, and all those little details—ha, she finally found someone who l o v e d her, to whom she could u n b o s o m herself with impunity, assured that everything would be accepted, without reprisal, and with love, warmly . . . And I had to accede and accept, to admire it all . . .

And she said: "Man must have a well-rounded education, he must perfect himself in body and soul, a human being must always be beautiful! I'm for the fullness of humanity. Sometimes of an evening I love to rest my brow against a windowpane and close my eyes, I can relax then. I like movies, but I love music." And I had to say "yes . . . yes." And she chirped that on awakening in the morning she must rub her little nose, feeling sure that I could not be indifferent to her little nose, and she would burst out laughing, and I too would burst out. And then she would sadly say: "I know I'm stupid. I know I don't know how to do much. I know I'm not pretty . . ." And I had to say "oh, no, no." She knew that I was gainsaying her not in the name of truth and reality but only because I was in love with her, and she therefore accepted these negations with pleasure, delighted that she had found an unquestioning admirer *a priori*, who loved, who agreed, who took and accepted everything, everything, kindheartedly, warmly . . .

Oh, what torture I had to endure to save this pretense of maturity, here, along those country paths leading through stubble fields, while yonder, peasants and lordships were tumbling and kneading one another without shame, and, from above, the pupa, suspended at its zenith, was horribly, mercilessly flinging its shafts of light, its billion arrows—oh, the warm kindness, the deadly, restrictive tenderness, the mutual admiration and affection . . . Oh, the gall these cute little women have, so greedy for love, so eager to team up in loving, so keen to become the object of admiration . . . How dare she, a mushy, wishy-washy nobody, acquiesce to my fervor and accept my worship, greedily and avariciously filling her appetite with my adulation? Is there anything on this earth and under the blazing, scorching pupa more terrible than that cloying, womanly warmth, that shy, intimate idolizing and snuggling? . . . And what's worse, in order to reciprocate and fulfill this mutual admiration scheme, she proceeded to admire me—and, with due attention and interest, she proceeded to ask me about myself—not because she was truly interested but to return the favor—for she knew that if she showed interest in me I would be all the more interested in her. I was thus forced to tell her about myself while she listened, her little head resting on my shoulder, interjecting questions from time to time to let me know that she was listening. And she in turn fed me with her admiration, snuggling up to me, enamored of me, told me that she liked me oh so much, that from the word go I had made such an impression on her, that she loved me more and more, that I was so bold, so courageous . . .

"You have kidnapped me," she kept saying, intoxicated by her own words, "not everyone would have dared. You fell in love and you kidnapped me, asking no questions, you simply kidnapped me, you weren't afraid of my parents . . . I love those eyes of yours, bold, fearless, rapacious."

And her admiration made me squirm as if the devil himself were flogging me, and the huge, infernal pupa exulted in its glory and pierced from above like the universe's ultimate portent, like the key to all riddles and the final denominator of all things. While Zosia, snuggling up to me, worked on me, and warmly, timidly, awkwardly, she mythologized me just as she chose, and I sensed that in her clumsy way she adored my attributes and virtues, she searched for them, all the while kindling the flames and warming up to me . . . She took my hand and nestled it in hers, so I nestled hers in mine—while the infantile, infernal pupa reached its zenith, its culmination, and scorched us directly from above.

Suspended at the very summit of space, it shot its golden, glistening rays on this vale of tears and between all possible horizons. All the while Zosia snuggled ever closer, bonded with me more and more, she led me into her. I was sleepy. I couldn't walk any more, nor listen to her, nor respond, and yet I had to keep walking, listening and responding. We crossed meadows, and those meadows of greenish-green and greening grass were full of yellow buttercups, but the buttercups were timid, nestled in the grass, the grass was a bit slippery, wet on the surface and a little damp below, steaming under the relentless heat from above. Snowdrops in great numbers appeared on either side of the path, but they were slightly yellowish, like weak tea, and anemic-looking. There were lots of anemones on the slopes and melons galore. On the waters, in damp ditches water lilies—pale, wan, delicate, whitish—stagnated in the scorching, sweltering heat. While Zosia went on cuddling and confiding. And the pupa went on hitting the earth. Dwarf trees, their core sickly, puffy, almost like a puffball, were so frightened that as soon as I touched one it fell apart. Little sparrows chirped in great numbers. High above were little clouds, whitish, pinkish, and bluish, as if made of muslin, wretched-looking and mawkish. No clear outline anywhere, everything smeared, silent and mortified, waiting in concealment, unborn and so undefined that nothing was separate or distinct, everything united with everything else into a swampy, whitish, faded, quiet pulp. Frail little streams murmured, spilled over, seeped into the soil and then steamed, or bubbled here and there, creating bleb and snot. The world was becoming smaller, constricting itself, shrinking and, while shrinking, it strained and pressed, it tightened round one's neck like a softly choking dog collar. All the while the utterly infantile pupa struck and terrified one from on high. I rubbed my forehead.

"What kind of a place is this?

She turned her poor tired and frail face toward me and said bashfully and tenderly, snuggling warmly into my shoulder:

"This is my place."

Something caught me by the throat. This is where she brought me. Yes, so all this was hers . . . But I felt sleepy, my head hung low, I had no energy—oh, to break loose, move away at least a step, push away to an arm's length, hit her with fury, say something unkind, shatter her—be bad, oh, to be unkind to Zosia! Oh, to be unkind to Zosia! "I must, I must," I thought sleepily, my head fallen on my breast, "I must be unkind to Zosia!" Oh, cruelty—cold as ice, life-saving, life-giving unfriendliness! It's high time to be unkind. I have to be unkind . . . But how can I be unkind while I'm kind—while she's charming me, suffusing me with her kindness and I'm suffusing her with mine, while she's snuggling up to me and I'm snuggling up to her . . . no help from anywhere! In these fields and meadows, among timid grasses just the two of us—she with me and I with her—and nowhere, nowhere anyone to save us. I'm alone here with Zosia, and with the pupa as it lies dead in the firmament in its absolute continuance, brilliant and blazing, infantile and infantilizing, closed, sunken, magnified within itself and standing still at the apogee of its zenith . . .

Oh, for a third person! Help, rescue us! Oh, may a third human being come to the two of us, oh, salvation, come and let me latch on to you, save us! Let a t h i r d   h u m a n   b e i n g come now, forthwith, a stranger, cold and indifferent, pure, distant and neutral, and like an ocean wave let him hit this steaming domesticity with his separateness, let him tear me away from Zosia . . . Oh, come, you third one, come, give me a base from which to oppose her, allow me to draw from you, oh, come, life-giving breath, come, great power, unhitch me, knock me aside and carry me away! But Zosia snuggled up even more lovingly, warmly, tenderly.

"Why are you calling out and shouting? We're alone . . ."

And she raised her mug to me. My strength failed me, dream assailed reality, and I couldn't help it—I had to kiss her mug with my mug, since she had kissed my mug with her mug.

And now come, oh mugs! No, I'm not saying goodbye to you, strange and unknown mugs of strange and unknown people who will read me, I say hello to you, hello, graceful bundles of body parts, now let it all begin—come, step up to me, begin your kneading, make me a new mug so I will again have to run from you and into other people, and speed, speed, speed through all mankind. Because there is no escape from the mug, other than into another mug, and from a human being one can only take shelter in the arms of another human being. From the pupa, however, there is absolutely no escape. Chase me if you want. I'm running away, mug in my hands.

> It's the end, what a gas,
> And who's read it is an ass!

W. G.